The Velocity of Blood

M J Williams

www.darkstroke.com

Discover us online:
www.darkstroke.com

Find us on instagram:
www.instagram.com/darkstrokebooks

Include **#darkstroke** in a photo of yourself
holding his book on Instagram and
something nice will happen.

To all those who should still be here,
I'm so sorry.

Acknowledgements

Custom dictates that the list of acknowledgments should be long, incomplete and absolutely not in order of importance. Suffice to say, the students and faculty on the MSt in Crime & Thriller Writing at Cambridge University have been amazing. Special mention must go to Sophie Hannah who made my dream a reality, to Midge Gillies, Elly Griffiths, Emily Winslow and Jenny Bavidge of Cambridge University's Institute of Continuing Education for their ceaseless encouragement, and to Jon Appleton, the most positive and thoughtful of tutors. To my fellow crime writing students, thank you for everything, especially our deliciously dark WhatsApp group. It's for a book, officer, honest...

The athletes of Cambridge University Athletic Club's High Jump squad have been wonderfully supportive, as has Coach Carol. We have to talk about something in between jumps, you know. Other mates...BT, Caroline, Dave, Jenn, Sarah plus Coffin Dodger Equity (Rod and John) are the most amazing people.

Other people in bookland have been ridiculously generous with their encouragement and support. Adam Hamdy, SJ Watson, Mark Billingham, Lesley Kara, Alison Bruce and Graham Bartlett are just damn good people (I'm sure I've inadvertently missed somebody out so please don't bump me off in script if I did). Laurence and Steph at Darkstroke – thank you so much for everything.

And finally...this novel would not have achieved successful fuelling without the coffee wizardry and world-class music recommendations of Rob, Sam and James of Dose Coffee, 70 Long Lane, London EC2.

About the Author

MJ Williams was born in 1975 and attended the London School of Economics, the Humboldt University of Berlin and the University of Cambridge. He spends his time on writing and his money on reading.

He can be found online at www.MJWilliamsWrites.com, @**MJWilliamsWrites** on Instagram and @**jumpingbackward** on Twitter.

Author's Note

I started writing this book on the train from Cambridge to London, England in January 2020. Little did I know that the world was about to enter into a global pandemic that would cost millions of lives. Covid was a worldwide tragedy. One of its effects, however, is that certain crimes happened less often as we were confined to our homes during various lockdowns and restrictions.

This wasn't the case with mass shootings in the US though. In 2020, there were 611 US mass shootings, up 47% from the 417 in 2019. Perhaps Covid gave the world a sense of false security with regard to school shootings. Anecdotally there seemed to be fewer *school* shootings, because for much the pandemic kids weren't physically in school. But that didn't mean they were safe. The number of kids (aged from 0-17) killed or injured by guns in 2020 rose to 5,241 from the 3,817 in 2019, an increase of 37%. But for whatever reason, there were fewer global headline-grabbing atrocities, so perhaps we all took our eyes off the ball a little.

Very recently though, the United States has seen two very public mass shootings, namely the awful events in Buffalo and in Uvalde, Texas. I don't have the words to express my sympathy for the victims because there are no words that can adequately describe the magnitude of my sympathy. I can describe my anger though. Because I'm absolutely fucking livid. Because this happens again and again and it's completely unnecessary and completely preventable. There were twenty mass shootings the week *after* Uvalde alone.

I've been asked how I came to write *The Velocity of* Blood a lot in the last few months. It's actually pretty simple. I wrote a book about a planned mass shooting in the United States because they happen. A lot.

By June 6th this year, the US had already had over 240 mass shootings. Let's not gloss over that. Over two hundred and forty mass shootings. In twenty-two weeks. Count to 240 now. One per second. Four minutes. That's a hell of a long time. And 240 isn't the number of victims. It's the number of the number of mass shootings. And as a mass shooting is defined as one where 4 people are shot or killed, excluding the shooter, that's a *minimum* of 960 victims in mass shootings alone. In the first twenty-two weeks of this year.

According to the US Bureau of Justice, 79% of multiple-victim homicides in the United States are carried out using guns. By way of comparison, 67% of single-victim homicides in the US are carried out using guns. Why the disparity? Because guns, awfully, tragically, are extremely effective at killing multiple people. They are one of the most efficient ways of doing so. And the damn things are too readily available. And as a writer, I'm going to write about reality. Even if it's fiction. I'm not a diarist and I'm not going to disappear up my own arse talking wank about "bearing witness to contemporary events." But I'm damned if I'm going to gloss over it either.

All that said, just writing about things isn't really going to fix them. What's needed is for the gun control lobby to be as well-resourced as the NRA. If you're taking the time to read this, and you're in the US, you can donate to the Giffords Foundation on giffords.org . And if you're not a US citizen and can't donate to a PAC, there are plenty of charities that can accept your contribution – the Brady Campaign to Prevent Gun Violence is a not-for-profit and can be found at bradyunited.org (these are the folks who get my donations).

The book isn't just about guns though. The initial prompt for the story came from a harrowing news report of a UK teenager who had committed suicide after being horrifically bullied. While the events, main characters and locations in this book are fictional, the story is generally based on actual incidences of bullying in the modern western world. There have been documented instances of 'everybody-but-x' social media groups in real life, and there have been deepfakes circulated of victims of bullying. If any of the events in the book have caused you anxiety, then might I point you toward www.samaritansusa.org in the United States or www.samaritans.org in the UK.

As I said, I started writing the book in January 2020 and started submitting to publishers in mid-2021. Darkstroke and I came together in January 2022. We started working on the edits in February and planned a publication date of July 4th as a tie-in given the cover design and the uniquely American nature of the book. (I should point out here that I *really* love the US. I spend as much time as I can there. I just wish there were fewer murders.). When the events at Buffalo and Robb Elementary School happened, we had some deep discussions about whether to delay publication or proceed (or just bin it).

We decided to proceed and I hope that's the right decision (a substantial portion of my royalties will be going to the Brady Campaign to Prevent Gun Violence). Obviously, I wrote a book, it's my debut novel and I'd like it to be published. And it is a tough topic and it is a hard read. I get that. And nobody has to read it. But if we were to delay, to *when* should we delay? Because after months and months of painstaking research, the one thing I know for certain is that there will be another mass shooting soon. It might not make the press. It might involve fewer victims than the ten poor souls who were murdered in Buffalo or the twenty-one innocents murdered at Robb Elementary. It might not be a racist, terrorist attack. It might happen on a day when the media and the world are focusing on something else. But it will happen. 240 mass shootings in twenty-two weeks is more than ten a week. More than ten a week. More than forty victims a week. Every week. And that's just in *mass* shootings (it doesn't include shootings with less than four victims).

From my point of view, the problem here isn't the book. It's the reality. And I appreciate you've bought a work of fiction here and do forgive me for getting on my soapbox, but if you want to change the reality, then please go to one of the PACs or charities I mentioned and donate something. Because I'd love this book to be obsolete.

MAJW, 4th July 2022.

All data is sourced from the Gun Violence Archive who can be found at https://www.gunviolencearchive.org/

The Velocity of Blood

Prologue

What if they *deserved* to die? What if they were monsters who tortured the weak just because they could? They'd deserve it then. All of them. Not murder. *Justice*. Execution. Every single one. Like fish in a fucking barrel.

How?

First, consider the barrel. It's not enough that the barrel is somewhere fish congregate in numbers. The fish need to be confined. A million fish in an ocean do not lead to success. One hundred fish in a barrel would be a world record. Nobody's ever done a hundred. Be *different*. Think big.

Second, consider the fish. Nobody talks about sharks in a barrel. Sharks have teeth. Sharks are strong. Sharks can fight back. And you get just as much recognition for a minnow as a shark. More so if it's a baby minnow. And, yes, minnows can try and fight back, but they're hardly equipped for it.

Third, it's called shooting fish in a barrel for a reason. Shooting fish. Not stabbing them. Not beating them. That doesn't count. It's shooting fish. And that means you need to source the right equipment. And that means Texas.

Welcome to Dallas.

Chapter One

Whittlesford, California. Six months earlier

The yellow school bus turned right and came to a slow gentle stop outside 1610 Chalcedony. Jack, the solitary pick-up at this, the last stop, hefted his backpack onto his shoulder and boarded. As he stepped up, faces turned toward him, and conversation lulled. A few smiles looked up from conversations or phones. He smiled nervously back and took his solitary place near the front. He eased his bulk into his usual double seat behind the driver and stared ahead.

The bus picked up speed north along Mission Boulevard, the driver keen to finish his morning. The sun shone through the windows on the right-hand side. Jack chose to sit in the shade, on the left. He closed his eyes and let his mind drift. He heard the muted buzz of the conversations behind him; some excited chatters about a forthcoming ballgame from a few of the jocks, a discussion about a movie from the girls, concern over a math problem from the nerds, a joke, a punchline and then laughter from the back row. His home, small but neat, faded in the rear-view mirror, his orange cat watching the bus through the kitchen window.

Jack dug his phone from his tight jeans pocket. He went straight to ESPN, although the chances of anything having happened since he last looked five minutes ago were relatively slim. The Chargers were still having a mediocre season. He subconsciously touched the badge on his jersey, as he read the latest op-ed on how to rescue the ballclub. *Maybe next year they could have a winning season. Maybe next year.* He sighed. He had the size for football – six foot three at sixteen years old – but even that frame and a XXL Shawne Merriman jersey couldn't hide that he was already more than forty pounds overweight. Not much fun in a beach town where surfers flew abs like flags. He sighed again and went back to his phone, this time more furtively.

He checked in the rear-view mirror and, confident he was unobserved, went to his apps. According to his fitness tracker, he had so far managed twelve consecutive days of walking more than 10,000 steps - his secret plan to lose weight. He smiled. *Surely it was simple*, he thought. *Calories in versus calories out. Do less of the former and more of the latter.* Then maybe he could look a bit more like everyone else, be a bit more like everyone else. He couldn't walk in the mornings – school was too far, and too early, and it would be too obvious. Everybody took the morning bus. But the bus home was much less busy as students dispersed home or to various different activities around town. Nobody had noticed he'd started walking home, a mildly circuitous route along the backstreets away from nosy eyes. He hadn't actually lost that much yet and looked the same. He'd decided that today was the day to address the calories inside of the ledger. A simple switch from regular soda to Diet Coke with lunch. A small adjustment to start with.

The yellow monster continued its noisy rumble along Mission. A right at the light onto Pearl and soon it was time to go. Jack lumbered off the bus. The other students greeted their classmates from different bus routes, a bewildering array of complicated handshakes, chest-bumps, and air kisses depending on friendship level, status, and gender. Jack navigated clusters of people, and then the smooth sweeping concrete walls of Whittlesford High School to his first class. English Lit.

Class wasn't due to start for another fifteen minutes, but Mr. Merle was already in his classroom. He was a kindly older gentleman, partial to wearing caramel cardigans in winter, even though his classroom marinated at an even seventy-two degrees throughout the year. Jack dropped his cellphone into Mr. Merle's fabric-lined bucket of technology. Students would be permitted to retrieve their devices again on the way out.

From the back of the class, Jack observed him. He was a good teacher, not a showbiz younger spark, full of gameshow tricks and faux friendliness, but a scholar with a lightness of teaching touch. Many a sceptical Whittlesford horse had been led to water and been surprised by the sweetness of Whitman, Twain, or Hemingway. Jack refreshed his memory of the assignment chapters, and the quiet trickle of students grew to a crashing waterfall as the latecomers just made it, depositing their cellphones just as the bell started. Mr. Merle peered up through his thick glasses, cleared his throat, and began.

Three lessons later, and Jack was hungry. His stomach ran like a Swiss watch, and each day at noon it chimed insistently. Pavlovian, this coincided with the lunch period, and so his gastronomic alarm clock only needed to endure around fifteen minutes of delay, that being the time between leaving class and reaching the head of the canteen line. Jack ambled, despite his hunger. He had learned to not be seen rushing to meals. Slimmer, swifter students swerved past him along Whittlesford's cream-colored corridors, posters waving in their wake.

Jack pushed his tray along the gleaming stainless-steel bars in the cafeteria. The canteen at Whittlesford ran to a regular schedule, with Monday lasagne as inevitable as Friday fish. Jack took the heftiest plate on offer. It looked normal in his large hand. Time for part two of the plan. He took a twenty-ounce reusable cup and pressed it against the metal tongue underneath the Diet Coke logo. It burbled and frothed, and he let it settle before topping up. He placed it carefully on his plastic tray, sliding along to the cashier and then carrying his meal to a quiet corner on the north side where it was nice and cool.

"I swear to fucking God, it's true!" On the other side of the cafeteria, Skyla giggled behind blonde bangs, savouring the attention of her crew. The In Crew. Status.

"Oh, come on. You're shitting me. What difference would it make? You're just making shit up," Trent snorted, supremely confident in his position. Abs and pecs and gleaming white teeth were what counted at Whittlesford. Add in a quarterback's arm and some recruiting interest from Division I schools, and Trent was as close as Californian schools usually came to organised religion.

"I swear I'm not. Fat Boy just took a Diet Coke. I was in line just behind him because Mr. Penderthy kept me late, and I swear he took a *Diet* Coke." Skyla relished both the gossip and the obvious comparison between her athletic swimmer's figure and the saggy butt of the joke. She deliberately stretched, lean, lithe, and on display.

"But what's the fucking point? Dude must weigh damn near three hundred pounds. What fucking difference is a diet soda going to make? It'd be like, ah…"

"Mowing the lawn with nail scissors?" This from Luke, Trent's favourite wide receiver.

"Painting the Superdome with a toothbrush," added Brie, Skyla's best friend, with long dark hair and thick natural lashes. She was less sporty than Skyla, but smarter. If Trent was honest with himself, he knew she had a bigger rack.

"Fucking Tammy with only one rubber," said Luke.

This really broke the boys up, Trent graciously extending a fist bump to Luke, who bowed his head theatrically to his king. The girls half-remonstrated, tightroping their way between sorority and credibility. Tammy had once been seen buying Canesten, although the rumour mill had embellished and adorned this to the point of penicillin and an STI. Truth is the first casualty of school.

"That's mean," said Brie, careful to maintain enthusiastic smiling eyes and dimples. She rubbed her knee against Luke under the table.

"Yeah, but seriously," said Luke. "I mean, what's the point? He's the size of a fucking house! And not just a normal house, a big house. A fucking mansion, with a double garage."

"And a pool," giggled Skyla again. "A pool full of Jell-O, just like his gut!"

"Ewwwww," shrieked Brie, and the girls shuddered together in delight. "I mean, ewww. Just imagine with his shirt off."

The king deigned to speak once more. "Do you *mind*? I'm

trying to *eat!*"

On the other side of the canteen, out of sight, out of mind, and out of earshot, Jack quietly ate his lunch. He was enjoying the relaxing cool air.

Chapter Two

So, hey everybody, and welcome to the latest edition of Killing Time, your friendly neighbourhood podcast about all things murder. Today we're going to be discussing the Whittlesford Massacre, which was a truly unique school shooting. I'm Nick-

-And I'm Chris. But first, before we really dive into this two-parter – because there's really a lot for us to discuss here, we'd both like to say thank you for tuning into this podcast, and we'd like to ask you a small favour. First, if you could go online to wherever you found this podcast and give us five stars, we'd be really grateful. It doesn't cost you anything, and it really helps us get the word out. If you have more than five seconds then if you could, leave us a review. That would be awesome. But if you only have five seconds, then spend one second per star, and that would really help us out.

Nick: Yeah, we'd be really grateful. And the second announcement before we dial into what happened at Whittlesford. If you could click on the link in our bio on Insta and Twitter, there's a real short survey which would really help us out. If you could fill that out, I promise it won't take you more than three minutes.

Chris: Yeah, no more than three minutes, unless you're special-

Nick: Dude! Are you allowed to even say that anymore?!!

Chris: I just did, so hopefully we won't lose all our special listeners!

Nick: *laughs* Yeah, they probably can't hit the pause button anyway! Anyway, if you can fill in that survey, I promise you it will not even take three minutes, and you go into a draw for a hundred-dollar voucher to spend at Amazon.

Chris: Yeah, because Jeff Bezos is really struggling right now, so we kinda wanted to help him out with some additional sales.

Nick: *laughs* You know, I heard Jeff Bezos actually lives in a house. You know, like a house he lives in on his own. Not a single room that he rents from a scary Jewish lady who keeps asking him when he's going to move out and get married.

Chris: Well, he is a billionaire. I guess he can probably afford to buy a house now. Anyway, your Jewish landlady gives you leftovers.

Nick: So…

Chris: So…

Nick: Today we're going to be talking about the Whittlesford Massacre, and in particular, why it was so totally unique-

Chris: Yeah, there's nothing worse than yet another normal school shooting. I mean, man, it's such a drag-

Nick: *laughs* Yeah, but Whittlesford was totally different. I mean, we've covered a bunch of 'em on the podcast, and none of 'em ever turned out like this. Jack Tolleson was literally one of a kind. What he did, never been done before. But, notwithstanding his uniqueness-

Chris: Wait, there's a but?

Nick: Well yeah, it's been a while since we covered a school shooting, as opposed to a serial killer like Bundy or Gacy, so I'm just going to mention to our listeners that Chris – spoiler alert here-

Chris: Jesus, really? Every time we do a school shooting you going to mention that I went to Virginia Tech! *laughs* Doesn't that ever get old?

Nick: Oh, I'm sorry. Too soon?! *laughs*

Chris: *laughs* Never too soon! But yes, I went to Virginia Tech, which I'm sure all our listeners will remember was where Seung-Hui Cho shot and killed thirty-three people.

Nick: I should know this, but does that thirty-three include him? Or was it thirty-two, plus himself?

Chris: Dude! Spoiler alert! If you ask if it included himself, then our listeners won't stick around to find out how it ends! *laughs*

10

Nick: *laughs* Man, that's harsh.

Chris: I always wondered if when a shooter offs himself at the end, it should be credited to his total or deducted from his total.

Nick: Deducted, how?

Chris: You know, like an own goal in hockey.

Nick: *laughs* That's a good point. If only school shootings had umpires to make those critical calls, and signs up in the cafeteria saying, 'don't shoot the zebras!'

Chris: For the benefit of our foreign listeners, I should point out that in American sports, umpires wear vertical black and white stripes. We wouldn't recommend having actual zebras in a school shooting. *laughs*

Nick: Yeah, that would be wrong. *laughs* No animals were harmed during the recording of this podcast.

Chris: *laughs* Anyway, it was thirty-two plus himself, which was, at the time, the deadliest mass shooting in America, although obviously we know it's been overtaken now. Interestingly at the time, in 2007, his thirty-two was the deadliest in America, but not in the world, because as regular listeners will know, that record at the time, was the 1996 Port Arthur massacre in Australia, although that's obviously now been overtaken by events. But yes, I went to Virginia Tech, and no matter what this douche says, there's no truth to the rumour that when you graduate from V-Tech, you get a graduation certificate like every other college plus a special pin to mark your actual physical survival.

Nick: Damn, you beat me to it. I was gonna-

Chris: Yeah, I know you were. Had to beat you to it. Anyway, let's get back to Whittlesford. The first thing we wanted to address in this podcast was the idea that there's such a thing as a typical school shooter. There really isn't. There's a lot of myths that all shooters are bullied, or all shooters are neo-Nazis, or all shooters are Goths or all shooters are whatever, and it's just not true.

Nick: Yeah, those myths and stereotypes seem to have sprung up over time, and we think – I mean, we have no proof – but we think they've come about because people want to be

11

able to find a reason for why they happen. Because if we can find a reason for why they happen, then maybe we can address that reason and do something about it. But when we look at mass shootings, there's only really one common factor in them all, at least as far as we can see-

Chris: Hey, don't spoil it. Let them see if they can guess. Come on, listeners, can you guess?

Nick: Yeah, guess the common factor and win a stuffed animal!

Chris: *laughs*

Nick: The common denominator – I mean, I think it's a denominator, but I haven't done math since like tenth grade – the common factor, is that shooters are overwhelmingly male.

Chris: When you say overwhelmingly male, do you mean they have beards and chop lumber?

Nick: Douche. I mean that there really are very few female shooters. According to our research, since 1982, there've been one-hundred seventeen mass shootings in America – defining a mass shooting as four or more victims in a public place, although different sources use different definitions which is like really annoying – but only three of those were by females. So that's, um, you can see why I quit math – it's obviously less than three percent. Whatever it is, it's like a really small number. So whatever the myths about shooters in general – bullied goths or whatever – the one thing that is true is that shooters are usually men. Or boys.

Chris: Or somewhere in between?

Nick: You mean like transgender? I don't know about that. We love transgender people on this show, love is love-

Chris: No, you douche, I meant between boys and men, like adolescents. That kind of in-between.

Nick: Oh right, yes. Yes, that would be true. It would be interesting to know about the orientation or sexual identity of shooters though. Although it might be hard to find out, given that the whole recognition of transgender thing is such a new phenomenon-

Chris: Yeah.

Nick: So the one thing we know is that shooters are usually

12

male. They're also more often white than of other races. I saw something somewhere that said fifty-eight percent of shooters were white, and I checked it against the last census which has sixty percent of the country being non-Hispanic white, so I guess that's broadly in line with the population-

Chris: I'm just wondering if you're going to try and justify that using math or stats, liberal arts boy!

Nick: Hell no!

Chris: *laughs* So when it comes to the actual identity of the shooters, the one thing we can be sure about is that they're male, and more likely than not, they're white. When it comes to the actual motivation though, it's much harder to get a handle on it.

Nick: Yeah, this is where the detail is sometimes hard to find. Firstly, mass shooters often kill themselves at the end of their shooting, which kinda makes it hard to question them. Sometimes they actually kill themselves like Jack Tolleson did at Whittlesford or Klebold and Harris did at Columbine, and sometimes – we think, anyway – they effectively commit suicide in death-by-cop at the end of the spree. It's almost like the end scene in Butch Cassidy where they come out guns blazing out of the bank in Bolivia and get shot down. They know what's going to happen and it's probably effectively suicide, just that they get someone else to do it.

Chris: You mean like sub-contracting it?

Nick: *laughs* Yeah, probably. It's obviously really hard to work out the exact motivation of that particular part of it, because they're obviously not around to interview. But it seems logical enough to me that it's suicide-by-cop? What do you think?

Chris: Yeah, it kind of makes sense. I mean, shooters are obviously totally fucked up, but that doesn't mean they actually want to hurt themselves. And shooting yourself in the head is pretty final but it probably also hurts too. Maybe they're scared of the pain it might cause them and that's why they get a cop to do it.

Nick: Oh, boo hoo fucking hoo. We should take a moment here to pause and consider the pain that these shooters went through when the last bullet went through their fucking head.

Chris: Yeah. Nobody ever thinks about them. It's a sad society *laughs*

Nick: *laughs*

Chris: So anyway...

Nick: Anyway...

Chris: Anyway, the point is that actually working out the motivation behind these shootings is really hard. I guess you can break it down into two different categories at first.

Nick: Yeah.

Chris: We'll talk about those two distinct categories in a moment because it really surprised us that all shootings could fit into those two categories-

Nick: Well, yeah. Everyone except Jack Tolleson.

Chris: Yeah, he was unique. But everyone but him. But first – we'd really appreciate it if you listened to this message from our sponsor. It's really important that we do this because it's because of the support from our sponsor that we've been able to do this, and we're now closing in on two hundred episodes. And in particular, we really and truly do love our sponsor, the completely fantastic Bullet Coffee. We usually record this podcast late at night, and we usually do our research late at night and we get through a lot of Bullet Coffee.

"Thank you for listening to Killing Time with Chris and Nick, your friendly neighbourhood podcast about all things murder. Here at Bullet Coffee, we ethically source the best organic coffee from around the world, before roasting it ourselves on-site in New York City. If you're in town, why not stop by at our flagship on Mulberry Street in Little Italy or one of our other locations around Manhattan, the Bronx and Brooklyn? And if you're elsewhere, we ship quickly to anywhere in the United States. You'll love our extensive choice of world coffee whether you like your coffee filtered, French pressed, espresso or any other way. Come check us out at BulletCoffee.com – total delight on your first order or your money back."

Chapter Three

The one question nobody has ever asked me – and I wish they would – is whether I think they deserved it. So much has been written about Jack, and most of it has been utter bullshit. Ill-informed total bullshit. And all of it has been awful, but nobody has ever really mentioned how bad it must have been for him to do what he did. And because of that, nobody has ever asked whether they actually deserved it.

Fine. I'll say it. Yes, they deserved it. All of them. Not just the ones who died, not just the ones he let go, and not just the one who was there at the very end with him. They all deserved it. My baby boy did nothing wrong. He was a quiet, kind, sweet boy, and he did nothing wrong. And then they picked him out and they drove him to that day. They whipped, and they drove him like a poor broken-down donkey. And then they have the fucking gall to say it was his fault when he finally kicked out? Bullshit. So yes, they fucking deserved it. I'll never say it in public, but I'm glad they're dead. They deserved it.

I obviously didn't go to their funerals. Why would I? I'm sure everyone thought the reason I didn't go was because it would cause a scene, or because it wouldn't have been the right thing to do, or whatever. Should you go to the funerals of people your son has killed? I don't know, to be honest. But I do know I don't care. That's not why I didn't go. Not because I felt guilty, or because I didn't want to cause a scene. I didn't go because you don't go to the funerals of people who don't deserve to be commemorated. And those kids didn't deserve a funeral with ceremony and flowers and black clothes and a priest saying they were taken too soon.

They did what they did, and they deserved to die. And if Jack hadn't killed them but just himself, if they'd driven him to just commit suicide, then I hope I would have done what he did and finished the job. Because they deserved it.

Jonathan and I spoke about it once. After the funeral of one of them. It had been on CNN, live broadcast, and I hadn't turned it off in time. And once it started, we somehow had to watch, some of it at least. It was nauseating. A eulogy talking about how he was taken too soon, what a promising career he had ahead of him. Complete abdication of any responsibility for what the little shit had done. No recognition whatsoever that he had brought it on himself and that he deserved to die. No mention of Jack, so desperate that he'd been driven to what he did by the little bastard in the shiny white coffin and all his friends.

Jonathan had put his arm around me, and we stood in the kitchen, watching in total, disbelieving silence. It was like watching a car crash, I guess, in slow motion. But we were both fuming. How fucking *dare* they claim the moral high ground?

Jonathan spoke first. He'd reached over to the TV remote and clicked the sound off just after the eulogy.

"I'm glad they're dead. Fucking assholes."

I leaned into him.

"Me too."

Chapter Four

It was a warm afternoon. The wind barely troubled the leaves on the palm trees, as Jack ambled home. His rucksack pressed on his broad shoulders, and he could feel the sweat warm and moist against his back. Red-mirrored Oakleys shielded his eyes from the sun. Wireless headphones broadcast the Chargers Podcast Network into his ears. They always found something new to discuss, even on a slow news day, and it helped make the walk home go by quickly.

Jack turned the corner into Chalcedony and saw his cat watching through the kitchen window, as he did every school day. That was their routine. Mr. Orange watched Jack leave every morning, and somehow, he knew, more or less, when Jack was coming home. He would wait patiently, sitting up in the window for his human to come home. Once Jack was actually indoors, Mr. Orange would prowl over to him and re-mark him with his scent, rubbing his chin against Jack's legs and hands. Occasionally he would stand by the cupboard where the kibble or Temptations were kept and miaow, hopeful for an unscheduled snack. But the unvarying routine was that of sentinel to 1610 Chalcedony. He counted them out and he counted them back. Once Jack and his mother were indoors, Mr. Orange would wander off, perhaps outside, to find a sun puddle to bask in, or a chair indoors to doze.

Today was no exception. As Jack's keys jangled on their way to the lock, Mr. Orange leapt down from the windowsill and trotted to the door. He greeted Jack with a half-miaow and batted his head against Jack's bare legs. Walking home in southern California is warm work. You need to wear shorts. And with baggy shorts, it's not like anyone can see if the thighs are a little chubbier than athletic perfection. Today was one of those days when Mr. Orange wanted additional treats, and Jack was powerless to resist him, especially if his mother was still at work and not able to tell him off. Truth be told, Jack had always been powerless to resist the miaow and slow-blinking eyes. He grabbed a fistful of Temptations direct from the packet and held out his flat hand toward the purring cat, who quickly devoured the pile before skulking off for a nap.

Jack kicked off his sneakers and peeled off his socks. Poured a glass of cold OJ from the refrigerator to fuel him during homework, and took it upstairs to his bedroom, where he discovered Mr. Orange had decided to stretch out on his bed. It was a double bed, and Jack shared it with Mr. Orange most days. It was pushed up against the wall, allowing for more space in his room for the usual teenage detritus. Sports posters adorned most of the walls, bright technicolour moments of athletic achievement. A life-size cardboard cut-out of Philip Rivers was propped against the wall, his arm cocked back, ready to hurl the football. That was the fun wall, as it were. Sports, sports, sports.

The other wall was more practical. Against it were two chests of drawers, one for clothes, one an old filing cabinet his dad had gotten when the Navy yard cleared out all their crap. A long plywood board lay across the top of both, painted chalkboard black to make a huge desk. His printer sat in one corner, his computer in the middle, and a neat pile of clothes occupied the other end of the desk. His mom would do the laundry and leave it there for him to put away, but more often than not, he would pick out clothes from the pile in the mornings, like a fabric version of buckaroo. Two bookcases flanked the computer monitor. They were jammed with well-thumbed, but not yet discarded, kids' books, and less well-thumbed school textbooks.

He gave the cat another gentle stroke behind the ears and fired up his computer. *Time to work.*

Homework today was History, or Advanced Googling, as Jack sometimes called it. He found textbooks dry and was forever getting distracted by his phone, Twitter, Facebook, Insta, TikTok and Snapchat. But he'd worked out that if he could find a decent podcast or online documentary, he could concentrate much more. Even when it was just on in the background, somehow it went in and tended to stay much more than if he just read a textbook. His dad always harked back to the old days when he would have to physically note chapters by hand, but that had gone out with the Ark. Jack wasn't even sure he could physically write cursive for more than an hour at a time. He guessed that was progress. The world had moved on, and Jack figured he might not be able to write neatly or quickly like his dad, but he was real quick typing and researching online. That was the way of the new world. New world methods to research old world facts.

Today's assignment centred around the Cold War, and specifically, the Cuban Missile Crisis. It was at least a topic which Jack found relatively interesting. He typed 'Cuban Missile Crisis' into Google and landed on a fifty-minute documentary on YouTube. *Perfect.* He reached into his rucksack for the assignment questions and fished the paper out from between the pages of the textbook he had no intention of reading. Then he pulled the blind down to darken his room, and carefully lowered his body onto the bed, trying not to disturb Mr. Orange.

As the documentary played on his monitor, he half-read the assignment questions, half-watched the documentary, and half stroked Mr. Orange, who snuggled with delight. It was a good documentary, even allowing for the dramatic voice of the narrator, and the background music which was low in volume but high in melodrama.

Despite the quality of the content, and his adoration of his cat, after ten minutes, Jack's attention began to wane. He figured he'd probably more or less worked out – or guessed – the answers to most of the questions, and his cellphone was burning a hole in his pocket. He turned the sound on each day when he left school, and even though there had been no notifications beeping, he felt the irresistible urge to check on the world. With Mr. Orange having settled on his left arm, and his phone in his left shorts pocket, it took an inelegant reach to be able to extract it with his right hand. He sighed as he saw the time; his concentration had barely lasted ten minutes. Maybe he could get one of those concentration apps to stop himself from being distracted.

He checked in, first on Twitter. Nothing exciting going on with the Chargers, or any other sports since he'd last checked. No messages for him on SMS or WhatsApp, although there were plenty of messages in his class WhatsApp group. He never really got involved in it, never voiced an opinion, and pretty much only ever contributed when someone asked a direct factual question. He felt good when he answered those. Useful.

The WhatsApp group was one of a number of ways that students at Whittlesford kept in touch with each other, alongside Facebook and Insta. A few used Twitter, but it was less popular. A couple of the higher-profile jocks had Twitter accounts which were clearly there to advertise themselves to potential college recruiters with athletics scholarships to award. Any embarrassing posts or pictures had now been deleted, and practically every post was either positive or religious, offering thanks either to God or to their coach. Facebook messenger groups existed both for the whole school, and for the different groups within it: football, both generic and 'PLAYERS ONLY', band, orchestra, and all the different groups and cliques, both formal and informal that form any group of humans.

The class WhatsApp group was universal, however. An invitation link would be emailed out at the start of every semester, and entry and participation were open to all, with no gatekeeper as admin. With that, however, came anonymity. Some students made it so everyone could see their profile picture, others made it visible only to their contacts. Not all those who did make their profile pictures visible, had an identifiable photograph. Some did, but alongside selfies and portraits sat sunsets and pets and distant photos, which made it difficult to work out the identity of the person chatting.

He scrolled back up the thirty-five messages within the

group. *Nothing important.* Some light joshing between two groups of football jocks was playing out in cyberspace. The jocks all had their pictures set to display, all wearing pads and eye-black. They often talked trash, offense versus defense. It was good-natured, but the underbite was clear. Status was everything at Whittlesford. *Like everywhere,* Jack supposed. And while the battle on his phone was nominally between one side of the football and the other, the reality was that if you weren't on either side of the ball, then you had even less status, and you'd have to prove it somehow else, music, academia, looks, celebrity connection. Anything had more status than being the grey kid that nobody remembered.

The hazing got a little spicier, narrowing in from tribal to individual. Jeff, one of the weaker football players on the defense, was being called out for some mistakes he'd made at today's practice. The momentum started to build as others chipped in, throwaway comments in themselves, but the weight continued to grow. Jeff was standing up for himself pretty well. Jack had caught up on the previous chat and was watching it unfold in real-time now, live and uninterrupted, as if he were at the game itself.

Jeff made a fatal error. He showed weakness.

Well, y'all can try and play safety. It ain't as easy as you think!

The reply came quickly.

Dude, when an average-to-good player plays that position, it's called safety. When a scrub like you plays it, it's called a fucking disaster.

Boom. The killer blow from a team-mate. Jack's phone lit up as the rest of the offense piled on. Flaming emoji after flaming emoji. Exploding bombs, coffins, triangular shits, flames.

One of Jeff's erstwhile defence-mates was the first to turn on him. Having initially stood with him, Gordon now saw the futility of his support and plunged the knife deep. He quoted the killer blow line and replied to it simply:

#True.

Four letters and a hashtag. Not much in the grand scheme of

things. But a biting, venomous reversal of support that breached the dam, and left Jeff with no allies.

#True was repeated again and again, all the way down the screen, by jocks, nerds, goths. Everyone piled in on the hapless Jeff. *#True* became the rallying cry. Even those who would never have dared pick on a football player, even those who had no reason to get involved, even those who were publicly Jeff's friends, repeated the hashtag. Some were neither contacts in Jack's own phone, nor set their pictures to visible. Their vitriol was poured anonymously and in great quantity.

Hastily created memes appeared. Coach screaming at Jeff with a huge speech bubble, "You SUCK!" and Jeff's own thought-bubble replying, *#True*. Jeff's girlfriend's thought bubble imagining, "I could easily do better", and Jeff's own thoughts again replying, *#True*.

Jack sighed. He didn't know Jeff especially well, had no reason to pile on, but also had no reason to not join in. Whatever. He decided not to. Then switched the WhatsApp group to mute, and flicked it over to archive. He'd come back and catch up another time.

He swiped onto his Insta. He followed a random collection of sports stars, musicians and surfers, but also some cat shelters, and a dude in South Africa who ran a lion sanctuary. Those were the ones he wanted to follow. He also followed various classmates and school sports teams, not through choice, but because it was easier socially than not following. He didn't post much himself. Just some sports pictures, beach sunsets, and the occasional picture of Mr. Orange. He followed far more people than followed him, but that didn't bother him. Some folks liked being the center of attention. He knew it wasn't really anything he had to make a decision about. He just wasn't, and he was OK with that.

He clicked through the timeline and saw a couple of new photos, clicked on 'like' for a couple of them. Then gently extricated his hand from underneath his sleeping cat and reached back to his computer to rewind the documentary. He left his phone face down on the desk, out of reach, so this time he would concentrate better.

Chapter Five

"OMG. He did it again! And it gets even better!"

"Say what?" Trent looked up from his phone. It was lunchtime at Whittlesford again. Chicken burger for him. Protein to build his muscles. Tight tee to show them off. Chicks dig guns.

"Fat Boy took a Diet Coke again. And, get this, he took the chicken salad too!" Skyla cackled, hoping she'd judged Trent's mood right. He'd been a little off with her this morning, nothing major, just a little distant. She wasn't sure if she'd done anything wrong. She was sure she hadn't. In fact, she was pretty sure she'd done everything she should have, from gazing adoringly at him, to not being clingy, to sending him a photo of her tits when she got out the shower that morning. She couldn't ask him because that was being needy. Boys didn't like needy.

"A chicken *salad?*" Trent inadvertently channelled Lady Bracknell. Not that he knew who she was. Or Wilde. Or whether being earnest was important, unimportant, or somewhere in between.

"Fat Boy took a Diet Coke again. And a chicken salad." Skyla giggled again, reinforced by Brie. Safety in numbers, although she wouldn't trust Brie not to steal Trent if she had the chance. Sure, Luke was good-looking and on the team, but Trent was the quarterback. The prize. Better looking. A giant fish in the only pond they could swim in. And maybe with the potential to go all the way, and make it to the NFL. Damn straight Brie would trade up if she could.

Trent finally paid attention. There was no reason he'd been distant. He was just a little tired from staying up late watching porn, and a little achy from a weight session in the gym, and a little bored with Skyla at the moment. The tits this morning were good, but sometimes he just wanted to chillax and zone out from what passed for conversation at Whittlesford.

"Wow. He must be serious," he said. "It won't make any difference unless he starts doing some exercise though. He's still a tub of fucking lard and Diet Coke and chicken salad ain't going to change that."

"Amen to that," replied Luke, fist bumping Trent with his right hand while his left groped between Brie's ass-cheeks under the table. She was squirming a little, hoping it came across as enjoyable flirty squirming rather than the annoyance she actually felt and was trying to hide.

"What kind of weights should someone that fat do for weight loss?" asked Brie, going for flattery of the boys. She looked rapt in attention, beautifully posed. Everyone at Whittlesford knew you needed to make boys feel clever. Then they think it's you that makes them feel great.

Luke removed his hand from her ass and listed a series of exercises, counting them off on one hand with the other. Brie wriggled to try and ease the thong from tight in her crack.

"Anything I missed?" he asked Trent. Maintaining deference was important. Luke could have a view, sure. Luke could even have expertise. But upset the quarterback and he'd suddenly find the ball being passed to the other receivers. He couldn't afford that. Neither in terms of status at Whittlesford or the impact on his numbers and potential scholarship options.

"Nah, bro. You're good." Validation.

Trent paused. Nobody filled the gap as thoughts crossed his forehead. They waited, attentive, but trying not to look too sycophantic. Skyla leaned in and was rewarded with an arm around her waist. Brie moved her hand under the table and lightly brushed Luke's cock through his shorts. He grinned, congratulating himself on his deserved treat.

Trent went on.

"I just don't get it. How can someone get to be that fat, so quickly, so young? I mean, what the fuck does he do with himself all day? Does he just sit in front of the tube and eat Mexican food?"

"We've never seen him at the beach," said Skyla. "He doesn't do any outdoor sports. He watches the football matches, and he's always wearing something with the Chargers on it, but I've never even seen him play pick-up. He just sits and watches from the shade."

The thought that she had never seen Jack at the beach because nobody had ever invited Jack to the beach did not occur to Skyla. The thought that even if Jack had been at the beach, she would not have noticed him because she focussed on tanning and selfies for Insta also did not occur to Skyla. If Jack had ever spoken to Skyla anywhere in public, it would have been an A-grade emergency. Flashing red lights, dial Nine-One-One. Run away fast before anyone saw her talking to the uncool fat kid. Put on a mask. Fake a seizure. Do anything, just get the *fuck* away from him.

Trent snorted. Further discussion of Jack was not worthy of his time. He pulled Skyla closer so he could feel the side of her tits. Nice. Drained the last of his soda. Football practice beckoned. Time to move.

The practice had been good. One of those afternoons when things just ran smooth, from the second Trent called 'Snap!' to the instant the receiver crossed into the end zone. Light contact, with Trent and the back-up quarterback both in red bibs so the opposition knew they couldn't tackle them.

The players sat on the grass after practice as the warm sun faded. The football field was practically league-level quality. They were only a mile back from the coast, but the hills inland of Whittlesford climbed quickly, dusty, brushy hills of light brown dirt and spiky plants. The turf they played on was on a terrace cut into the hillside and it was immaculately manicured and flat as a pancake. Natural, not Astro. Somehow the school always managed to keep it lush and watered, even when California saw drought. Bleachers ran the full length of the long east side, gleaming white concrete rows cut into the hillside. The set-up cost considerably more than the school library and was considerably better attended.

25

Coach had addressed them post-practice and was clearing away cones while they stretched. Cliques within cliques had formed, same as any team. The giants of Offensive line and Defensive line sat together. The skill players – quarterbacks, receivers, running backs – formed their own little pod. An inward facing circle of six, not by design, but nonetheless deeply unwelcoming to any outsider who wanted to join.

The talk was standard teenage locker-room talk - football, specific moves, pro football, chicks, who was getting the most action, who wasn't. Some of it was even true. General trash talk, which chicks were hot, which chicks were not, which ones would give it up easy. They, none of them, had their cellphones with them which ensured more actual conversation than happened at pretty much any other time of the week. They couldn't leave until coach left and slowly went through their stretches and cool down.

Luke reached forward and clasped his hands fully around his feet, supple hamstrings barely noticing the strain. He pretended to smile with the exertion. He was actually smiling with self-satisfaction.

"Damn, I don't know how you can do that," said Tom. He was one of the running backs, nimble, agile, quick – and yet not as flexible as Luke.

"Just always been able to do it, I guess. Not like them big boys on the line. Swear some of them can't even *see* their feet, never mind touch them!" Luke chuckled.

This was maybe a step too far. Trent frowned. He knew if he agreed with his friend, then it would get back to the O line. And next time a blitz came at him, one of them might just let the rusher through to teach him a lesson. But he didn't want to throw Luke under the bus either. Hmm. He chose the middle ground.

"Ha-ha, they ain't that bad," he said. "They got so much thick strong muscle on their legs, it's just harder to stretch that than your itty-bitty speedy skinny legs." He said it with a smile, striking the right balance of gentle admonishment.

Luke had realised his mistake and was grateful for the recovery line thrown in his direction.

26

"Fair. They're still good athletes. Not like some." He paused. "I bet Fat Boy can't even touch his knees, never mind his toes!" A good attempt to deflect.

"Which one's Fat Boy?" Tom looked nervously at the O line. He didn't think they were within earshot, but it wasn't worth the risk.

"Not one of them, stupid. Fat Boy! Jack whosis! The fat dude who always wears a Chargers shirt. In our class."

"Oh! Dude, you shoulda said so. Yeah, he's fucking fat. Gross." The other skill players shuddered in sympathy. Most of them didn't actually know who Jack was, but that didn't matter.

"He's started a diet," announced Trent quietly.

"He's done what?" asked Tom.

"A diet. Skyla saw him a couple times this week. Diet Cokes and salad. At least, I think he's started a diet. If the great big fat fuck got that big always eating Diet Coke and salad, there's really no fucking saving him."

More chuckles.

One of the other wide receivers chipped in.

"I don't know, Trent," he said with mock seriousness. "Maybe someone from Scripps can roll the fat fuck back into the ocean if it gets too bad."

Chuckles turned to guffaws and fist bumps. The chosen few stood and worked their way through their final stretches before reaching in. "One-Two-Three-WIN," was the call. They prowled off the field, with more bravado and self-confidence than if they'd just won the Super Bowl.

Jack was nowhere to be seen. He was miles away, walking home, listening to a podcast and completely ignorant of any discussions about him.

Chapter Six

"Dude, that's sick! How did you do that?"

"It's not that hard. It's called a deepfake. Just took a little while. It's not perfect yet though."

Luke manoeuvred the mouse on the pad, and the clip began to play again. It was *Raiders of the Lost Ark*. One of the most memorable movie openings in history.

Indiana Jones hacks his way through the Peruvian jungle. He beats the booby traps in the chamber. His strong jaw and manly stubble are illuminated by the golden glow of the idol, its lips twisted in a deathly rictus. Good and evil, right there, and yet it's Indy who's stealing the idol, and every kid who ever watched that movie wanted to be Indy when they grew up.

Indy weighs up his bag of sand. Feels about right. He sweeps the idol off its pedestal, and replaces it with the sandbag. Turns in triumph to leave the cave. He hears the chamber beginning to self-destruct and runs to escape. Survives the double-cross by his sidekick and dives under the descending stone gate. He retrieves the idol, takes a deep breath, and then hears a diabolical noise. As he looks up, he sees the biggest boulder in film history roll toward him, grinding ominously. Truly a work of cinematic art.

Except it wasn't a boulder in this clip. Not *that* boulder anyway. It was big and spherical, like a boulder. But it wasn't made of stone. Nor completely rigid. It was a little floppy, like a giant soft cheese, or lard. And as it started to roll, Jack's face appeared on it. He was puffing and panting and sweating and crying.

The signature theme tune kicked in. Swashbuckling brass,

trumpets blaring. Dah-de-dah-DAH, dah-de-dah. Heroism as soundwave. Recognisable to practically everyone in the western world, a reminder that the world is full of bad things, scary things, evil things, but there's not one of them that can beat Dr. Indiana Jones.

Except this time, the trumpets were not underlining the triumph of good over evil. They were the accompaniment to a carefully planned and specifically targeted character assassination of Jack. He had been transformed into a monstrous bulging ball of fat, chasing after Indy. His face was on the ball, but even that had been altered. His cheeks were chubbier than in real life. His eyes had been narrowed and looked piggier than they normally did. His skin was pockmarked with pimples, some especially swollen and green, ripe for popping. Sweat was rolling down his forehead, but not in a masculine, athletic, running-the-glory-relay-leg-in-track kind of way. Sweaty and furtive and disgusting in this context. Rolls of fat bounced up and down, around his boulder-waist, swelling up under his armpits.

Trent chuckled again.

"I want to get the eyes right first," said Luke, as if he were a portrait artist working on a commission. "I want them to be a little pudgier."

"Hmm. What else? Because I think it looks pretty darn good already."

"You're too kind," said Luke elaborately, affecting an educated Harvard drawl. "But an artist is never satisfied with his work, and most masterpieces are in fact abandoned rather than completed."

They laughed again and fist bumped again. Luke settled back down at his PC in his bedroom, while Trent stood and stretched. It's hard work bullying the weak. Crouching over a computer monitor isn't great for the posture.

He took a deep breath and settled down on Luke's beanbag. He half-watched over Luke's shoulder as he finessed the deepfake, and half flicked through his WhatsApps. There was nothing in his various group chats. Well, nothing he needed to respond to, just a smiley selfie from Skyla with hearts attached, of her at her desk in her bedroom. She was wearing a V-neck top and he could see her cleavage.

He typed back.

So cute. But you'd look even cuter without the T-shirt.

...

She typed back.

Oh, would I? Dude, my mom is home. Later xx

Skyla added extra kisses to texts when she said no to Trent. Kisses or winky-faces or hearts. She couldn't afford to lose Trent, but she didn't want to get caught sending nudes either.

Trent was undeterred.

*Honey, you're killing me. Literally. So fucking hard because of you. No blood left **anywhere** else x*

This was a lie. He wasn't hard, just bored. He wasn't Machiavelli. This wasn't part of a master plan to bend Skyla to his will, or to assemble a huge collection of photos of her topless or nude. He had no intention of posting the pictures – and he already had quite the collection – on a revenge porn website, to blackmail her. He was just a little bored, and when he made Skyla send him pictures, of her breasts or her ass or her cunt, he felt good. Sometimes he masturbated to them there and then, sometimes he did it later, and sometimes, like now, he just wanted them because he wanted them, and because he was bored.

You're crazy. I like it when you get hard because of me. Give me one sec xx

He smiled and sent her the heart-kiss emoji. Waited.

The picture wasn't long in coming. Skyla sent him a bathroom selfie. Obviously made sense – she could lock the door of the bathroom and be undisturbed. Most of his nudes from Skyla had been taken in the same bathroom. In this one, she'd taken off her T-shirt and bra, and was holding her breasts up a little from underneath with her left arm. Her nipples were erect, and he knew that she would have played with them to get them right for the photo. Her right arm was extended upwards to take the shot. The picture was carefully

30

cropped. Right on the top edge of it, Trent could see her full, pink mouth gleaming with freshly applied lipstick and her glowing white smile. Her tongue was sticking out. He liked that. He couldn't see her eyes or her nose though. Skyla thought this made her anonymous.

Trent smiled. He felt good.

Fuck!!! You are *so* beautiful. Going to have to do something about this x

He signed off with the waving hand, the eggplant, and the water splash emojis, and then two heart-kisses.

Come hard for me, baby xxx

Trent was still not hard. And he had no intention of getting hard, not in Luke's room. But he was satisfied, for now. He swiped through his apps until he found the one he was looking for, tucked away in an app folder he'd named 'Orchard.' It was where he kept all the crappy Apple apps he didn't really use like iTunes, and the App Store, and Facetime. To all intents and purposes, this one app looked like a standard math calculator. It was even called 'Calculator'. But it wasn't just a calculator. It was a hidden filing system app.

He opened the app and keyed in the code. Zero-four-two-five-decimal point. The calculator disappeared and was replaced by an array of icons. Folders with different girls' names on them. He prodded at Skyla's folder, and it opened up. There were many screens worth of thumbnail pictures of Skyla in various forms of undress. Topless, nude, one of the top of her head taken from above as she sucked his cock one time. She didn't know he'd taken that one. She didn't know he had kept the others. He promised her he deleted them, had told her nudes and selfies were all about connecting in the moment together with her, when they couldn't actually be together. Obviously a lie.

He idly flicked through a couple of pictures, focusing in on a couple of particularly explicit ones that Skyla had been especially reluctant to send. Her fingers stroking her cunt. He smiled, then remembered why he was there. He'd actually forgotten, had gotten distracted, by the picture of her pink

31

painted nails stroking her pink denuded lips. He clicked on the '+' icon and added her latest picture to her folder, saved it for all time, and nobody could ever know it was on his cellphone.

He closed the app and then went back to the regular Photos app. He deleted the picture, then deleted it from the deleted items folder. If Skyla ever asked to borrow his phone – which she had done, once or twice – he knew he could hand it over, and if she went through his pictures, she would not see that he had kept, against her explicit requests and despite his explicit promise, every single picture she ever sent him, plus quite a few of her she didn't know he had taken. Plus, quite a few of other girls he had kept, although for the most part, they didn't overlap with when he had been seeing Skyla. For the most part.

He typed back to Skyla.

Damn that was good xxx

He put his phone away and levered himself up from the beanbag. Time to check on progress by Luke in *Raiders of the Lost Ark*.

Chapter Seven

I used to be blonde.

I know, it sounds so silly saying that. But I was always really proud of my hair. When I was in high school, everybody used to say, "I wish I had your hair." It was the same in college. Girls used to pay a small fortune to have highlights or lowlights, or a full head of hair dyed, and I had it for free. People used to point it out, not knowing I could hear them. I'd hear store clerks say to customers that what they were looking for was where the blonde girl was. I had long blonde hair, soft and silky, and it just stood out. When we went to Harvard for mixers, I got noticed just for being me.

Jonathan told me years ago, when Jack was a baby, that it had been one of the first things he noticed about me. He was on shore duty back when Jack was born, and we thought we were so lucky that he could be home for that and the first few months. We'd met in a restaurant in Boston. This was all way before the internet and online dating. I was with a bunch of girlfriends, going out for a birthday. Jonathan was with a bunch of his friends from the Navy. They were all eating huge steaks and drinking beers. When our cake arrived, their table sent over a second bottle of champagne, and then we invited them to join us. We knew they were military, of course. They all had short hair and boisterous confidence. When they came over, we added chairs and another table to make it boy-girl-boy-girl and Jonathan sat next to me. I thought he was good-looking, but I wasn't really looking for anything serious. I was just finishing college and I was pretty ambitious. I only found out later, after Jack was born, that Jonathan had talked his buddies into sending over the bottle because he'd seen my hair and thought I was hot.

I mean, I didn't think he wasn't cute, but it wasn't really on my mind. I was out with my girlfriends after all, and you don't leave with a boy you've only just met, or at least you didn't back then. And we'd been out for dinner, I mean there was wine, but because of the food, nobody had gotten that drunk. But Jonathan sat next to me, and we talked, and when the evening broke up, he asked for my number, and I said yes. I can't even remember if I thought I would hear from him again, but it just seemed easier to give out my number than not to. I remember being impressed that he didn't try and kiss me that night. He seemed a bit more serious, more of a thinker than I'd have imagined sailors could be. He'd been to college too, obviously Annapolis, and he asked me about Wellesley and what I would do next. I remember I said Madison Avenue because I didn't want to tell him I wasn't sure, and he was definitely the kind of person who always knew where he was going. He was quiet but strong inside, and I found that attractive.

Our first date was actually just daytime coffee. It seems back to front, going for coffee after sort of having had dinner already, but Jonathan was different. It was a beautiful, cold, clear day, and we met downtown. Jonathan suggested coffee to go and so we walked around the Common and just walked and talked. The next thing I knew, we'd been walking for about two hours holding more or less empty coffee cups and then he kissed me gently. Stone cold sober, at lunchtime on a bright Saturday, next to the statue of George Washington near Commonwealth. I remember feeling his stubble, already sharp by noon, and not really thinking anything. And then we went for lunch in Back Bay, and he kissed me again when he had to get back to the ship, and I had to get home.

It was a complete stroke of luck when you think about it. Since it happened, I've often thought why specific things happen to specific people and tried to work out why. Jonathan wasn't stationed in the north-east. His ship just happened to be there that week. We hadn't been to that restaurant before, but one of the girls had seen a good review

34

of it, and they had good desserts so that was why we were there. And it's just fate. Sometimes there's just no point trying to work out why? If you tried to work out why everything happened, you'd just go crazy. And I don't believe everything happens for a reason. There's really no deep meaning to what happened.

I remember getting back to school that evening and my roommates either teasing me or interrogating me. They were impressed that he was a naval officer, and kept singing the music from *An Officer and a Gentleman*. They thought he should have come and picked me up in his dress whites when I graduated. I was more reserved. I'd never dated anyone in the services, I wasn't sure about being left on my own while he was deployed, and I wanted to be my own person, not 'wife of' somebody else. But the ship was docked in Boston for two weeks, so we saw each other while he was there. And when I was with him, I was just me. I didn't have to pretend to be cool, or clever, or anything. I was just me. On his last day we sat by the duck pond and made out, and we agreed we'd stay in touch. And then we wrote, old-fashioned paper letters to the Fleet Post Office. When his ship docked again three months later, I flew down to Jacksonville, and we spent the weekend together. We didn't even discuss it in the letters, but he got a hotel, and we spent the night together, and that was the last time I slept with anyone for the first time.

It was strange, in a way. I wanted to be my own person, and yet I ended up marrying the military. But when Jonathan and I first got together, he was deployed on his first ship, and so that gave me the freedom to do my own thing. So I went to law school when I graduated and that worked well. I clerked for a judge in Massachusetts, and when Jonathan docked somewhere, I'd usually fly down, and we'd have a mini vacation wherever he was. I'd always be waiting for him in port, and that way we had more time together. It was fun, although a bit of a charmed existence, because in our first year, year and a half, we were effectively only meeting up for vacations and not normal life. When a hotel maid services the room every day you're together, I guess you don't notice clutter or if only one of you is a clean freak.

After I left law school and got my own place in New York, Jonathan kept tidying all my stuff when he came home because he was used to it from the Navy. I had to tell him off. He could tidy his stuff, and he could tidy our stuff, but he had to leave mine alone. That used to drive me mad. I'm not especially messy, but then again, I'm not in the Navy. I didn't date while he was away, although I could have done. It just seemed inevitable that we would wind up together and get married.

I remember the actual wedding day, although everyone says that theirs goes so fast. Jonathan was in his dress blues, and I wore white. I had my hair piled up and a tiara, and I'd been running, running, running so I could fit in the darn dress. These days, I suppose I'd have signed up for a bridal bootcamp. But back then, I just ran every morning before work around Central Park and then figured I'd spun up my metabolism for the rest of the day. I'd take the subway to work ahead of time, run the park, and then shower in the office. I stayed off the desserts and wine, and when the day came, the dress fitted and I said 'I do' in a small church, back home in Massachusetts. Everyone said we looked good in the photos, and we did. Jonathan's crewmates were the guard of honour and we walked out underneath their cutlasses. I remember seeing the first photos come through. We had small, heart-shaped paper shapes to throw instead of normal confetti, and one of them was caught in the middle of the picture, a silhouette frozen in time, and that was the print we used for our thank-you cards.

I've still got that picture. It's aged well. None of my other friends from college married anyone in the military, and when I used to visit, I would see a picture of their wedding day in their house. Wedding dress fashions do vary, but for the most part, all my girlfriends look good, contemporary. Their husbands have dated, on the other hand. There are unfashionable lapels, or sideburns, or beards, and so on. And when I look at my picture, Jonathan is in his uniform, and they obviously don't age. And he always had short hair, and you'd expect a navy officer to have short hair, so he doesn't look like he's from another time. And the only difference is that I had my blonde hair piled up, and the sun was shining, so you can see just how golden blonde I was. I used to be blonde. Before.

I remember when Jack was born, he had dark hair. I didn't care, obviously, just as long as he was healthy. I didn't know if he was going to be a boy or a girl. I didn't care about that either, but I think Jonathan might have preferred a boy. But Jack arrived a week or so late, and he was born with a lot of hair for a new-born, soft and fine, but lots of it, and very dark. We had two weeks to name him, and my mom told us to hold out in case his hair colour changed. Apparently mine did when I was a baby, but he stayed dark – Jonathan's genes – and so we called him Jack Jonathan. I wanted a name people couldn't shorten, and Jonathan wanted initials that worked if he turned out sporty. I guess JJ is pretty catchy, well, not an embarrassing set of initials anyway. Some people just don't think, and there are some terrible names and initials out there. We just wanted Jack to have a name that would help him fit in, however he turned out, nothing out there or fancy.

I always smile when I think of Jack as a toddler. He was just your standard excitable little boy, always wanting to play. He had Jonathan's dark hair, but my eyes and nose. And when Jonathan was deployed, I never really bothered about set bedtimes, as long as he was asleep. I mean, it doesn't really matter where a toddler sleeps, as long as he does, and I figured him sleeping on me on the sofa was fine, and it made up for me being at work all day while he was with childcare. When he snuggled, he would grab a bunch of my hair and almost suckle on the end. I still had long hair back then. Long, blonde hair. Before all this happened.

Chapter Eight

Nick: So welcome back, and thanks for listening to those messages from Bullet.

Chris: Yeah, thanks. Now, back to the good stuff. I mentioned that you can pretty much put all shooters into one of two boxes. Well, everyone except Jack Tolleson. The first category – and we'll come back to them – is the shootings where the shooter didn't kill himself at the end. The cliché is that they always do-

Nick: Usually in the cafeteria-

Chris: Yeah

Nick: Survival tip, kids. Bring your own lunch to school. And eat it outside!*laughs*

Chris: *laughs* Yeah, the cliché is exactly that. But actually, only in about half of the cases does the shooter kill themselves at the end. And from what I've managed to research, they don't usually fail to kill themselves because they ran out of bullets, although that does seem to have happened to Dylann Roof in Charleston-

Nick: Yeah, he went full Winchester.

Chris: Yeah, but that's the only one I've found. So it's probably not, I don't know, involuntary survival? Not in that way? And similarly, I tried to find out if any shooters had tried to kill themselves, but fucked it up and again, I'm not aware of any times that's happened. But when I think of a couple of relatively recent occasions where the shooters have survived – I'm thinking of Holmes in the Aurora movie theatre or Cruz at Stoneman Douglas High-

Nick: We'll be covering Stoneman Douglas High in the future, although we probably should wait until the trial is done and dusted.

Chris: Yeah, that one's going to be really interesting. But the interesting thing with both of those shootings is that the shooter was apprehended by law enforcement after the event. They'd stopped shooting, hadn't tried to kill themselves, and either had escaped the scene, or were about to. Now you'd think that would make it easier to actually work out the motivation behind the shootings, but it doesn't. Obviously, at that point, the shooter is going to be tried, and one way to avoid the chair – if they've done it in a death penalty state – is to plead insanity. And so the narrative we usually get after the event is probably twisted a bit by the need for their lawyers to present a decent defence, and that's often an insanity plea.

Nick: Yeah, although in the case of Holmes at Aurora, it didn't work, and he's obviously doing life without parole.

Chris: Yeah, although Colorado was a death penalty state at the time, so maybe the fact that he was so fucked in the head meant he got life without parole rather than the needle? I guess the point is, what we hear from the shooters during the trial phase kind of has to be taken with a pinch of salt, because they're trying to get the best result they can. I mean, there's no way they're going to be found not guilty, but they're still trying to get the best result out of the situation, so the information we get is going to be specifically tilted toward one particular narrative.

Nick: Yeah. The other situation is when the shooter does kill himself, and we assume it's because of desperation. They've done what they've done and there's no way out, so suicide is the best answer.

Chris: Yeah, this is where Tolleson is so completely unique, because in all of our research, nobody has ever done what he did, how he did it, and especially why he did it.

Nick: Yeah, obviously we can't question the shooters who off themselves about their motivations, but we need to build up a picture based on other stuff. This is where we sometimes get journals and stuff like that.

Chris: Yeah. In some cases – Harris and Klebold for example – we get journals, and we can get a sense of what was going through their minds. And this is where, you know, you and I disagree to a certain extent.

Nick: Yeah. I guess, my starting point is that – and I'm talking about kids more than adults here – people sketch and draw all kind of shit in their notebooks during class, and sometimes it doesn't mean shit. It's just bored sketching. But after the event, because we all want to have a reason, a magic explanation, every single cartoon or sketch during math suddenly gets much more importance? Like, for example, when I was in elementary school, every kid drew cartoons of American warplanes with stars on them and German planes with swastikas on them. And swastikas looked kind of cool, because in elementary school, you don't really know the whole story. And sometimes you just doodle because you're bored and the next thing you know, you've done a page of swastikas. Did I grow up to become a neo-Nazi school shooter?

Chris: I don't know, man, did you? I mean I kind of feel you should have mentioned it if you did. You know, before now. Not live on air!*laughs*

Nick: *laughs* For the record, I did not become a neo-Nazi school shooter, or any other kind of school shooter. I even rent my room from a Jewish lady. Never once shot her! *laughs*

Chris: *laughs* Not once.

Nick: But anyway, my point is, nobody really knows. I mean, we never hear about all the kids who sketched stuff they probably shouldn't or said stuff they probably shouldn't and yet who never got involved in any crime, never mind a school shooting or something similar. I guess I just get annoyed when people look at sixteen pages of Eric Harris's notebook and say, this is definitely what he meant, and this is definitely why he did it. I mean, I heard one dude on the internet say that if Harris hadn't done Columbine, then he would have definitely ended up being Ted Bundy because his notebooks were full of hate and misogyny and so on. And the truth is, we'll never actually know, you know? Not for sure.

Chris: Yeah. I do see your point, but this is where we have

different opinions. I totally get that kids in school sketch all kind of crap. Probably ninety percent of it they never want to see the light of day once they're adults. I mean, thank God I grew up in the sketchbook era rather than the smartphone era because there really is no place to hide in the smartphone era. But I guess my view is that the notebooks or online postings of kids who turned into shooters are valid specifically because they turned into shooters.

Nick: Yeah, I kind of see that argument, and I agree with you about the smartphone era. I kind of think that Congress should bring in a law that automatically seals everything you posted online once you turn eighteen.

Chris: Like what?

Nick: Well, you know that if you're a juvenile offender, once you're eighteen, you can get your records sealed? So nobody knows you got caught shoplifting a half-dozen Twinkies when you were fifteen, because, yeah, it was a crime, and yeah you were dumb and yeah, you got caught, but you kind of get a fresh start once you're eighteen? Because after that, you're an adult and you should know better?

Chris: Yeah. Well, unless you're special, you knew better when you were fifteen too, you just didn't act on it.

Nick: *laughs* Exactly. Well, I think Congress should bring in a law that automatically wipes or seals everything you put online before you were eighteen because you and me, we got to make our mistakes when we were kids and nobody can drag up my notebook entirely filled with swastikas that I sketched during math because I was bored, and then blame everything I ever did on those swastikas. Or like when football players get caught out because they liked or retweeted a joke that was close to the line when they liked it in high school, but which is way off limits today. Anything after you're eighteen, fair enough, but underage? I think we have to give that stuff a pass, because kids do stupid things. It doesn't seem right to attach adult meanings to juvenile posts and journals.

Chris: That would be a good law. But maybe – and again,

this is where you and I have different views. I mean, you're wrong, but I respect your right to be wrong. This is America, godamnit-

Nick: Douche

Chris: *laughs* I respect you even more now. I agree with that law, but I think that if a crime is committed that's in line with the stuff in your journal or the stuff you posted online, then I think we can probably attach greater meaning to that stuff than, I don't know, that time you experimented with the liquor cabinet when your parents were away and retweeted some jokes you shouldn't have done?

Nick: OK, well maybe we agree to disagree on that one.

Chris: OK, but the point is that sometimes we get evidence in the form of journals or online activity, kind of speaking to us from beyond the grave. And sometimes it's not even from beyond the grave. I mean, we haven't had the trial yet, so I don't know how it's going to be presented, but from what we've seen so far, Nikolas Cruz at Stoneman Douglas High posted a shit ton of hate stuff online, including that he wanted to recreate the Texas Tower shooting. So we can kind of get a sense of motivation from that.

Nick: Yeah.

Chris: Sometimes, though, we don't get any of that - no journals, no online presence, no actual clues about what they were thinking, or least what they were writing before the event. Obviously in the pre-internet era, the only stuff would have been paper journals and maybe there was less investigation going on back then?

Nick: Yeah.

Chris: And sometimes, even in the internet era, there's nothing to go on. The Las Vegas shooter, I forget his name-

Nick: Paddock. Stephen Paddock.

Chris: Thank you-

Nick: You had like one job! *laughs* Hashtag-Fail!

Chris: I know! Paddock left behind no notes, no online presence, no red flags, hell, not even any yellow flags. Just planned it, did it, and then shot himself. We really don't know anything about why he did it, and so there's a bunch of *guesses, some of which are conspiracy theories and some of which are maybe more sensible guesses, but the truth is we just don't know.*

Nick: Yeah, and this is kind of the case with Jack Tolleson at Whittlesford in that we don't have any journal or online presence. We have eyewitness accounts, both of that day, and of his life generally, because he was in high school and so he was surrounded by people – which is different to Paddock, who was loaded from real estate, didn't have a job where he interacted with many people and generally kept a low profile. What we do know about Tolleson is that he seems to have planned this over a considerable length of time, but we don't actually have any evidence of what he was actually thinking during that time. We don't have a journal, we don't have any online presence. Well, we have an online presence, but there's nothing out of the ordinary. Just usual high school stuff.

Chris: Exactly. So to understand Tolleson, especially because what he did was so totally different to any other shooting, we need to rely on other stuff, and we'll get right into this in a moment.

Chapter Nine

Another glorious day in the neighbourhood. Friday fun day. Jack arrived home and chilled in his room with Mr. Orange. He didn't do homework on Friday nights, but he knew he should because it would hang over him for the whole weekend until he forced himself to do it on Sunday, after football. He figured everyone was due a relaxing evening at the end of their working week. And he was no exception. And he didn't feel the urge to rebel against Sunday working. His dad worked the hours the Navy told him to, and his mom always seemed to be half-working. She'd sit on the couch while he watched football, reading and marking papers, or pecking away at her laptop.

Jack was alone in the house, save for Mr. Orange. He checked the time, and quickly stripped naked. He didn't want his mom walking in on what he was about to do. He went into her bedroom and looked himself up and down in the full-length mirror. He wasn't sure if he was making progress or not. It was day nineteen of his fitness drive. He'd started on a Monday, and this was the third Friday.

He frowned as he examined his naked body. He started at the top. He had his father's hair, not like his mom's golden flowing tresses. His was thick, dark, and unruly. He didn't use product, didn't know how to. Or why. His hair started each morning relatively in place, held by water from his morning shower. By first coffee break it would start to wilt, and by lunchtime it was limp. It was too long and needed cutting, but he'd seen a video on Insta that said bigger people should have longer hair. A big person with short hair – well, that just looked like a tiny ball balancing on top of a great big fat one.

He moved further down. He liked his stubble, thick already, even at his age. This was a saving grace as far as he was concerned. Early into puberty gave you some status. There was nothing worse than being the last kid to sprout pubes. One kid at school would be forever known as the *Mexican Hairless*. Not because he was Mexican. He looked at his crotch. Smaller than a porn star, and surrounded by thick dark pubic hair. He rarely changed in front of his classmates. He was not an athlete, but at least he wouldn't get mocked for being bald down there.

He wondered briefly how it went for the girls. The internet was full of stories about girls being pressurised into waxing or shaving. The bush was dead. Did that mean girls who didn't grow hair early were the cool ones? He wouldn't know. He didn't have any close female friends, and had never been kissed, had never seen a girl naked in real life. It never occurred to him that he was in the same boat as most of his classmates. Nor that most of the girls his age hadn't seen a boy naked yet either.

He ran his hand over his stubble again. He figured he could grow a full beard pretty easily by now. He'd false started over the summer break and not shaved for a week. He had thought it looked a little patchy, even though an objective observer might have said it wasn't. It was the itch that put him off though. After a week it had gotten scratchy, especially around his neckline, and he had given up and shaved it off. He decided then that the best look was one that said he *could* grow a full beard, as evidenced by stubble, but without the hassle of actually doing it.

He forced a smile at the mirror. His wires were due to come off soon, but until then his teeth were obscured by metal. He'd wanted to go with Invisalign, but it wasn't covered by insurance. Instead, he had railtracks running across his teeth. He'd gotten used to them by now. It would probably feel weird when he didn't have them anymore and, to be fair, only a couple of people at school had Invisalign. Most people had railtracks. And while stories were rife about interlocking while making out, that wasn't a bridge his tracks had crossed yet.

He looked at the rest of his body. Even after nearly three weeks he wasn't sure. He'd foregone a lot of favoured food during that time. And walked a lot, although he was actually enjoying the walks. Private lessons with Professor Podcast. He thought he might have lost a little weight, but the handles around his waistline seemed to have grown, not shrunk. The thought never occurred to him that they looked bigger because the portion directly above had shrunk. He focused in on his arms. They looked spindly to him, especially next to his ginormous torso.

He sighed and held out his phone. He carefully positioned his hand and the phone in front of his face, and snapped himself in the mirror. He was charting progress. Insta was full of 'before and afters'. If this worked, he'd try and find a way to shift them together like a time-lapse, tracking his journey from fat to fit. For now, he hated it. He was big, and white, and wobbly. He was a wobbly whale with a huge ass. No wonder he hadn't gotten to kiss a girl yet.

He stood on his mom's bathroom scales. One pound lighter than last week. Whoop-de-fucking-do. A pound. Just one bag of sugar. He'd started the process by weighing himself every day, but found that disheartening. There were days when he'd weighed more, not less. He'd gone back to Google and discovered that his weight could change lots over a twenty-four-hour period. The smart dieter focused on measurement in inches, not weight in pounds, and they weighed themselves once a week, at the same time of day, preferably naked, or wearing as little as possible. It was advice he'd started following. Maybe once he was closer to his 'after' photo he'd start an Insta profile called that: *@TheSmartDieter*. His gleaming smile illuminating a six-pack as he held hands with an equally photogenic girl. He smiled at the thought.

For now, though, one pound only this week. Three pounds in total. For a new total of 251. That was 251 bags of fucking sugar. He returned to his room and got dressed, doing the math in his head. At a pound a week, it would take him nearly a year to get down to 215. That was his target. 215

was what LaDainian Tomlinson had weighed when he lit up the Chargers when they were back in San Diego. Admittedly, LT was five foot ten and not six foot three. He was also a Hall of Fame running back and not a high school student, but Jack liked the idea of connecting by numbers. 215 it was. Thirty-six pounds more needed.

He entered the number into a spreadsheet on his laptop, and a chart updated to the right. Only three data points, but at least pointing down. But it was still too slow, too damn slow. He cast a glance at his own small mirror in his bedroom. There must be more that could be done. Hollywood did it all the time, bulking up for one role, and then slimming down for another one. He wanted to do both, to bulk up his muscles and slim down his fat.

He clicked on the browser, animated and urgent. Where could he find the magic bullet? Hollywood's greatest weight losses? His Google search led him to clickbait after clickbait; Tom Hanks in *Philadelphia*, Matt Damon in *Courage under Fire*. He lost interest, disparaged by the constant need to click through to the next page, and how Hanks and Damon looked in those movies. One was ravaged by HIV, and the other by PTSD. Neither was the look he was going for. He wanted to look, hmm, the athletic side of normal. The muscly side of normal. He leaned forward towards the laptop and his stomach butted against the edge of his desk. His great big stomach. His shoulders sagged. Fuck it, he just wanted to not be fat. Mr. Orange could sense he was upset. He padded along Jack's bed, and deftly sprang onto his desk. Butted his head against Jack's, marking him, and distracting him. Jack smiled.

"Temptations?"

Mr. Orange chirped a half miaow of delight and sprang down from the desk. He trotted briskly down the stairs to the kitchen cupboard where the treats were kept, looking over his shoulder to make sure Jack was following.

While Mr. Orange was tucking in, Jack carried on researching on his phone. There was a lot of overlap between articles that spoke about beach bodies and articles that claimed to maximise your number of followers on Twitter or Insta. Hmm, one interview with an Insta fitness babe proclaimed the benefits of jumping rope. He wasn't sure about that. He'd only have room to do it in the yard, and then people would see, and he would look disgusting. All that fat wobbling up and down. Plus, the noise of his sneakers slapping onto the ground. Hmm, not good, but maybe she had a point? Boxers were always jumping rope, and they had bodies he wouldn't mind having. It was only in the real heavyweights where they carried any spare fat. Guys like Ruiz. Came out of nowhere and sparked out the Brit in the seventh round. Then he partied, and ate solidly for six months before getting his ass handed to him in the rematch. But generally, yes, pro boxers had a good look to them. Maybe the fitness babe had a point.

He looked her up on Insta, to see what content she posted. Actually quite promising. Every day, she posted at least one exercise routine; stretching, strength, or HIIT. What the fuck was HIIT? Ah, High Intensity Interval Training. Cardio-type stuff. Hmm, maybe Jack wasn't for high intensity just yet, but the rest of the content seemed pretty decent. Maybe this was the way to go about it. The fact that she was invariably wearing the skimpiest gym outfit didn't hurt either. He joined her 326,000 followers.

He poured himself an OJ and went to the couch, flicking on SportsCenter in the background.

He quickly went through her posted content and saved it, dividing the individual items neatly into folders. Abs, upper body, lower body. Then found some other influencers. Most were like the original fitness babe. Young, slender women, with perfect smiles, and skimpy outfits. They seemed to focus mainly on abs and booty exercises. It was all about the booty, it seemed. He checked through their content and followed a half-dozen or so identikit models. They all looked the same, yes, but they all looked the same because that was what looked good. That was the right way to look.

There were quite a few men plying the same trade, although they presented themselves differently. They had a different version of skimp. Practically none of them were wearing a shirt, whether exercising indoors or outdoors. Shorts, yes, but baggy. Nobody wanted to look at their junk while they flexed and strained, but top half was usually naked and showing off a six-pack or with a sleeveless top to emphasise the straining guns. Several of them wore olive green and highlighted their former military credentials, Marine Corps. SEAL Team. Delta. It was yet another pissing contest but, in fairness, they looked like Jack wanted to look. He followed a few of them too.

He finished his OJ, newly energised. He'd effectively just engaged a dozen personal trainers, for free. If he could get into the routine of doing a couple of their training sessions a day, it would surely help. He knew he wasn't going to look perfectly buff within six weeks. Those kinds of promises were bullshit, probably only achieved by the likes of Barry Bonds and the rest of his juiced cronies. But this was another step in the journey, an incremental step. The feeling of satisfaction he enjoyed at that moment was as if he'd done the first training session already. He savoured the warm healthy glow and smiled as his mom pulled up outside their home. Time for a snack before heading out to watch football.

Jack arrived at Whittlesford early, as he always did, to watch the game, keen to secure the best seat. It was the season opener, and the whole student body seemed to have showed up, even twenty minutes before kick-off. It was open seating, but social pockets had already formed. The swim team, in matching tracksuit tops fresh from practice, occupied one corner and devoured fast food. The boys were tall and broad-shouldered with short wet hair, the girls equally statuesque, but with longer and more obviously dishevelled locks. Huge sports bags were cast around them. Jack had never worked out why they needed so much stuff. Surely it was just shorts or a swimsuit, a towel, and some goggles.

Other groups formed, either by synchronised arrival, or by social magnetics. Some groups were tighter than others. The math club geniuses tended to sit by themselves. Jack knew a couple of them, but he would never impose on their company. For one thing, he was content to just soak up the atmosphere. For another, the brain trust was on a different level – one frizzy-haired redhead girl was intimidatingly clever – and even if Jack had wanted to join, he figured he would just get in the way of conversation way beyond his comprehension.

Other groups had lower barriers to entry, if any at all. There were sprawling groups of common interest, or near neighbours, or just force of habit of sitting in a particular spot. There was a gentle order and routine, anticipation of the game rather than fever pitch excitement. This was California after all, where fever pitch was set a notch or two lower than the firebrand football games in East Texas.

The Friday night floodlights snapped on, illuminating bright green turf. It was nearly game time. The home team warmed up in one of the end zones, doing drills back and forth, jocks in motion and collision. The school band assembled in neat rows and columns, scarlet uniforms festooned with rows of buttons. Whittlesford's musical kids sub-divided themselves into stoners, who grew their hair and played crackly, guitar-heavy grunge, and the ones who played band. A couple of the truly gifted vocalists and drummers were accepted into the stoner-led crowd but playing in a high school band was never cool. As they began to play, they walked back and forth to the direction of the conductor on his plinth on the fifty-yard line. Short staccato strides in time to the beat.

They were followed by the cheerleaders, all gleaming white smiles and shaking pom-poms. Tiny girls were launched into the air to be caught by chunkier girls, and the smiles stayed constant throughout, like synchronised swimmers. They were jocks in their own right in terms of the training required, but not widely recognised as such.

The band worked their way through the repertoire. It was a standard playlist that had never changed during the three previous football seasons Jack had experienced at Whittlesford. Show tunes, marching tunes, a couple of reworked pop songs, and then always finishing with *The Star-Spangled Banner*. Everybody would stand and remove their caps for that, the same as at every football game, at every high school, across the country.

This evening, there was a twist. A new tune had been added, which threw Jack a little. He had been watching the band, and the cheerleaders, on autopilot. Still enjoying it, but more as background. He'd been watching the cheerleaders both because they were pretty and because they were impressively athletic. As the usual penultimate song tailed off, he'd shrugged his shoulders to stretch out the kinks, waiting for the national anthem to be announced so he, like everyone else would stand. But the band had kept playing where they would usually tail off. The brass stepped forward amongst their formation and blasted out the theme to *Raiders of the Lost Ark*. It was an old movie and an old tune, but one that everybody recognised, a tune made for mass brass bands. Instant visions of Indiana Jones with Fedora and whip.

The song clearly took the band conductor by surprise too. Jack could see him laughing, as could the rest of the crowd. The tune obviously amused the players; Jack could see them break their warm-up and exchange fist-bumps, laughing. It must have been a prank, or a bet laid down by one of the players. The conductor let the band play out a few more bars, and then brought the Raiders march to a close.

The announcement rang out over the speakers and the spectators rose for *The Star-Spangled Banner*.

Chapter Ten

There was something different about Brie today, but Jack couldn't work out what it was. She looked hot, for sure, but he couldn't see what it was. He occasionally lusted after her, but that was nothing unusual. Most of the guys at Whittlesford lusted after her, and probably more than a few of the girls did too. She was tanned, toned, and with long shiny dark hair. Her father was a dentist, and early wires had paid off with a gleaming Hollywood smile. Jack would often slouch from his corner in the classroom and stare, unnoticed. He sometimes imagined Brie when he jerked off in the shower, thinking of a neatly trimmed bush and of her shuddering in ecstasy as he went down on her, before she did the same to him. She wasn't his only crush, wasn't his only object of lust, but she sure was hot.

Today, though, something was different about her. He couldn't quite put his finger on what it was. Immaculate white sneakers with immaculate white socks. Nothing different about that. Sometimes she wore sneakers, sometimes flip-flops. Today was a sneaker day. They were the plain white Nikes, probably designed for tennis, even though he didn't know if she played. Of course she would though. They probably had their own court, or membership at the Pines Country Club, but there was nothing unusual about her footwear. Daisy Dukes, and a plaited leather belt showed off those toned, tanned legs. Again, fairly standard. In the winter months, she would sometimes wear skinny jeans, but only in winter. The rest of the time it was shorts, or occasionally a mini-skirt. She had on a white shirt through which he could see the outline of a white lacy bra. He knew that after school she would untuck the tails and tie them under her tits, showing off her midriff, but only after school – no exposed midriffs allowed on campus. She often wore white shirts, or checked shirts, or tees with slogans, so there was nothing different there either. And yet, something had caught his eye as she walked past him with her gang. He'd smiled in her general direction. Not a personal smile to a friend, nor a 'will you be my friend' smile, but a general positive smile that he hoped didn't look creepy or needy. She hadn't noticed, or maybe she had. Either way, she hadn't smiled back, just continued on her way along the corridor, her backpack over her shoulder

He paused and leaned against the wall of blue aluminium lockers, closing his eyes, and bringing his hands to his face as if he were fatigued. The vision of Brie floated before his eyes. That was it. There had been a black circle on the collar of her shirt. Only on one side though. Asymmetrical, Discordant. That was what had made him pause and wonder what was different. He wondered what it was, but his mind quickly moved on. Fashion wasn't his thing, certainly not female fashion. Probably a new brand or something.

"I got one for you too!" Brie said, giggling, and extending her hand toward Skyla. They were sat in a corner of the canteen, killing time between class. The boys were hanging out doing boy stuff, and Brie and Skyla were just hanging, iPhone on the table, 50Cent playing *Tryna Fuck Me Over* just loud enough to prove rules about music didn't apply to the cool kids, just quiet enough not to actually force a teacher to do something about it.

"You're so funny! Did he really not notice?"

"I don't think so. He did a double-take, but I don't think he saw what it was."

"Probably too busy looking at your rack!"

"Ewwww!!!"

Skyla looked in her hand at the disc that Brie had just given her. It was a small circular pin about an inch across. In the centre, a black and white orca was venting a small plume of water through its blowhole. Around the edge of the pin, white letters picked out 'Save the Whale.'

"Too funny," repeated Skyla.

"It's so cool! He really hasn't got a clue," giggled Brie. "Are you going to put it on?"

"Actually, I have another idea. You wear yours today. Monday, I'll wear mine too. The day after that, we get someone else to wear one as well. And the day after that-"

Brie positively cackled with laughter.

"And the day after that, another one, and another one, and another one, until the whole school is wearing one, except Shamu! This is the best idea ever!"

"You're going to need more pins!"

"I know!! Actually, I know…why don't we order a bunch of them from Etsy or somewhere? We can sell them to everybody else, one at a time. We could even mark up a little."

"Great idea!"

Brie looked on her phone. She tilted the screen to share it with Skyla. Etsy sold them for a buck twenty each, but there didn't seem to be a bulk discount. She quickly did the math.

"How about we buy a hundred between the two of us? Costs us sixty dollars each, and then we sell them for two dollars. We clear forty dollars each in profit, maybe more if we can charge more than two dollars."

"You are so smart! I'm in!"

They linked pinkie fingers and shook. Brie placed the order online while Skyla retrieved her own cellphone and transferred sixty dollars over to Brie on Venmo.

Chapter Eleven

Thomas sighed. He hoisted his heavy gut up, putting his heart and lungs under considerable strain, and then he sighed again. His arms, dripping with fat visible even through his bespoke pinstripe, gestured a helpless shrug. The shrug was helpless, even if Thomas was not. Oh no, in a world of relative comparison, Thomas was absolutely powerful, and absolutely rich. The two, unsurprisingly, were linked. But even though he ruled his kingdom like a mediaeval despot, and there were no threats to his crown, his goals remained relative. He wanted more money. More success. Not more than competitor x, or competitor y. Just *more*. More for him. And when some idiot came and pitched an idea to him, he would listen. He had learned a long time ago that even the most badly presented person could have an idea that was pure gold. Conversely, even the most polished presenter could have a truly awful idea and needed to be cut off at the knees.

Today was one of the latter. The pitch was being delivered by an earnest young woman. Mid-twenties, with long dark hair hanging loose. Slim and sporty, with an amazing smile. She genuinely believed in her pitch; he had seen that right from the opening sentence. It hadn't impressed him. Some of his best commercial successes had come from movies where the only thing the producers had believed in was the forecasted profits. He didn't care if producers believed in the message and the meaning. He cared about dollars. Lots of dollars. And given that commercial success was inversely proportional to the complexity of the message, this pitch was already beginning to bore him. However, he was still intrigued by the woman in front of him, by which he meant he enjoyed watching her beg and was debating what she would be like in bed. The thirty-year age gap was irrelevant. What Thomas wanted, he usually got. And what he wanted right now was for this woman to be on her knees, sucking him.

He nodded both sagely and plausibly. "Run that by me again," he said. "Pretend we're in an elevator, and you've got thirty seconds."

Alina paused, composed herself and then smiled.

"Of course," she said. "A genuine elevator pitch." She held his gaze.

"The Whittlesford Massacre was different. It was totally unique, and it touched American hearts in a completely different way to any other school shooting, so the film about it should be completely different to any other film about a school shooting."

She paused. The best pitches were like movie trailers themselves. Speak slowly. Pause. Emphasise meaning. Go again. Ramp up.

"*Bowling for Columbine* was the first commercially successful movie about a school shooting. It took over fifty million dollars at the box office, versus a budget of less than five million. And since then, we've had many more shootings but no more commercially successful movies."

Pause.

"There is a gap in the market; a significant, commercial, gap. This picture will fill that gap."

Pause.

"The gap is large and commercially viable. Documentaries and factual podcasts have seen exponential growth in the last five years. The Netflix generation *devours* them, but we can't remake *Bowling for Columbine*. We need to make something different. We need to make something that the modern viewer is crying out for."

Pause.

"We need to make a movie about the *victims*, not the shooter. But about the victims; the people that Jack Tolleson killed that day at Whittlesford High."

"This is a picture that sits perfectly in the intersection between commercial success and critical appraisal. It needs to be made, because Whittlesford was *different,* and because people need to know *why* it was different. They want to know about it, and they'll *pay* to know about it."

Thomas smiled. *Good pitch technique.* Although honestly, did people think that good pitch technique was something he hadn't seen before? He liked her though. She was his type. Young and idealistic. He enjoyed women like her. He enjoyed watching them supplicate in front of his bulging wallet, and he enjoyed fucking them. He kept a running total on his phone of how many he'd fucked. At least one a week found their way into the Notes app on his iPhone; a name, a guess of their age, a brief sentence of what they looked like, and how well they fucked. He wondered what would be written for this one. *Alina, twenty-fiveish, long dark hair, swallowed, but hated it.* Not that that would stop him.

He paused and briefly touched his left hand to his temple. His right was gently holding a super shiny chrome pen. He pretended to think. At the same time, he pressed his right foot onto a button under the desk.

"OK. I see where you're coming from. It's interesting, maybe, but you're not planning on mentioning the shooter at all within the picture? Literally not one word?"

She tried, but failed, to conceal her excitement. In her mind, this was genuine interest.

"No, this is the unique selling point of the movie. Nobody wants to hear about the shooter and, personally, I don't think society should publicise their names. But we owe it to the victims to memorialise them."

She paused.

"*America* owes it to the victims. And because of that, Americans and citizens worldwide will go and watch this movie. In the theaters, and in their homes by subscription."

Thomas nodded, again, sagely and plausibly. Much practice, but honestly, what the actual fuck was keeping his-

A knock at the door, and his assistant walked in. Thomas feigned annoyance.

"I'm sorry to butt in, but your next appointment has arrived…"

Thomas looked at his watch, again in a credible demonstration of annoyance. He knew he had no other appointments. That was why he had to press the button under his desk.

"I'm very sorry, Alina, but we are out of time. Hmm." He pretended to consider, pretended to look at his computer screen, which showed not a calendar, but the performance of his stock portfolio. The numbers were green. Richer. Definitely warranting a reward. Like fucking a twenty-five-year-old brunette. Not just any twenty-five-year-old brunette, but one he hadn't fucked before. It kept the scoreboard ticking over.

"Hmm. I'm back-to-back for the rest of the afternoon. Are you free later? We could discuss over an early dinner."

He knew the answer would be 'yes.' He honestly couldn't remember the last time anybody had turned down a second appointment with the king. He couldn't tell if Alina knew how dinner would go, but it didn't matter. She would find out soon enough.

She nodded brightly.

"Sure. What time and where?"

He looked at his assistant, who was familiar with the routine.

"Your last appointment is a little open-ended…" she said.

"Ah, OK. In that case, can you come back here at 6.30 p.m.? We'll have worked something out by then."

"Yes, that works." Alina stood and collected her valise. She extended her hand to Thomas. Anybody could make an entrance, but pitching required a strong exit. Put the ball back across the net, smile, and be confident. No last minute whining.

"Thank you very much for your time, Thomas. I will see you here at 6.30." Strong, confident. No abbreviation nor informality. Polished and professional.

"Looking forward to it."

"Me too." She smiled again, consciously relaxing her face

so he could see her dimples.

They shook, and the assistant walked her out. Thomas stared openly at Alina's ass. Toned, he thought. Very definitely toned. He was definitely going to fuck her, maybe even before dinner, maybe before and after, although he'd probably need to pop a bluey to manage the second one. Then kiss her off. She was over twenty-one. No harm, no foul.

He chuckled to himself. They were always so earnest, so naïve, the twenty-somethings. They'd grown up on a constant diet of emotions and righteousness. Generation emote, celebrating every aspect of humanity, regardless of whether it warranted it or not. He'd become skilled at pretending to care. He frequently mentioned his Foundation and the good works it did, although – cue sigh – he wished he could do more. The doe-eyed innocents lapped it up, but it always ended the same way. With him emptying himself into them, or onto them, in a hotel, or a limo, or his office, and mentally moving onto the next prospect before he'd even zipped himself back up.

He certainly had no intention of making a movie about the victims of Whittlesford, though. Literally nobody gave a shit. A movie about the shooter, whatever his name was? Maybe. But *Bowling for Columbine* hadn't been called Klebold and Harris. Nor was it named after Scott, or Rohrbough, or Sanders. School shootings were named after where they happened. Location, not cast. And if there was one thing Thomas knew, it was how to turn a buck making movies.

As she descended in the elevator, Alina smiled. If there was one thing she knew, it was how to make men want to fuck her. And women, although that particular skillset was less useful in a world where men held most of the power. Making men want to fuck her had been what had gotten her into the building in the first place. There were hundreds of would-be filmmakers who wanted ideas financing. There were hundreds of hot women who wanted to make films and needed financing, and there were hundreds of good ideas for films.

She clutched her valise. A movie about the victims of

Whittlesford. Did Thomas think she was serious? She couldn't think of anything worse. Who, in their right mind, would want to go and watch a movie about that? It was hardly date night material. *Oh, hey honey, it's our third date, and I'm feeling kind of horny, so I got us back row kissing seats to watch ninety minutes about a bunch of bullying little shits who got shot in the head by some fat wacko in a high school in California somewhere. Are you wet yet?* She giggled inwardly at the thought. How could Thomas be so stupid?

She caught sight of herself in the mirror of the elevator car. *That* was why Thomas could be so stupid. Because she looked hot. Slim legs from hours on a treadmill, and a skirt above the knee, hose that looked demure, but showed the merest hint of stocking top when she crossed her legs. A dark suit jacket with a narrow, but deep vee so cleavage was on display if one looked. And men did. And heels that lengthened her legs and made her taller, but not so tall that middle-aged short men in management positions couldn't see down her top. That was important. And a silver brooch on her lapel that concealed a tiny camera lens and a microphone. Because Thomas was a fat, disgusting pig who still believed in the power of the casting couch and she was going to expose him. Ironically by pretending she wanted to make a movie about another fat, disgusting pig. Her mind wandered. What was the collective noun for fat, disgusting pigs? A jelly? A smear? A blob?

She would have to be deft this evening to escape his inevitable attempts to fuck her, but she was confident. Everything would be recorded, either by the camera in the brooch, or the lens in the snap of the valise. And then, well, that would be a movie. One starring Thomas, rather than financed by him. She smiled again. That movie would make her more money, and make her more famous, than anything she could ever have done about whatever the fat kid at Whittlesford was called. She was going to be so famous that she'd be on Oprah. She'd be known just by her first name. Just like Oprah. Or Kanye. *Malala.*

Chapter Twelve

Over the weekend, Jack had forgotten about the black circle on Brie's collar. That didn't mean he hadn't thought of her. He had, but only once and only naked, with his dick in his hand, in the shower. The rest of the time, he was focused on his usual weekend, or on other fantasy girls.

There hadn't been a school football game on the Friday evening, so Jack had walked home after class. He had quickly dashed off his homework. He wasn't especially enthusiastic about his assignments, but he hated working during college football on Saturday or pro football on Sunday more than he hated missing Friday afternoon sunshine. He'd learned to get home and just get it done. His grades were probably better as a result, the subject matter nearer in his memory but that wasn't the point. He just wanted to have the weekend free.

He'd gone to the movies on Friday night, not really with anyone, but not really on his own either. The school WhatsApp group had discussed a new release – the latest CGI superhero flick – and a bunch of people had agreed to meet at the local AMC theatre. It was kind of an open invitation. The discussion had ended with one of Jack's classmates saying that they were going to the 8 p.m., IAWTCA, Whittlesford-speak for *If Anyone Wants To Come Along*. About half a dozen had given a thumbs up, and Jack had followed suit. None of the beautiful people had, obviously. They would never respond to an open invitation like that. They didn't follow an agenda, they set it. And beautiful people had dates on non-football Friday nights anyway.

The movie had been watchable without being good. Jack had foregone popcorn and soda, but just drank water from a bottle in his backpack. After, he'd hung out with the crowd, mainly guys, for a little while as they talked about the movie over ice cream at Geno's next to the theatre. He'd passed on the ice cream, too.

The rest of the weekend had gone quietly. He'd watched a lot of sports, and a Netflix documentary. He'd helped his mom with a couple of chores around the house and in the yard. The small lawn in front was plastic, polka-dotted with holes for real cacti, but the back yard had more live plants. His mom had trimmed various spiky protrusions, and Jack had bagged and taken them out to the trash. He'd also maintained his walking levels, hitting his 10,000 strides early each morning before the sun had gotten too hot. Calories out needed to be bigger than calories in. Like homework, he knew better than to put it off or it would impinge into sports TV time. His cat had looked curiously at him as he left the house for his Sunday walk, and then trotted along behind him for a few yards before deciding to turn back. When Jack had returned, Mr. Orange was fast asleep on his bed, but awoke to give a half-miaow before returning to his slumbers.

He smiled at the memory. The weekend seemed a long time ago. Instead, he was on the bus as it pulled into Whittlesford. Amongst the pockets of students loitering around before class, he saw Brie in the distance, another white shirt, sleeves rolled up, and the black dot on the collar again. She was striding toward Skyla, arms outstretched for a public Monday morning hug. Skyla had on a tight pink tee and black mini-skirt. The tee also had a small black circle on it. He thought it must be some new fashion brand, presumably a women's one, or he'd have seen it on the boys too. Whatever. He wouldn't be following the trend.

Jack was content with his fashion choices or, more specifically, his conscious lack of them. He wore cargo shorts pretty much every day of the year, only wearing long pants when he had to, or when it was really cold. 'Really cold' in Whittlesford was limited pretty much to January, and even then only after sundown. If he was at a late ballgame, he might wear jeans or cargo pants, but he usually stuck with the shorts. They were less sweaty. And if he wore a thick hoody, the temperature seemed to average out. Pretty much every tee he owned came from the Chargers, and each year he would get a new game jersey for his birthday. They were designed to be worn loose, which was good. Offset the sweat-inducing properties of 100% polyester.

The day passed without incident. It was just another day of school. Some days Jack felt like the bug, some days he felt like the windshield. Today had been neither. There had been a couple of genuinely interesting lessons; a lab that had actually been exciting – affinity series chemistry, making things go bang. The chemistry teacher was a wildly enthusiastic mad scientist who made everyone laugh as they learned. He was ex-army, but the most liberal ex-military Jack had ever met. He just lived for blowing shit up. God only knew what he'd gotten up to in the service. God only knew what he got up to at home. He was a class favourite though, and he made the class stand a good distance away as he'd lowered a chunk of caesium into a flask of water and gleefully explained what had made it explode so violently.

By the end of the week, the little black dots had become more prevalent at Whittlesford. Maybe a dozen or so people were wearing them, mainly amongst the cheerleaders and football players. Not so many of the ordinary people. Jack realised that they were not brand marks but pins, little black save-the-whale pins. He loved animals, always had, but he'd never worn pins or asked his mom to sew patches onto his backpack. He agreed with the sentiment, sure. Everyone had seen *Blackfish*, the documentary about orcas in captivity, and everyone had been sickened by it. It was a topic that was somewhat close to home. SeaWorld was a relatively short drive down the coast, as was Scripps. Jack didn't have any burning desire to get a pin though. Just this week's fashion, although he wondered where they came from. He hadn't noticed save-the-whale pins in the stores and he had no intention of spending any money on one. He was just Jack, content to let fast fashion pass by while he carried on with things that mattered to him. Like his cat, football, and his fitness project.

Chapter Thirteen

I used to be blonde.

About a month after Jack's funeral, I looked in the mirror and saw I'd gone grey. I don't think it happened overnight, but I couldn't tell you when it actually had. Jonathan had gone back to the *Nimitz* by then. His commanding officer had stretched the regulations a bit, but he still only got thirteen days of sick leave for bereavement. He didn't want to go back. I didn't want him to go back either. But what could he do? It's not like he could go and join another Navy. And he didn't have that long to go until he earned his full pension entitlement. I guess that's one good thing about the service.

Jonathan and I never really talked in much detail about money. I made good money, he made good military money, we had one child, one college fund we'd taken really seriously, and we weren't especially extravagant. We didn't go to Europe every summer on vacation, didn't drive fancy cars.

Even so close to Jack's death, we knew that things were going to be different financially. I know that sounds so crass, but food costs money. Stuff costs money. I remember the first time I logged into my computer after it happened. I was expecting a ton of unread emails. I always dreaded that. I was the one person who never had any unread emails in their inbox. And I actually panicked as I booted up the PC, as I always did, wondering just how many emails would be crashing down on top of me. And to being surprised by…not nothing, but next to nothing. The crazies hadn't found my email address by then. But clients knew who I was. The shooter's mother. More than half of my clients disengaged, 'under the circumstances.' They thought I should take some time to focus on family, and they would get in touch in a few months. That kind of thing. So it was obvious that there was going to be less money coming in from my work.

It's kind of hard to remember that first week after it happened. The Navy actually did a pretty decent job of getting Jonathan home real quick. And they did an even better job of dealing with the press. Nobody does silence quite as well as the Navy.

I remember when Jonathan came in that evening. It was late, around nine. The cat was on the windowsill, looking out. Jonathan unlocked the door to come in and then locked it behind him. He dropped his duffel. I was in the lounge, just staring into space, I think. I did a lot of that. I still do. I got up and walked toward him. We didn't say anything, just held each other. The floodgates just opened, and we cried and cried and cried. At some point – this sounds so selfish – I got cramp from how I was standing, and I had to move him over to the couch. And then we just cried more. There wasn't much eye contact. I don't know why. I don't think I could face him. He'd been away, and I was supposed to look after our baby. And I hadn't. Jack was dead. He told me later that he couldn't face me, because he hadn't been there when our baby died. Neither of us knew it, but we were both blaming ourselves for letting each other down, but more for letting Jack down.

We didn't eat that night. I could hear Jonathan's stomach growling, and normally I would have made a comment, but not that night. I wasn't hungry either. I can't even remember if I did eat anything that first week. I know I must have, but I can't remember what it was.

At some point, Jonathan spoke, slowly. He was exhausted.

"Where is he? Have you seen him?"

"Yes. He's in the county morgue. They told me you could go see him in the morning."

"OK."

Jonathan didn't ask anything stupid like 'is it OK?', or 'does he look OK?' I kind of wished he had. I guess he knew what Jack would look like: dead, waxy. Because of how he'd done it, his face was intact, and they had cleaned him up in the morgue. He had on a white rubber hood around the back and side of his head, kind of like a wetsuit hood. He didn't look like he was sleeping. I've read about people who say that, but he didn't. He looked dead, and lonely, and cold. So cold. I wanted to hug him and warm him up.

"The BLO told me the cops want to talk to me tomorrow as well. I'll go and see Jack first. They can wait."

The BLO was the Base Liaison Officer. I nodded.

"OK, I'll come with you."

I didn't want to come with him. I didn't want to go back to that horrible building where my baby was cold and dead. But I knew I had to go with Jonathan. I just needed to go with him. Not for him. I'd been there on my own. He would be OK going on his own. But I needed to go with him for me. I don't know why. I'd been on my own since it happened, well not really on my own, because there had been cops and interviews. But I'd been on my own. And now Jonathan was back, I just couldn't let him go without me. I needed to be with him, just to go together. Better or worse, richer or poorer. I just couldn't not go.

He nodded. OK. I don't know if he understood why.

"I haven't started the paperwork yet. Or the online stuff." I paused. How stupid. Our baby was dead, and I was talking about legal formalities. I don't know why I said that. I think I wanted Jonathan to know that I hadn't started without him. I wanted him to realise that I needed us to do things together. I needed there to *be* an 'us'. I needed him to know that. I couldn't face shrivelling on my own, solitary confinement in a town full of people.

He understood.

"Thank you."

I think he was about to say it could wait, but then he stopped himself. I think he realised that if he said that, he was helping me justify my decision, and you only say that when someone's decision needs justifying. Jonathan knew that. He's rarely ever said something he regretted. He thinks.

I thought he might ask more questions then, but he didn't.

66

I guess the BLO had filled him in on some details and the press had definitely published enough. I just assumed he'd read it. But he just sat on the couch next to me, and we held each other's hands, or held each other properly. But mainly we just stared into the silence. It was awful, but it wasn't, because he was there and I was there and that was something, I guess. It was less awful than the first day, when I'd been staring on my own.

At some point that first night, Jonathan gently eased himself away from me and got up. He went to the kitchen and came back with two glasses and a bottle of Scotch whisky. He's never been a hard liquor drinker, but he'd been given that bottle by a guy from the Royal British Navy who'd been seconded to *Nimitz* one time. It had sat in a cupboard, unopened, for years. He didn't ask, just poured two shots, and passed me one glass. We sat, and sipped, and stared. After we finished sipping, he refilled the glasses. We drank a lot that night, but I don't remember actually getting drunk.

When it was time, Jonathan put the cap back on the bottle. We left it, and the glasses on the coffee table, and went up to bed. Jack's bedroom door was closed – I'd closed it because I just couldn't look at anything in there any more – and Mr. Orange was sitting by it. I just opened it. I didn't look in, but I opened it, and the cat slinked in.

We brushed teeth and took turns to go to the bathroom. Usually, when Jonathan came home on leave, we'd skip the toothbrushing, and go straight to bed the first night, bedside lights low and make love. Absence makes the heart grow fonder and all that. As Jack got older, we had to be more subtle about it, hurried quickies and so on, but we still managed. We both had needs, after all. I knew I did. I'd always look forward to that first night home, like a ridiculous teenager. Sometimes I'd break out the French underwear. That first night Jonathan came home was different. Jonathan went first. When I came to bed, he'd already turned out the lights. It was pitch black.

I slipped into my side of the bed, on the right. Even though Jonathan is away so much, I still only really sleep on one side of the bed. It's a huge bed too, we kind of went crazy when we bought it, but that was because Jack used to come and snuggle in the mornings when he was little, so we figured what the hell, and got a super king. It was a super king that I barely use a third of.

I lay on my back and stared into the darkness. I knew Jonathan was awake. His breathing was too quiet, too measured. I could sense that he was looking up into space too. I rolled toward him and lay my head on his chest. I just needed to not be lying in that great big bed on my own. He had his left arm around me. I could feel the metal of his wedding ring on me, cold from where he'd washed up before bed. His right hand was stroking my hair, but he was miles away. I could feel it.

We just lay there in the dark, not moving. It really was pitch black, deadly silent. You could hear the house breathe. I don't know how it started. I really don't. But one minute we were just lying in silence, not moving, just breathing, and the next, well, the next minute, my husband was fucking me, and I was fucking my husband. It was easier that it was dark. I needed to do it to him. I needed him to do it to me. And yet, I couldn't have done it if we'd left the lights on. He came inside me, hard, and stayed in me after, as he softened. When he pulled out, we'd swapped places. He was on his side, his head on my chest. We were both lying on the cold, wet patch of sex beneath us, but we didn't move. We just stayed like that until one of us, it must have been me, fell asleep.

I woke up first the next morning, but I always do. Jonathan has this weird ability to get up at any given hour and switch on straightaway, obviously because of his job. But when he's on leave, he can turn it off like a switch. I woke up at five, which was obviously stupidly early, but I got up anyway. I left him to sleep and went downstairs. Mr. Orange heard me making coffee and padded down the stairs after me, from Jack's room.

I remember, when I was a kid, my dad told me how animals deal with death. Not elephants mourning other elephants or stuff like that, but animals and humans. If, one day, the human leaves the house as normal and doesn't come back, then the dog or cat or whatever wonders where they've gone. They don't know that they're not coming back. It's the same if you have two dogs or cats or whatever. If one disappears, then the other one – especially if they're a bonded pair – doesn't know what's happened to them. And they'll look for them, or look for their missing human. But if the animal sees the dead person or dead animal, then they know, and they don't look for them. And Jack was obviously in the county morgue and his cat didn't know that, and he kept looking for him.

I made a cup of coffee and wondered why I'd got up. I could feel the pile of unread envelopes and paperwork quietly staring at me from the corner of the kitchen table where I'd stacked them. I sat down and pulled them in front of me. It was regular mail. Some of it important, some of it junk. There was nothing personal or handwritten. I sipped my coffee and sorted it into piles. All the advertising and flyers went into one pile. The real letters I kept close to me. I flipped them into two piles. A 'deal with it' pile, and an 'it can wait' pile.

Jonathan's post went into a separate pile, all of it, whether important or not. Some of it was mailing list stuff like catalogues, but he would always want to decide whether to read it or bin it.

I was doing OK while I was sorting the mail. It was all for me or Jonathan, and I think that made it easier. Jack never really got any mail. I guess that's normal for kids these days. But then I saw an account statement from Jack's 529 college savings plan, and all of a sudden I wasn't OK any more. I didn't get a panic attack, or start crying, or anything like that. But I went from being OK in my head, displacing with activity, to not OK and just staring at the envelope.

Looking back, I can't honestly say what threw me was the fact that Jack wouldn't be going to college, and that we wouldn't be there to watch him graduate, or anything like that. I get that for some people when they lose their child, they feel robbed of all the moments to come: graduation,

69

marriage, grandchildren, that kind of thing. But I just felt robbed of Jack himself.

I took a fruit knife and slit the envelope open. We'd been saving for college since Jack was born. We'd known we'd do that from before we'd even gotten married. Jonathan's college had been free because he went to Annapolis. The Navy doesn't charge you to go there, obviously. I'd gotten some financial aid for my undergraduate and a partial ride through law school, but even when we started saving, we could see that tuition was just getting more and more expensive every year. So we'd researched it in detail pretty much the minute we got pregnant and had started putting money aside.

When I looked at the account statement I just saw numbers floating in front of me. I couldn't really take them in. I blinked hard and looked again. Obviously we weren't far away from having to pay for Jack actually going to college, so the fund was pretty much finished. It does this thing where it switches into government bonds and low-risk stuff as you get closer to having to actually pay tuition, kind of like an insurance policy in case there's a Wall Street crash the week before you have to write the check to the school.

I hate myself for what I thought next. I only thought it for a second, a couple at most, but I'll always hate myself for thinking it. We'd saved and invested so carefully for Jack's college and his college fund had just over $150,000 in it. It was pretty much enough to cover four years tuition at a private college anywhere. And because we'd started so early, we'd never really missed the money. Sure, right at the start it had felt like another level of tax on top of state and federal, especially while I was paying down my own student loans. But Jonathan and I enjoyed doing it, enjoyed putting Jack first, and enjoyed knowing that he would be able to go to school without worrying about the money.

I saw this big number in front me on the page. And then – and I truly hate myself for this – the thought flashed in my head. *What happens to this money?* The account was controlled by me – 529's have to be in one parent's name only, and obviously Jonathan was always deployed. Jack was the beneficiary, and I saw that number in front of me, and my brain asked what happened to it now. Did it go to me, to me and Jonathan? Could we use it to tide us over if nobody wanted to hire me again? It couldn't go to college, because Jack was dead, and then I started hating myself for even thinking that. And I haven't really stopped hating myself ever since.

Chapter Fourteen

Chris: Thanks for listening to that message. In fact, while it was playing, I made myself a fresh cup of Bullet coffee. Love this stuff...

Nick: ...What the listeners don't know is that you're a really annoying douche at the best of times, and now you've had yet another coffee, I might just have to go postal on your ass-

Chris: Haha, guilty, but could you imagine the irony if there were a mass shooting in the recording studio of a podcast about mass shootings?

Nick: We'd be like so famous

Chris: Nah, dude, you'd be the "Also killed..."

Nick: The what?

Chris: You know, the "Also killed..." I mean, let's be honest, I'm going to get top billing. The news would say something like, "Last night, Chris Hicks was shot in a tragic," blah blah blah. I mean, you'd still get a mention, but you'd be an also. Like, "Also killed was Nick Smith blah."

Nick: Oh, I see. So you'd get three blahs, and I'd just get one blah?

Chris: Sorry, man. I mean, there just never seemed a good time to tell you that you wouldn't even get top billing during your own murder-

Nick: Douche. You are such a douche.

Chris: Anyway-

Nick: Anyway-

Chris: Where were we?

Nick: Whittlesford. Whittlesford, California. Home of the Whittlesford Wacko. The House that Jack killed. Tolleson the terrorist. Porky's Revenge...

Chris: OK, OK, enough with the nicknames. Let's go back to the beginning. How much do we actually know about the shooter in this case?

Nick: OK, so Jack Tolleson was seventeen. His weapon of choice was a Kel-Tec RDB. It's the first time I think I've seen one of those used anywhere in a school shooting, or indeed in any mass shooting. It's a bullpup, which basically means it's got a barrel as long as a regular rifle, but by bringing the trigger and pistol grip assembly forward ahead of the magazine and the breech, the actual length of the weapon is much smaller than a regular assault rifle. Uh, I have it here somewhere – yeah, so a regular Bushmaster assault rifle-

Chris: Popular with many mass shooters!

Nick: Haha, yes, the preferred weapon of the mass shooter. The Bushmaster has a twenty-inch barrel, and the whole weapon is about thirty-nine inches long. The Kel-Tec that Jack Tolleson used similarly has a twenty-inch barrel, but is only about twenty-seven inches long.

Chris: So what do we think that means? The choice of gun?

Nick: Well, we kind of have to start with the fact that Jack Tolleson was both under eighteen and in California. The second part means he wouldn't have been able to buy any assault rifle, because they're illegal in California. And we don't know for sure, but we kind of assume that he bought it in Texas – I'll explain why in a moment. But the key point is that we can more or less assume that he didn't buy it in California, because nobody would have been legally allowed to buy it in California.

Chris: I can feel a 'but' coming on....

Nick: Well, yeah, kinda. We don't know for sure where it came from. There's no national registry of guns, after all. It's not like the DMV, where law enforcement can find out who's the registered owner of any vehicle. So even though we have the weapon itself, after its last shot took his head off, we don't know where it came from. However...

Chris: However...

Nick: Just because assault rifles are illegal in California doesn't mean that they don't exist. It's not beyond impossible that Jack Tolleson could have bought the gun illegally in California, from someone who owned it illegally. It's an unusual weapon, admittedly. Not a spray-and-pray Uzi or Mac-10 which were real popular with gangbangers in South Central, and they're also illegal, technically.

Chris: Do we think that's likely, that he bought it in California somewhere?

Nick: Not really. I'll explain why Texas is much more likely in a moment, but the main issue around California is that how would a regular high school student, from a small beach town in California know where to go and who to talk to about buying an illegal gun? There's a lot of myths about shooters all being too Asperger's to communicate, and Jim Jeffries did a decent comedy routine about it, but in reality, Jack Tolleson seems like a regular guy. He liked watching sports, was polite and well-mannered in class. He wasn't incapable of holding a regular conversation, so that's not the issue. And he didn't lack money. The issue is just that we don't think he would know where to go.

Chris: And because it's pretty hard to get hold of one in California, we think he went out of state to get it?

Nick: Yeah, we think so. And this kind of paints a more determined picture of Tolleson. This really doesn't seem to be a Falling Down kind of moment where he just snaps. Not that school *shooters generally snap in that way. But he definitely seems to have planned this. In fact, I would say he really seems to show far more planning than pretty much any other shooter I've read about. At least, that's my read, at least based on the travel he did in the build-up to this.*

Chris: To side-track just for a moment, are there any shooters where we think it was a snap kind of moment, or some kind of spree?

Nick: That's a good question, and the answer is, I'm not sure. But the reason I mention the planning and the extra level of determination is that Tolleson went from having zero access to any gun – being under-age and in a state with tough gun laws – to using a military-style weapon. If he'd been in a different state-

Chris: He could have gotten a friend to buy it for him?

Nick: Yeah, exactly, like with Klebold and Harris in Columbine. At the time they got the weapons, they weren't old enough, so a girl in their school bought some of the guns for them. She thought they were for target practice-

Chris: Well, technically...

Nick: *laughs* Dude, that's harsh! She thought they wanted to shoot paper targets. And in fact, she went to prom with Eric Harris, just before the shooting. So I think it's fair to say she genuinely didn't have a clue what he wanted them for.

Chris: You think? I mean, I'd date a hot chick even if she might be about to start shooting-

Nick: I know you would. You'd date a fat chick even if she might be about to start shooting. But the rest of the world is often not as desperate as you, and so-

Chris: Douche

Nick: Truth hurts, my friend. Truth hurts.

Chris: Fair. Guilty. I mean, I am guilty. I don't feel it, obviously.

Nick: Obviously.

Chris: Anyway...

Nick: Anyway, so Tolleson, being in California, doesn't have the option, even at a gun show, of getting a friend to buy him this kind of weapon. Nor does he have the same option as Lanza at Sandy Hook, who used his mom's Bushmaster to shoot her first and then go to the school-

Chris: Whose mom has a Bushmaster?? I mean, my mom is pretty tough, but even she doesn't have a Bushmaster. Oh, unless you're listening to our podcast and thinking about robbing her, in which case she has five Bushmasters.

Nick: Five Bushmasters and seven German shepherds?

Chris: Exactly. Maybe more, I haven't checked recently. But seriously, whose mom packs a Bushmaster?!

Nick: Well, Lanza's mom apparently did. And I don't know for sure, because nobody knows for sure, but I think he might be maybe close to a snap kind of shooting as you put it. He had mental health issues, we know that, and we know that he planned it, per the official inquiry. But he used his mom's guns, and also, his shooting was over incredibly quickly. I have it here somewhere – he shot 154 times within five minutes. So that speed to me suggests a huge amount of anger, some kind of blind rage, possibly. It's not impossible – to me at least – that Lanza snapped, was enraged, got his mom's guns, shot his mom, and then went to the school. With Tolleson, we don't see that. We see anger, sure, and we definitely see hatred, but they seem to be much more of a slower burn. Both in terms of the painstaking preparation and practice, but also in the actual shooting itself. I wouldn't want to say that he savoured it, exactly, but he seems much colder and more-

Chris: Organised?

Nick: Yeah, organised is a good word. He's planned it, he has a specific aim in mind, and it's a specific aim which he thinks will mean he's never forgotten about-

Chris: It's interesting you say it like that. Some shooters, I get the sense that they want to be famous. So it's kind of like a positive notoriety, if you like? They know what they're doing is illegal, but they still want to be famous for it. The terrorist mass shooters like the guy in New Zealand and the guy in Sweden, they want the chance to broadcast their political manifesto, and for that to happen, they need to stay alive. But when you look at mass shooters like Paddock, you get the sense that they want to kill as many victims as they possibly can, and when they end it with a bullet in their own head – as they always seem to do – they want to know that they've achieved that aim.

Nick: OK, but I can feel a 'but' coming on.

Chris: But with Tolleson, you said 'he thinks it will mean he's never forgotten about,' like you're implying that Tolleson thinks his default setting is to be forgotten about.

Nick: Good spot. Seriously, man, excellent attention to detail. Was law school one of the many educational establishments you already flunked out of, or is it one you *aim to flunk out of at some point in the future?*

Chris: Douche.

Nick: You know I'm right…

Chris: And you know I am. Maybe?

Nick: Yeah, well, with Tolleson, we certainly get that sense. We know what he actually said in the classroom at the end. Well, we have one surviving witness and we have her account of what he said. We don't know how reliable that is, obviously-

Chris: You think she made it up?

Nick: Um. No. Probably not, at least not consciously. I'm not sure how reliable a witness I'd be if I sat and watched that carnage go down. And um, to consider the question again, we know from other kids at the school that she had been a complete bitch to Tolleson. Although, to be clear, that's not a good enough reason for buying a Kel-Tec and shooting all your classmates!

Chris: That's an important public service announcement. Under no circumstances, can you take a rifle to work and shoot Karen from accounts unless-

Nick: Even!! You mean 'Even!' not 'unless!'

Chris: OK. Under no circumstances, can you take a rifle to school or work and shoot anyone even if they've been a bitch to you. Even if it's Karen in accounts.

Nick: There are women all over America called Karen in accounts who are sleeping easier tonight because of you. I mean, none of them will ever actually sleep with you, but they'll sleep easier now…

Chris: Douche…

Chapter Fifteen

Jack positively sauntered up the hill to the expensive houses where Trent lived. There was nothing wrong with his own home, but this was a different league. Near the top of the hill, set a ways back from the coast, but still with an unbroken view over the Pacific. So high up in the hills that nobody would ever be able to build into that ocean view, although there were rumours that these properties came with ordnance legally preventing that anyway.

The lot size was difficult to work out. Each house was shielded by thick spiky hedges, with ornate wrought-iron gates and tall trees lining the drives. The streets were still marked by the royal blue street signs universal across the county, but the individual house numbers were stylishly embedded into the gate pillars, blue or green mosaics. A few houses had names as well as numbers, and they looked to have yards in front and in back. There were detached outbuildings away from the main houses too, although you couldn't tell if they were for vehicles or staff. The cars he could see parked inside each set of gates were European, not domestic; Mercedes, Porsche, even a red Ferrari, gleaming like new. This was something else.

He heard the babbling brook of voices as he passed one house. Classical violins playing softly in the background. It sounded too refined to be a school party. He paused, curious, as the music came to a gentle halt. Through the hedge he could see a formally dressed party of about twenty people gathering around a white muslin canopy held up by four men. The men wore dark suits and light ties, and white skullcaps. As he passed the gate, he saw an ornate wooden board which announced the marriage of Stephen and Helene Berman. Ah, a Jewish wedding. Jack smiled. He'd never been to one before, a Jewish one, but was curious to see how it differed. He dawdled by the gate. Respectfully eavesdropping, as it were. The ceremony itself did not seem to last long, although he didn't have much of a view. He heard the glass break and every voice shout. He understood what mazel tov meant. The string quartet was replaced by Neil Diamond. *Beautiful Noise*. He smiled and resumed his walk. Jack wondered what his own wedding day would look like. Probably not Jewish. But what if his wife was Jewish? How did that work? Ah well, one day.

He could see the party house way before he reached it. Parked cars lined the road out front – there had clearly been overspill from inside the house. Not all European this time, although there were a few chunky Volvos of the kind parents bought for their kids when they worried. But mainly the small domestic run-arounds favoured by teenagers all across America. Even from a distance, he could smell pungent meaty barbecue smells, of char-grilled chicken, German franks, and fried onions. He was hungry and licked his lips without noticing he'd done so. The waft had reached him before the party noise, hip-hop loud but not blaring. It was a party, sure, but it was a party in a rich neighbourhood.

The property itself sat on the street corner. It had a prime view directly out to sea. At least three stories high, and red brick, not stucco. Like most of its neighbours, it guarded its borders with a low brick wall, topped with a six-foot dark green hedge, laced with spiky thorns. The hedge was neatly trimmed; no vulgar topiary cut into the top. He could just about see through it, and into the front yard. Or maybe it was the back yard. Either way, it was enormous. Tall conifers sat just back of the hedge, haphazardly placed at the edge of a grass lawn, cut in contrasting stripes and fresh as Wimbledon. Two Hispanic men in kitchen uniforms manned the barbecue while a third handed out bottles of beer from buckets of ice. The party was in full swing already, it seemed.

Jack paused for a moment. In the wind, he caught the faint

acrid whiff of marijuana drifting alongside the more attractive smell of the barbecue. Hmm. This made him pause. Not really his scene. But then again, being invited to a party wasn't his usual scene. But he had been, so he should go. Hmm.

He cast a glance through the hedge again. His classmates had divided into pods of activity, groups of friends sticking close to each other, but he couldn't see Trent. Where was the host?

He suddenly heard him, close by. Very close by. He jumped.

"Brie!" Trent spoke louder this time.

Jack realised, with a start, that he'd actually walked past where Trent was sitting, in the corner furthest away from the house. He was wearing his usual white muscle tee and was taking a puff from a joint before passing it to Brie who sat nearby. Skyla sat on the other side. Trent sounded pretty drunk already. Or maybe stoned. Or maybe both.

Jack ducked down instinctively, then stopped, feeling faintly ridiculous. Why duck down so the host who invited you to a party can't see you? Why duck down in broad daylight outside a house where you're expected?

He wanted to keep walking to the gates, but his legs wouldn't let him. His quads strained as he tried to pick up his feet, but they were too heavy. He knew he was bright crimson already, could feel it. This was way too cool for him. He did not fit. He found an element of respite, and his feet let him take a step backwards, not forward, but back, so he could see into the yard, guarded a little better by the stout trunk of one of the conifers.

He could see Trent and his cronies sat in a circle under the trees. They were far enough away from the others to be able to stub out the joint if anyone came over. Or maybe they wouldn't bother. There were four girls and three boys. The boys wore Abercrombie jeans and muscle tees and sat in poses designed to show off their biceps. The girls wore shorts and skimpy tops and sat in poses designed to show off their cleavage. They had brought their own bucket of beers from the main gathering. It was a party within a party. The VIP area for sure, whether it had a red rope or not.

Trent was a little tipsy already, or maybe it was the joint. He was less careful than he usually was when Skyla was around. More blatant checking out Brie's curves. It was a little cooler in the shade of the trees than out on the lawn, and he could see her nipples harden through her top. She did have pretty big tits, and that long dark hair. Trent wondered if she shaved her cunt. Skyla was very blonde and kept it waxed. Maybe it was time for some variety.

He drained his beer and belched loudly and shook his head from side to side, blowing out breath like a horse. He rolled his shoulders over and back.

"I think," he belched again. "I think we need a game. Spin the bottle!"

He reached forward and placed the empty Heineken in the middle of the group. Challenge laid down, an empty bottle as gauntlet.

Skyla was in a quandary. She couldn't protest too much, or she'd be the square. But she couldn't let Trent make out with anyone else or she would lose status. Laughing stock. But she couldn't make out with anyone else either, not in public. She couldn't win. Fuck, fuck, fuck. Light protest.

"You're crazy," she said, leaning in and kissing Trent full on the mouth. He kissed her back, enjoying her desperate tongue forcing its way between his teeth, and her desperate hand touching his body, and the desperate look he knew was behind her closed, desperate eyelids.

Tom laughed.

"Dude, that's a sick idea, especially as there's three of us and four chicks. I like them odds!" He smiled. Either way, he was going to get some action tonight. Great party.

Brie looked round and counted. She was a little tipsy, and the joint had gone to her head a bit.

"Wait a minute…" she said with elaborate over-acting. Decent comic effect. "I don't like those odds at all. I have an idea. Wait here!"

She levered herself up and stumbled in the direction of the

Hispanic servers, pinballing into trees and classmates along the way. The barbecue server looked confused, and then light dawned on him. He led her into the house.

"What the fuck is she doing?" said Tom.

"I have no idea," replied Nancy. "Seriously, no idea."

Brie stumbled back, carrying a heavy white bucket in front of her and a Sharpie between her teeth. She drunkenly moved Nancy further away from Skyla so there was a bigger gap between them. Dropped the heavy tub into the space. Morrell Snow Cap Lard, twenty-five pounds of it, catering pack size. She giggled. This was hilarious, a fact lost on Luke.

"Brie, what the fuck?"

"Shush!" She was concentrating as she wielded the Sharpie. She spelled out the name "J-A-C-K," in big drunken block capitals on the bucket of lard.

"This is sick," she said. "Best idea ever. So, we have one too few boys for spin the bottle. And we need even numbers or it's not fair. But we all of us know, there's only three guys really worth making out with here. So here is Jack. Fat Boy. Butter butt. And whoever gets this has to make out with the bucket of lard." She giggled to herself again.

"Awesome idea," said Trent. He wasn't the one who'd have to stick his tongue in a bucket of lard. He'd try and rig his spin so he got to stick his tongue in Brie. And maybe his fingers too, although that might have to be later.

"So," Brie announced, "spin the bottle. Whittlesford rules. It must spin one full spin at least or you lose your turn. If it points to a member of the opposite sex, you have to make out for a minute the first time right here. Two minutes the second time right here. And third time, you get to go hide for ten minutes. If it points to someone of the same sex, you both have to want to make out for it to happen. Same rules apply. And if you get that disgusting fat fuck Jack, then you have to do *everything* in public."

"Ewwwwwwww," from Skyla was echoed by Nancy and Erin. Skyla knew she'd been outplayed by Brie, knew it from the way Trent was still checking out her rack. But there was no way out. She'd have to play and hope she got Trent. If she got Trent, then maybe she could get him away from the group, give him a BJ in his room, or in the bathroom. Before that bitch Brie did. Or if she got one of the girls, maybe she could convince them to make out and turn Trent on that way. She'd done it before. Boys liked it when girls made out in front of them. She enjoyed it too, not that she'd ever tell anyone. Making out with girls was something you could only really do in front of boys, preferably at parties and for a dare. If you did it without an audience, dykey rumours started. Love might be love, but you wore the T-shirt at Whittlesford, you didn't live the life.

Trent leaned forward to spin the bottle. He looked round at the group like a dealer flicking out cards for poker. To his left, Brie, then Luke, Erin, Tom, Nancy, the tub of lard, and then Skyla. If he span the bottle clockwise, one full spin minus a little bit would land on Skyla and would be void, not a full spin. If he span it one full spin plus a little bit, it would point to Brie. Perfect. And any more than that, and he'd be happy with Erin or Nancy anyway. He just wanted some action. He tapped a druMr.oll into the sod, and span. Touchdown. It landed on Brie.

He leaned across to her and kissed her, to catcalls and applause. It was a long, deep kiss. She was good, uninhibited. He opened his eyes during the kiss and saw her do the same, dark, brooding eyes savouring it. She reached a hand out around his waist and pulled him closer, the other accidentally resting palm up on his crotch, against his swelling cock. Trent had his arm around her, his forearm accidentally grazing the side of her tits.

"One minute!" called out Luke, not cool with the action in front of him. But like Skyla, he couldn't object too publicly either. So he called it just once, and let the pair take their time finishing it off. More catcalls and applause. The rest of the party were starting to notice now, looking over from their groups by the barbecue and beers.

Brie disengaged, lingered. She batted her eyelids at Trent and attempted to look down demurely, or as demurely as possible, given that her nipples jutted out through the cotton, firm and aroused.

"It's my turn I think," she said, smiling at Trent.

"Yup, dealer's left."

The kiss had sobered her up a little. She'd enjoyed it, a lot. She wanted to do it again. She held the bottle, trying to work out its weight and how hard to spin it. Like the turn before, she had to go around one more spin than her preferred destination or it wouldn't count. She span it hard, and it twirled and rotated quickly, before coming to a slow and grinding halt. It pointed at the heavy white bucket, and the group erupted with cheers.

"You started it, you gotta finish it!" Trent was delighted she wasn't about to kiss another guy before he got to make out with her again.

"Oh, man," she giggled at him. Fun Brie, happy Brie, chilled-out Brie, perfect-for-you Brie. "I guess I do."

She reached over the bottle and took the lid off the bucket. It was about three-quarters full, thick white fat gleaming up at her.

"Um...how do I do this?" she asked herself.

She now had an audience; not just the bottle spinners, but all the rest of the party too. They were staring in confusion at the sight of Brie holding a bucket of lard on the horizontal and approaching it with over-acted romantic ardour.

"Oh, Jack," she said loudly. "Oh, Jack. I've counted the days until I could taste your disgusting jelly-like fat again, your hideous wobbly face, and your revolting porky body. Take me, Jack. Take me. No! Take me to *bed*, Jack. Not Dairy Queen!"

The crowd burst into laughter, in on the joke now. A couple looked around for Jack, but that was all. They weren't expecting him to show up.

Brie pulled the tub toward her and stuck her tongue in it, twisting her head this way and that, so everybody could see her making out with the lard. She screeched out, playing to the crowd.

"Oh, Jack, Jack. Have you ever actually managed to see your dick underneath all that fat? It's just that it's so small and thin. Use your fingers instead. Use your chubby, hairy fingers, you disgusting fat fuck!"

She kept it up, waiting for someone to call time. Eventually she paused and looked round, her mouth covered in lard, her face glowing from the exertion and the attention.

"Really? That has to be a minute by now!"

Trent looked up from his watch.

"Actually it was about three, but it was so funny watching you make out with that fat fuck, we decided to let you keep going."

Brie burst out laughing. Fun Brie. Annoyed-but-fun Brie.

"Why you…." She launched herself at him, pretending to try to tickle him. Trent fell back with laughter, enjoying the impromptu wrestle and the weight of her breasts against his chest.

"Help! help! I'm being attacked by a strange chick who gets off on fucking buckets of lard! She just made out with fucking Shamu!" he shouted.

The wrestling match broke up and Brie wiped the fat off her face. She'd felt Trent's cock against her in the tussle and had pushed her boobs into him a little harder.

"Is Jack even here?" asked Luke. "Didn't you invite him?"

Trent snorted.

"Yeah, I invited everyone, but you know he's not going to come," he announced loudly. "One, the fat fuck would die getting to the top of the hill. Two, if he were here, we'd know it. The fat fuck is kinda hard to miss! We wouldn't be able to see the fucking sun!"

The assembled crowd laughed, and one shouted out, "Where's Shamu?" More laughter and then a chorus started up, repeating the name of SeaWorld's famous killer whale.

Trent stood and dusted himself down. He raised his arms in the air like the conductor of an orchestra. The crowd followed his direction and chanted, "SHA-MU, SHA-MU, SHA-MU."

He motioned them to sing more softly. Then brought them louder and faster, louder and faster, racing along at breakneck speed and chanting the name of a two-thousand-pound whale to underline just how fat Jack was. A *dead* two-thousand-pound whale.

Trent brought them to fever pitch, his toned biceps contracting in the sun. At peak excitement, he brought his arms together and mimed an explosion, shouting, "BOOM!" at the top of his voice. Laughter and applause reverberated. It was a great party.

Trent reached down for his bottle; more beer needed, and more food. The game of spin the bottle was over, and Skyla was relieved. Brie a little disappointed. They strolled toward the barbecue, where the servers had waited for their young, spoiled clients to return, talking quietly in Spanish with blank expressions. You don't bite the hand that pays you to feed it.

The crowd walked away, but Jack remained stock still, hidden behind the tree, and on the other side of the hedge. He closed his eyes, even though they were hidden behind his shades. He couldn't bring himself to move. Frozen. His mind was a total blank, no conscious thought at all. No subconscious thought either, a void. Not a single synapse fired. He realised his mouth was open. It took him a conscious effort to close it. He swallowed, but didn't know why. But it felt like that was what he needed to do. He did it again and again.

Jack suddenly became hyper-aware of his surroundings. He could hear every voice, every rustle of leaves. He could smell every scent, every flower and every waft from the barbecue. He could feel the warmth from the sun on each individual pore on his body. As he took the sensations in, his consciousness stepped outside his body until he was viewing himself from above. From this vantage point he could see his own brain whirring and computing. And then he watched his own brain realise the origin of the Save the Whale pins, universally sported at Whittlesford. It had nothing to do with whales at all but was just a universal joke, about him, for everyone to laugh at. Everyone. Well, everyone *except* him. His mind flicked from image to image, memory to memory. He genuinely couldn't think of anyone he knew in school who had never worn one of those pins.

He breathed out. It was the first breath he realised he'd taken since Brie had returned with the bucket. He must have held his breath. And yet he was breathing out, not in. He took one more deep breath. Turned, and walked back down the hill. Away from the rich house and the party.

It was easier walking down than up the hill, but still his sneakers slapped on the ground. He didn't notice their cushioning. He walked blindly. There were no tears. Not at first. He walked too close to one of those privacy-guarding hedges and noticed the sharp sting on his arm from its thorns. He looked down. He had three or four spikes in his arm, but he must have only noticed the last one. It was still oozing. He pulled them all out between his thumb and middle finger, and blood seeped from the tiny puncture marks. He looked down at the ocean in the distance and could make out his block a little way inland of it, further south. He gritted his teeth as the tears came, and he walked slowly home.

Chapter Sixteen

It's only a small town.

I guess we decided to move out west when Jonathan got a promotion, which meant transferring to the Pacific Fleet. He was offered it, but that's just the Navy's way of telling you politely. I'd only taken the New York bar, but getting qualified in California wasn't the end of the world. It was a heck of a lot better than it could have been, Pearl Harbor or Yokosuka. And there would be more chances for Jonathan to progress out west, and the weather was a good draw too. I guess we were slightly different from a lot of military families. I was earning. To be honest, I was earning a good deal more than Jonathan, although that's probably more to do with what the Navy pays its sailors than anything especially enlightened on the behalf of the legal profession. But we could afford a nice house with a yard and a sensible commute for me, and decent schools for Jack. He would have been about four at the time. He was sad to say goodbye to his friends, but he seemed ok about it. We just figured he would make new ones.

I guess I never thought much about the fact that moving would mean I would need to make new friends too. I just sort of assumed I would. I was never a complete Navy wife. I had my own job, and so my life never orbited my husband's in the way that some wives' did. I had my job, I had Jack, and I had various hobbies. In New York, I was always super-organised – I guess I had to be – and so I never needed to beg a favour of another mom to collect Jack from this or that, or to cover for me. Looking back, I realise that meant the other moms never had a favour to call back in when they were scrambling. I would have helped, of course I would have, but I just don't think I was ever really asked, not for a same-day emergency.

When we moved out west, I kind of fell into a more social world. I guess I didn't realise how frantic New York was until I wasn't there. In California, the pace was more laid-back. I guess the weather helps. I mixed with other moms more, not military moms for the most part. I didn't make a conscious choice to not be part of the military set, and when Jonathan was on leave, we obviously mixed with his friends and their wives, but we didn't live on base. As I said, we were slightly unusual for a military family in that I had a decent job, even adjusting for California wages instead of New York ones.

There was more of an overlap in California, socially. I mean, in New York, nobody from work ran with the same running group I did, or went to the same Pilates studio I did, things like that. I had a bunch of acquaintances in New York, even friends, but nobody was ever-present. New York is like that; very big, lots of individual connections, but nobody you see in more than one setting, not really.

In California, it was different. If you run then you're probably going to run along the oceanfront, and you'll see everybody else who runs. It's not Podunk, but there's only a few decent Pilates places, so you cross over a bit more. Stuff like that. Plus, Jack was in school by then, so there were kid things. I didn't make an active plan to socialise more, but all the moms would sit on the bleachers in Little League and pass the time of day. Usual stuff. Nothing too deep. And once in a while there would be a moms' evening out for some chick flick the men didn't want to go to. It was kind of interesting too, because some of the moms I liked were people whose kids Jack thought were douches.

I stayed in touch with my East Coast friends, and so I guess I never really felt isolated. My best friend from law school stayed in New York and did the Wall Street thing. Whenever we went home to visit my parents in Massachusetts, we'd talk about meeting up for lunch, but it rarely happened. We didn't mind though. That's the benefit of smartphones these days; I still had that sense of friendship, a confidante, and it was important, especially when Jonathan was deployed.

Like I say, California was different. It was a small town before all this happened, and it feels even smaller now. Wherever I go, I see people. People who know. And they can't help but stare. People I've never met, people who don't even have kids, never mind at Whittlesford, but they just stare anyway. I don't think I'm being paranoid, but maybe I am. Yesterday I was in WholeFoods downtown and I'm sure one woman followed me. She was young, thirtyish, pushing her boy round in a stroller, and she had that 'I think I know you from somewhere' look, but she didn't say anything. I suppose I'm used to it now. I used to run away and hide, in the washroom, or the elevator, but I still needed to buy food for me, or for Jonathan if he was home. I don't know if people expected me to starve, but after the initial shock, I had to eat something. To stay alive.

It's a different look from people at Whittlesford. Especially people who I knew before. It's such a small town that you can bump into people several times a day, and there's sort of a shorthand greeting. The first time you say hello, and then the rest of the day people either just smile or flick their eyebrows just enough to say *hey*, but not enough to stop and talk. Nobody does either to me anymore. They just look at me with dead eyes. They hold eye contact for that fraction too long and then they get embarrassed and look away. Nobody has ever started a time-of-day conversation with me since that day. I've literally stood in line for ten minutes at the grocery store in between two moms – moms whose kids weren't even involved – and watched the conversation go over and across me like a game of tennis, but I was the net, and I had no feelings and couldn't speak.

It sounds so crass to say it, but obviously I don't go to school anymore. Because Jack is dead.

Chapter Seventeen

Jack woke early that morning. In his half-sleep, he'd hoped he'd been dreaming but knew he hadn't. He'd hoped the world would be a little lighter in the morning, but it wasn't. And he still had to go to school. He couldn't drop out, and besides, he *liked* school. Well, not the people. But he liked most of the lessons. They were interesting. And so were some of the teachers. And even if he didn't, that wasn't the point. He had to go to school. That was his life. That was what he was meant to do.

He showered and brushed his teeth as normal. He didn't jerk off. He didn't loiter in the bathroom to wait for the steam to clear, to see his naked reflection in the mirror. Instead, he trudged directly back into his bedroom where he towelled himself dry. He was sullen and he was angry, and he rubbed the towel so hard against his body it left red marks. Who fucking cared? Nobody wanted to see it anyway. Rather than sit on the bed and put his socks on facing the mirror, he knelt, facing the bed, and put them on. Got dressed and went downstairs. Watched TV while he ate cereal, kissed his mom goodbye, and walked to the bus stop.

It was grey that morning. The sun hadn't burned off the ocean mist, but Jack reached into the cargo pocket of his shorts and pulled out his sunglasses anyway. They were Oakleys. Sporty, wraparound Oakleys. He put them on. Nobody could see his eyes now. He didn't bother checking his cellphone while he waited for the grinding yellow monster. Nothing good would come of it. He would just go to school, learn as best he could. And then come home. And repeat. Five days a week, until he could leave for good.

The bus arrived, and he quickly took his seat. He didn't look down the bus as he usually did. He was too embarrassed. The story would have done the rounds by now. Brie and the bucket of lard. *Fuck that. Fuck them. Fuck all of them.* He slumped in his seat and looked out the window. There was silence behind him. That *never* happened. Sure, there were days when the chatter was higher or lower, when people were more or less tired, or desperately cramming for a quiz in school, but it was never *nothing*. It was today though. Quiet as a morgue. And he knew why. He wasn't sure if they knew he knew. They were still wearing those fucking black pins though.

He couldn't bear the silence anymore, and dug out his earbuds. Jammed them into his ears, and hit play on the first icon he saw on Spotify. He had no idea what he was listening to. It didn't matter. It was better than the silence behind him; heavy and judgmental. If he'd looked back, he might have seen a couple of looks of well-hidden pity, even concern. But he didn't look back.

He kept his sunglasses on all day. A few teachers noticed but didn't raise it. Obviously something wrong, but nothing major or he wouldn't be in school, so they acquiesced and left him alone. Didn't make any comments, or ask him any questions in class. Benefits of being a quiet and reliable student. He was allowed an off day. Maybe it would have been different if he'd had a lab class like Chemistry where he might have to wear safety goggles. But he didn't so he didn't. He just sat behind his dark glasses and avoided eye contact with everyone, even the teachers. From time to time, his mind wandered away from lessons, and his eyes began to water, but he blinked them away. He took out his phone when he felt close to losing it. The wallpaper was of Mr. Orange on his lap. That was always good for distraction.

He said not one word at Whittlesford High that day. Not to the driver, to classmates, to teachers, or the canteen staff. He spoke only to his mom when he had to and his cat when he wanted to, before and after school. He yawned loudly at home so he would seem tired rather than upset. He didn't go online once. Didn't check WhatsApp or Facebook or Insta or Snap or TikTok. When he was outside of 1610 Chalcedony, he had on his sunglasses, and he said nothing. When he was inside his castle, he battened down every hatch and made no contact with the outside world. Just sat and watched TV and fed his cat. And inside of him, the waterfall of tears started to turn red. Bright, angry red.

Chapter Eighteen

The next day started a little better. He boarded the bus and noticed immediately that there was someone in his seat. Justin. He was in a different class, not someone he knew. But he knew him enough to know that he didn't usually carry two crutches and have his left leg in plaster up to the knee.

Justin shrugged. He wasn't one of the jocks, nor one of the nerds, nor one of the cool kids. He was just one of the kids. Average height, average weight, average looks, average grades. In any other environment, he'd be the one being ignored. The original grey kid. But for obvious reasons, he wasn't ignored. Not really. Not like Jack.

"Sorry, Jack. Hope you don't mind if I sit near the front. Easier for me to get on and off that way."

Jack looked down the bus to see if there was a spare place Justin would usually sit. There was, but there wasn't. He saw the kid who usually sat next to Justin swing round and sit sideways, his sneakers dangling into the aisle. A very clear message. Don't sit next to me. Jack blinked and squeezed himself into the seat opposite Justin. It was on the sunny side of the journey, and he felt the heat on the back of his neck. He started sweating almost immediately.

"Sure. What did you do?"

It was an obvious question. And under the circumstances, it was a question that Justin could answer without risking his street cred by talking to the kid made out of lard.

"Skateboard. Overcooked it on the quarter-pipe and tore a bunch of ligaments and stuff. I get this for six weeks."

"Yowch. Does it hurt?"

"Like an absolute motherfucker."

For a moment, Jack thought the conversation might fall into place and pass the time on the journey. But Justin seemed to catch himself. He didn't need to be an asshole to Jack, had no need to score points off him. Why punch a man when he was down? No need at all. But Justin was also aware of his own status. Today he would be the school celebrity. He would grin ruefully as he explained the accident. Thank fuck he'd done it doing something cool and not something embarrassing. Maybe one of the girls would offer to carry his backpack and help him with doors. The possibilities were endless. But he could forget all that if he was seen to be too tight with Jack. The wretched stench of distaste was highly contagious. And Justin had no desire to catch it.

He sighed and rearranged himself so he was looking out of his own window. Jack's usual window. But looking away from Jack.

Jack took the hint and flipped his sunglasses back down. His jaw clenched with anger. *Whatever, asshole. You'll get yours one day.*

He planned to keep himself to himself that day. Just get through the day. Put his buds in during the breaks and concentrate on his phone. Look busy. Just get through the day and then get home. Get safe. For the most part, it worked. Until it didn't.

Walking between classes, he became aware of one of his classmates trying to get his attention. He cut out the tunes and looked up. Haseeb was a quiet Indian kid, scrawny, and weighed a buck oh-eight on a fat day. Very quiet. Never went to parties, never in any trouble, always in the top two or three in class, but better on math than essay subjects. He was a nerd, but a friendly one.

"Wassup, Haseeb?"

"Hey, Jack. I was wondering, I missed math this morning. I chipped a tooth." He pointed at the offending corner. It looked pretty crooked. "Is there any chance I could borrow your notes over lunch? I can just copy them out and give you them right back. And I can actually read your handwriting."

Why not? A small thing but Jack felt a tiny warm glow. Nice to be needed. Nice to be, well, nice.

He rolled his backpack down his arm and fished out the notes. Smiled.

"Take your time. Tomorrow is fine, if that's easier."

"Thank you." Haseeb paused. Jack still had his shades down, trying to read Haseeb's eyes. Did he know? Maybe the world didn't revolve around Jack. Maybe it was just a short thing. Jack would get roasted for a week or two and then they'd move onto someone else. Maybe it wasn't even a thing.

No.

As Haseeb slipped the notes into an immaculate folder in his own backpack, a familiar sound turned left at the corridor corner and glided toward them. Laughter. It was Trent and his posse, girls squealing, boys fucking with each other, trying to push each other into the faded metal lockers with hefty thuds and clangs. Background tunes today provided by Curtis, proclaiming the ease of executing a 187, California penal code for a homicide. It was the kind of hip-hop by poor black kids that rich white kids liked to play and sing along to, minus the n word.

Jack knew who it was before they turned the corner. So did Haseeb. To be fair, so did everyone, but even he was surprised by Haseeb's reaction.

Haseeb thanked him again, quickly. But then he turned on his heel and stepped quickly away from Jack. The first stride was a ridiculously long one. Comically long. And kinda pointless. It wasn't like he was going anywhere. They were on a break. There was nowhere to go. But it was suddenly blindingly apparent that Haseeb just needed to put some clear actual physical distance between himself and Jack. Like Jack had shit his pants. But it wasn't the stench of shit that had made him move. It was the far more contagious stench of failure. Even studious Haseeb, whose mom still drove him to school every morning and who'd chosen his medical school in seventh grade, couldn't have demonstrated more clearly just how untouchable Jack now was. He was the physical embodiment of shit and leprosy.

Chapter Nineteen

From: Killing Time Podcast
To: L.Wenger@harvard.edu
Subject: Research / Podcast Enquiry

Dear Dr. Wenger,
I hope you don't mind the direct approach. We host a podcast called Killing Time and are in the process of researching a future episode which will cover the tragic events of the Whittlesford High School.

The Whittlesford tragedy was obviously completely unique. In all our research, we have never seen a tragedy like this before and as a result, we are keen to understand exactly why what happened, did. From our perspective, the only way we can make sense of the uniqueness of the tragedy is to focus on Jack Tolleson, what he was feeling at the time, and in the build-up.

We came across your name in our research around personality disorders and violent criminal acts and wondered if you might be available for a call to discuss the case from a psychiatric perspective. We would be happy to speak with you off-the-record for background, on-the-record for quotation, or if this might interest you, we could discuss you joining us as an expert on the podcast episode.

We look forward to hearing from you.
Best regards
Chris Hicks
Nick Smith

From: L.Wenger@harvard.edu

To: editorial@KillingTimePodcast.com
Subject: Re: Research / Podcast Enquiry

Dear Chris and Nick,

Thank you for your email. It's flattering to hear from you.

Obviously I can't comment on the specifics of this case, but I'd be happy to jump on a call with you to discuss the broad aspects and pathologies that have been at play in similar events. Only by understanding the psychiatry of these individuals (and then crucially, by actually treating them) can we take steps to ensure that these tragedies are prevented.

I am usually free on Wednesday afternoons (between 2 and 5, EST). Perhaps you could let me know when might suit for a call / Zoom.

Best regards,

Lea

Professor Lea Wenger, M.D., Ph.D., M.A. (Cantab).
Harvard Medical School, Faculty of Psychiatry.

Chapter Twenty

It was a little before four in the morning when Jack awoke. There was no particular reason why he had. His bladder wasn't full. He hadn't twitched in his sleep and startled Mr. Orange. Occasionally that would happen and the cat would pounce on his leg through the duvet and if Jack was unlucky, he'd get clawed. He didn't blame the cat though. Not his fault.

This time was different. He felt himself slowly surfacing through the fug of sleep, that half-conscious state of awareness. He knew where he was, could see his bedroom through a dark and hazy filter. He rolled back onto his stomach and tried to fall back asleep, but it wouldn't come. The dark green glow of the digits on his alarm clock didn't usually stop him from sleeping, and they didn't now. It wasn't light that prevented him from sleeping. Nor sound.

It was dread.

When Jack was in elementary school, he'd both loved it and hated it. He hated the first day back after vacation. Hated not being able to sleep in. Hated leaving his cat. He would kick up the occasional tantrum, and his mom had to practically force him out of the door. But once he was there, he seemed to enjoy it. Before he was there, even. When he saw all his pals, he did what kids always did. He would shake off his mom's hand and charge headlong into the mass of kids playing whatever game it was, football, soccer, tag. He was just one of the crowd. The girls kept themselves largely to themselves and the boys avoided them. Girls were yukky. One girl played football and roughhouse games with them. Honorary boy. She was bigger than some of the boys at that age, but overall, they were all more or less the same size. A couple of kids were at the far ends of the bell curve, height-wise, but it didn't really matter. Nobody was trying to dunk.

As the years had progressed, so had the kids. Their personalities came through. Genuine friendships developed. Sleepovers and pool parties. And in tandem with the friendships, also enmities. Nothing too serious, but the kids learned who they liked and who they didn't. One boy in Jack's class was an early September baby and much bigger than anyone else. He was quickly nicknamed Tank. His greater strength was appreciated on the football field but feared in the playground. Tank was a bully, and everyone learned quickly to avoid eating candy within view of him. Even after several calls from the principal's office, Tank's mom refused to believe her boy was doing anything wrong. Until every kid bar Tank himself was invited to a joint party at Soak City. Then she got the hint. When Jack's year moved from elementary to middle, Tank disappeared. He was last heard of going to a private prep school.

Middle school had followed the same trajectory as elementary, more or less. Groups developed. Musical kids became more musical, started nascent bands. Sporty kids set off on the journey to becoming jocks. Nerds dived headlong into their books. The division between genders stayed broadly the same. And the kids who were average at everything got along just fine.

High school was where things started to go wrong. The cordial division between boys and girls was ripped apart by the onset of puberty. Swelling chests turned girls from objects of derision to objects of desire. Still objects, but now desirable ones. The first pair to make out achieved heroic status. Well, heroic for the boy. The girl, not so much. But for the first time, status became apparent.

High status was earned by being a jock. Or by making out with girls, preferably plural. Or by being a girl who boys wanted to make out with (but woe betide if the girl in question actually did make out with more than a boy, singular). Status was grudgingly given to nerds who were at genius level. They were mocked, of course, but being nicknamed 'brains' was still status.

High status was unachievable by those with average ability, with one exception. Those without a musical ear, a professor's brain or a rocket arm were doomed to mediocrity. Unless they were hot. As in every facet of life, beauty, or rugged good looks, trumped actual achievement or good character. The handsome and the beautiful glided through school, secure in their certainty that good things would come to them. They largely revelled in the admiration and deference of the not-so-handsome and not-so-beautiful.

At Whittlesford, and likely every school in America, there was a substantial group who even the kindest observer would describe as average. They weren't stupid or ugly or mean or bad. Just average. They made up the crowd, and hung out with other people within the crowd. There were friendships, and romances, and arguments, and tears, and victories, and losses. But all within the same group, surfing the B-grade wave to a decent white-collar job via a decent college. There was comfort to be had in the group. Safety in numbers, one might say.

Jack was realistic about his academic abilities. He knew he was smart but not Harvard smart. Not Stanford smart. Maybe UCLA smart. Or Berkeley smart. But he was more than smart enough to know where he stood at school.

Jack had been deliberately and specifically separated from that comforting herd. He was outside of the group, lacking any status beyond that of contagious disgust. And the worst thing about it was that he knew.

He knew what it meant too. He knew that once you were outside the group, it was hard to get back in. He didn't know *why* he had been selected for exclusion, wasn't aware of any transgression or misstep. But he knew he had been.

He knew he would never be approached by one of the beautiful people. The beautiful girls who took endless selfies on the beach of their toned, tanned bodies, and dazzling white smiles didn't approach guys like him. They never had though, and he had known this and accepted it. Not being approached – or even being actively avoided – by the beautiful people didn't bother him. That had always been the case. Well, since the onset of puberty.

Now, though, it was becoming apparent that his presence was intolerable to more than just the beautiful people.

When he went to watch school football on Friday nights, he would usually get there early, so he could watch the drills. He would be huffing and puffing a little as he made his way up the bleachers, middle-middle for the best view of the fifty-yard line. There were no assigned seats because there weren't really seats, just solid white stone rows cut into the hillside and looking down onto the field. He was usually one of the first spectators there. Definitely the first spectator who didn't have a sibling who was playing, accompanied by parents. He would arrive early and get a soda from the stand before he took up his usual place.

He wasn't a jock, had no status amongst the athletes, but he did have an encyclopaedic knowledge of professional sports. He was known to have this. As such, he could occasionally join in discussions with the jocks, despite not having actual playing credentials. As long as he kept it factual. Jack was smart enough not to venture an opinion on either existing players at Whittlesford, nor how the game should actually be played. He had sports knowledge credibility, but not that much.

Now, though, he knew that this privileged position was over. It had been a simple ceremony, the withdrawal of those privileges.

On a normal Friday night, he would sit in those white bleachers and watch practice, and read ESPN or Sports Illustrated on his cell. As other spectators arrived, they would naturally fill up around him. Not because he was so damn popular, of course. But because he was sat in the prime spot. And he was one of the ordinary people, so sitting next to him neither gained nor cost status. He was in the mass of ordinary. Just one of the guys. There would be light conversation about plays and players, about pro sports and school sports, about life and school. That had been the norm since he first arrived at Whittlesford three years before.

The most recent Friday had been different. He'd arrived at his usual time, bought his usual soda and huffed up to his usual spot. He wasn't quite the only person in the bleachers, but it was close. A few gaggles of competitive parents were in front of him, taking photo after photo of their kids. Talking to the principal who always put on a clean white Ralph Lauren button-down and starched khakis to meet and greet parents. He usually wore shirt and tie in school. This was his Friday night uniform. He stood close to the field, available and approachable for parents. As always, he looked up at Jack, the number one fan, and snapped off a casual salute. A polite acknowledgement that Jack was there, even though he probably didn't know who Jack was by name. Whittlesford was a big school, and Jack was neither a genius, a jock, nor a stoner. And it was those three groups that most frequently caught the attention of the principal.

It had been an absolutely spectacular evening. The bleachers faced west, and the sun was setting over the Pacific in the distance, bright orange and purple. Dozens of small dark clouds sailed the skies, adding another dimension. Jack had seen hundreds of spectacular sunsets. That's what California does. But this one was so good he huffed his way to the top row and took a photo. Even on an iPhone, the colours popped, the vivid sunset, the bright green of the playing surface and the scarlet of the endzones. It was magical. He put it up on Insta, and hashtagged it #GoWhittlesford.

As game time approached, the floodlights turned on with a loud clang, one at each corner and one each side in the middle. An inflatable tunnel unfolded itself from the home locker room. Whittlesford's finest would make their entrance like professional gladiators. The visitors did not get a tunnel.

The stadium started to fill up. Small-ish groups of maybe four or five crammed into cars. Some had been to the beach after school or out for food before the game. Some carried take-out from Jack-in-the-Box. As they came into the stadium, the usual form was for students to detach from their parents, if present. The parents usually sat together, about three rows up.

It was a family occasion, but most knew their kids wanted to sit with their friends. By sitting on the third row, parents could watch the game without watching their teenagers. A happy state for both parties. The students would start to fill up from where Jack sat, more or less. Middle, middle. Prime viewing on the fifty-yard line. If he knew them, he would wave or nod, and they would sit with him. If he didn't, he wouldn't, but they would sit nearby, and standard school football conversation would ensue. Light and easy.

That hadn't happened on Friday. Jack had been in his usual spot, received his usual salute from the principal. And then as the crowd slowly filled the bleachers, Jack realised that great care was taken not to sit near him. The first group chose to sit behind him, a couple of rows further up. Fair enough, maybe an even better view. The next group walked past Jack to join the first and slowly but surely over a thousand people filled up the bleachers at Whittlesford High, leaving one boy in the middle of the prime viewing spot, isolated in the middle of his own exclusion zone. When it was impossible to avoid sitting on the same row as Jack, they filled in from the crap seats first, at the end zones. When it was impossible to avoid sitting near Jack, they competed not to be nearest to him, hurrying toward him then sitting down away from him. The last person – the loser – then sat with their back demonstrably facing Jack, pretending to engage animatedly with the people on the other side.

It was impossible for Jack not to realise what was going on. He was in what had always been for him a place of comfort, a place of happiness and warmth and companionship and belonging. It had become his place of humiliation, a ten-foot exclusion zone around him, formed of air and nothing. He hadn't just been ignored by the beautiful people. Or the jocks who were injured or played a sport other than football. Or the nerds. Or the stoners. He had been systematically and obviously excluded by everyone. The artists, the musicians, the wealthy, the less-wealthy, the social campaigners and the average. *Everyone*.

Even as he sat and watched the game, his mind was

computing what had happened to him. He wasn't stupid. He understood. It was contagion. He was so undesirable, even the nobodies would not sit with him. Even the nobodies, his previously fellow members of the ordinary people, feared being contaminated by association. Everybody feared it. And he knew it. He might as well have had a fucking bell around his neck. The Whittlesford leper.

He'd realised what was going on but couldn't bring himself to move. He sat through a turgid first quarter. Ordinarily, the first break coincided more or less with him needing a leak. Ordinarily he'd leave his bag in his seat and whoever was sat nearby would guard his bag. Sometimes he'd pick up another soda on the way back, or Nachos. Sometimes he would share them with the bag guarder. Certainly offer, but tonight nobody was within ten feet of him. He put off going to the restroom and practically crossed his legs, hoping for a short second quarter. Mercifully, it arrived, thanks to running plays that didn't stop the clock. As the crowd stood at the halftime break, he walked out amongst them. They didn't maintain separation during that. He stood in line to use the urinal, and then walked out of the stadium. He wondered when they would realise that he wasn't coming back. Would they sit in the prime spot then? Or would they make jokes that he had even infected the concrete with his disgusting fatness?

He reached for his second pillow and placed it over the first, gently easing himself into a half-lying, half-sitting position, taking care not to wake his cat. He knew he wouldn't get back to sleep. His head was whirling, half full of bullying that had already happened and half full of what he knew would happen.

He didn't know exactly what form it would take, but he knew he couldn't stop it. He knew it was inevitable. Every day. And it was that total conviction, no, that actual *knowledge*, that it was inevitable that burst the very breath out of him and he turned onto his side and sobbed, pulling the pillows into his face so he did not bother his cat or his mom. It wouldn't be fair if he woke them.

Chapter Twenty-One

The new normal was quick in coming. Like a hot new technology, the pace of adoption was swift. One moment, Jack had just been one of the crowd. Not hot, not ugly. Not smart, not stupid. Not a jock, not a nerd, not a musician. Not anything really. But normal. Taller than average, and bigger than average, but there was no reason for him to be picked out especially.

But he had been. And the sheer pace and vehemence of his exclusion was striking. Network effect in action. His untouchability was known to one, so it was known to all. His exclusion was known to one, so it was known to all. That status – not even a viewpoint, but a reality – had moved at the speed of light along the information superhighways that connected everyone at Whittlesford and few more people beside.

If he thought about it, it had started with the pins. He hadn't known what they were, or whose idea they had been. But they'd spread through school like mono. One day the cool kids had one, the next day their extended entourage had one, and the third day, everyone had one. Small black dots on the collar or chest or wherever was obvious. Jack had originally dismissed it as standard eco-virtue signalling. Until he'd found out what they actually stood for.

He had plenty of time to think about it. There's no hour as long as one where nobody will talk to you. No week as long as one where not one single classmate will mention even one word to you. Not about schoolwork or chicks or parties or football or the Aztecs or the Chargers or even if Whittlesford would make it to State that year. Jack had so much time.

He had his daily commute, slumped against the window on the shady side every morning. Some days he'd be ignored completely by everyone on the bus. They wouldn't even look up as he boarded. It was as if he didn't exist, as if he was thin air. Except he was fat and disgusting, not thin at all.

He preferred the days when he was ignored. They were better than the days when he wasn't.

On the days when he wasn't, he would board the bus, and the bus would be silent. A clear sign that something was up. If he was being ignored, there would be the usual hubbub, a mix of conversations from the studious to the silly. But the sound of silence was the warning of imminent incoming.

The cowardly wolf-pack sought safety in numbers and safety in anonymity. They would wait until Jack had taken his seat. Normally. Once he'd sat down, there would be a catcall or a holler. SHA-MU! Maybe one voice. Maybe all of them. But he knew better than to turn around. He knew he couldn't react. He'd made that mistake once, whipped his head around. If it was one of the younger kids, smaller maybe, maybe he could clock him. He might be fat, but he was big. He could deck a kid a couple of years his younger, surely. That would make them stop.

It hadn't worked out that way. His head had whipped round, angry and indignant and immediately the bus had fallen silent again. He couldn't tell exactly where that morning's abuse had come from. Every single passenger was staring perfectly face forward with a blank zombie face, clearly prearranged by all of them, every single one. He'd given up, blinking away the tears he hadn't realise were already dripping out of his eyes and faced forward. As he did so, the bus erupted into laughter, and he heard high-fives.

It was obvious that the better days were the ones when he was ignored. At least then he was free to let his mind wander. He entertained fantasies of what life might be like. A girlfriend perhaps. Friends for sure, like the kind his dad had - big, beefy men from the navy who came round to barbecue when they were on leave. They had smiley wives and the yard would ring with laughter and the clink of bottles of Bud. Friends who would chat and tell stories, some tall and some just long, sometimes over and over again. The shared history of friendship with a little light-hearted ribbing. He imagined one day having a house of his own and a girl of his own and friends of his own. Of course it was better when his mind was filled with happy unreal thoughts rather than the abject misery of his reality.

Some days the wolf-pack became more creative. The harbinger of doom would be the same. A sudden hush when he boarded the bus. The remarkable coincidence of not one of them looking forward. The first time it happened, he'd known something was up. He just wasn't sure what. He'd worked it out soon enough though.

It was just a tub of lard, but his shoulders sank. He felt heavy, heavier than he'd ever been. Even as he collapsed down into his seat, he was back outside Trent's expensive house watching Brie make out with the tub of lard and hearing the Shamu chorus. He could feel his jaw physically shaking and he was short of breath. He tried to breathe, but his rhythm was just fast and shallow. He could barely get any air into his lungs. He was drowning. Drowning in a barrel of lard.

The laughter behind him made it worse. He thought, no, he *knew* they had seen him react and they had laughed even more. That had made it worse, and he'd just spiralled until somehow his body knew to give up. *Just give up, Jack. You tried. It's OK. Not everybody gets to win. Just surrender. Let yourself go. It won't hurt any more if you let yourself go. It'll just be like sleeping.*

He'd imagined sleep, sitting there on the bus. Transported himself back into his safe place. His big double bed and his cotton bedsheets. Mr. Orange wasn't there though. This was his safe place, not his happy place. He mentally went to bed and reached over to the nightlight. Flicked a switch and it was over. Wouldn't that be better?

Some days it wasn't a tub of lard. Some days they didn't shout Shamu. Some days they didn't make loud noises when he eased his bulk down onto the seat, mimicking the springs giving way. Some days, they left a pack of Twinkies on the seat and some wiseass left a betting book next to it, detailing odds on how long they'd last before Shamu gave up and ate them. But some days they ignored him completely and those days were his favourites.

Chapter Twenty-Two

I remember the day itself very clearly. Obviously, I guess. I was working from home, in the study. I had a hair appointment in the afternoon and so it would just save time to work from home. I used to work from home quite a lot. Jack, well, he'd left for school. Obviously. I used to really like working in the study. It was a nice mix of work and family. There's a real big desk, dark wood, and a proper office chair. Big screen, actually at the right height to work. Our wedding picture in a dark frame and a picture of Jonathan and me with Jack when he was born. He was so tiny in Jonathan's hands, but still pudgy and with all that that dark hair. On the wall, Jonathan and I had our combined ego wall, his graduation photo from Annapolis, mine from Wellesley and law school, bar certificates, Jonathan's citation. And we'd consciously left room for Jack's, for when he would grow, for what he would become. The gap on the wall is still there. I don't know what to do with it. Even now.

I don't think I ever had any wishes for Jack. Not to be a lawyer, or a doctor, or President, or anything like that. It's a cliché I know, but I just wanted him to be happy and healthy. Before he arrived, I remember having lunch with a girlfriend and she said with mine and Jonathan's genes, he'd probably end up being a Navy lawyer, like Tom Cruise in *A Few Good Men*. I remember laughing and thinking that would be a lot better than being a real sailor. I worried about Jonathan when he was deployed, but if I'm completely honest, it wasn't like he was in the Marines or the Air Force. He couldn't get shot down over enemy territory or captured in Afghanistan. It's been a long time since a Navy ship was sunk. Maybe that's what I used to tell myself, but it seems bitter that I worried about Jonathan.

Jonathan used to joke about what Jack would turn out to be. When we were picking out names, Jonathan said he had to have a name that would sound good for a World Series, or Super Bowl winner. He used to joke about Jack making hundreds of millions of dollars and keeping us when we were old. We'd be sitting in the owner's suite, watching Jack throw touchdowns or fastballs and being proud and rich. When it came down to it, though, I always knew that Jonathan wanted Jack to be smart first. Achieve in school, go to a good college, and then have choices. I guess that's a pretty good ambition for your kid. Although I know Jonathan would have been deliriously happy if Jack had turned out to be an athlete too.

Anyway, on that day, I was working from home. I'd made a proper pot of tea – procrastinating, if I'm honest. Then I'd settled down in the study and started reviewing a very long contract on the screen. I had music playing in the background. I can remember the sound. It was a Finnish composer I like. Sibelius. It's gentle classical music, very soothing, and not distracting. I can only work to instrumental music, or my brain hears the words and then I get side-tracked and start singing along. I had Sibelius on Spotify and my phone bluetoothed it to a speaker on the coffee table in the study. I was making steady progress, now that I'd started.

I remember everything else in that room. It was a bright day, so I'd closed the white shutters to cut out the glare. I was sat in my big chair, dark leather. The cat was on the sofa, on his cushion. He wasn't purring, just sleeping. I had on blue jeans and heeled mules, and a white T-shirt that I was planning to change out of after the hairdresser because even with the cloak they give you, the hair still gets everywhere. So I was looking nice enough to go out into town, because small towns can still be bitchy, but not so smart that I was going to have to handwash a top that was covered in my hair after wearing it once.

I'd gotten to a natural break in the contract and was contemplating going into the kitchen and sneaking a cookie from the jar, instead of lunch. My cellphone rang. I had this stupid ringtone – *I fought the law and the law won* by The Clash. Jonathan had changed my ringtone years ago because well, I was a lawyer, and I hated the song, and I hated the fact that I didn't have just a normal ringtone like a grown-up, but it had become part of us, part of our story. So I kept it and that morning, it rang. Sibelius stopped, and that fucking song started.

It was one of the other moms. Erica. She was breathless. There was a shooter at Whittlesford. Her husband was a County Sheriff, and he'd told her about the nine-one-one alert, all units.

I remember the world just stopped for me, there and then. Somehow I was standing up and I could see all 360 degrees around the study, without actually looking. The bright screen. The dark leather chair. The cat on the sofa, immobile and sleeping. The rug, dark red. Bookshelves of law books and reference books and fiction. My teapot. The empty cup. The white shutters. My stupid mules. And the ego wall with its gap. That gap for what Jack would become. I hung up and immediately dialled Jack's cellphone, but it was turned off. I left a frantic message, but I remember thinking that wasn't a bad thing, because he'd been complaining about the battery life and how he just had to have a new cell. I guess I was rationalising even then.

I started moving without even thinking, got in the car, and drove to Whittlesford. I was on complete autopilot. Jonathan was deployed, and I obviously couldn't call him, so I called the Base Liaison Officer while I drove. Speed dial on hands free. I'd never needed to call Jonathan when he was deployed before, but he insisted I had that number stored in my cell. It was close to lunch, and I got the answerphone, and I left a damn message. It's a straight drive to Whittlesford, seven minutes max, and I remember even thinking that this was good as it meant I didn't have to jump red lights on the way. Which I obviously would have.

I was thinking all kinds of crazy thoughts. How many kids there are at Whittlesford. What the chances were that Jack would be hurt. It's a decent sized school. How unlucky would he have to be to be one of them, even to be in the room? I didn't think to call my mom or dad. I just drove. In my head, I was convinced it was going to be all right. I just kept doing the math. 1200 students at Whittlesford. It's awful, but I even remembered the Aurora shooting, in the movie theater, because Jonathan had wanted to watch the Joker movie when he was home on leave, and we didn't go in the end. I actually remembered there were less than twenty victims in Aurora. I tried to work out what the chances were that Jack was one of them given the size of Whittlesford. It seemed so small, tiny, that I was sure he would be OK. He probably wouldn't even have been in the same building. I tried to call Jack again, but it was still switched off.

While I drove, the school alarm notification system texted. There was a system, like most schools, to alert parents for things like fires or floods or anything else that needed an evacuation or a lockdown. I knew it also covered active shooters because some of the moms of the younger kids had gotten angry about a planned lockdown drill. It had frightened their kids and made them not want to go to school. California also texts every cellphone in the case of things like a child abduction and the chime is different for emergencies, but I didn't need the confirmation. I'd heard the truth in Erica's voice. I couldn't read the text anyway because I was driving. I think the car radio was on, because I always left it on, but I don't actually remember it.

Before I even got to the school gates where the buses pull in, I had to stop. There was police tape a good hundred yards from the gates and moms were standing around, shouting. I remember noticing that it was mainly women and that the voices were higher pitched. More moms would have been at home, but I guess the men work downtown or in the Navy yard or were deployed and had further to come. Police officers were shouting on a megaphone to stand back, stand back. Cars were all over the road, parents just abandoning their vehicles and charging to the tape. It was total chaos, growing as more people screeched to a halt. More police arrived, half pointing toward us to keep us back, half pointing toward the school, crouched behind vehicles or shields. They were pointing their pistols at the school. A command center van pulled up behind them, bristling with aerials and antennae.

A local TV crew pulled up in a white van, its logo on the side in blue. Three cameramen jumped out and started filming. One of them pointed his camera at the school building, and one of the others started filming the anchor, as he did a piece to camera. I couldn't hear him, but I could see him, his back to the school, wearing a sport coat and striped tie, holding his microphone with its logo-ed collar close to his mouth, squinting against the sunshine as his hair blew in the wind.

I recognised one of the few men there, just catching his face through the growing crowd. Tom was on the *Nimitz* with Jonathan, but he was home on leave. He just looked so calm. Reassuring. He's a bit older, not tall but he's solid, about a mile wide. As I ran toward him, one of the TV cameramen pointed his lens at him from close-up and Tom just looked squarely into it and said, Fuck off. Now." The cameraman fucked off.

We sort of hugged, didn't really say anything. We just stood there and waited. He had twin girls in ninth grade, and he was trying to message them, but nothing was coming back. I tried to text Jack, but my WhatsApp just went to one tick. We both knew that didn't necessarily mean anything. A lot of teachers at Whittlesford used to make students put their cell phones in a bucket or a box during class. Most parents thought it was a good thing. Before all this happened.

More and more parents were arriving. People were standing behind the tape, guarded by the police officers and just watching. The megaphone kept telling us to stand back, stand back. It was so noisy. I suddenly noticed a news helicopter hovering overhead, low enough to hear the rotors whupping around. And then we saw one girl, maybe in tenth grade, burst out of the fire exit door at the back of the cafeteria building and run as fast as she possibly could toward us. The police were screaming at her to get down, get down, but she just kept on running and running and running. She was in a blue checked dress, fists clenched, black spectacles bouncing up and down and she just ran like her life depended on it and she collapsed into the arms of one of the police officers.

She was the first. Another girl followed, and then a boy. He had dark hair, and my heart skipped a beat, but then I saw he was younger than Jack, younger and skinny. I recognised one of the Phys Ed coaches at the fire exit door, in a bright red Whittlesford polo shirt, grabbing the kids from inside and pushing them towards the cops. He was practically flinging them out of the door one at a time, screaming GO GO GO! But he didn't run himself.

The police line started receiving the kids. It seemed like once more of the boys started running out of the cafeteria, the police changed their strategy. They made the kids all lie down on the ground, face down with their hands out and up, like starfishes. Officers patted them down and searched them for weapons. Once they were clear, the police questioned them. They didn't seem to know anything, but someone said a boy had a gun and had been shooting. An older boy. Someone thought there had been two shooters. Someone thought there had been one. It was rumour piled on top of hearsay on top of confusion on top of chaos. The police were trying to get a description, but none of the kids running from the cafeteria had seen anything, just heard it.

We all just waited. Some moms saw their kids and screamed, wanting to go get them, but they were held back at the tape. Kids were getting searched and cleared and then screaming for their moms and then loud tears as they just held, held, held. Tom and I had been joined by other parents from kids in various different grades and we just stood and stared at the cafeteria building, still trying to text or Whatsapp.

One of Tom's daughters made it out of the cafeteria, and he hollered at her, his huge booming voice. She tried to run straight toward him, but the police intercepted her. Every kid was being patted down now, boys or girls. She cleared the cordon and ran into his arms and collapsed, tears streaming down her blotchy red face. He held her in his huge, tattooed arms, but still looked over her shoulder for the other twin. He was trying to ask where her sister was, but she was hyperventilating and couldn't get the words out. Then he saw her twin run and he exhaled the longest breath I think I've ever seen. He was so relieved. He scooped his other child up, and tears ran down his cheeks, over his stubble. And then he saw the rest of us, still waiting and, well, I don't know what that expression was. Maybe embarrassed. I'll never know.

While the kids were running out, the police SWAT team had moved in. Initially they'd covered the kids running, but now they were physically moving toward the door. When the Phys Ed teacher finally turned and ran from the school, my heart fell. That must mean the cafeteria was now empty. I still hadn't seen Jack. The number of kids who'd run from the cafeteria wasn't enough to have been the whole school, so it seemed pretty obvious that hundreds were still in the other buildings. But I started to worry more. I don't think I knew at that moment. But I'd been convincing myself that the math favoured Jack and with so many students, he was bound to be OK.

I remember the next moment extremely clearly. It was loud and noisy and then we heard a single gunshot, and it all went quiet. We didn't know what the shot was. We stared at each other. And then, maybe thirty seconds later, another single shot. I was frantic by now, and so were all the moms who hadn't found their kids yet. Another thirty seconds, another single shot. I counted four shots, each with a thirty second or so gap between them. And then, maybe a minute later, we heard the last one. A single flat gunshot, and the sound of breaking glass.

We didn't know it was the last gunshot then, of course. We stared at each other and our phones and waited, but it was quieter now. TV crews on the other side of the school were broadcasting live pictures of kids escaping from classrooms and buildings over there. I kept looking between my cellphone and the buildings, but I couldn't see Jack. One by one, the group I was standing with thinned out as they spotted their kid. They didn't say anything as they left, just ran to where their kid was and hugged them tight.

I try not to think about that moment, but I can't help it sometimes. I'll be doing something else, not consciously trying to keep myself busy, but doing something. And then I'll float back to that bright day. It's like I'm a statue on a traffic circle, immobile in my ridiculous mules, while the world continues to spin around me. Looking through a periscope view on the world from hell. And I don't think I actually did, but in my memory, while I was waiting, I was thinking about Jack as a baby, as a toddler, as a little boy. How he'd picked me a flower from the yard once, yanked it out with soil falling off the root and came to give it to his mommy and then climbed onto my lap for a cuddle, and I dropped what I was working on and just hugged him back and kissed him all over his soft chubby cheeks.

I think that maybe the moment I knew was when I realised there were only two of us left in that particular group, standing there. The math had gone to fifty-fifty in my mind, which was stupid because this was just one group, and there were still plenty of other pockets of parents waiting and hoping. We just stood next to each other, two moms wondering where our babies were. I don't know who did it. It might have been me. But we stood next to each other and stared at the school. And then we were somehow holding hands, my right in her left. I had my cell in my left, she in her right. And then her boy made his way through the line of police, tears streaming down his face, and she let go of me. Ran to her boy. And I think that's the moment I knew that Jack had gone. I still told myself that he would be OK, bargained that maybe he'd just been hurt, or he'd locked himself in a closet or something. But I think that's the moment when I knew.

I was looking blankly down at my phone when I saw a pair of black polished boots on the grass. I looked up and saw a police officer. His expression was blank. I couldn't read it.

"Mrs. Tolleson? I'm afraid you need to come with me."

I was numb. I nodded. I didn't even ask if Jack was OK. Just followed him under the tape and through a group of other officers and into the command center van.

An older officer sat in the van. Maybe late forties. Grey and spiky. He had more stripes and badges than the young patrolman who'd fetched me. A captain. He motioned to the first officer to close the door behind him.

"Please. Sit."

I didn't even say anything. Just folded into one of the chairs in the van. A standard office chair, on wheels, rotating away from a bank of black and white computer monitors.

"I'm incredibly sorry, Mrs. Tolleson, but I need to ask you some questions about Jack. What was he wearing to school today?"

"Uh, jeans. Jeans and a Chargers shirt. Shawne Merriman. Number fifty-six. Is he OK? Tell me he's OK."

I remember the sounds coming out of my mouth. It wasn't me that made them, but obviously I had. When I remember it, I can actually see myself speaking, as if I were filming it from over the captain's shoulder. I don't even know why I asked what I asked, because by then I knew.

"I'm sorry, Mrs. Tolleson, but Jack has died. We're sure it's him. I'm very sorry."

At that moment, I don't have a skeleton. I'm just a mass of soft, unsupported tissue, collapsing into a wheeled office chair in a command center van. My baby is dead. My husband is deployed and doesn't know. I'm hyper-ventilating, fast and shallow. A female officer I didn't even know was there is touching my shoulder. I shrug her off. How dare she?

"Someone needs to tell his father," I say. I hear the words again, and even though this is the worst moment of my life, I notice their incongruity. I would normally refer to Jonathan as my husband. He's not a badge or a trophy, and I don't say, "my husband," to prove a point to single mothers, but that's what he is. My husband. A man I met by chance one evening in a restaurant in Boston and built a life with. But now, I call

118

Jonathan, 'his father.'

"Where is he?"

"He's on the *Nimitz*. I tried to call the Base Liaison Officer earlier. I left a message." Saying I left a message sounds like the most ridiculous thing ever.

"OK, we can take hold of that for you. What's his name?"

"Jonathan Tolleson. Commander Jonathan Tolleson."

The original patrolman who brought me in leaves. Closes the door quietly behind him. I'm struck dumb. What happens next. I don't know. I stare, glazed. There are no tears. Why are there no tears? Surely there should be tears. My baby is dead. My poor sweet baby is dead.

The captain steadies himself. Maybe he's relieved that I'm not hysterical. He takes a deep breath with his shoulders but not his mouth. Conflicted.

"Mrs. Tolleson, I'm incredibly sorry to have to break this to you. But. We believe Jack was the shooter."

That's the last thing I remember.

Chapter Twenty-Three

Chris: Hi, Doctor Wenger. It's Chris Hicks. Nice to meet you, and thanks for taking the time.

Dr. Wenger: Hi, Chris. Good to meet you too, even on Zoom. I never asked, where are you and Nick based?

Chris: Oh sorry, I guess we should have said. We're in New York, not too far from Boston, I guess, but Zoom makes everything easy I guess. And when it's just us, we record the podcast in a recording studio which lets us have it at weird times for a discount. We just get better sound quality that way. When we have guest experts, we usually record the Zoom or WebEx, or conference call, or whatever.

Dr. Wenger: Oh, cool. So how exactly can I help you?

Chris: Well, as I emailed, we're looking at covering the Whittlesford tragedy on the podcast. It was so different and so unique in how it ended, it kind of seemed to Nick and me – he sends his apologies, his day job got in the way – that it probably would have had a unique beginning also. And we did some research, and we came across some of the papers you've written which mentioned the mental issues around school shooters and thought you seemed someone we should talk to, to, you know, make sure we got the facts right-

Dr. Wenger: OK. Well, like I said, I'd be happy to help. What would you like to ask?

Chris: Actually, before I ask anything, can I check if you're OK if we record this conversation, or would you rather check any quotes we would want to use, or do you want to just be off-the-record entirely?

Dr. Wenger: I'm glad you asked. Let's make this first conversation off the record, just for background. I don't mind if you record it to save you taking notes, but not for publication or quotation just yet? There's a lot of nuances in this topic, and it's very easy to upset people when that nuance is misunderstood.

Chris: Cool. We can do that. I guess before we start, what got you into this field to start with? I mean, everyone always asks Nick and me why we do what we do, so I'm kinda intrigued as to what brought you to it.

Dr. Wenger: It's a fair question, for both of us I guess-

Chris: *laughs* Yes

Dr. Wenger: I did Natural Sciences for my undergrad in England, kind of like pre-med in the American system. That led me to med school here – Harvard because Cambridge – the English one - had good connections to Harvard. And then I went the psychiatry route. At one point I took an elective which included working with offenders within the corrections system. And I guess, it struck me then that medicine can obviously help people who've been victims of crime after the event. And maybe I could do something useful in helping prevent people from committing those acts in the first place-

Chris: And that was your PhD, I believe.

Dr. Wenger: *chuckles* Someone's been doing their research. Yes, I focused on personality disorders found within convicted violent offenders in the British penal system – back in the English Cambridge – and then moved back over here to take up a post within the faculty. And since then, that's been one of the focuses of my research.

Chris: Fascinating. So I guess you're probably the best-placed person to tell us – and I guess listeners generally – what made Jack Tolleson do it. I guess the starting question is the obvious one. Was he mad, or bad, or both?

Dr. Wenger: Well, I guess I'd start by saying that we tend to shy away from those distinctions within psychiatry. And also, I want to be clear that I can't comment on Jack Tolleson specifically at all, having never met him. However, there's usually a lot more nuance in the psychiatric condition of most people – even those who haven't presented with particular symptoms to a physician or committed any criminal or violent acts. And when we look at similar cases involving people who commit violent or illegal acts, there's usually a number of things going on with them-

Chris: Forgive the interruption, but I'm curious as to why you said violent or illegal, as opposed to violent and illegal.

Dr. Wenger: Oh, the two can be very different. Self-harm, destruction of your own property, punching your own walls, that kind of thing. Definitely violent, but not strictly illegal. There's plenty of risky behaviours that patients can get involved in which aren't violent but are illegal; usually stuff like drug-taking, promiscuity, especially involving sex workers in certain jurisdictions, sometimes even petty theft and shoplifting things you don't need and won't even sell, purely for the element of regaining control, at least in the eyes of the patient. And obviously there are some things which are both illegal and violent, ranging from deliberately starting fist fights in bars to the kind of awful things we've seen happen far too often at places like Whittlesford or Sandy Hook.

Chris: Right. Gotcha.

Dr. Wenger: So we wouldn't categorise a patient, or even the act of a shooting like Whittlesford as mad or bad. The bad – that's a legal judgement. Did Jack Tolleson break the law doing what he did? Yes, obviously. Was he mad? Well, obviously I can't comment on him personally. But in similar cases, what we've seen, is that some of the people committing these kinds of acts are actually sick in that-

Chris: Well, yeah, I mean shooting up teenagers in a school is sick-

Dr. Wenger: No, no I want to be very clear here. I can't talk specifically about Jack Tolleson, but if we talk more generally about similar events, in some cases we find that some of the perpetrators are very clearly suffering from specific mental health disorders, so I mean sick as describing someone who is unwell. This is one of the nuances I mentioned in my email. I completely understand why society uses the terms it does. Saying someone is sick is a convenient shorthand for the rest of us to categorise an individual or their actions as being something that a quote normal unquote person would not do, especially when that action is designed to maximise suffering of the victim. Then we say that the perpetrator was a sick person, but society uses it as a pejorative. In my field, we use it as a statement of clinical fact.

Chris: Ah, OK. So what mental disorders do you think he had? Was he a psychopath or a sociopath?

Dr. Wenger: Well, again I can't speak about Jack Tolleson specifically, but I would also be a little careful about using those terms in a general forum-

Chris: How come?

Dr. Wenger: Well again it comes down to how society uses medical words and they have certain nuances which are either inaccurate, unhelpful, or both. I do understand why broader society uses them, but my field has to be a little more cautious.

Chris: So what is the difference between the two?

Dr. Wenger: Ah, now. We tend not to use the term 'sociopath' in psychiatry. However, psychopathy is a recognised type of personality disorder. It tends to be associated with antisocial behaviour, a reduced ability to experience empathy or remorse and bold or egotistical traits-

Chris: And how does that differ from sociopaths?

Dr. Wenger: Psychiatry doesn't tend to use the word sociopath, although obviously, it's popularly used in the media and personally, I'm not sure that using either term in a non-medical concept is helpful-

Chris: Why is that?

Dr. Wenger: Both of those terms have generated their own pejorative identity in popular usage. Calling someone a psychopath or a sociopath is a term of abuse as much as anything. In my view, they dehumanise the subject and they also downplay the fact that this person is actually ill and therefore should be being treated, both for their benefit and that of society-

Chris: OK, so you think we should be treating shooters rather than locking them up?

Dr. Wenger: I didn't say that, but what I would say is that psychiatric intervention is like other branches of medicine. If we treat people with a contagious disease, we make them better, but we also do good for society. Because nobody else can catch it. The effective contagion of mental illness isn't my research specialty but clearly other people in society can be harmed by people with brain diseases, as we have seen in the pathologies of some offenders. If we treat people with psychiatric illnesses, then we make them better and hopefully we also avoid damage to other members of society by preventing them acting out their risky or destructive behaviours.

Chris: Ah OK. That seems fair, I guess. So how would you categorise Jack Tolleson?

Dr. Wenger: Well, I can't categorise him, as I said – I never met him and I really have to keep my comments general. However, if we look at the disorders suffered by people involved in similar acts, we do often see that they are suffering from depression and anxiety, and sometimes these can be linked to social exclusion. This goes back to basic human mindset. If we are cut off from the herd, we die, so when we see this kind of orchestrated exclusion from a group, that leads to almost primeval fear at the expected physical trauma that our ancestors knew would happen to them if they no longer had the protection of group membership.

Chris: Wait, so how does that work? Did Tolleson shoot everybody because in his head he was sure they would do it to him first?

Dr. Wenger: I'm afraid I really can't talk about him specifically, but perhaps I can explain the generalities like this. Right from the start, humans have survived on this planet despite not being the biggest or the strongest species. We've done so by forming groups, societies. There's always been a competition for resources on the planet – water, food and so on – and the way individuals maximise their chance of survival is by being part of a group. Now, those groups aren't universal – that's how we've formed competing tribes and so on – but generally speaking, being part of a group was a sound way of avoiding being eaten by a predator.

Chris: Safety in numbers?

Dr. Wenger: Yes, exactly. Now what's interesting is that when we look at modern day society, we see multiple phenomena. Firstly, the world is much safer than it ever was. Generally speaking, even if you get cut off from society, you're probably not going to die. We don't have predating animals roaming the streets of New York-

Chris: You clearly haven't been to Brownsville recently, doc. *laughs*

Dr. Wenger: Quite, but that's one phenomenon which is quite interesting. That the world is much safer. At the same time, society is much more connected, thanks to how we live both physically and digitally-

Chris: How do you mean?

Dr. Wenger: Well, generally speaking we live in much more concentrated conurbations than we used to. Megacities of millions of people are not unusual, but they were practically unheard of even in the mid-19th century. And we've consciously formed far more groups in various guises. Sports clubs, hobby groups, corporations, universities and so on.

Chris: Ah OK. And the digital world, you mean social media?

Dr. Wenger: Yes, but not just that. For adults in employment – I should say in specific types of employment, the digital world increases their social connections far more than was possible in previous years. We think nothing of emailing or conference calling people in multiple cities around the globe. For those either not in those kinds of jobs, or not in any kind of job just yet, the workplace media is missing, but the rise of social media has also heightened social connectivity.

Chris: OK I get that, but how do we get from this to Tolleson deciding to murder his classmates?

Dr. Wenger: Well, let's stay away from this specific case. My point is that the concept of society has become something you can't really escape on the one hand, and that you really don't want to escape, on the other. We are all much more connected to this thing called society, and society has done a really good job of promoting itself as something desirable and good.

Chris: Isn't it? Something good, I mean?

Dr. Wenger: Well, overall, yes. But the point I'm trying to make is that in the modern, safe, world, opting out from society is no longer physically dangerous. And yet if one either excludes oneself, or is excluded by the group, the sense of panic that can engender is exactly the same as if one were cast out into a wilderness full of dangerous predators in ancient times-

Chris: Wait, so what we're saying is that Tolleson felt he was under physical attack by a bunch of students calling him names and hazing him a little-

Dr. Wenger: No, I'm still not commenting on this case specifically. But what I am saying is that when we look at laboratory tests and clinical studies, we find that a socially excluded human can demonstrate exactly the same sense of panic, the same biochemical response in the same areas of the brain, as if they were suffering physical trauma. The fact that it's emotional trauma that's causing those neurons to fire is frankly irrelevant.

Chris: Really?

Dr. Wenger: Yes. I could show you Mr.I scans of clinical subjects subjected either to physical trauma or emotional trauma and you'd see the amygdala – that's kind of like the threat management area of the brain - firing identically-

Chris: How does that work?

Dr. Wenger: Well, basically, we can photograph the brain using an Mr.I. And we can record the number of electrical impulses firing in response to various stimuli. And what's interesting and relevant here is that regardless of whether we show most patients physical or emotional trauma, you wouldn't be able to tell the difference in intensity or speed or duration of response. Now that doesn't apply to everyone, and there are some people who don't especially react to things that would normally scare the rest of us, but generally speaking, emotional trauma can generate the same response as physical, actual threat-to-life physical trauma. And there in some specific patients, those feelings of potential abandonment are so terribly painful – far beyond what it seems the rest of us experience – that they experience huge trauma and logically a huge emotional response to that trauma. And there are a number of known mental health disorders which can lead to that exceptionally painful and fearful response.

As Dr. Wenger continued, Chris pulled out his cell, below the line of the camera perched on top of his laptop. He whatsapped Nick.

"On the Zoom to the shrink now. You were so right to dodge this, bro. She won't comment on Wacko Jacko at all and she's talking pure shrink. No juice whatsoever. Boring AF."

The reply came quickly.

"Nothing useful at all?"

"Nope. I mean, she's kinda cute but not much use for the podcast. Way too generic."

"Told you. Give it ten minutes then kiss her off, fifteen if she's hot. We need some juice."

"Fifteen then ;)"

He leaned toward the webcam. In camera, he was feigning interest as the psychiatrist diligently clarified potential illnesses, the detail of which would be of no interest to his target demographic. Out of shot, his hands were scrolling idly through Insta bikinis on his cell.

Chapter Twenty-Four

Cyberspace wasn't just the means to ensure Jack's isolation. It was a battleground in its own right.

There were various different social media groups at Whittlesford, and Jack was a member of some of them. WhatsApp, Facebook, Messenger, Snap, Insta, TikTok and so on. Standard year group, check. Football fans, check. Baseball fans, check. Basketball and Lakers fans, check. De facto study groups that had sprung out of multi-person chats about assignments and then grown, check. He wasn't a member of the cool kids groups or the actual football players' groups. He was so far away from crossing that red velvet firewall, he didn't know for sure that they existed, he just assumed. Assumed correctly, as it happened, but that didn't mean he was ever going to be invited.

Each of those groups became a theatre of combat in its own right. If he asked a question, it was ignored. If he answered one, no comment, neither disagreement nor thanks. It was like he wasn't there to begin with. As if he was the ghost, rather than the one being ghosted. He soon learned to stop contributing. He became, paradoxically, more focused in class. He knew there was no chance of cadging notes, or a steer from a classmate. He found solace in the anonymous company of strangers on the internet chat boards that discussed the Chargers or the Lakers. But he couldn't stop watching society at Whittlesford continue without him, pressed up against the glass on the outside. He saw friendships blossom and wither, hazing and praising, break-ups and make-ups. He saw the life of a small California town neither blossom nor wither, but just *be*. Rolling along at a speed of twenty-four hours per day. And he knew he would never be part of it.

The shift from indifference to attack took a while in coming. He didn't know why, and if he had have looked back, he would have realised that it was just inevitable. Sometimes cyberspace follows reality and sometimes it's the other way around. From his spot as a member of various groups across social media, he had a perfect view of everything that was said or not said. Perfect vision but zero power.

It started light, or at least that was what the protagonists would have claimed. *Gentle hazing*, they would have said, just replacing a 'Yo'momma so fat' joke with one about Shamu. Just a joke. It must have been funny because everyone laughed. Just a joke. And then another one, and then another one, and then another one, and then another one. Over and over again. An inexhaustible list, but just jokes. Everybody gets fun made of them now and then.

After a day of such jokes, there was a pause. Why, Jack wasn't sure. Had they thought they'd gone too far? Unlikely. The speed at which things went viral was drummed into students at Whittlesford in one of the earlier classes. The lesson should have been called *Risk Management for Horny and Stupid Teenagers*, but was just called *Taking Care On the Internet*. Either way, kids in school were more savvy about what to put on the internet than their parents had been twenty-odd years before. But jokes in a WhatsApp group? Just light-hearted fun. Nothing to see here. But then it restarted.

It wasn't a perpetual wall of bile, either. Life went on at Whittlesford and its social media planned it or discussed it. School, college, music, movies and sports. Who was dating who. Teenage sex in its usual format, where many more people were discussing it than doing it. But alongside the daily spin of the earth about its axis, there was usually room for a joke or a meme about Jack. Manipulated photographs of whales were especially popular. And if not an active comment naming him personally, his isolation and exclusion continued. Meet-ups polled availability for all but him, both school and social.

Jack had turned off his notifications on the apps. But when he did open them, he couldn't help but see the counter waving at him, quantifying just how many posts or messages had happened since he'd last visited. The numbers themselves were depressing. So much life he wasn't allowed to be part of. He observed friendly discussions wistfully, but couldn't take part. He tried a couple of times to redeem himself by being helpful. No dice. A valuable steer on an assignment was met with technological tumbleweed. He posted a link to a data source for a history assignment and there was no comment in the WhatsApp group for the rest of the day. As if it had been coordinated as such. He resolved not to try it again.

His resolve only lasted so long. Jack was helpful by nature in the first place. In one of his darker, lower moments, he bargained with himself that even if he was the group bitch, at least that made him *part* of the group. He wanted to be part of a group, any group. He was just so very tired of being alone. He was playing with his phone in his room, idly scrolling through clickbait quizzes. He couldn't help but look at the number of unread messages in the class Messenger group. A physics assignment was causing problems. Nobody had worked out how to do it yet, or if they had, they weren't sharing. But Jack had.

He figured he would try one last time. He could be useful to the group. Maybe they'd let him stick around. He might have someone to talk to on the bus or in class. Maybe if he was super nice and super helpful, his pariahdom might end. He quickly took a photo of the solution he'd come up with and added it to the chat.

Little face avatars appeared next to his post as individuals viewed the answer. Dozens and dozens. But no actual response. No smileys or thumbs-up or monocles or thank yous. Nothing.

And then there was one. From Luke the wide receiver.
#FuckOffShamu

Below it was a video clip. The opening scenes of Indiana Jones recovering the icon in *Raiders of the Lost Ark*. Jack couldn't help but click on it and watch. As Indy ran, the trumpets blared. He made the connection with the school band playing the soundtrack before football but still didn't know why.

And then he did.

He saw the big white ball turn into his face, expertly deepfaked. That huge orb of blubber chased Indy along the subterranean passageway, while the brass pounded away at his ears. He knew why the band had started playing that tune before football. He knew why he'd heard it in the hallways at Whittlesford and behind him on the bus. And he watched that flabby ball of fat, with his face on the front of it, lurch and spill itself after Indy and he was disgusted with himself. He turned his phone off and cried in his room. He was hideous, and disgusting, and there was nothing he could do about it. They were right.

Chapter Twenty-Five

Nick: So anyway, from what we know, it does look like Tolleson planned this for quite a while. We have a trip to Vegas, where he was supposed to be watching a football game, but he went to a rifle range instead, and he specifically asked to practice on bullpup rifles like the Kel-Tec he ended up using in Whittlesford.

Chris: To be clear, there was nothing suspicious about the range in Vegas.

Nick: Haha good point. Yes, for the sake of our legal liability, we should say that the rifle range in Vegas did nothing wrong, and for the sake of legal fairness, Tolleson did nothing wrong by visiting the range in Vegas. He didn't lie about his age, he wasn't intoxicated, he did nothing illegal. He booked some time at a range, like thousands of tourists do every year in Vegas. It was his first time firing a gun, like it is for thousands of tourists in Vegas. The guy who taught him to shoot only remembers him because the other customers that day were a bachelor party group and so Jack Tolleson ended up with a one-on-one lesson.

Chris: Don't tell me, he was a quiet boy, kept himself to himself?

Nick: Haha, they always are, aren't they? But I think that applies more to the serial killers who end up with an entire sorority buried in their front yard. But actually, more or less. Apparently, he was a polite teenager who'd always wanted to shoot, on a family trip to watch the Raiders, and whose dad was sleeping off a hangover from the night before. He had specifically wanted to try the Kel-Tec or similar bullpups, which was unusual, but not unheard of. They often get first-

timers wanting to try out particular guns they've seen on TV or read about in a magazine.

Chris: But the fact he went to Vegas a while before the shooting happened does suggest a pretty long-term plan.

Nick: Yeah, I think that's fair. He decides he needs to do it. He goes to Vegas to test-drive a bunch of guns. And then we think he goes to Texas specifically to buy the gun.

Chris: When you say, 'we think'?

Nick: Well, we know he bought a return plane ticket from LAX to Dallas-Fort-Worth, and we know he flew the outbound leg but not the return leg. We know he bought a Greyhound ticket from Dallas to El Paso, and then he took the train from El Paso back to LA. He spent the whole journey locked in his cabin, didn't talk to anybody, wasn't rude to anybody, wasn't friendly to anybody. And we know he did that journey having taken out a lot of cash.

Chris: So what do we not know?

Nick: Well, we have no cellphone record or email record of him discussing buying a gun. We know he downloaded a burner app on his cellphone, but we don't know who he called or texted from it. There aren't any records of it. So we assume that he bought the gun when he was in Dallas. That would explain flying into Dallas-Fort Worth, but travelling back on the train-

Chris: Why?

Nick: He wasn't old enough to own that gun. He wouldn't have been allowed to take it on the plane, and nobody would have been allowed to take that gun to California by air anyway.

Chris: Ah, OK. Makes sense. Did the ticket conductor not wonder what was going on? I mean, how many kids take a train ride that costs more and takes longer than a flight, during the school semester?

Nick: It's a fair question. I guess the first thing is that while Tolleson was seventeen, he was a pretty big guy; well over six feet and he was kind of fat, so he didn't look like a standard seventeen-year-old, I guess, and maybe the trains are full of nerds. But he had a ticket, bought on the internet, and he was quiet and polite, so I guess the Amtrak staff just let him get on with it.

Chris: Fair enough. I'm guessing the train staff work for tips, so they probably realised they weren't going to get anything off a maybe-teenage train nerd anyway and concentrated on the other passengers?

Nick: Yeah, probably. But this is kind of where the whole Tolleson personality thing gets interesting anyway. He didn't have mental health issues-

Chris: Woah, woah, woah. Jack Tolleson, the Whittlesford Wacko, didn't have mental health issues?

Nick: Lol. OK, fair point. I'll rephrase. He didn't have diagnosed mental health issues. He wasn't socially awkward. He was a solid, quiet student. He didn't post anything twisted online, and he didn't leave behind a bunch of diaries with swastikas in them or video messages where he proclaimed a manifesto. He wasn't treated well at school – we'll get onto that later – but he's about as far away from the stereotype of the school shooter as you can get.

Chris: Do you think that's why he was so, um, maybe not the right word, but so um successful?

Nick: Successful?

Chris: Well, you know. He had a firm aim about what he wanted to achieve, and he actually achieved it?

Nick: Oh. OK. Maybe? I guess? If I think of Klebold and Harris, they didn't achieve what they aimed to do in more than one way. The propane bombs they set didn't detonate, either in the cafeteria or their cars, and they also apparently got bored very quickly during the shooting and gave up relatively quickly. And obviously there's a ton of different narratives around their motivations, but certainly from the basement tapes and the journals, there seems to be a lot of pure anger and rage within them. And maybe that's why their murderous intent wore off relatively quickly? Or maybe they were so consumed by rage that they failed to set their bombs off properly?

Chris: Yeah, that's where I was going. Tolleson seems to be much more controlled. I mean, I know the usual thing to say in these circumstances is 'oh my it was such a shock, nobody could have seen it coming.' But the truth is that in quite a few cases – Stoneman Douglas High, Virginia Tech – you could have seen it coming and to be honest, people did see it coming but action wasn't taken. But with Tolleson, it genuinely seems to be the case that nobody ever thought he'd be the kind of guy to do something like this.

Nick: Yeah, he wasn't treated well at school, but he didn't react badly to it, at least not publicly. But obviously, something wasn't right under the surface. Plus, hundreds of kids get bullied and they don't go around shooting people. But I agree that the high degree of calculation within this – starting with the gun research, the practice and so on – probably does explain why Jack Tolleson got done what he wanted to get done, where others haven't.

Chris: Yeah. That makes sense.

Nick: And that's probably a good moment to pause and listen to these messages from our sponsors. We know you tune in to listen to us, and not to listen to commercials, but the commercials really allow us to carry on making interesting podcasts for you, so we'd really appreciate it if you listened to them and didn't skip forward.

Chris: And, as always, if you really really really enjoy the podcast-

Nick: Really really really?

Chris: Yeah. If you triple-really like the podcast, we'd be really grateful if you could support us via Patreon. This unlocks members-only content, and you even get a free coffee mug with the Killing Time podcast logo on it. Guaranteed to help you skip the line at most neighbourhood coffee stores...

"Thank you for listening to Killing Time with Chris and Nick, your friendly neighbourhood podcast about all things murder. Here at Bullet Coffee, we ethically source the best organic coffee from around the world before roasting it ourselves on-site in New York City. If you're in town, why not stop by our flagship on Mulberry Street in Little Italy or one of our other locations around Manhattan, the Bronx and

135

Brooklyn? And if you're elsewhere, we ship quickly to anywhere in the United States. You'll love our extensive choice of world coffee whether you like your coffee filtered, French pressed, espresso or any other way. Come check us out at BulletCoffee.com – total delight on your first order or your money back."

Chapter Twenty-Six

Jack Tolleson Signed Coloring Book Artwork from Murderantiques.com
CLICK HERE FOR IMAGE
$750
ADD TO CART
Jack Tolleson Half-completed Coloring Book Artwork. Signed and dated on reverse.

Jack Tolleson is notorious for committing the Whittlesford School Shooting, in Southern California in November 2020. This was a truly unique event in modern American history. He had no previous criminal record before he killed. This artwork of a Mexican street scene comes from a coloring book for adults. It is half colored in using felt tips and is signed three times, once with his full name, and twice with his initials. The signings with initials include the date, one week prior to the shooting. We have not seen any signatures dated closer to the killing than this unique piece.

CLICK HERE FOR MORE ITEMS FROM JACK TOLLESON

CLICK HERE FOR MORE ITEMS FROM SCHOOL SHOOTERS

CLICK HERE FOR FREE VALUATION IF YOU HAVE ITEMS TO SELL

Chapter Twenty-Seven

I guess I don't know which exact memory of Jack is my favourite. It's tough to pick one thing, you know.

Ever since he was tiny, Jack was just fascinated by animals, especially furry ones. He would squeal at the TV, and point if there were ever lions or tigers. When he was in his stroller, he'd always try and pet any dogs we went past. I was always scared that they would bite him, but they never did. He just had a way with them. And when sometimes they came up to him, for a sniff, he would burst with excitement, bright red and giggling, even if it was the biggest and fiercest German shepherd. And somehow, they would react to him, and just nuzzle him while he petted them, even if he did that thing kids do, when they pet dogs and cats like they're painting a wall with a roller. They never barked or even growled at him. They just let him adore them.

When he was about six, he came back from school, and he'd decided we needed to get a dog and a cat. He was quite strong-willed like that, sometimes. He'd decided that we should get a Labrador and a kitten, and they would be friends. Jonathan was deployed, obviously, so I tried to push back a little. Little things like that did used to annoy me a little, especially the idea of a dog. As much as Jack promised he would walk the dog, I think every parent knows the kid won't do it every day. And every mom knows that if her husband is in the Navy, she'll be the one walking the dog all the time. So I pushed back on the dog, but I did a bit of research about cats. And we lived on a nice quiet street, and we had a decent sized yard and so I thought why not. And one day I surprised Jack after school by taking him to the animal rescue shelter, where I'd found out they had some kittens that needed homes.

It was the end of March, I remember. College kids were arriving into SoCal for spring break. It was sunny but not overly warm. But it was kitten season. I'd been planning this for a little while, to surprise Jack and had rung around a couple of shelters. It was a Friday afternoon. I told Jack we had to do some shopping and his little face sank. He wanted to stay home but he knew he couldn't stay at home on his own. I felt so bad then, like I was playing a trick on him, but I also knew I was going to make my little boy extremely happy, and so I got a warm glow inside about it at the same time.

He'd been asking pretty much constantly about getting a puppy or a kitten for three weeks, but he was quite good about it. He'd ask first thing in the morning and then he'd only ask again if we saw a dog or a cat, or if there was one on TV. And if I was having a hectic time of it, he would know not to push it. He wasn't being calculating or anything, but he was always aware of how other people were feeling. Empathy. If Jonathan came home from leave and was too exhausted to play with him – which he often was, because it's not like they fly them home in club – Jack would just curl up on his dad's lap, that first evening home, and just hug him, wouldn't act up.

So anyway, we got into the car, and he knew this was mom shopping not Jack shopping so he didn't pay any attention really to where we were going, just sang along to the radio. Such a pure, high voice. And then I pulled into the kerb and looked at him in the rear-view mirror, and told him we'd arrived. He looked to his right, confused. There weren't any real shops there, just a laundromat and a rickety looking nail salon. I smiled at him.

"Other side."

He looked left, across the street. The penny dropped and he saw the hand painted – tired and fading hand painted, not artsy hand painted – sign that said 'Paws Rescue Centre', and a picture of a smiling black cat with a red neckerchief. His little eyes went wide as windows and his little jaw dropped and he just beamed out of every little inch of him. He was so excited, my little man, and he fumbled at his seat belt before I opened his door. He held my hand as we crossed the road, squeezing it so tight, even though recently he'd been trying to avoid letting me hold his hand, especially anywhere where kids from school could see us. But that day, he squeezed my hand so tightly, and we went in.

The old lady behind the counter was a sweetie, the perfect grandmother, looking down over her eyeglasses.

"Well, hello young man. How are you today?"

"I'm-I'm- I'm," Jack just couldn't get the words out. He kept walking in line, picking his feet up and down. He was so happy and so excited, and his little hand was crushing my fingers with all his might.

"I'm Jennifer," I said. "I think we spoke on the phone?"

"Yes, we did. And that means you must be Jack. I'm Valerie, and I understand you want to give a kitten a lovely home to live in."

"YES! Do you have any orange ones?" he shouted. "I want an orange one, or orange and white."

Valerie beamed with delight and motioned us to follow her back into the shelter, through glass double doors.

There were eight kittens, about eight weeks old, in a big comfy room, with scratching posts and cat trees and scuffed furniture. One little grey one was fast asleep in a little basket, curled up between his mother's paws. Another little calico was dozing in another nearby basket. For the rest of them, it was kitten furball mayhem, scrapping and leaping and pouncing and charging around the room, the chased becoming the chaser and back again. Jack was absolutely beside himself, and I quickly took my phone out and took a couple of pictures for Jonathan.

"So, young man, have you seen one you'd like to say hello to?"

Jack pointed at a fluffy orange bundle that was waiting to pounce down from the cat tree. "Him!! Can I have him?!"

"Please," I added automatically.

"Oh! Please! Please, can I have him?"

She reached into a tub on the sideboard and pulled out a foil tube of cat snack, kind of like toothpaste or a running gel. She ripped the end off and then passed it to Jack with a smile.

"You'll need this."

She then scooped up the little kitten and held him close to her chest. Then she scooched down so she was the same height as Jack. The kitten wriggled gently but settled against her.

"Now, just squeeze a little bit onto the end of your finger, and then hold it out."

"It smells fishy!"

"Well, of course it does. Cats like fish." She was so gentle and kind. She could have run a shelter for kids as well as cats.

Jack walked closer and held out his hand, covered with the fishy gel. The little orange kitten caught the scent in the air and wriggled around, whiskers twitching, nose flaring. He craned his neck towards Jack's hand and then started licking it all off. He put his front paw on Jack's hand to stop him taking it away and carried on licking it all up. Jack was completely beside himself, entranced and bright red with happiness. I managed to take another couple of pictures even though I don't actually need them. Even now, I can just close my eyes and remember my little boy beaming with delight while a tiny orange kitten licked his fingers clean, while *his* tiny orange kitten licked his fingers clean.

By now the kitten had worked his way from Valerie to Jack. Valerie had moved Jack's arm round to hold the kitten from underneath while he started gently padding on Jack's chest. Tiny little purrs sang out in time with each softly clenching paw. I took yet another picture.

"Shall we have this one then, Jack?" I asked. He mouthed 'yes', but no sound came out. He was completely drowning in the staring blue eyes of the kitten.

Jack called the kitten Mr. Orange. To him, it was obvious. He was a boy kitten, well, a snipped boy kitten, and he was orange. So, of course he was going to be called Mr. Orange. I tried to gently steer him away, but then again, I'd seen

Reservoir Dogs. Tarantino and Tim Roth, and a sliced ear that made me shudder when I first saw it, and I always hid behind a cushion if it came up on television. My six-year-old little man obviously hadn't seen the movie. I suggested Garfield, I suggested Marmalade, I suggested Ginger, I suggested Carrot, but Jack insisted he was Mr. Orange and he lived at 1610 Chalcedony. And so I gave up, and Mr. Orange he was.

The name grew on me quickly. It's funny how that works. To everyone else on the planet, I'm sure if you mention the name Mr. Orange, you think of sharp black suits and black ties, a heist that goes wrong, and Stealers Wheel as the background to Michael Madsen doing something unspeakable with a cut-throat razor. But to me, when I see or hear the name, I remember a clear spring day when my little boy practically exploded with excitement and fell in love with a little orange kitten barely bigger than my hand.

That clear spring day he stretched out his little arms so he could carry the cat carrier and I worried all the way back to the car. Not really worried that if he dropped it, the cat would get hurt. It would only have been about a foot drop. The cat would have been fine. But I worried because I knew that if Jack felt he'd hurt his new cat, he'd burst into tears and be inconsolable. So I let him carry it, but I only really breathed again once we were back in the car. I turned the carrier so the barred door-grate faced Jack and then strapped it tight using two seatbelts across each other.

I drove home carefully, avoiding the potholes and slowing early for traffic lights. Jack was feeding Mr. Orange some more of the cat treats through the bars. When I pulled into our driveway and cut the engine, I could hear Mr. Orange purring softly. I turned, and he was wide-eyed, up against the door of his carrier, curious but also happy. My little boy might have picked out Mr. Orange, but I think Mr. Orange was quite impressed with the little boy too, especially bearing in mind all the snacks he'd been given.

We took Mr. Orange in and made sure all the doors and windows were closed. We had a hand-out from Paws about kitten care, and Jack had solemnly promised to Valerie that we would keep Mr. Orange in one room for a week, then the downstairs for two weeks, and then the whole house for a month. He'd been disappointed that Mr. Orange wasn't allowed to live in his room, but we compromised on the kitchen / diner. Valerie had said he'd been housetrained, but I figured I'd keep the little fluffball away from carpets until he'd proven that he actually was. Jack was fine, as long as he could be near his cat. And Mr. Orange seemed to enjoy being in the kitchen too, as cats tend to.

As it turned out, Mr. Orange had been well-trained, and we never had any puddles or messes to worry about. But what really impressed me was Jack. Other moms told me they had to berate their kids to feed their pets or tidy up after them, but Jack dutifully fed Mr. Orange every morning when he got up and emptied out the litter tray. I had to remind him to wash his hands afterwards, but I never had to remind him to do the litter tray. And every evening he would stop what he was doing at six, without prompting, and come and feed Mr. Orange.

So I guess I can't pick one specific memory of Jack that's my favourite. It's more the whole thing about him and Mr. Orange.

My little boy loved his little cat from the minute he set eyes on him, and that little kitten loved his little boy. Where there was one, there was the other. When Jack went to school, Mr. Orange would jump up to the kitchen window to watch him get the bus, and then quietly pad up to his room and sleep away the day on Jack's bedcovers. When it was time for Jack to come home, Mr. Orange would look out for him through the window and trot down to welcome him in.

He had a special miaow for welcome home, that he only ever used when Jack came home. If I went to fetch something and then came back, I swear that cat didn't even notice if I'd been out, unless I'd been picking up fish tacos. But if Jack so much as went to the newsstand, Mr. Orange would know and be waiting for him with that miaow. And even when Jack was dead, the cat would wait for him at the usual time, looking out the window.

Chapter Twenty-Eight

TRANSCRIPT: NRA PRESS CONFERENCE

Fields: Good morning. I'm Catherine Fields, president of the National Rifle Association of America. I'd like to welcome you here for our discussion of the topic that's been on the minds of all parents in America since the tragic events at Whittlesford. Before we begin, I'd like to suggest we take a moment of silence to reflect and pray for the victims.

Pause

Fields: Thank you.

Fields: Like most Americans, we were shocked by what happened. Like all Americans, we've been discussing the various options available to protect our children, and at this point we would like to share our thinking with you. And for that purpose, I'd like to introduce Wayne LaPierre, our Executive Vice President.

Fields: We won't be taking questions during this press conference, but we will be available in the next few days for 1-1 discussions, so please do reach out to us at that point.

Fields: Thank you. Wayne?

LaPierre: Thank you, Catherine. Good morning, everybody.

The National Rifle Association - four million mothers, fathers, sons and daughters - joins the nation in horror, outrage, grief, and earnest prayer for the families of Whittlesford, California, who have suffered such an incomprehensible loss as a result of this unspeakable crime.

Out of respect for the families, and until the facts are known, the NRA has refrained from comment.

While some have tried to exploit tragedy for political gain, we have remained respectably silent. Now we must speak for the safety of our nation's children because for all the noise and anger directed at us over the past week, no one, nobody, has addressed the most important, pressing, immediate question. How do we protect our children right now, starting today, in a way that works?

We must face the truth. Politicians pass laws for gun free school zones; they issue press releases bragging about them. They post signs advertising them and, in doing so, they tell every insane killer in America that schools are the safest place to inflict maximum mayhem with minimum risk.

How have our nation's priorities gotten so far out of order? Think about it; we care about our money, so we protect our banks with armed guards. American airports, office buildings, power plants, court houses, even sports stadiums are all protected by armed security.

We care about our president, so we protect him with armed Secret Service agents. Members of Congress work in offices surrounded by Capitol Police officers. Yet when it comes to our most beloved, innocent, and vulnerable family members - our children – we, as a society, leave them every day utterly defenseless, and the monsters and the predators of the world know it, and exploit it.

That must change. The truth is that our society is populated by an unknown number of genuine monsters, people so deranged, so evil, so possessed by voices and driven by demons, that no sane person can ever possibly comprehend them. They walk among us every single day. Does anybody really believe that the next Jack Tolleson isn't, right now, planning his attack on a school?

How many more copycats are waiting in the wings for their moment of fame from a national media machine that rewards them with wall-to-wall attention and a sense of identity that they crave, while provoking others to try to make their mark; a dozen more killers, a hundred? How can we guess how many, given our nation's refusal to create an active database of the mentally ill?

145

The fact is that a database wouldn't even begin to address the much larger, more lethal, criminal class - killers, robbers, rapists, gang members, who have spread like cancer in every community across our nation. While that happens, federal gun prosecutions have decreased significantly, to the lowest levels in a decade, so now, due to a declined willingness to prosecute dangerous criminals, violent crime is increasing again for the first time in nineteen years.

And there's another dirty little truth that the media tries to conceal. There exists, in this country, a callous, corrupt, and corrupting shadow industry which sells and stows violence against its own people, through vicious, violent video games and blood-soaked films. A child growing up in America today witnesses sixteen thousand murders and two hundred thousand acts of violence by the time he or she reaches the ripe old age of eighteen. Throughout it all too many in the national media, their corporate owners, and their stockholders act as silent enablers, if not complicit, co-conspirators.

Rather than face their own moral failings, the media demonizes gun owners. Rather than face its own moral failings, the media demonizes lawful gun owners, amplifies its cries for more laws, and fills the national media with misinformation and dishonest thinking which only delays meaningful action, and all but guarantees the next atrocity is only a news cycle away.

Worse, they perpetuate the dangerous notion that one more gun ban or one more law imposed on peaceable, lawful people will protect us where twenty thousand other laws have failed.

As parents, we do everything we can to keep our children safe. It's now time for us to assume responsibility for our schools. The only way to stop a monster from killing our kids is to become personally involved and to invest in a plan of absolute protection.

The only thing that stops a bad guy with a gun is a good guy with a gun. I'll say that again. The only thing that stops a bad guy with a gun is a good guy with a gun.

A good guy with a gun would have stopped Whittlesford from being in pain this morning.

A good guy with a gun would have stopped Jack Tolleson from committing his monstrous acts.

The only answer is a good guy with a gun.

There's going to be a lot of time for talk and debate later. This is a time; this is a day for decisive action. We can't wait for the next unspeakable crime to happen before we act. We can't lose precious time debating legislation that won't work. We mustn't allow politics or personal prejudice to divide us. We must act now for the sake of every child in America.

Thank you, and God bless.

Chapter Twenty-Nine

Rock bottom was reached one day in math. It would have been news to Jack that there was any further he could fall, but fall he did.

He had chosen to sit in his usual spot at the back. Only the teacher, Mrs. Potter, could see him. She was a tall, pale, redheaded woman from Kansas. Jack was generally diligent in math. He wasn't in his dad's league at math and physics. He was good enough, though, and he knew his dad got a bigger smile from Jack's math grades than he did stuff like history. So he paid attention and took notes and was generally diligent. Allowing for obvious lapses like checking out the girls if he had a chance to do so unobserved.

So there he sat, quietly minding his own business, not putting up his hand to answer any questions. Hell no. He wouldn't have done that before the wolf-pack had turned on him anyway, and he sure as hell wasn't going to draw attention to himself now. He just quietly took notes, neat handwriting on his pad, and whiling away the lesson. If pushed, he wouldn't claim he understood everything, but he'd have taken an even bet that he would remember it. His dad had drummed that into him. If you hear it, you might remember it. If you say it, maybe you remember it. But if you write it down, you will remember it.

Midway through the class, the door burst open. An out of breath Tyler panted his way in: average student, average intelligence, average cool status. One of the grey kids.

"So sorry I'm late!" A gulp of air. "I had a doctor's appointment. I think I told you about it. They were running late." Another gulp of air.

Mrs. Potter seemed amused that Tyler had turned up at all. A solid excuse like a doctor's appointment usually translated into a de facto pass for the rest of the day. Wonders would never cease.

"Calm down. Deep breaths. Yes, you did tell me, and thank you for making the effort to come in, even though we're obviously nearly done. You need to catch up the notes...now, who's got good handwriting for you to copy from and will volunteer to lend them to Tyler?" Her blue eyes flicked around the room. She looked for someone to do a good deed.

A mutter from the front. "Shamu's got decent handwriting. For a whale."

Sniggers and giggles bubbled up in the classroom, half-surreptitious. But not surreptitious enough. And it was immediately obvious that this wasn't the first time Mrs. Potter had heard Jack called Shamu. She stood on a tightrope, wondering whether to let it go or make something of it. Jack could see cogs turning in her head, her tongue pushed against her cheek as she decided on a course of action.

Please, God. Don't say anything. Please, Mrs. Potter. Just let it go. It's easier that way. You get to leave this class when the bell goes. I don't. **Please,** *just let it go.*

Jack's eyes caught hers. He willed her, implored her, to just move on. She didn't nod. She just silently acquiesced.

Relief. Intense relief. Jack exhaled, surprised. He hadn't even realised he'd been holding his breath, but maybe, just maybe, he'd caught a break.

Wrong.

Mrs. Potter turned back to Tyler. She opened her mouth. "Tyler, I think you could do a lot worse than borrow notes from Sha-"

She realised what she was about to do, and her cheeks flushed bright red. She knew the fat kid was nicknamed Shamu, that much was clear. She knew he had good handwriting. That was clear too.

But clearest of all was the fact that the only name she could summon at that moment was Shamu's. She had forgotten Jack's actual name and she knew it. Her pale porcelain cheeks turned scarlet as she realised Jack knew it, and that everyone else knew it, too. The whole class was snickering now, low guttural expressions of glee. A couple were puffing up their cheeks, making themselves look fat like a beached whale.

Jack was stunned. *How could she do this? How could one of his own teachers know his hideous nickname but not his actual name?*

Vacantly, he held up his hand, holding his notes. Showed her the escape door. He would never know why he did that.

"Ah-wonderful-you-have-a-volunteer-thank-you-so-much," she said, panicked, pointing toward Jack. She hurriedly turned back toward the board and frantically started recapping the previous points. She looked toward the class, but couldn't look Jack in the eyes. She couldn't even look in his general direction. Instead, she taught the remaining three-quarters of the room and ignored him.

Jack had flipped down his shades from the top of his head. He'd done so in the knowledge that he was about to have to blink back tears. He was surprised to discover they weren't coming.

No more tears? Had he run out? God only knew, he'd cried enough.

No.

No more tears. Jack's call.

Fuck you all.

He didn't know what he was going to do, but he knew he was going to do *something*. It was going to be big, and it was going to be painful, and it was going to be violent, and by the time he'd finished with those fuckers, they would never forget his name again. Every single one of them would remember his name for the rest of their miserable shitty lives.

Chapter Thirty

How do you eat an elephant?
One bite at a time.
Jack sat, at his desk, in his room. Not mad. Not enraged. Thoughtful. He pulled out an old wire- bound notebook from his bookshelf. Flipped to an empty page and took up a ballpoint.
What do you need for this to work? What makes you unforgettable?
For this to be truly memorable, for you to be truly memorable, you need triple figures. Nobody's ever done a hundred. That guy in Norway got close. But he's that guy in Norway. If he'd done a hundred, you'd remember his name.
So, by definition, you need at least one hundred people. But nobody gets one hundred percent on a test like this. So you need more than a hundred, in order to get a hundred. And you need to keep them in one place while you do it. Like the concert in Vegas or a nightclub. Problem One. The barrel.
You need a weapon. One that works. One that has the capacity to do what you need it to do. Stuff like rate of fire, accuracy, range. Reliability. You're not going to get much time to clear it if it jams. Problem two: the gun.
You need to execute. You can't afford to miss too many. You need to get it right first time. Nobody has ever gotten two goes at getting this right. So you need to practice. Practice makes perfect. But you've never done this before. Nobody has. Well, nobody you can actually talk to. But you'll need instruction. Guidance. Coaching. Feedback. And then you'll need to practice. A lot. Problem three: execution.

Three problems. One elephant. One bite at a time.

He paused. Actually, four problems. What he needed to do was to research, discover, plan. But he had to be careful. The internet had eyes. He knew he couldn't search via Facebook, or Instagram, or Twitter. There were eyes everywhere. Boy, did he know that. This needed to be a surprise. He scribbled the four problems in his notebook; old-fashioned pen and paper.

He thought for a moment. *How to be anonymous online. Nothing wrong with googling that.*

A string of articles appeared. He read them carefully. The first rule of being anonymous online, Google told him, was not to use Google, or Bing, or Yahoo. The latter was irrelevant. Nobody used Yahoo anymore. Only old people had Yahoo email addresses, and everybody hated Bing. The article recommended a browser called DuckDuckGo. Never heard of it. Stupid name.

Several articles discussed using VPNs: Virtual Private Networks. Jack's eyes glazed already. He wasn't a tech geek, wasn't interested in that part of the world, and he wouldn't know how to connect to one if he tried. But there was something called Tor, an anonymous browser. He'd heard of it somewhere before.

He typed in DuckDuckGo.com and searched again. That was it, an anonymous browser that had been connected to the Silk Road and Dread Pirate Roberts. Ironically, the guy had gotten careless, and was now doing life without any possibility of parole. Ever. For not doing anything like what Jack was planning. He needed to be careful.

He read further. So many acronyms: Unix, Linux. Well, he assumed they were acronyms. He had no idea what they stood for. The websites that discussed staying anonymous were largely tech websites and assumed a level of pre-existing computer knowledge that Jack didn't have. Nor was he likely to acquire that knowledge without talking to someone. From the results of the story of Silk Road, he couldn't even trust asking someone online. They could be anyone.

This was more promising: an article for investigative journalists. This could be a better angle. Investigative journalists were the respectable side of anonymity. Protecting government sources, and exposing cover-ups, like in the movies. It was not without risks, but was respectable, at least. First Amendment basics.

The article was detailed and, unsurprisingly, well-written. It detailed the pros and cons of various messaging systems, some of which he'd heard of, and some he hadn't. Had he known Facebook owned WhatsApp and Insta? He wasn't sure, but didn't trust Facebook anymore. There had been so many data leaks.

The article talked about how Tor worked. It was easier to understand in general terms, but still didn't light Jack's fire. It mentioned something called TAILS. The Amnesiac Incognito Live Operating System. You'd download the software onto a USB stick, then plug it into any laptop around the world and could use that computer to browse via Tor, message, research, do anything. And no records would appear anywhere.

It sounded promising, but Jack was cagey. He didn't need cops kicking in his door. Not until he'd executed his plan. He leaned back in his chair and frowned. Drummed his fingers on his desk. *How to check? How to be sure that TAILS was actually secure itself?* At some point, he had to trust in something. And, at the moment, there wasn't a whole lot he was willing to trust.

Inspiration struck. Journalists. He quickly went to the LA Times website, and clicked on 'How to give us a tip.' The instructions mentioned secure messaging apps like Signal. He went back to the article. It mentioned Deep Throat which Jack thought was a kind of blowjob. It turned out that it was a confidential informant who had brought down President Nixon. He clicked to the Washington Post. Their section on anonymous tips was much more detailed, but it still didn't verify TAILS.

He drummed his fingers again. Used DuckDuckGo to search for articles about TAILS. One was written by a journalist from the Post who lauded the system. TAILS had been vital in uncovering illegal acts by the government. He checked out the journalist on Wikipedia. Renowned, three Pulitzers. OK, TAILS sounded good, verified as best it could be.

He dug around in an old breakfast bowl of crap at the corner of his desk. Small change, padlock keys, an old fridge magnet with a picture of him and his parents in it, and a Chargers keyring USB, still in its cellophane, from a giveaway at a game one time. He deleted his internet history and rebooted his laptop. Then downloaded TAILS onto the disk. He rebooted the laptop again and got to work, confident as he could ever be that nobody was watching what he was doing.

And nobody was.

Chapter Thirty-One

How do you eat an elephant?

One bite at a time.

Problem One. The barrel.

How do you get one hundred people – minimum – in a small space from which they can't escape?

Think.

They probably need to be there voluntarily. This is a one-man operation. It would be difficult for one person to herd over a hundred and then execute.

You can't invite them somewhere and expect them to turn up. You'd be lucky to get a half-dozen people show up to anything you invited them to, never mind a hundred. And you'd have to lay on something spectacular for people to show anyway. Because they wouldn't be coming for you. They'd be coming for whatever event you laid on. And it would have to be a good one. Free burgers and beer wouldn't cut it. You'd need a celebrity. Scratch that. Can't be done.

If not an event you organise, then they need to be there already. They need to be there already at something that someone else has organised. OK. This is better. This makes sense. Vegas worked because thousands of people were fenced in at a gig. Nowhere for them to go. Norway worked because they were on an island. And unarmed. Nowhere to go. No way to fight back.

Hmm. Fighting back. You don't just need over one hundred people. You need the right kind of people. Minnows. Not sharks.

What's the difference between sharks and minnows?

Size. Minnows are tiny. Sharks are huge. Go for the

smaller ones. They're smaller, weaker and can't swim away as fast. You can gobble up more than one with a single bite.

Strength. Minnows are weak. They're less than three inches long. That's not much muscle. They'll break easily. Not like a shark.

Anything else? Yes. Juvenile minnows don't think as straight as adult sharks. They're more likely to panic. Less likely to know what to do. Adult sharks are probably more likely to realise there's strength in numbers. They could counter-attack. That would be harder to resist.

So, panicking juvenile minnows, trapped in a barrel. That's the best chance of success. And you know you only get one chance.

Location next. Where can you find more than a hundred juvenile minnows, enclosed in space?

Easy. Whittlesford High School. Jack was almost relieved. It was better that way. Symmetrical. Just.

Where in school did over a hundred people gather?

Hmm. Biggest crowd would be the football field. He liked that idea. That would be just. Friday night lights out. But it was a bad idea on many levels. Not especially enclosed. Too many exits and too easy to escape. Too many sharks. Hyped up football players wearing pads and helmets. Their parents. No. That would not work at all. He crossed out 'football' in his notebook.

Forget about the sharks for a moment. Consider the barrel.

Consider the barrel.

The best barrel in school had to be the sports hall.

He closed his eyes. Remembered the layout before sketching it out on his notebook. It was a long rectangular multipurpose building, with a huge variety of crisscrossing floor markings for various sports. The basketball court markings were in the middle and the backboards could be raised up and down via pulleys on the ceiling. The court itself was in the middle of the hall, stretching the full ninety-four feet in length, with long run-offs behind each hoop.

Along all of one long side was a bank of seating, bleacher

style benches in blond wood. They could be pushed in and pulled out of the wall, like a chest of drawers, but they were usually left out. Too heavy and too much hassle to push and pull. And the hall was plenty big enough for all its uses, from sporting to graduation, even when the bleachers were empty.

Jack focused his mind's eye. How many rows of benches were there? That would determine how many people could be in the hall at any one time. He counted with his ballpoint in mid-air, remembering the last time he'd been in there. Maybe twelve rows? He started doing the math but quit once he realised he was way over the numbers he needed. He had the right barrel in terms of size. Capacity. The number of minnows the barrel could take.

Next problem. How do you seal the barrel?

His paper notebook jottings continued. One set of double doors leading directly into the main hall from the entrance hall. Changing rooms and showers were off the entrance hall, not the main hall. In the hall itself were three sets of fire escape doors, big heavy, green-painted metal doors, with a push bar to exit. No windows at the ground level, just a ring of opaque shower-style glass around the top of the hall, letting in some light, but not much. There was another set of green metal doors in the hall, on the opposite side to the bleachers, which led to a big storage area, full of cones and balls and nets and suchlike.

Jack considered the layout. This could work. If he could block the doors, this could work. The fire exit doors were windowless metal – obviously because a sports hall would have balls and jocks flying around at rapid speed – and so nobody in the hall would notice if he blocked them from outside. They opened outwards. Fire exit doors always did. He'd need something heavy to block them. Or wedges underneath. Why not both? Cover the bases.

The main double doors to the hall from the lobby had those windows with the embedded metal wires criss-crossing it. Same reason, but he figured it would look odd to have the main doors without any windows. But they opened into the hall. Was that more problematic? Hmm. Not if that's where he positioned himself. And if he came in and started it, then he wouldn't have to smuggle anything in. Just walk in and start. He could walk to the sports hall, carrying a sports bag. And then start.

He considered it. If he was at the main doors, the obvious reaction was for the minnows to swim toward the fire doors. Away from him. They would assume the doors would be open. And when they couldn't get out, they might turn round and charge for him. Or would they? Maybe they'd swim to the other fire door. No. scratch that. Some of them would already have gone there. They'd all go for their nearest door, surely. So they would know pretty quickly that all the doors were blocked. Would any of them swim towards him, to try and counter-attack? That was an unknown. But he figured it was unlikely. Even minnows know they're minnows.

He quietly ticked each fire door on his sketch. Noticed the storage room door. It was a pretty big room, he remembered. Big enough to house all manner of apparatus, from pommel horses for gym to the high jump bed for track. Would any of them escape to there?

He considered it. Placed himself in their shoes. Yes. Logically, yes. If someone was at the main door, then they would run literally anywhere they could. So that included the storage room. He couldn't remember if there was a fire exit from within the storage room. But it was usually jammed full of crap, so he considered it wouldn't be easy to navigate through. Not under fire. It would be a barrel of its own.

Jack stopped. He quickly drew a large emphatic tick through the page on his notebook. He ripped the page out of the notebook and looked at the page beneath, to see if he'd gone through or left an indentation. Maybe. He tore that page out for good measure.

He went into the bathroom and tore the paper into tiny pieces before dropping them in the lavatory. Unzipped his fly and pissed over them. The water turned dark yellow. Then he flushed them away

He had found his barrel.

Chapter Thirty-Two

It was a blazing hot afternoon as Jack walked the back route home. Uncomfortably so. He could feel the sticky sweat between his backpack and his skin. His pace was ambling at best. But it was still better than being in school.

His buds sweated in his ears, and he was glad he wasn't running, or they would slip out. He was a while away from running shape anyway. There had definitely been progress, but he still wasn't about to start running in public. Certainly not anywhere near school. Or near Whittlesford in fact. He idly contemplated asking his mom for a gym membership. Gyms had treadmills. Discreet, indoor treadmills. Presumably with cooling aircon. He could lock himself away like a training montage in Rocky and come out ripped after fifteen minutes. Yeah, right.

He heard a ping in his ears over the music and realised he must have turned on notifications by mistake. He hooked his phone out of his shorts pocket. It was WhatsApp. Not Mom but the Whittlesford group chat. He stopped walking and his head slumped. He just couldn't escape it. He didn't want to think about school, didn't want to think about people at school, didn't want to see them, hear from them, have anything to do with them. He just wanted to be left alone. He turned off notifications and set the school group to mute.

He felt a small sense of relief as he swiped left across the school chat and archived it without reading. Replaced the phone in his pocket. He regained a certain amount of composure as he resumed his ambling. It had felt good to be able to turn it off. His gait took on some of the rhythm of the music in his ears. A passer-by would have assumed he was happy.

The track came to an end, and he didn't like the one that followed, so he pulled out his phone again to select something else. Maybe something more chilled. Friday afternoon sunshine music. Maybe something from his mom's playlist. Beach Boys maybe. Something happy. Maybe even Pharrell.

Eurgh. In the two minutes or so since he'd replaced the phone in his pocket, there had been fifteen messages posted in the WhatsApp chat. He cringed. He knew, just knew, that at least one of them would be trash talking him. Shamu the whale. And he knew it would be one of the anonymous ones. Cowards, hiding behind a blank profile pic, only displaying their phone number and no name. It could be literally anyone at school.

An idea appeared between his eyes and his sunglasses, and he stopped again. Did he even have to be part of the group? There really wasn't anything useful on there anyway. And nothing that was useful was only posted there. School stuff went up on the school website and was auto-emailed also. The days of joining impromptu movie theatre trips were over too. He knew where he wasn't wanted. That much was clear. Clear as crystal.

Would it be running away? He didn't care. He just wanted it to stop. Just wanted to carry on with his life. Anybody who said you should stand up to bullies clearly had never faced hundreds of them. Hundreds against just him. Fuck it. Why not?

He went to the group chat. To do what he needed to do, he couldn't help reading it. Sure enough, he was being insulted by a series of anonymous numbers. One had set their profile pic to a donut. *Whatever, asshole.* He tapped through to the Group Info page and scrolled down. Exit Group. He paused. He'd never actually seen anyone leave the group. Either nobody had ever done it, or it didn't announce it. He took a deep breath, surprising himself. Why? He was allowed to leave if he wanted to.

He tapped on Exit Group. The chamber of hate dissolved to nothing in front of his eyes. He smiled in wonder. Was that all that it took? A weight had been lifted off his shoulders. His feet felt lighter, and he realised he was actually smiling. For the first time in a long time, he actually felt, well, genuinely happy. Truly so. It was a sunny Friday afternoon in Whittlesford, California, school was out, and he was walking home to his family. He was actually happy. He decided to detour home via the Starbucks on the corner of Ocean Boulevard and treat himself to an ice-cold Frappuccino. It would accelerate the homework, he told himself. He realised his mom would likely be home and thought about messaging her to see if she wanted one too. He decided not to. Would be a nice surprise for mom, and they could both feed the cat the whipped cream.

His mom was in the study when he got home, frowning as she stared at her screen. Deep in concentration. He wandered in and placed a mocha Frappuccino, with whipped cream, onto the coaster by the mouse mat. He was halfway done with his.

She looked up at him. Raised her eyebrows.

"What?"

"To what do I owe this pleasure?"

"I think you're supposed to say thank you, mom. I didn't break anything, I'm not in trouble. It was just real hot, so I stopped and got one for me. And I figured you might want one too. So thank you might be better," he grinned. Sass. In this case, well-founded sass.

She smiled back. "Thank you, honey." She chuckled. "I think I'll be another hour or so. Did you eat already?"

"Nah, but I'm not hungry. I want to get homework done before I forget what it was about. I'll be upstairs."

He went to his room and turned on the PC. The ice had melted in his Frappuccino, diluting the taste. Still a little sweet though. He dug his phone out of his pocket so he could sit down.

What the fuck?

There were notifications on the lock screen. Twenty-eight of them. New messages within Whittlesford HS. The group he'd left.

What the FUCK?

His mouth opened. It stayed open. His eyes widened. Flight or fright? Freeze. His biceps had tightened, and his weight was more on the balls of his feet than it usually was. His body had recognised the imminent threat.

How the fuck had this happened? He'd left. Not twenty minutes ago, he'd stood on the sidewalk and left the group.

Someone had added him back. Without asking. An anonymous number. Not someone he knew. Well, not quite. Someone he knew, who didn't want him to know who it was, had added him back.

The first post since he'd been added back just read:

Aww, Shamu. Don't leave us.

Underneath was the whale emoji.

The pile-on followed as he scrolled down. It was still continuing. He could barely keep up. Endless whale emojis and Shamu-so-fat jokes. All anonymous.

He repeated the steps he'd taken earlier. Exited the group. And waited.

He held his breath as he waited. Within minutes, he'd been added back again, by the same anonymous number. The next post read:

You can run, Shamu, but you can't hide. Actually, scratch that. You can't run AND you can't hide. You're too fucking fat for either.

More whales followed. Laughing face emojis. Flames to show the burn. He hurled his phone onto his bed. It bounced and hit the wall but didn't break.

How was this possible?

He went straight to Google. Followed the instructions and blocked the anonymous number. Whoever the shithead was, he wouldn't be able to add Jack back to the group.

It worked. Briefly.

A different anonymous number added him back.

*We told you, Shamu. **Don't** leave us.*

We?

He'd known it wasn't just one person but seeing the 'We' hit Jack like a ton of bricks. He was in his room, his ordinary

162

bedroom, but he was still surrounded. There was no hope.

More whales and laughing faces followed. *#Owned* trended, and was followed by photos of real whales.

One by one, the anonymous participants added profile pictures that were visible to all. They all used the same picture. One by one, anonymous chat participants changed their photos to a beached orca. They all used the same photo. Exactly the same photo. A beached orca dying in the sun while people stood and watched.

He clenched his jaw and blocked the other anonymous number as well. He'd never needed to block anyone before. Never had cause to. Never had any major arguments with anyone, never needed to raise his fists in person, nor take the online nuclear option. And now, in the space of ten minutes, he'd had to do it twice.

He didn't leave the group yet though. He needed to think about this. He put his phone face-down on his desk and researched more. OK. There was a different way. He could change the settings on his phone so that only his contacts could add him to groups. Surely nobody would do that. Not if they couldn't be anonymous. He changed the setting. And then left the group again. Hopefully for the fear that it wouldn't work. Fear that one of his contacts would add him anyway. Fear that it would never stop.

He collapsed onto the bed, pulled both pillows over his head, and the tears started to flood. If he hadn't been alone in his room, it would have been noticed that he, a strapping seventeen-year-old, six foot three in his bare feet, had subconsciously retreated to the foetal position.

Chapter Thirty-Three

Jack sat on the bus and focused on his cell. He could only be added to WhatsApp groups now by his contacts. He would know who they were. He didn't have many friends, but that wasn't the same as not having many contacts in his phone. You accumulated them over time, like sand in your shoes. There were people he'd been friendly with in previous years, who'd drifted apart. Moved out of state. No actual major fallouts or arguments. Just life moving on, Twenty-four hours per day. That was before he'd become untouchable.

He scrolled through his contacts and considered how much he needed them. Many of them, he just didn't. Maybe it was better to just be on his own. By definition, if he was on his own, he couldn't be betrayed. Maybe it was safer that way. Was deleting all his contacts a nuclear option? He wasn't sure.

What if he needed them again? Not for friendship, but for something important. Like asking about homework, or if someone had tickets to a game they were selling. Would he regret deleting them? He was lost in thought as the bus bumped its way along the noisy asphalt.

Hmm. It wasn't quite the nuclear option. His iPhone backed itself up every month. If he did need to go back, he would be able to retrieve the numbers via a backup. But maybe it would send a good signal to remove all his contacts. If he removed them, they would no longer see his last seen status or his picture. They would know they had been deleted. Nobody would like that. It kind of evened up the score a little. And if he needed to check anything school wise, there were still Facebook and Instagram groups. Those actually had people's real names on them, so his chances of getting bullied there were maybe a bit less likely.

His right thumb swiped on his contacts ruthlessly. Delete, delete, delete. He was left with only relatives. That was fine. Imagine if they lived in the middle of nowhere, one of those hick towns in the Midwest that was really just a crossing. Or in Australia. In the outback. Then there wouldn't even be hundreds of people in his school to abuse him. It would just be him and his family, and his cat in the Australian outback. He smiled at the thought and then shuddered. Australia was full of spiders and snakes that bit. Not good for Mr. Orange. He wasn't much of a hunter, but like all animals, he followed the principle that might was right. Smaller animals were fair game. But just like at Whittlesford, smaller creatures developed strategies to survive and thrive. Tiny snakes and spiders were normally more poisonous than bigger ones. Full of venom. So Mr. Orange would have to be an indoor cat in Australia. No more basking out in the yard. He smiled at the memory.

His contacts were gone now, and his phone physically felt lighter in his hand. Come to think of it, why did it even have the phone function? He rarely called people. People rarely called him. It was just internet access that he needed. And now his only contacts were his family, he felt safer. Less threatened. And he could always go to the Facebook and Insta groups if he needed to. He had control of that though. He could choose to go or not. He had choices.

For the first time in a long time, Jack put his phone away during the bus ride. He leaned back in his seat and shrugged his shoulders. Stretched his neck. He felt OK. Even on the shady side of the bus, it was still warm. He gazed out the window, enjoying the view of the Pacific in the distance, and the warmth of the vinyl against his back and underneath him. A contented sigh even escaped his lips.

Chapter Thirty-Four

Chris: ...And welcome back to the podcast, and thanks for listening. If you have a moment, please do go to wherever you get your podcasts and leave a 5-star review. It won't cost you anything, and it would really help us grow our listeners and allow us to carry on making these podcasts.

Nick: Yeah, it really does make a big difference to us. Apart from anything else, Chris is basically unemployable, so we need the advertisers.

Chris: Douche.

Nick: True though?

Chris: Well, yeah. Guilty. *laughs*. Hashtag-trueee! Anyway, on to the last part of this week's podcast, which as you'll know is all about Jack Tolleson and the Whittlesford Massacre. We've spoken about the level of planning that seemed to go into this particular shooting, and it does look like he spent a lot of time planning this, and also practising it. But what we don't have any actual tangible evidence of is why. We have the testimony of one survivor, but we don't have any actual diaries or video statements or tapes, so he wasn't like some of the others.

Nick: Do we have anything from the families at all?

Chris: Tolleson's family? Or the victims' families?

Nick: Tolleson's, I guess.

Chris: No, we don't have much. To be honest, we got the usual crap from the mother-

Nick: Don't tell me, he was a quiet boy, kept himself to himself, we never thought he would do this-

Chris: Right. Here's a life hack for you: don't hang out with anybody who's quiet and keeps themselves to themselves. They're always the ones who are going to shoot you.

Nick: Always. Like Dennis Rader, quiet, kept himself to himself. Hobbies: gardening and serial killing.

Chris: Exactly! *laughs* So, the answer is, no we don't have anything in terms of legacy writings or otherwise. And we don't have anything in terms of internet history or otherwise. But what we do have is the testimony at the inquest of the survivor, and this is maybe one of the reasons why the Tolleson shooting attracted so much attention.

Nick: Because people called him fat?

Chris: Exactly.

Nick: I mean, I don't want to be an asshole or anything, but I've seen the pictures. He even looks fat in the autopsy photographs. It's not like he wasn't fat.

Chris: Dude!

Nick: Oh yeah, because you never speak ill of the dead. I forgot you were such a beacon of, of being polite! Not to mention, you're positively bulimic...

Chris: *laughs* Fair. Anyway, before we get into it, we need to say that all bodies are beautiful, all body shapes are beautiful, and nobody should ever make fun of you because of your body shape.

Nick: Man, it's such a good job that this is a podcast, so nobody sees you trying to keep a straight face.

Chris: Douche.

Nick: OK, but seriously. The idea that kids commit school shootings like Tolleson because people call them fat is just dumb. People get called fat all the time. Or get called skinny, or weird, or nerdy or stupid or whatever. And they don't go out and commit even one murder-

Chris: Not even one?

Nick: OK, maybe one. Two, rarely. Three at an absolute maximum-

Chris: *laughs* Asshole.

Nick: But you see my point? People get bullied all the time. It's always happened, and it always will. And it just doesn't make sense for one fat kid to get some shit for being *fat and whoops, next thing, he's gone and bought himself a Kel-Tec and shot up a school? I mean, seriously, have some fucking perspective!*

Chris: Yeah, I guess this is where we talk about the kind of shit he got, although I guess bullying isn't exactly the remit of the podcast. Not really.

Nick: Hell no. we know what our readers want, and it's murders, the more the better.

Chris: Yeah, Tolleson really let the side down there.

Nick: Complete amateur!

Chris: *laughs* Still memorable though.

Nick: But it's a fair point. What kind of shit did Tolleson get and is that the reason, the real reason why he did what he did?

Chris: Hit me.

Nick: So one thing we do know is that Tolleson was overweight-

Chris: Was he a little bit overweight, or was he like Jabba sized? Planet-sized?

Nick: He was pretty overweight. I don't, uh, I don't like know what his BMI was, but he was pretty overweight. No danger of making the track team, put it that way. And we know that he got a nickname-

Chris: Was he like the fattest guy in school?

Nick: uh, I don't know that, but I think so. I mean, it makes sense, but it doesn't say that anywhere in my notes. But he did get a nickname as a result...

Chris: Hit me.

Nick: Shamu.

Chris: *laughs* Oh man, I shouldn't laugh but that is actually pretty funny. Southern California, size of a whale – it's perfect!

Nick: A locally sourced nickname?

Chris: *laughs* Yeah. Man, actually do you think we should hit them up for a sponsor contribution? The Save the Whale guys?

Nick: *laughs* I'm not sure that pitch would fly. Besides, the whale is dead? He died at Whittlesford!

Chris: *laughs* Oh man, that's harsh-
Nick: Too soon, or too late?
Chris: LOL. Good cue to hit the advertising jingle though...
Nick: Hit it!

Chapter Thirty-Five

The morning lessons had passed neither quickly nor slowly. Just another day at the office. Jack had enjoyed some aspects and found others tedious. Just like every kid in America that day probably. He'd written down homework assignments and deadlines by hand, enjoying the safety that his paper notebook represented. Nobody could get to him via that. It wasn't Harry Potter. Bullies couldn't suddenly make nasty comments appear in his notebook. Jack had taken control back.

He took his lunch, as usual, to the quiet corner of the cafeteria. Another chicken salad, another glass of iced water. Fuck them. He had the right to eat what he wanted, when he wanted. He got to decide if he wanted to put on weight or lose a little. He didn't feel especially angry about it today. Just a quiet resolve that he got to decide what he ate for lunch. His body, his rules. He didn't give a fuck what they ate, after all.

He surfed the net as per usual during his break. Sports updates, professional and college. Cats. Same old, same old. Then the thought came into his head, and he couldn't get rid of it. Was he missing out on anything? He doubted it. FOMO? Well yes, obviously. But *Fear Of Missing Out* on what, exactly? He didn't know. Maybe that was the point of FOMO? You never knew what you were missing out on. Not at first. You just knew you were. Maybe... No. Do a day without it. Don't look. Just do a day without it. A day without any Whittlesford group. Pretend you're a secret agent from the movies. You have to stay off social media for a day or you get captured by the enemy. You can do a day, surely.

Heck, pretend you're in the Navy like Dad. He doesn't get to check on Facebook when he's on shift.

He nodded and imagined the hands of a clock turning. Do a day without it. You can check general internet. But leave social media alone. No groups, no Facebook, no Instagram, no Snapchat. OK. Why not? He took up his phone and held his thumb down onto the Facebook icon, pressing it down until it wobbled around. He moved it into the folder where he kept all the crappy apps he didn't use but couldn't delete. He repeated the process with Facebook Messenger, then Insta, then Snap. Then he paused. He didn't post much on Twitter, but he did use it to follow sports people. He moved it into the folder too. Five icons swept away into the cupboard with five swipes of his thumb. His wallpaper picture of Mr. Orange on his lap was more visible now the apps had gone. If only everything could be swept away so easily.

He paused. What about notifications? He went into the settings and turned them all off. Then returned to Safari and ESPN. Perfect lunchtime reading. Some of those athletes would be enjoying chicken salad too. And he would exercise that afternoon as well. Maybe not as vigorously as them. But he would walk home and spend the calories. Resolute.

He thought for a moment, then set the timer on his phone. In twenty-four hours it would sound his favourite notification noise, a commentator shouting 'touchdown.' He could do twenty-four hours. Discipline.

He made it through the day and through the night without breaking his fast. A couple of times, he wanted to check on Twitter. A couple of times, he felt his phone burning a hole in his pocket. Sometimes he didn't know what to do with his hands. They felt jittery at the end of his arms. But he made it through. He found himself paying more attention to the TV, although weirdly it was harder to concentrate on one single thing than on two. He hadn't just watched TV without playing with his phone for so long, and once he'd read all the stories that interested him on ESPN, he could hit refresh as much as he wanted, there just wasn't any newer news to be had.

When he awoke the next morning he felt better. He had put his phone away a while before bed, bored with the information options available to him. He'd just watched regular TV in the last hour before brushing his teeth. Some true crime thing where the viewer always realised from the start that it was the ex-boyfriend who'd done it. It had been interesting without being engrossing. Then he'd kissed his mom goodnight as always, brushed his teeth and then crashed out. He had slept soundly, falling asleep quicker than he usually did.

He didn't put two and two together about the quality of his sleep and the lack of cellphone usage until later. He felt the urge to check social media at the same time he would usually do though. He was determined though. He went to the timer app and checked that instead. Only five hours to go. He had nearly done twenty-four. Although a good eight of those had been sleeping. Maybe they didn't count. Whatever.

He listened to music on the bus to school that morning. He'd exhausted all the sports news over breakfast, then while waiting at the stop. So he put in his buds and listened to music instead. Just background for the journey. He never considered it his commute, but in reality, he was no different to any other working man. Live one place, work another, get from A to B at the start of your working day and from B to A at the end. And watch or read or listen to something on the way. He could read his phone on the bus, but for some reason he couldn't read anything written on paper. That made him queasy and puking on the school bus was a bad idea. The smell would linger as would the reputation.

After twenty-four hours, over a tuna salad this time and iced water, his phone shouted touchdown at him, and he jumped. He obviously realised twenty-four hours ran from lunchtime to lunchtime, but his mind had wandered while he watched highlight film of Chargers touchdowns. LT carving up defences, low-slung and speedy like a pinball ricocheting his way into the endzone. He turned off the timer. He'd done it. Twenty-four hours. Did he feel any different? Not really. He'd noticed a sense of space around him, but space was just another way of saying empty. But he'd proven, at least to himself, that life could go on without needing to use Whittlesford's social media.

So now what?

Should he look now? Why not do another twenty-four hours?

Well. He knew he could do another twenty-four. He'd proven his control. His discipline. Maybe the way to deal with it was only to look at it once every twenty-four hours. Maybe that was a better option than opting out altogether. That way, he could be part of the group, but only when he wanted to. Only when it was doing something useful for him.

His tongue slid subconsciously under his top lip and his head tilted from side to side as he weighed up the options. No harm in having a look.

He opened Facebook. In the top right corner, the messenger icon was red, furious at being ignored. Didn't Jack realise Zuckerberg's entire wealth was based on people constantly using his app and seeing the advertising he sold? How dare he! He tapped it. In twenty-four hours, there had been twenty or so messages in the school group. It seemed a little light compared to normal. Some days, there were hundreds. Most days there were at least fifty. Nothing especially important. Just stuff.

His scroll started with the oldest messages first. Usual chitchat. Did anybody know what the assignment was, was band practice still happening, that kind of stuff. But then his heart skipped a beat.

A new comment from Skyla. Two minutes old. Not about him, as such. But. But, but, but.

We all need to be nice to Evan today. One of his friends deleted him as a contact yesterday and he's still sad.

Evan was one of Jack's contacts. Had been. Not a friend, not a close one. Just one of the guys in school who Jack occasionally talked to about football and baseball. But his number had been in Jack's phone from a time when they had hung out over the summer. Jack didn't have anything against him. But he wasn't family and so he had been deleted. He couldn't actually remember the last time they had messaged one-to-one. Long enough ago that he didn't have a message to delete when he'd removed him as a contact, put it that way. He didn't know Evan was tight with Skyla though. But it was clearly aimed at him. Bitchy.

That wasn't the worst bit though. What followed was worse.

Brie. Pretty, dark-haired Brie, replied to Skyla:

Dude!!!! Wrong Group!!! #EAWBS!!!

Skyla immediately responded:

Doh! #EAWBS.

What the fuck? There was only one school group for everybody. At least, only one that Jack knew about. Sure, there were football groups and band groups and math groups and baseball groups and groups for pretty much everything. But there was only one main group. One group for everybody. Jack frowned. What was this other group?

His right hand automatically put his phone down and then flipped his sunglasses down from the top of his head to over his eyes. He didn't realise he'd done it until it was darker. Subconscious. Maybe not. He didn't want anyone being able to see his eyes right now, that was for sure.

His forehead grooved tramlines as he thought. Evan and Skyla. Skyla and Evan. They didn't have anything much in common, as far as he could see. Skyla dated Trent. Evan wasn't a jock, just a regular guy. Liked sports, liked his music. Smoked weed now and then, but not a regular stoner. He wasn't going to be a member of a sub-group that Skyla was. She wasn't going to be a member of any sub-group that he was. So there had to be a second group. One with a wider membership. A wider membership that Jack wasn't part of.

He felt the heat rising through his chest, through his now sweating armpits and up his neck. His biceps contracted and he clasped his hands around his phone, close to his chest. He kept his head stock still and moved his eyes around the cafeteria. A cursory glance would have shown a pretty normal scene. Teenagers being teenagers. Some eating, some talking, some looking at their phones, some hastily writing out homework or reading up for quizzes. Last-minute cramming. But Jack's glance wasn't a cursory glance. It was a targeted one, hidden behind his shades.

He didn't know what *#EAWBS* meant. He could guess that the W was Whittlesford. And the S was presumably school. He didn't know what the B was. But he knew there was a group which he hadn't been invited to join. And he would bet that Brie and Skyla had probably set it up. He kept his head motionless and looked over at the corner where they usually ate. They looked like they normally did at lunchtime. In fact, they looked very, very like they normally did at lunchtime. Not glancing in his direction at all. Which itself was suspicious. Because the comment was clearly aimed at Jack, and if you make a comment aimed at someone, especially if you get caught out, you're going to find it hard not to look at them. As Jack ranged his eyes around the rest of the cafeteria, he realised that not one single person was looking even vaguely in his direction. Not even close. Everyone seemed magically to be drawn by something or somebody in the opposite direction to him. That was unlikely.

And that meant, that everybody else knew what *#EAWBS* was. Everybody at Whittlesford but Jack.

He went into Facebook again, into the search box.

Searching for *#EAWBS* took him to a series of posts about aircraft. Something something Wide-Body.

He removed the hashtag. Just searched for EAWBS.

It was a group. A private group. 257 people were members. Only members could see who was in the group and what they posted. It was visible, meaning anyone could find the group. The Group had been created two weeks ago. It was located in Whittlesford, California. It had one administrator and moderator. An obviously fake Facebook profile called *Goaway Whales*. The profile picture of the admin and the group was the same. A beached Orca.

Jack knew.

There was a separate Facebook group for literally everyone in school but him.

Not *Everyone At Whittlesford But Jack.*

175

Everyone At Whittlesford But Shamu.
#EAWBS.

He didn't tear up. He didn't start crying. His head started nodding slowly instead. He leaned forward and forked his healthy salad into his mouth. *OK then. OK, assholes. If that's how you want it. It's going to have to be **all** of you.*

Chapter Thirty-Six

How do you eat an elephant? One bite at a time, remember.
Next step. Equipment.
What do you need? How do you get it? It's shooting fish in a barrel. So you need something to shoot the fish with.

Like every kid in America, Jack had grown up seeing guns on TV. But he'd only ever fired them at fairgrounds. Air rifles. He'd enjoyed it. Much more fun than cramming himself into a rollercoaster or a bumper car. But it was something he didn't do often. Even though dad was Navy, he wasn't really into weaponry. Well, not that kind of weaponry. Dad was more into big guns. The kind mounted on the side of warships. And even if he had been, he was away so much, Jack figured he wouldn't have bothered keeping one at home. And if he had, it would have been locked away and no way Jack would have been allowed anywhere near it.

How do you get hold of a gun?
No idea. I've never done this before.
How do you get hold of anything?

He scribbled down a quick list on his notepad.

Buy it. Borrow it. Earn it. Steal it. Win it. Receive it as a gift. Get someone to buy it for you. Beg for it.

Was he even allowed to own one?

He didn't know anyone who would buy one for him. Hell, he didn't know anyone who would walk into a liquor store and buy beer for him, not that he needed anyone to. And this was a different league. Felony big leagues, not the misdemeanour minor leagues. So scratch that.

He didn't curse as he scratched through that option on his pad. He wasn't angry. Calm. Cool. Methodical. One bite at a time.

He discounted 'borrow it' for the same reason. He didn't know anybody, and he wasn't about to ask around for an introduction. That would be insane. Indiscreet.

He paused and considered 'receive it as a gift.' Who would give him a gun? Not a ridiculous question. Shooting was a legitimate hobby. It was in the Olympics. He went through the list of potential givers. Relatives and family friends. Not likely. Another consideration came into his head. A gift like this would take time. If he suddenly declared an interest in shooting, then he would have to be into it for a while before he could plausibly ask for one as a gift. That would take too long. He wanted this over with already. He scratched that option out.

Buy it. Earn it. Steal it. Beg it.

He scratched out the last two options. Stealing a gun meant stealing something from somebody who had a gun. Notwithstanding the fact that he didn't know who had one, that was a dumb risk. Stealing something from someone with a gun would end badly. And he realised that he would also need ammunition. It wasn't just about the gun. Shooting fish required a gun, sure, but it also required bullets. Lots of them. Begging for it wasn't even an option.

Earn it? No. A legitimate way of obtaining some things, but not a gun. Nobody got paid with a gun itself.

He would have to buy it. He drew a circle around that option on his pad. Inserted the TAILS flash drive into his computer and went to work. Time to research the Second Amendment.

In California, he was screwed. The state had the most restrictive gun laws of any in the Union. In theory, he was able to possess a rifle or a shotgun at seventeen, but he couldn't buy one. Eighteen-year-old minimum. California also banned assault weapons and large magazines. Handguns were only for over twenty-ones. So even if he could buy one, he wouldn't be able to buy the right kind of gun.

Unless...

He turned the page over in his notebook. Printed out 'BUY IT' in block capitals at the top center and then drew two lines

178

coming off it. Marked them as 'Legal' and 'Illegal.'

He considered illegal for a moment. Then divided that again with two more lines. Marked them as *Black* and *Cheat*. One bite at a time.

Black was the black market. The totally illegal option. He knew guns were bought and sold illegally. But that required connections he didn't have. Plus he figured he'd just get robbed. He'd have as much chance of buying what he needed as he would buying weed. Not his scene. And he wasn't about to drop all his money on being given the gun equivalent of a dime bag of oregano rather than weed. He crossed out the *Black* option.

He frowned. Money. He made a note on a new page. He would need to pay for this. But not now. One bite at a time.

He looked across at the other two options. If nobody could get what he needed in California, where could it be gotten? He googled state gun laws. Time to shop around. Literally. It seemed California had the most restrictive gun laws of any state in the Union. Ordinarily, he would have been pleased by that snippet. But now it was just fucking annoying. Pricks.

He realised he was getting agitated and took a deep breath. Chill. Think. Plan. Execute. He cast a glance behind him and noticed Mr. Orange had found himself a spot on his bed, stretching out in a sun puddle and dozing away. He smiled and got back to work.

He found himself a couple of websites that graded the states based on their gun laws. One website was from a shooting magazine. Their highest grades went to the states with the least restrictive laws. The other was from The Giffords Law Center. Their highest grade went to California, for having the most restrictive laws. The name Giffords rang a bell somewhere in his mind and he briefly fell down a Wikipedia wormhole. That was it. An Arizona Congresswoman who'd survived being shot.

He made brief notes as he went along. Brief bullet points, like he'd been taught in school. Numbers for the main point, letters for the subsidiary points. Bullet points. Ha, ha, ha.

First things first. He wasn't old enough to buy what he

needed. He would have to pose as eighteen, or twenty-one or wait until he was. He wasn't going to wait. So that left posing as eighteen or twenty-one. This was *Cheat*. The illegal-lite option. Still illegal. But in a slightly more legal way. The transaction would be legal. Just that his taking part in it wouldn't be. He needed more information.

California was out. Nobody could get what he needed, without resorting to the black market. And for obvious reasons, that had already been discounted.

This was annoying but OK. He felt a warm thrill of satisfaction as he realised he was making progress. Discounting unfeasible options was just as much progress as following up good ones.

If not California, then where?

Stop and think for a minute. If you're going to get it somewhere else, that means you have to go somewhere else. And if you have to go somewhere else, that means you have to get back from somewhere else.

He clicked on Google Maps. The nearer the better. Less time to be away. Less cost to get there and back. Arizona and Nevada were nearest.

He cross-referenced versus the shooting magazine website. Arizona looked promising. The least restrictive state in the Union. He was surprised, given it was one of their Congresswomen who'd been shot in the head in Tucson. Maybe it would be different if she'd died.

He dug a little deeper into the website. It was clear that wherever he went, he would need to buy via a private sale. If he bought from a dealer, there would be background checks. Federal requirement. He wouldn't pass those. He wasn't old enough and he would need a real ID, not a fake one.

From what he could work out, if he went private sale, then he just needed to look old enough. He clicked on a link that took him to the classified advertisements. Private sellers aplenty. Everything from historic revolvers to military-style assault rifles. The tone of their listings made it clear that they didn't tolerate lowball offers but equally didn't believe in much paperwork. Second Amendment zealots. One even made it clear, with block capitals outlining 'PRIVATE SALE = NO TAX, NO PAPERWORK TO SIGN.'

Arizona was favourite so far. No need for background checks in private sales. He clicked on Nevada for thoroughness. No good. Nevada required a background check even for a private sale. Scratch Nevada. A pity, in a way. He could have maybe caught the Raiders. Or maybe the Raiders would have been a good reason to go. He'd need a reason to go on a trip. But he hadn't determined exactly what equipment he would need yet. And different guns had different laws and different states and, and, and.

His head suddenly filled with questions branching off potential problems, and problems branching off questions. He was losing focus inside his head, and he was actually looking around in mid-air.

Stop. Think. You need to get your shit together. You need to plan this, cool, calm and collected. You need to research this, cool, calm and collected. If you get side-tracked, it isn't going to work.

He relaxed a little. Looked back at his notepad. Saw indisputable progress and calmed down a little more.

He thought a little more about the elephant. Maybe he needed a different bite. A more strategic bite.

What do you need?

A gun.

Well, obviously.

What else?

At least a hundred bullets. More. Because you're not going to get it perfect. Nobody ever has.

What does that mean?

Your gun needs to have a big magazine. And more than one magazine. Lots of bullets.

OK. What else?

It needs to be reliable. It can't break or jam.

OK. So you need to research that. What else do you need it to be?

It needs to be small enough to get in school. And to be brought back from wherever you buy it, without being

181

noticed. Because you won't own it legally and if you get stopped, you're fucked.

OK. How do you solve this? What do you choose?

You can only choose from what's in front of you. You can only choose from the choice available.

What is that choice?

He went back to the classifieds. Filtered for Arizona. Hundreds of advertisements. This did not help much. Literally every kind of firearm seemed to be available, right down to muzzle loading single shot rifles for historic re-enactment.

Stop and think for a minute. What will work best?

I've no idea. I've never done this before.

Nobody, who's ever done this, had ever done it before. But they made it work. Think.

OK. What did they use? When they did it, what did they use?

Now you're thinking. That's better. You're learning.

He googled US school shootings. Realised Vegas wasn't on there and changed the search criteria to *mass* shootings rather than *school* shootings. More detail. There were pages and pages of them on Wikipedia. He'd heard of a few of them, but not many. There were lots of smaller ones. It seemed anything over four victims counted as 'mass.' That was about ninety-six too few for what he needed. He refined his search. Ah. That was what he needed to search for. *Deadliest* mass shootings in the US. That was it. That gave him a list, sorted by descending casualty count.

He clicked through the details, starting at the top. Las Vegas. The Orlando nightclub. Virginia Tech. Sandy Hook. Most of the shooters had used semi-automatic rifles although a few had used semi-automatic pistols. He thought about it for a minute. Virginia Tech was pistols. So they clearly worked. Vegas had used bump stocks to turn semi-automatics into automatics. That had been more effective. But he knew bump stocks were illegal now.

Hmm. Think.

Pistol.

Pro. Smaller and easier to hide, both on the way back from Arizona and on the way to school.

Con. Smaller magazine. Much smaller.

Rifle.

Pro. Bigger magazine. Apparently more accurate.

Con. Much bigger. Harder to hide.

He googled the AR-15, a rife which seemed to be the weapon of choice for mass shooters. Nearly 40 inches long. That would be hard to conceal. He would need a really big bag. Maybe a field hockey bag. They were pretty long. But he didn't play field hockey and it would look weird.

The pistol would be easier to move, no doubt of that. But the default magazine size was about a dozen rounds. That would need a lot of magazines to get to a hundred. Nine magazines, and that would only get him to 108 shots. And he wouldn't have time to refill the magazines. Having two guns wouldn't solve anything either. He still needed the magazines. Extended mags were available – Glock made them up to thirty-three bullets – but the default mag was still only a dozen. Hmm.

The rifle option had its advantages. They were mainly military or military rip-offs and as such were designed for accuracy and a high rate of fire. Exactly what he needed. They also looked scary, which he figured was helpful. From a distance, it would be harder to see a pistol. He wanted them scared. He wanted them scared, and panicking, running around like headless chickens. He wanted them terrified. All of them. Rifles were more accurate too. A longer barrel. He would be more efficient with that. Less wastage.

He went back to the AR-15. A thirty round magazine made life much easier. By a factor of a lot. Half a dozen magazines would bring him up to 180. He wouldn't have time to refill them either. Actually, he would need more than half a dozen. Although it was still more efficient than the pistol option, forty inches was just too damn long. What would happen if he cut off the shoulder stock? Could he fire it from the hip? What did that do to accuracy? He discovered that some rifles came with folding stocks, but they were few and far between.

He went back to the shooting website. Composed himself. Imagine this is a legitimate purchase, he told himself. You want to buy a semi-automatic rifle, but you want it to be smaller. Compact.

Jackpot. He discovered something called a bullpup, something he'd not heard of before. A peculiar kind of rifle where the firing pin and magazine sat behind the pistol grip rather than in front. Whatever. The important thing was that they seemed to run only to about twenty-seven inches long. Still pretty long, but a big difference. He took a ruler from his desk drawer, a battered clear plastic relic of junior high, with gouges along the metric side from elementary school sword fights. He measured out twenty-seven inches. Still too long for his current backpack. But much, much easier than forty. He listened acutely to see if there was any likelihood of Mom coming upstairs and then went to his wardrobe. Took out a sport bag from the bottom. At a push, he reckoned he could get something thirty inches in there.

He went back to the gun magazine website. Top ten bullpups. He discounted anything longer than thirty inches and he was still left with four choices. Typed them into Google for further research. A bearded fat white man, middle aged and wearing camouflage was on YouTube. He wasn't unfriendly. He stood in front of his jeep in what looked like it could be Virginia woodland, two bullpups laid out on a light green towel on the hood.

Jack leaned back and was about to click play when he realised the time. Close to dinner time for Mr. Orange, although there was no sign of stirring just yet. He made a mental note of the search terms and then shut down TAILS, hiding the flash drive in the bowl of small change and other crap. He pulled out the pages of scribbles from his notebook and flushed them down the toilet in tiny pieces again. He went back to his room, where he stood up and stretched, reaching high and touching the ceiling, relieving the hunch in his back from his research. He felt good. He leaned down and scooped up his cat and carried him downstairs to feed him. Mr. Orange purred in his ear.

Chapter Thirty-Seven

Jack sat in the canteen at Whittlesford. He scrolled through Sports Illustrated on his phone while feeding chicken salad into his mouth. A large glass of ice water sat to the left. His cell was propped up on the edge of the tray, to minimise the glare, and he would click on a story with his little finger to avoid having to relinquish the fork he held in his right hand.

Monday lunchtime at Whittlesford meant Jack was reading Monday Morning Quarterback. He'd preferred the Peter King years, but the newish guy, Albert Breer, was pretty good too. This week's column focused on seniors in college and where they might wind up in the draft. It seemed it was never too early to speculate on the draft. Ordinarily Jack would have enjoyed the piece, but not today. Today, he was fuming.

He wasn't fuming because he disliked the athletes that Breer wrote about. Generally, he liked them. Well, liked the way they played football. He didn't know them as people. He wasn't fuming because they'd lucked out in the lucky sperm competition and been born with physical attributes Jack would have loved to have. Not at all. Fair play to them. He wasn't even fuming because he just knew they were getting as many girls as they wanted.

He was fuming because the high school to college to pro ball conveyor belt was something he would have dreamed of following and yet it was open not to him, but to Trent. And Trent didn't deserve it. Not because of his strength or vision or skill or commitment to training. Jack would concede Trent had all of those. That motherfucker didn't deserve that glide because of how he behaved. To Jack.

Jack didn't over-analyse it. Didn't sit there and talk to

himself or an imaginary counsellor. He just felt it. In his gut. Deep within the red, pumping muscles of his heart was a constant burning hatred. When he felt it rise up and begin to consume him, his jaw subconsciously clenched. His eyes widened a little. He found himself staring at nothing in particular. Hatred expanded into loathing. And he was going to do something about it.

His eyes flicked back to the article, and he carried on reading, only half-engaged. His fork moved automatically back to the plate. The clang indicated that he'd finished the salad, but he hadn't realised. He placed the fork down on the plate, neatly.

The article dove into the detail of Alabama's quarterback, previous Heisman winner and now the presumptive number one draft pick. There were many ifs between now and draft day, but if, if, if…that twenty-one-year-old was likely to wake up one morning with a contract worth over thirty-five million dollars and twenty-four million of that guaranteed. Nice work if you could get it.

The vision of so many dollars lightened Jack's mood and he engaged in a little light fantasy. What would life be like if he had that. He imagined a bigger house, with a yard big enough for one of those ride-on lawnmowers. Maybe a pool in back. A fishpond for Mr. Orange. And a huge TV room where Jack and his hot wife would laze around and watch movies between making out. He pictured himself driving them to dinner in a Mercedes and then tipping the valet parker with a crisp twenty.

Hmm. He frowned. The image of dishing out money had triggered another thought in his mind. What he was going to do would cost money. He'd only considered it in passing before. He needed to think more about that.

Jack rarely thought about money. In that way, he was like Trent. But for very different reasons.

Trent never thought about money because his parents were loaded. He had a small Mercedes and always wore immaculate new sneakers. It was rumoured his parents had given him a credit card on their account, and he was allowed to spend pretty much what he wanted. Like everyone else in school, Jack was aware that some people had more money than others, and it didn't really bother him. The parade of fashionable clothes and latest model iPads didn't really impress him.

Jack didn't really think about money because he didn't really spend it. His allowance was generous but not over-the-top. Above average compared to the other students at Whittlesford, from what he could work out. It didn't really matter anyway. It frequently went unspent and was swept into his savings account at the end of each month. Christmas and birthday presents from relatives usually took the form of cash, and likewise moved into his savings, quietly earning interest.

Not wasting money was a family trait. His mom made good money in the law and his dad made decent money as a Commander, but they didn't spend it ostentatiously. It wasn't about being frugal or holier-than-thou. It was just that the things they enjoyed really didn't cost very much. Jack was the same. What little money he did spend went on Chargers items, but that wasn't very much.

Most of his leisure activities involved watching sports and he tended to do that on TV. Not technically free, but cable was part of the household budget and so not up to him to pay for it. He'd watch the Chargers a couple of times a season in person, but truth be told, the view was better from the couch. Better replay, explanations, everything. If he was honest, the only reason he went to the games live was because he felt he should, as a fan. He had a goal to visit all the stadia in the NFL, but that was more of a long-term ambition. Not that he'd get to finish it.

A bit like his savings account. He'd had it since he was a kid. He wasn't saving up for anything in particular. Not like some kids who saved for a new surfboard, or a car or stereo. He knew a couple in school like that. Some had done deals with their parents, who'd agreed to match the savings to get the object of their desires. Jack wasn't like that. He knew he had a college fund. And while he liked the idea of cruising along Highway One in a convertible black Mercedes, he would have balked at actually ever spending that amount of money on one.

He shut down the browser on his phone and went to his banking app. His savings account paid a shitty rate of interest, but it was easier than having two separate apps on his phone. His savings account currently had a total of $6,041 in it. More than he thought he had. He clicked on transactions. It showed a series of incoming payments, sweeping money across from his checking account each month, the day before the next month's allowance was due to arrive. There were a few larger deposits around his birthday and Christmas. He searched for withdrawals, but there was nothing showing within the six-month limit that the app provided.

Just over six thousand bucks. A lot less than Trent would have earned if he'd made it to the NFL, but more than enough for what Jack needed. He wondered briefly what would happen to what was left over in his account. Could he leave it to Mr. Orange? He would miss him.

He signed out of the app and took his empty tray to the rack by the exit.

Chapter Thirty-Eight

Problem three.

You've never done this before. But you need to get it right first time. So you need to practice.

Did the others practice? Hmm. Maybe.

The Vegas guy had enough guns to start a small war. So he must have. He'd owned guns for a long time.

Virginia Tech bought his legally. Presumably he practiced on a range somewhere.

Columbine, that was different. A similar situation to yours though. They'd gotten a friend to buy some of their weapons for them. Because they were like you. Under eighteen. So they must have practiced somewhere, albeit illegally. At the very least, they would have practised loading and reloading, maybe dry firing. Their situation was a little different in that there were two of them. Crowd control must be easier with two. You don't have that advantage. And you still need to get to a hundred. On your own.

You need to get to a hundred, on your own, on your first go. And last go. And it has to be a real hundred. Not ninety-nine plus you. A hundred of them minimum. Or you'll get an asterisk. Like Barry fucking Bonds, who is never getting in the Hall because of that asterisk.

Where can you practice? How can you practice?

Bad news. You can't practice anywhere in California. Under eighteens need to be accompanied by a parent or guardian. That means mom, and no, that one won't work. So you need to go out of state. Or you need to do it illegally. Like in a wood or a quarry or something. And that's a stupid fucking idea, because if you get caught, you're fucked.

There's another consideration. Can you use the practice to test out your potential equipment choices? That would make sense. Athletes have their preferred sneakers. You never saw Jordan play in Reeboks. Strictly Nike. So good they named them after him. Maybe sneakers are much of a muchness, maybe guns are much of a muchness, but while you're there, you might as well try and find out if you have a preference. Why try and break the world record wearing Nikes if your feet are too wide for them? Why not practice and then take your shot at the hundred while wearing ASICS if that's what works best for you?

OK so you need to go out of state. Where?

Where needs to be determined by three aspects. Where can you go to try out a range of different guns? Where is it not unusual to go and try out a different range of assault weapons? Because it could look odd. And where can you go, ostensibly to do something else, because if Mom thinks you're going somewhere purely for the purpose of firing guns, then this could all be over before you've even gotten started.

Three considerations, then. Choice of weapons. Appearance of normality. Plausibility for the visit.

You need a town with lax gun range laws. Where under eighteens can shoot, supervised by local staff. Where they give actual proper shooting lessons. Where people regularly go to shoot assault weapons for a fun one-off. It can't be too far away. Preferably a day trip. This is getting expensive already and hotels don't like under-age guests. And it needs to have football or baseball or something that makes it worth visiting for, as far as Mom is concerned.

Thank you, DuckDuckGo. Las Vegas it is.

Chapter Thirty-Nine

I don't think I should have to move.

This is my home. This is Jonathan's home. This was Jack's home. We came here, we built a life here and this became our home. People talk about a fresh start, but I don't want that. My memories of Jack are here. Well, here and New York. But I have far more of them here. The end of his toddler years. Elementary and junior high. Blotchy watercolours taped to the refrigerator. Pictures of daddy on board a ship. Paintings of the three of us at the beach, making sandcastles. I look at the refrigerator and although the paintings were long gone when all this happened, I can still see them. He would bring them home, I would stick them onto the refrigerator, and we would take a selfie of us with the picture and send it to Jonathan.

This house is Jack. He deserves to be remembered. His room is still the same. The cat still sleeps on his bed. I guess he finds his scent comforting. Or maybe he just sleeps where it's comfortable.

I don't think I should have to move. What happened wasn't down to Jack. Not really. After it happened, one of the psychologists asked me when I thought I'd lost Jack, when he had disconnected from me, from Jonathan. I could have punched him. He was older and patronising, a bow tie, and a stupid beard. We didn't lose Jack. We didn't have a moody teenager who listened to death metal backward and locked himself away in his room. We didn't have a rebel with long hair and a history of minor infractions against authority. We didn't raise a boy on violent video games and guns. We had a normal boy, sweet and kind. He wasn't the strongest, fastest,

191

funniest, or smartest. He wasn't the weakest, slowest or dumbest. He was normal.

I spent a lot of time thinking about that. Were there any warning signs? Did I miss anything? The simple answer, is no. We were a normal family until one day we weren't.

People always assume that because we were military, we had to have guns in the house. Everybody seems to think they know more about my own family than I do. I hear them on the radio, I see them on TV. They're not experts. That's not how the media works. The media wants contentious opinions. Social media is even worse. But I guess you knew that anyway.

Anyway, for the record, we never had guns in the house. Never. There's a difference, I guess, between the Navy and say, the Army or the Marines. Jonathan wasn't, isn't into guns. He's always been fascinated by machinery, and that's why he did engineering at the Naval Academy and why he joined the Navy. Sure, he finds weaponry interesting, but torpedoes and missiles and rockets and stuff like that. But he also finds engines and cogs and wheels and aircraft fascinating. I've never seen him hold a gun. We didn't have them at home, he doesn't hunt, we don't have a gun cabinet. It just isn't his thing. And I guess some leisure activities, you only get into if your parents do them, and we never had guns.

Years ago, one of Jonathan's crewmates lucked out and got London, England for a shore assignment. You can do that, be seconded to an embassy as an attaché. He met an English girl there and got married. When they came back and had kids, she was terrified about guns. They're pretty much illegal in England, apparently. She saw risks everywhere she looked. I grew up in this country and you'd have to be blind not to see they exist, but they just weren't part of our lives. I obviously remember when things happened, like Sandy Hook or Vegas. But you never think it's going to happen. I thought those things were rare. It's only after it happened that I realised it doesn't matter how rare it is. Jack is still dead.

When I'm in town these days, I see the faces of other moms and they either look away quickly or stare. I don't think they know they're doing either. Nobody holds a normal look at me. The mothers of the boys and girls who didn't come home that day tend to stare rather than look away. I sometimes wonder if they're trying to chase me out of town. They have an opinion, and they practically glare in their justification of it. They're wasting their time.

I don't think I should have to move.

I'm not going. I did nothing wrong. This is my home. It's still Jack's home. I remember him. And he deserves to be remembered.

There's one person in this town who doesn't stare. Father Martin. We weren't, aren't a religious family particularly. We need a religion because Jonathan is in the Navy and you kind of have to put something down on the form. But we never really did church either for the religion or the social aspect. This is California, not Texas.

I guess it was about three months after it happened. I was coming out of the dry cleaner. I know, it sounds stupid. But I'd lost so much weight, my clothes didn't fit so I had to have them altered. I'd stopped getting things altered in the place I used to go to, because it was around the corner from Whittlesford. I'd found this new place, via Yelp. A polite and friendly Asian man and his wife. I think they knew. How could they not. My picture had ended up everywhere after it happened, that picture of the three of us, the last time Jonathan had been home. I'd put it up on Facebook at the time and obviously the media had used it.

Anyway, I was coming out of the dry-cleaners, and I saw Father Martin. I didn't know who he was then, of course. I just knew he was a priest. He had on the black shirt and the white collar. And he obviously recognised me, and I saw he recognised me, and he just looked at me with such compassion, such openness. He's English. I don't know how he got here. But he's English, in his fifties, going grey. Slightly overweight. He was walking his dog, a chubby little Labrador puppy with a pink collar. He's not married. I think he might be gay. This is California, after all. And he looked up and he saw me, and I think that's the only time, of all the people I've seen since it happened, where someone has looked at me and shown genuine warmth and compassion. A recognition that I'd been through something too.

He looked at me on the sidewalk, and I guess I must have slowed down because he actually said good morning. Maybe priests do that all the time, I don't know. Normal people don't, I guess. It might be California, but random strangers don't say hello to each other, even here. But he looked over, and he just said, "Good morning." It was a low, clear voice. Understanding.

I said, "Good morning," back.

And then he said, probably the only time anyone has said it since it happened, definitely the only time anyone has said it this way since it happened, "are *you* OK?"

I remember exhaling deeply at that moment. It was obviously such a stupid question, but it was said with so much warmth. It was genuine. It was concern. It was about me. For the first time, someone had actually asked about *me*.

I don't think I actually replied. I just shrugged. He motioned toward his dog, and asked, "would you like to join Daisy and me for a walk?"

I nodded. Thank you. We just walked. He didn't say anything. I looked at him a couple of times to see if he was expecting me to say something, but he wasn't. Didn't. I just followed him on what felt like a random meander through the residential streets. I don't remember seeing anybody else there. I don't remember actively thinking anything. In a way that was peace. Because not thinking meant not feeling. And I'd done so, so much of that. So we just walked, maybe for thirty minutes, and then I realised we'd looped back around. His church was one block over from the tailor. He motioned to it, and said, "This is us. Come in whenever you like. Or come on the walk. It's a regular fixture."

"Thanks. I have to get home but thank you." A lie, and he saw it, but he didn't mind. I had nothing to get home for. Jack was dead. Jonathan by then was back on the *Nimitz*. What on earth did I have to get home for.

"Mrs. Tolleson. Forgive me, but if I may…" His polite

Englishness, rich words, yet hesitant, quiet. Understated. "I wonder if I might draw your attention to something. The Bible speaks of universal salvation. It is not for man to question or determine who gets to be saved. That's a choice the Lord makes. To put it another way, the most put-upon character in the Bible was Judas Iscariot, and he was still deemed worthy of salvation. Everyone can be saved. But only by the Lord. Not by man."

I nodded dumbly. I half wanted to scream that it was too late. My baby was dead. So were others. But I just nodded. I mouthed a silent thank you.

"As I say, Daisy and I work to a routine. We'd be glad of your company again. Same time every day."

I smiled and nodded. He turned gently and retreated inside his church. A modern, cream-bricked building with a service schedule behind glass. St. Botolph's Church, Father Martin Croft, M.A. (Oxon). I stood there for some time. And then I headed back to my car and drove home.

Chapter Forty

Jack smiled as the stewardess approached with the beverage cart. He politely asked for a coke, passed on the lemon, and enjoyed the sickly-sweet flavour. He was squeezed in tight, at the back of the plane. He could barely move his knees. The guy in front had tilted his seat back just after take-off but back row Jack didn't have that ability. His seat didn't tilt. But he was quietly content as the plane raced westward from McCarran to LAX.

It had gone smoothly. Much more smoothly than he had hoped for. An early morning direct flight from LAX to Vegas. They were barely in the air an hour. Then a nine-buck shuttle from the airport to the strip. He'd gone inside and gotten himself a coffee from the Starbucks inside Caesar's Palace and then settled down to wait in the lobby. It was a weird experience, sitting and waiting. He was bright and alert, even without the caffeine, and even in the absence of any natural light. He'd read somewhere that casinos never had clocks or natural light, so the gamblers never realised how much of their money or their lives they were pissing away. He looked around as he held his coffee like a prop and realised he was in far better shape than ninety percent of the other patrons. It looked like they were filming a zombie movie.

His ride didn't take long to show up. A white shuttlebus for one of the Vegas machine gun ranges lurched to a stop by the door. It was one of those strange vehicles you only ever saw near airports. It had an irregular-shaped fiberglass body crafted onto a regular chassis. He got up and walked over. He wasn't nervous. He wasn't about to be completely honest, but he wasn't nervous. He was doing nothing wrong, after all.

Not yet.

The driver was a friendly Latino in his forties, in a bright red polo. He was running a little fat and had a permanent smile in the middle of a thick goatee. His arms were tanned and covered in tattoos. Jack could make out the globe and anchor on his left forearm. *Semper Fidelis* below it. Ex-Marine. Jack had met a few through his dad. They were good guys off-duty, not really like their reputation on duty. Or maybe they were just polite with him.

The Latino had checked his tablet and realised he just had the one pickup from Caesar's. If he looked a little surprised that someone of Jack's obvious age was at the Caesar's, he didn't say anything. Just greeted him with a cheery wave and motioned him aboard. Jack was the last pickup of this particular run, and he joined six young men in the shuttle bus. They were a group, in their twenties, and clearly a little worse for wear after a big Saturday night.

Jack had his story all worked out in case they asked. And they did. Just a bunch of guys on a weekend break and the chat was easy and light-hearted. Jack's story was easy to remember because it was broadly similar to the pretext he'd sold to his mother for the trip. The Raiders were playing that afternoon. True. He was a big football fan and that was the real reason for the trip. Not true but it could have been. His mom, dad and older brother had known they would want to sleep in on the Sunday after arriving on Saturday and were fine for him to go off and blast away at a few targets before they had a family day at the football before flying back that evening. Totally false.

It was the same story he'd told the shooting range when he'd rung up to book. He'd scratched around for a reason for a seventeen-year-old to be in Vegas on his own and he couldn't find one. Not easily. But a seventeen-year-old could be in Vegas for another reason. Football. With the family. What could be more wholesome than that? And an early Sunday morning shooting session was likely to be the least popular given how much money Vegas took on a Saturday night in the bars. So it wasn't surprising that the youngest son, the eager beaver who wouldn't have been able to drink the night before, was keen to do something on a Sunday morning. And that particular range had a minimum age of ten years old to shoot. Yes, ten. He'd been amazed. With no need for parental or guardian accompaniment. He'd asked this very specifically when he'd spoken to the owner on the phone. The old guy had chuckled and set his mind at rest.

"Young man," he'd drawled. "This isn't California. You can come and join us, and we'll teach you how to shoot a bunch of different guns. Your poor hungover father won't need to come along because we'll have you properly supervised all the way through. And then we'll drop you back home in the shuttle and you can go and bring your dear old dad some Alka-Seltzer and a cup of joe. After all, I presume he's paying for the break." He'd chuckled again. This clearly wasn't the first time he'd had that inquiry. Jack was grateful for the confirmation. Vegas was full of gun ranges, full of the opportunity to spend a couple hundred bucks on automatic weapons, but not many of them didn't require a parent to be present. And while he had no idea how seriously they would card him, he didn't want to take the chance.

The bus headed north along the strip. It was a much shorter journey than he had bargained for, barely leaving the Strip before turning off west for a couple of blocks. The range itself was a squat rectangular building of grey brick, with the company logo picked out in dark red. It was possibly the least garish thing in Las Vegas.

The dirty half-dozen fellow shooters fell out of the shuttle a little more languidly than he thought they might have. Clearly not that awake yet, despite each holding onto a paper cup of coffee for grim death. The Latino chuckled behind them.

"They're so fucked," he said gleefully. "They're tired after a night out and now they're drinking way too much coffee. They going to get jittery. And they ain't going to like the loud bangs none too much neither."

Jack smiled politely. He waited for the group to check in at the reception desk and then made his way to follow them.

Wow. The desk was hosted by a beautiful brunette, tall and lithe and dressed like the chick in Tomb Raider. A tight black vest restraining either a wonder bra or a wonder rack. Shiny black leggings, with a thigh holster on the left side, although he couldn't see if the gun in it was real, or just for effect. Perfect teeth and red lip gloss, giving a radiant smile, even at this hour of the morning. Clearly a business where tips mattered. She greeted Jack with warmth, perhaps grateful that he didn't try to hit on her like the hungover six. She checked his ID with barely a pause. California driver license, tick, fine. Please join the others on the black leather couches over there for more coffee and a safety briefing.

The safety briefing had been given by the owner – Jack recognised the voice as he introduced himself. Jerry was a white-haired wizard of a man, in his sixties, barely five feet nine, and with a beard like Santa. He drawled clearly and calmly, setting out the ground rules without being a killjoy. His khaki shirt was adorned with patches, including that of an NRA Instructor on one shoulder, a bright red triangle. He wore a holster on his hip, not on his thigh, with a gleaming black pistol inside.

"Remember folks," he said, "we do want you to have the best time so you come back and give us more money. But these things are very, very good at killing people, so you do need to do what we say, when we say it. You don't get lucky if you get hit by one of these. It's not like on the TV."

He paused and smiled. He had seven clients, six in one group, and Jack.

"Now then. You six probably all want to shoot together? And you, young man, you're just happy to be here."

He smiled at Jack, almost paternally.

"Now what we'll do…what we'll do. Yes, we'll divide you six into two threes, and at half time, you can swap round if you like and that way, you all get to shoot with one another. More or less. So you decide on your threes and one group go with Chad over there, and the other three go with Esteban, him that picked you up. And young man, if it's alright with you, you get the bonus of a one-on-one lesson with me. Save you having to listen to these young men telling you stories of a night when you weren't there. Saves them having to lie too." His eyes twinkled.

With that, he walked Jack over to the long glass counter. Pistols sat in racks below the glass. All were for rental. On the back wall sat all the long guns in their racks, with chains securing them to the metal housing. The receptionist stood behind the counter, waiting for him to choose. At the far end of the counter stood another man, wearing a red polo to match those of Esteban the driver and Chad. He was a tall native American, with longish dark hair and similarly faded tattoos on his forearm. He made no motion to help serve, but just stood and observed. Like the others, he wore a pistol on his hip.

It initially freaked Jack out, once he realised what he was there for, but then he relaxed. He didn't know any of these people here. The six guys seemed like nice guys, but he'd met them less than a half hour ago. They could be incompetent with guns, they could be evil, they could still be drunk and just hiding it well. Jack didn't know. And neither did the range staff. But they were about to hand over weapons to them. So yes, of course there would be a guy behind them all at the firing points, with a loaded pistol to prevent any accidents or misunderstandings.

Under the package Jack had booked, he got to shoot six different guns, although it seemed that owner's privileges meant that Jerry could bump that up to however many he felt like. Jerry was a quiet zealot, subconsciously trying to sell Jack on the value of shooting, on its worthiness as a fine traditional sport. No hard sell. Just quiet competence and enjoyment. He proclaimed gentle disbelief that Jack had gotten to seventeen without ever having fired a gun outside of a fairground.

"Now Jack, you'll have to remind me, I know you mentioned one particular gun you said you'd seen in a magazine and wanted to try?"

"Er, yeah. I saw a feature on bullpups and thought they looked interesting. But obviously, I never shot one. I'd really like to know how to shoot properly though. And maybe go fully automatic after that."

Jerry motioned to two such rifles stacked side-by-side in the rack.

"Well, why don't we take those two and try 'em out? In fact, let's treat this like hockey, not football. Let's take a pair of guns for a third of your time, and then we do two changes. Rather than three guns per half, we do two guns per third. That sound OK to you?"

That sounded very OK to Jack. Very OK indeed.

He paid rapt attention as Jerry explained the workings of the bullpups. In the red corner, and fighting out of Florida, the Kel-Tec RDB, weighing in at seven pounds and just over twenty-seven inches long. Fired .223 calibre Remington and able to take any AR-15 compatible magazine, although the ones they had there held thirty rounds. And in the blue corner, fighting out of Israel, the Tavor bullpup, which fired a heavier calibre bullet and was a shade longer, at just over twenty-nine inches.

They took two boxes of ammunition with them to the range, one for each weapon. Once inside, safety goggles and ear defenders on, Jerry led Jack to the far shooting lane, away from the party six. He patiently and quietly explained to Jack how to load the magazines, how the guns worked and how to shoot. Plus a little troubleshooting in case of a jam or a misfire. He was a good teacher, quiet and enthusiastic, although he stopped and caught himself a couple of times when he was about to launch into a war story or two. Like Esteban, he had a marine corps logo tattooed on his forearm, although his was faded and blotchy in comparison.

Once he figured he'd spoken enough, he stood back and passed Jack the Kel-Tec.

"The American should really get to go first," he said, smiling. "The Israeli can have a turn afterward."

Jack had been paying attention. Frankly, paying attention like nothing he'd ever been taught before. The targets were sent out to ten yards away on an electric pulley system controlled by a keypad set into the wall of the firing point.

He carefully loaded the magazine with thirty rounds of Remington. Clicked it into the magazine well and heard it click. He pulled the stock into his shoulder, snug and firm. The more stable the better. He reached forward with his left hand and pulled back the lever to chamber the first round. Cocked and loaded. He paused, wondering if he was supposed to wait for the OK from Jerry.

He felt Jerry's hand on his left shoulder.

"You're all good there, Jack, just release the safety and squeeze. Easy does it."

Jack flicked the safety with his right thumb. Click. Live.

He took a medium deep breath all the way in, then exhaled. Paused three-quarters of the way through. Held the breath there. Looked down the sight and lined up the crosshairs at the middle of the circular target. The party of six had chosen pictures of charging soldiers to shoot at. Jack had gone for circles. He figured the less he looked like he was there for what he was actually there for, the better.

He pulled the trigger.

It was almost a let-down. He had been expecting a huge kick of recoil and an enormous bang, maybe a burst of flame, like in the movies. But it was nothing like that. It wasn't silent. He had heard a flat crack and he'd involuntarily blinked his eyes, but it wasn't that loud. And there wasn't much recoil in his shoulder. And no flash. He looked through the scope again and saw where his bullet had pierced the target. High and to the right.

He repeated the process. Same result. And again. Same result. After five shots, he had a pretty tight group of bullet holes, but they were all high and to the right. Not too far away. If he'd been aiming for Trent's solar plexus, he would still have gone through his right pec. Maybe the sights were off a little. He paused and felt Jerry's hand on his shoulder. He kept the weapon pointing down the range like he'd been told, took his finger off the trigger, splaying his fingers visibly away from it, and thumbed the safety back on. He cocked his head back to listen as Jerry lifted the ear defender off his ear.

"You need to squeeze a little slower there, Jack. A little slower and a little smoother. You're going high and right because you're pulling that trigger oh-so-slowly and then when you get to the end of the pull, you can't quite believe she hasn't fired yet and then you're jerking it. When you jerk it, she's going to fire high and right. Remember how much travel the trigger has before you even get close to firing. Pull it in a ways first, and then slow it right down. A little quicker at the start, and then a little slower at the end. Otherwise, you're doing just dandy." He dropped the can back on Jack's ear.

Jack stood straighter and flexed his neck. Relax. Then he retook his position. Ticked off the checklist in his mind. Safety off. Organise the breath. Initial travel of the trigger. Gentle squeeze. Perfect. Not quite dead centre but damn near close enough. If he'd been aiming at the centre of Trent's forehead, he might not have hit the centre, but it would still have been in the forehead. He repeated the process. Single shot by single shot.

When he'd emptied the magazine, he paused, remembering the next step of the procedure. Release the magazine. He carefully placed it onto the bench in front of him, next to the ammunition. Tilted the rifle onto its side, keeping the muzzle pointing down the range. He looked into the open breech for a tell-tale flash of brass. Nope. No unfired rounds lurking in there. He tilted the breech so Jerry would be able to look in also. Jerry nodded and motioned to the bench. Jack put the rifle down and took a step back.

Jerry was beaming at him. He extended a warm hand and shook with Jack.

"Young man, that was excellent. I was worrying that you'd maybe started a little late in life, but you really got the hang of it quickly. You should be very pleased with yourself."

Jack was grinning like a lunatic. Happy. Not happy because he would be able to do what he wanted to do. But just happy in the moment. He could feel his face reddening, although he wasn't sure if that was because of the joy or the embarrassment of praise.

They fired some more magazines with the Kel-Tec before moving onto the Tavor. The Tavor was louder and gave more of a kick, but aside from that, Jack didn't detect much of a difference. Beginner's lack of nuance maybe. But both felt solid and sound in his hand. Both were easy to shoot. Both were easy to reload. And even when they sent the targets out to thirty yards, the limit of the indoor range, they came back shredded in the middle.

He knew then. He would be happy with either.

He had two-thirds of the session left, and he thought it would be suspicious if he asked to spend all the time on one particular gun. He chose two semi-automatic pistols for the middle period, a Glock nine millimetre and a .44 Magnum. Jerry chuckled at his plainly movie-influenced choices but patiently taught him the basics of pistol shooting. Again, it wasn't especially taxing mentally. His arms and eyes were getting a little tired, but these things were designed to be simple. You couldn't expect cops or soldiers to do complicated math when they were being shot at. So the guns they used were as simple and robust as they could be.

They paused before the final period of the session. A quick drink of water from the cooler and a leak. Jack wanted to revert to the bullpups for more practice, but he figured it would look odd if he didn't use the opportunity to go fully automatic while he was there. While he was humming and hawing, Jerry nudged him along a little. They compromised on bringing the Kel-Tec bullpup back to the range alongside a Colt Commando. He shot the Kel-Tec on semi-automatic for accuracy, and the Colt on full automatic for thrills. It was a tremendous rush going full auto but even then, he realised its limitations. He'd emptied a thirty-round magazine in a matter of seconds, and the target bore considerably less damage than he'd inflicted going semi with the bullpup. His fish would be in a barrel but that didn't mean he could afford to miss. And he would need a heck of a lot of bullets if he was going to use thirty of them so quickly.

The session ended just in time. He was real tired now, and his hands were starting to feel a little sore. He saw the party boys across in the other lanes, posing for photos taken by their instructors and realised it would look odd if he didn't ask Jerry to take a couple of him too. He handed over his cellphone and posed. Smart. Don't stand out. Just look normal. Use your own phone, not someone else's.

He washed up in the restroom once he was done, scrubbing the oil and grime off his hands. He kept his paper targets for no other reason than everyone else did. Clearly you were supposed to keep them as souvenirs. He folded his neatly, blank side facing outward. Shook hands again with Jerry and tipped him ten bucks. Jerry seemed touched. Maybe the younger shooters didn't usually tip. Esteban drove them back down the strip, collecting the next batch of customers as he did so.

Jack walked into Caesar's as if he were meeting his family. Instead, he went to the restroom, where he washed his hands again, taking care and time to remove all the residue. He washed his face too, scrubbing especially hard where his cheek had been in contact with the stock. He looked in the mirror. Couldn't see any marks. No dust or oil. He discarded his targets into the trash. Deleted the photos from his phone.

He waited in the Starbucks again for twenty minutes. He was supposed to be going to the ballgame that afternoon, not back to the airport and he didn't want to be caught in an immediate lie. Then he took the nine-buck shuttle back to McCarran. His wait time in the airport was uneventful although paranoia had him wash his hands for a third time. He did not need the trace of gunshot residue to set off any alarms as he went through security.

The flight he took back home was cheaper because most people would fly back at the end of the weekend. By flying back early, he'd saved himself over 120 bucks, money which could be spent elsewhere.

He arrived at LAX on time. Then hung around arrivals, eking out a soda watching the Raiders game on one of the TVs bolted to the wall. He was supposed to be at the game, so he'd better know what happened in it, just in case his mom asked. Nobody else would ask, obviously. Plus hanging around at the airport minimised the chances of anyone spotting him back in Whittlesford before he should have been back. The Chargers won, but Jack took no pleasure in it. The purist would have it as a pretty decent game, with long spiral passes carving through the clear warm Nevada air to speedy receivers. Muscular ground play from cannonballing running backs. But Jack couldn't get excited. Maybe the first time ever he hadn't enjoyed watching a football game. It felt like homework, prepping for a quiz his mom would set.

On his cellphone, he kept an eye on the departures board from McCarran. Once the flight he should have been on showed as boarding, he sent his mom a quick WhatsApp and then switched his phone off. Prayed that the plane didn't crash. If it crashed, he would have some explaining to do about why he hadn't been on it. When LAX arrivals announced touchdown, he switched his cell back on, relieved. Whatsapped '*Touchdown LAX xxx*' to his mom, and then made his way back home.

He was ready for the next bite of the elephant.

Chapter Forty-One

The window opened one Thursday evening. Jack and his mom sat at the table in the kitchen, eating dinner. Pasta with beef ragu. Nothing fancy. Just wholesome normal food, quick and easy for a working mom and her seventeen-year-old son. Jack had been doing homework in his room when his mom hollered up and asked if he wanted dinner or rather fix something himself. Fifteen minutes later, she hollered again. Some evenings he would take his plate up to his room, some evenings he'd eat in the kitchen. Today was the latter. No particular reason. Just happened that way.

SportsCenter was on in the background – Jack was listening to it, but his mom was ignoring it as she went through emails on her iPad. The cat was in the living room, asleep on the couch. Beef ragu didn't do it for him. If it had been tuna, he would have been screaming for morsels from their plates.

"Jack!! Did you hear what I just said?"

Jack stopped looking at the TV and looked at his mom. A grin spread across his face.

"Um…you won the lottery, and I don't have to go to school ever again?"

"Wise-ass. No. I have to go out of town for work next week. Leave early on Wednesday morning, back Friday night. Will you be OK?"

"You mean will I burn the house down while you're gone?" Jack was sassing his mom, but his mind was already computing. Out of town business trips came along now and then, but not with any regularity or convenient schedule.

A thought occurred to him.

"Where are you going?" He tried to make it sound casual.

Disinterested.

"Phoenix. Well, technically Glendale. So not too far."

Fuck. Or maybe not. What impact did this have?

"Cool. I'll be fine, Mom." Even in that moment, he knew he needed to seem more interested in SportsCenter than her trip. That was what he usually did.

"Want me to bring anything back for you?"

Yeah, can you bring me back a semi-automatic rifle and enough ammunition to kill a hundred people please? Thanks Mom!

"Um…I already have Cardinals and Diamondbacks. If you see a Suns one? That would be cool." He waved in the general direction of the refrigerator. It was covered with magnets of sports teams from across America. When he was younger, the refrigerator had served as the gallery for all his pre- and elementary school artwork. At some point, his drawings started being held up by colourful enamel magnets of football, baseball and basketball teams. The drawings had long been placed into scrapbooks and boxes in the attic, but the sports magnet collection remained.

"Phoenix Suns. Sure, I'll try and find one." His mom reached out and touched his forearm and gave it a squeeze. He didn't resist, just smiled at her.

"Thank you."

When he was little, he loved climbing up his mom's body for cuddles and hugs. At some point, he would try and fight her off because he was a big boy now, and he didn't like her holding his hand in public, ever. And now he was at the stage where he'd relented, and he let his mom touch him again. She seemed to need it more than him.

Jack turned and focussed on the TV, but his mind was already spinning. He didn't have much time, but this was clearly an opportunity that was too good to miss. Ordinarily he would watch ESPN for hours, finding new items of interest even in the repeated segments on slow days. Today it dragged but he continued watching. Paranoia told him to stay in the kitchen so his mom wouldn't think he was planning anything in response to her trip. His bare foot tapped up and down under the table, the drumming masked by the noise of the TV. After what he judged to be a decent amount of time, he stood and took his empty pasta bowl and placed it in the washer. Then went upstairs to his room.

He slouched back on his bed, half sitting up, half lying and stared into space. No need for the flash drive or the computer for this. Just think.

Mom going out of town. You have three days to get what you need. You could even execute.

Woah there, cowboy. One bite at a time.

As he processed his thoughts, he saw he was waving his arms out in front of him, like the guys who directed planes at the airport.

Mom is out of town for three days. That gives you a window to do what you need to do.

OK. What do you need to do? Exactly what do you need to do?

I need to source the equipment. And then I need to execute.

OK. First bite of the elephant.

What does this mean?

I have a window. A three-day window.

Is it definitely three days?

Probably. She rarely comes home early from trips. But not guaranteed. Definitely two days. She's never come home from a trip more than a day early.

Jack cast his mind back to previous trips. When he was younger, she travelled rarely. Hardly surprising given his dad was always at sea. Sometimes it was unavoidable, and he'd been foisted on a classmate for the night, something that had been occasionally reciprocated in the pre-teen years. Grandparents were too far away to babysit.

Once he was sixteen, his mom was able to leave him overnight although she hadn't liked doing it to begin with. The first was a single night away, on a work trip. He'd gorged himself on pizza then watched porn in his room with the sound up, exasperated when his mom kept whatsapping him to make sure he was OK and interrupting his viewing. She'd come home the next day to a relatively tidy house, a happy and overfed cat and the box from Dominos neatly jammed into the trash. She'd checked the trash for cigarette butts and beer cans out of paranoia more than anything else and been reassured. Since then, there had been a few more trips. Mainly business but there was one time when his parents had gone out of town for their wedding anniversary, a rare treat that his dad was home on that date. They'd driven to a cabin in Tahoe and hadn't whatsapped except to say good morning, good evening, and to send a photo of them holding hands by the water. It was cute and gross at the same time.

He refocused his mind.

Wednesday morning to Friday evening.

OK. You definitely have two days. Very probably three. If she comes home on Thursday evening, that could be a problem. If she comes home Friday morning, that's less of a problem. Because you're supposed to be in school and she wouldn't expect to see you at home anyway. Unlikely that she comes home Friday morning though. If she doesn't need to be there on Friday morning, then she'd leave on Thursday night, surely. Phoenix isn't far.

His arms were still waving in the air, and he realised he'd added in circular head movements as he worked through the possibilities. It was almost like a logic problem – if I pull this string, then the ball drops into that pocket and then z follows y follows x.

Mom going to Phoenix presented another problem though. Phoenix was a big city, sure, but there was a risk that if he went there when she went there, he could bump into her. He would know the hotel she was staying at – she always emailed him the travel details – but he wouldn't know her full schedule. To get that, he would have to ask her and that would be weird. He'd never asked because he wasn't interested, but also because he could always get his mom on her cellphone if he needed to. She always kept it with her, and she always had it face up on her desk, even during meetings. Parents' privilege. People understood that. And that in turn meant there was never a need for him to have her full schedule so he could call different landlines at different times of the day.

Does this mean Phoenix is a bust?

Probably.

Probably?

Yes. Arizona would have been good. It's nearby. It's easy to get to. And you can get what you need. All of those things. But you either need to go to a different place in Arizona than Phoenix, or a different place overall. The risk of bumping into Mom in Phoenix is small but it's not zero. And if you do, it doesn't matter that it was a one in a million chance. You'd be fucked.

OK.

Not Phoenix then. You need to come up with an alternative. And you've got less than a week to plan and execute. No pressure.

Chapter Forty-Two

Jack frowned as he stared at the computer screen. He sighed and leaned back on his chair, which creaked loudly in protest. He wasn't concerned. If it was going to break, it would have broken forty pounds ago, not now. And nobody was in his room anyway. Mom was downstairs watching TV. Mr. Orange was out in the yard, catching some rays with his eyes closed. He'd stir soon enough, once it got close to dinner time. But for now, he was contentedly dozing. Jack could see him out of his bedroom window.

He wouldn't say Plan A was a bust and he needed to go to Plan B. Because he'd never had a plan B. Plan A, by definition, is only plan A if there's a plan B. Else it's just a plan. And Jack had purposely not planned too far ahead. Phoenix had been favourite though. Slack gun laws and not that far away, plus a good reason to visit on his own to watch the Cardinals. But now he needed to adapt.

Think. Start from the beginning.

What do you need to achieve?

I need a weapon and a lot of ammunition.

Does it matter how long the journey is?

Yes and no.

It matters because once I've bought it, then I'm a felon. And if I get caught with it, then I'm fucked. And the whole thing is off. So the longer the journey, the more likely I am to get caught. Assuming the risk is constant, then it increases with every hour of the journey.

Is that the most important thing?

No. The most important thing is being able to buy it in the first place. Because if that doesn't happen, then the rest of it is irrelevant.

OK, so was Arizona the only place you could do that? Is it all over now?

Well, no. Not the only place.

Was it the best place?

I don't know. I've never done this before.

Stop saying that. Think. Plan. Research.

Jack fished out his flash drive and turned on his computer. Used TAILS to open Tor, and then DuckDuckGo. As anonymous as he could be.

He researched without scribbling notes. He returned to the shooting magazine website which had a league table ranking states in terms of their gun laws. Top five: Arizona, Alaska, Idaho, Kansas, Oklahoma. Aside from Arizona, all were a long way away. Hmm. Might have to be Arizona after all. He quickly went to the classifieds. There really wasn't much outside of Phoenix or Glendale. And they weren't really feasible because Mom would be there. A few in Tucson but not much.

He dug further into the detail on the states. The top five surprised him. Not because of which states were in it, but which were not. He would have guessed the Deep South would be more represented. Texas, Georgia, Mississippi, Alabama. Places like that. Either that or backwater places in the northwest where the militias hid in forests. OK, Kansas was very definitely a backwater, but it wasn't that kind of backwater.

He read further. There were different reasons for the league rankings and some of them didn't apply to him. He really didn't give a shit that Alaska lacked a competitive shooting scene. He looked at other websites. Different sites had different league tables, and in some of the others, Texas was higher. As was Georgia. Hmm. That could work. Cowboys, Texans, Falcons, Braves, Rangers, Astros. Plenty of reasons to go to either, although quite the journey.

Stop. You're getting distracted.

OK.

The league tables don't matter. You're not trying to qualify for the play-offs. This is a one-off game. All you need to know is how does the law work for private sales. If it means you can buy what you need from a private seller, without a background check, you should be fine.

Should be? That doesn't help. I have to be.

OK, so what you're saying is, you need is a state where it's not only legal for eighteen-year-olds to do this, but where people love guns and hate gun laws? Where they believe the Second Amendment was a gift from God himself?

Yes. That's exactly what I'm saying.

Texas then?

Texas.

He thought for a minute, considered further options. Could he get what he needed in Texas? Dallas was a much bigger city than Phoenix or Tucson, so he assumed he probably could. More people surely equated to more sellers. And buyers. Texas might not be the nearest place, but it was probably the best place.

Don't assume. Check.

He went to the classifieds, and this time filtered first for Texas, and then dropped down the menu for Dallas. Pages and pages of listings with the most recent – posted only a few minutes before – in the top slot. He clicked forward four pages, and he had only reached yesterday's postings. Lots of guns for sale.

The language was similar to that which he'd seen before. The dealers promised the lowest prices in the state. That was no use to him. He needed private sellers and no background check. The private sellers had zero tolerance for lowball offers or paperwork. That was much more promising.

He searched specifically for the two bullpups that he'd tried in Las Vegas. There were a half-dozen available, or at least had been within the past fortnight. Mainly the Kel-Tec, the American one. Patriotic gun buying? Sounded like Texas.

The scale of the listings was extensive. This rich choice boded well. Although maybe the listing stayed up after the sale had happened? The only way to check was to call or text. Some of the classifieds were from dealers. No good. They would background check. But the private sales wouldn't. He reached for his cell but then stopped. Realised he would need to get a throwaway phone to stay off the radar. A burner.

He checked through another couple of listing websites. There definitely seemed to be enough choice. It was a long journey. He would need to get there and back while Mom was out of town. But it was doable. He nodded to himself with quiet satisfaction as he disconnected the flash drive and shut down his computer.

He was going to Dallas.

Chapter Forty-Three

Nick: So anyway, he had this nickname, and people called him Shamu. Like the killer whale. And one student told police that at one point, a bunch of kids in school were wearing Save the Whale pins as like an in-joke against him?

Chris: Yeah but dude, that's just like regular bullying. It happens to everyone.

Nick: Yeah, true. I guess bullying has changed a bit over the years though. From what we know, Tolleson got shit both in person and online

Chris: I thought we didn't have any legacy from his social media or anything.

Nick: Well, we don't have anything from him, himself. But we know that bullying does extend to online, especially via social media. There's a statistic somewhere, uh-here it is. Between 2007 and 2017, the rate of teenage suicides in the United States rose fifty-six percent, and accelerated faster in the last five years than the first five, according to the CDC.

Chris: CDC?

Nick: Uh, CDC is, uh, the U.S. Centers for Disease Control and Prevention's National Center for Health Statistics. That's the source. And we know that the incidence of depression and anxiety is rising quickly and we know that this has been linked to social media bullying.

Chris: So do we know that Tolleson was bullied online?

Nick: Well, we know a bit. We don't know what happened on WhatsApp, because WhatsApp is encrypted and not even WhatsApp can see what he received. And if anyone was bullying him via WhatsApp, they've obviously not come forward. I mean, why would you? If you were chatting shit to a kid and he overreacted-

Chris: Overreacted?? Come on, dude, there's overreaction and then there's overreaction

Nick: Well, yeah, but you know what I mean. If you were chatting shit to a kid, and you figured it was just in fun, and one day he goes into school with a Kel-Tec and shoots it up, you're not going to be running to the cops saying, 'I made him do it. I made him do it!'

Chris: Fair.

Nick: So we don't know about his WhatsApp really. He was a member of a couple of groups but nothing major was posted there. He was on Insta but he rarely posted, rarely interacted with anyone, and tended just to use it to follow sports and exercise people. And cats. He liked cats and animals. There were rumours that there were specific groups that specifically excluded him-

Chris: Excluded him how?

Nick: There were rumours that some kids had set up WhatsApp groups or Insta chats which they didn't let him join. Those haven't been made public, so we don't know exactly how they functioned

Chris: How you mean?

Nick: Well, we don't know if they were specifically set up for everyone in theory, but Tolleson was excluded. Or they were just groups which Tolleson wasn't eligible to join, so he wasn't really being excluded.

Chris: Like what?

Nick: I mean, like, say there was a WhatsApp or Facebook group for Cheerleaders. Tolleson wasn't a cheerleader, so he wouldn't have been eligible to join that. I wouldn't call that being excluded. Or say there was one for all the football team – he wasn't on the football team, so he wouldn't get to join that either. I wouldn't call that actually being excluded. And he was on the class WhatsApp and Facebook groups so it's not like he was excluded from those things?

Chris: Yeah. *laughs*

Nick: What?

Chris: No, I really shouldn't say this

Nick: Since when has that stopped you?

*Chris: Um. *laughs* I was just thinking. Was there a group for fat kids? I mean, if he couldn't be in the football group or the cheerleader group, he could have just started a group for all the fat kids? That way he could have been excluding the hot chicks and the jocks, rather than him being the one excluded.*

*Nick: *laughs* Man, that's harsh.*

Chris: You see my point though. Not everybody gets to join every group. That's not exclusion, just fact.

Nick: Well, yeah. And to be fair, we don't actually know what groups he wanted to join and wasn't allowed or eligible for.

Chris: Yeah, we don't know. But since when has not knowing stuff stopped us mentioning it in our podcasts?

*Nick: *laughs* Yup. Four years of speculation and still going strong. Please listen to us!*laughs**

*Chris: *laughs**

Nick: Yeah. So. Anyway, we know there are rumours that he got shit for being fat and we can kind of assume that some of it carried on online.

Chris: Yeah, I get that, but you can just turn off your damn phone, surely?

Nick: This? From you? You spend more time on your phone than almost anyone I know!

Chris: Yeah, but I'm a really busy guy-

Nick: You're not! You lie around all day, doing jack and looking at hot chicks on your phone.

*Chris: Well, there is that. *laughs**

Nick: I don't think it's quite as simple as turning off your phone. I mean, every so often, I try and do a digital detox and then I like realise there's a reason we invented smartphones. Because we need them.

Chris: Totally. Especially around mealtimes. UberEats!

Nick: You could always learn to cook!

Chris: You can't cook either! You live on leftovers from your landlady.

Chris: Fair. Anyway, the point is, if he was getting shit

online, he should either have turned his phone off! Not shot everyone! Or given shit right back – it's not like you get punched in real life if you give shit back. Everyone has a weakness, don't they?

Nick: How do you mean?

Chris: If he'd turned the tables on whoever was giving him shit. Work out their weak spot and go after them. If it's online, surely everyone's equal.

Nick: I guess. Although I guess in person, he was a pretty big dude, I mean not just fat, he was a big guy, height wise. I wouldn't have wanted to get into a fistfight with him.

Chris: You wouldn't want to get in a fistfight with anyone.

Nick: Fair point. I'm a lover not a fighter…

Chris: I think you mean neither a lover nor a fighter.

Nick: It's just a dry spell.

Chris: Whatever.

Nick: Asshole.

Chris: *laughs*

Nick: Anyway, the point is that Tolleson does seem to have been bullied, but we still don't really know why, out of all the thousands of cases of bullying that happen, this one ended with him in a classroom with his classmates and a loaded Kel-Tec-

Chris: Even though we don't know, what do you think might have been the reason? Care to speculate?

Nick: Why not, I guess. I guess…it's a tough one. People get bullied all the time, and I don't mean like it's fun being bullied, but that's not a reason to go and shoot up the school. And we don't know exactly how or why he got bullied. I mean, I don't want to speak ill of the dead, but he did commit murder so maybe I don't feel quite as bad…maybe he got bullied a little and he was just like over-sensitive. Maybe he just got bullied a lot because he was an asshole.

Chris: Yeah, I guess the obvious point is that anyone who did what he did is an asshole. He was an asshole on his last day, so it's not impossible he was an asshole before and that's why he got bullied.

Nick: Yeah, I guess. We know that he hadn't been having

any treatment for any mental health issues, so we can assume that anything that was wrong there, hadn't been diagnosed yet.

Chris: Yet?

Nick: Well, I guess I'm kind of tending toward the idea that he was mentally ill, and it just hadn't been diagnosed. Some kind of sociopath, maybe. Because it just doesn't seem feasible that he did what he did because some of the kids who he spent some of his time with made fun of him for being a porker. I mean, that's a hell of a stretch.

Chris: Yeah, that makes sense. I guess…

Nick: And on that note, we're running out of time, so thank you very much for listening, as always. If you've enjoyed this podcast, please do go and rate us with five stars on wherever you downloaded the podcast. If you click on the link in our bio, you'll also get directed to a prize draw for an Amazon voucher, and you can also buy some <u>very</u> cool merch we have on offer. Next week, we'll wrap up the Whittlesford Massacre but until then this has been….

Nick and Chris together: Killing Time.

Cue music.

Chapter Forty-Four

How can you get to Dallas and back with a gun?

Getting to Dallas was easy. Direct flight, hundred-odd bucks. Getting back was the problem.

The best option was to drive, but it was damn near 1500 miles, and he would need to break the journey for rest. Plus rent a car. And the big car companies who would do a one-way rental were the big car companies who didn't rent to under twenties. Scratch that.

A carpool minimised contact with other people. Hopefully bringing it down just to one other person. But Jack reckoned that two people in one car for thirty hours would lead to conversations he didn't want to have. He couldn't pretend to sleep for the entire time. What if he got mugged or fell asleep and they stole his bag? Plus most carpools wanted someone to share the driving. Scratch that.

Greyhound direct was over thirty hours. Cheap. Wi-Fi. But cramming his frame into a bus seat for thirty hours didn't appeal. He wouldn't need the money after he was done anyway. Scratch Greyhound.

Train was the better option. The train had rooms where he could have privacy. Seclusion was expensive but worth it. No need to worry about having his backpack stolen if he dozed off. Still over twenty-four hours of travel. So he figured he would need to sleep at some point, even if right now, he felt so wired he would never sleep again. But the only route out of Dallas went south to Houston first. Around the houses in a state where Jack felt he would have already outstayed his welcome. He wanted to get back west as soon as possible.

OK, so what are you saying? Compromise: bus then train?

Stage One. Get out of Dallas as fast as you can. Leave the scene of the crime.

Stage Two. Go in the right direction. Go straight west. Greyhound. Head for El Paso. Pick up the train there.

He'd sacrifice privacy on the first leg in return for it on the second leg. The first leg would be overnight. Even if his fellow passengers weren't asleep, Jack could pretend he was. Minimise contact. Minimise conversation. Avoid being memorable. For now, at least.

That left him a few hours to kill in Dallas before the Greyhound left. It could work. But he still needed to be sure he could get what he needed in the first place.

For the first time, Jack felt a little under pressure. The window was open, but it wouldn't stay open forever. For this to work, he needed to jump through it during the time available. And unlike some of the others, he couldn't control the timing. It was what it was, and he would have to work within those constraints.

He breathed in deeply. In his bedroom, he was surrounded by all that was familiar and comforting. He could smell the faintly floral waft of fresh bedsheets. His mom had placed the new linens on the corner of his desk as she did every couple of weeks. He'd fished an old sweaty T-shirt from his laundry basket and put it on his desk chair, and then moved a gently protesting Mr. Orange onto it while he changed the sheets. The cat found Jack's scent comforting. Put the T-shirt on the chair and he would wait and watch the sheet-changing process. Put him on the chair without a T-shirt and he would either sit with his back to Jack, sulking, or if especially affronted, jump down and prowl out of the room. If he hadn't done the latter, he would leap onto the bed and spread himself out on the new linen, depositing hair and marking his ownership.

He scribbled in his notepad. He was about halfway through, and the book looked odd. The wiro binding was too big for the number of pages that remained in it. He had gotten into the routine from day one. Scribble on paper, nobody can see that. Rip the paper and the subsequent sheet out at the end of each session. Rip them to pieces, piss on them, flush them down the can.

He needed four things:

He needed a weapon.

He needed ammunition.

He needed to get to where he was going to buy it.

He needed to get back from there.

He frowned again. When he scribbled it down like that, it seemed so simple. A four-item shopping list. Most people wouldn't even write a list for four items. Four is easy to remember. If his mom sent him to Krogers, he wouldn't forget one item out of four. But this was a lot more complicated than that. For each item he needed, he needed something else to be able to get it.

First things first. You need a weapon. And ammunition.

This would need cash. Not just money. But actual cash. Folding stuff. He knew from his initial search through the classifieds that this would be a cash transaction. This suited him. It was anonymous in the first instance

You need ID.

Sellers were clear about not wanting to do much paperwork, but it wouldn't be a bad idea if he had a fake ID. He snorted as he realised he would probably be the first person in history to make a fake ID that made him look eighteen and not twenty-one. He figured he could probably pass for twenty-one in a slack bar but why risk it. He didn't want a beer. He wanted a gun.

To buy a gun and ammunition, he needed a seller. And a way to contact them. Most of the classifieds listed phone numbers and said to text rather than call. He didn't want to use his own cellphone. The prefix was clearly a California number. And out of state residents couldn't buy guns in Texas. So he would need a Texas number.

He needed his seller to be reliable. Problem was, there were only reviews for business sellers. Gun dealers. And dealers would do an ID and background check. So he would be going blind in this regard. He considered it for a minute. His tongue flicked across his teeth and his head bobbed from side to side as he thought. That could work. Line up two sellers, one after the other. The second one would be the insurance policy in case the first one didn't show, or dicked him around. He made a note. He would have to build in additional time in case the first seller was a bust.

Getting the cash was easier than he'd thought. He'd gone to his bank in person, for the first time since he'd opened the account. His daily ATM withdrawal limit was three hundred bucks, so he'd gone to his bank in person for the first time since he'd opened the account. He withdrew fifteen hundred bucks from his savings account. Years and years in the making. Not so much from especially diligent saving. More that he just never spent much money. He'd planned a plausible reason for when the teller asked him what he needed it for. Buying a motorcycle. He'd even found one for about the right price on Craigslist. But the teller had paid absolutely no attention whatsoever to him, just counted out the money in twelve hundreds, four fifties and five twenties, her eyes already on the next customer in line. He folded the crisp new notes into his wallet and walked off, dazed that it had been such a non-event.

He searched online for burner phones, and DuckDuckGo took him to an online review site. He learned quickly that he wouldn't need a new physical phone. There were apps that supplied burner numbers which he could use for texting and calling. The article highlighted the advantages of a disposable number for online dating, to avoid giving your real number to stalkers or batshit crazy women. If only.

He clicked on Hushed, which sold itself as the best provider of second numbers. He liked that. Second numbers. There was clearly a market for them, judging by the number of reviews. Then again, the reviews might be fake. You couldn't tell. Nothing online was real any more.

He quickly purchased a Texas number from a selection available and a prepaid seven-day bundle for fifty texts. It might show up on his bill at the end of the month, which his mom paid, but it was only two bucks. And it wouldn't matter by the end of the month anyway. He sighed. Knowing that he was coming to the end brought him grief and relief at different times but in equal measures. Either way, it fatigued him. He sighed again, blowing the air out between his lips.

Next on his list was ID. There were dozens of fake ID websites, offering drivers' licenses from pretty much every state in the Union. There were not, however, online reviews to help him. Not surprising given there was no legitimate reason for having one. Not like a burner. It was a minefield. He briefly considered school. There were definitely people in school who had fake IDs, both amongst the jocks and the stoners. But it would attract attention if he asked. They weren't friends. Just acquaintances. And the more he thought about it, the more he figured that if he did ask, and if they were willing to help, then they'd probably point him toward someone local. Who did fake California licenses. And that was no use to him whatsoever. He needed a Texas one.

He found a website that looked relatively professional and searched around it. The company sold them 'for novelty purposes only' and maintained a Twitter presence. At least they still seemed to be in existence. He decided to risk it. He found the address of a student dorm at SMU and entered that in as his fake address. Made himself a year older. Paid eighty bucks for the license and twenty-five bucks for two-day delivery to his house. He'd have to make sure he intercepted the mail before Mom did. He didn't get much mail and she would be sure to ask him.

The next stage was more tricky. It required two simultaneous transactions. Well, practically. He needed to make sure he could travel there and back. Then make sure he could get what he needed. Then book the travel. It would be pointless lining up the purchase if there was no travel availability. Pointless booking the travel if nobody was selling what he needed.

He decided on a three-step strategy: research, coordinate, execute.

He went first to the classifieds. Two separate websites.

He found three recent listings in Dallas for versions of the Kel-Tec he'd shot in Vegas. Prices ranged from seven hundred to a thousand bucks. He quickly created an account for the website, which in turn required him to create a quick disposable outlook email account. Sent all three sellers a polite email, asking if the weapon was still available, if it came with extra magazines and ammunition and asking the seller to email or preferably text his Texas cell number.

He searched for the Israeli weapon next, the Tavor. Ouch. Prices started at fifteen hundred bucks and that seemed to be just for the weapon, no mention of extra magazines or ammunition. He broadened the search for bullpups in general. A few more choices, including a Steyr that was painted gleaming white. Presumably originally for winter warfare over in the Austrian Alps. He sent similarly polite emails or texts to each potential seller.

Summing the sent items from his bogus email account and the sent texts from his burner number, he had eight potentials broadly within Dallas. That should surely be enough.

While he waited for replies, he shifted focus to travel. Plenty of availability on outbound flights from LAX to Dallas-Fort Worth. He didn't need to push the button and book a flight right this minute. It could wait a moment.

He knew his mom would be leaving early to fly out to Phoenix, in order to get a full day's work in. Phoenix was one of those short flights where you barely felt you'd been in the air for a moment before they grabbed your coffee cup and told you to put your tray back. But it still beat a five-hour drive. If there was a problem at LAX and Mom couldn't take off, well, that would be a problem. Although if she couldn't take off, it would likely be because of the weather rather than the aircraft, and that would mean Jack couldn't take off either. That would be problematic in one way, but not the other.

He turned his attention to the return leg. In a perfect world, he'd be able to do it as a day trip, flying both ways, but that wasn't possible for the obvious reason of bringing an illegal firearm with him. In a nearly perfect world, he'd be able to get back on Thursday, just in case Mom's trip was shortened and she came back early. But that wasn't possible either.

He paused and considered. Assuming he could get what he needed, how long would he need to spend in Dallas itself? On the one hand, as little as possible. On the other, he needed to budget for at least two meetings, in case one of them was a no-show. Or if he had to buy the weapon and the ammunition from different sellers.

That brought up another question. Where would people normally meet to do this? It was a legal transaction. Well, it would have been had Jack been eighteen. But with the seller holding a gun and the buyer holding a fistful of banknotes, where would people normally meet? The websites recommended a well-lit public place. That made sense. He was in two minds. On the one hand, this was supposed to be a completely legal transaction. On the other, it wasn't legal the way Jack was doing it. But it was still probably better to treat it as if it were. No meeting in deserted spots late at night. One website recommended meeting in the parking lot of a gun store. That would make sense, but then it might look weird if Jack blatantly didn't have a car there. Everyone had a car, surely. The only way he could get a car was if he rented one. Would that mark him as an out-of-towner? Probably. When Jack and his family went on vacation, they often rented vehicles at their destination. He remembered being disappointed as a kid that their rental in Orlando came with Georgia plates, not Florida ones.

He paused and considered this in more detail. This was a legitimate purchase. He was an eighteen-year-old student, living in Dallas, and buying something he was legally allowed to buy. Would he have a car? Yes, probably. But not always. Some students didn't have cars. Some had motorcycles. And some rode bicycles everywhere. Or maybe his car was being fixed or he'd lent it to a buddy. Was he overthinking this? Probably.

Another potential location was a parking lot next to a police station. Jack balked at this. Surely this was insane. If he got caught, they might as well just toss him through the windows into the cells. But actually…maybe this was the most sensible idea of them all. A felon would surely be

227

cautious about transacting right next to a bunch of cops. A legitimate buyer wouldn't think twice. Not in Dallas. Apparently, some police stations had designated areas nearby specifically for this purpose, but there didn't seem to be an easy way to check exactly where they were. He wasn't about to ring the Dallas PD, not even using the burner.

He realised he was losing focus and wasting time. He didn't get to decide the location all by himself. It would also depend on his seller. Who had presumably, possibly done this before. He quickly went back to the classifieds. He wanted to check if his sellers had any other items but there was no information on that. Nor was there a rating system like eBay or TripAdvisor. Hmm. That would have been helpful. Park that thought for the moment. Stop worrying about what you can't control. Concentrate on what you can.

He played around with Google Maps, Greyhound, and Amtrak. If he arrived during the day in Dallas, then he could meet his buyer in the afternoon or the evening. Hopefully downtown. Preferably not too late. But it would be plausible for him to be a college student, and therefore available in `the afternoon. And his seller probably had a job and therefore would want to meet after work.

He mentally built in late afternoon and early evening for completing the transaction. He assumed the first meeting could be a no-show and he therefore factored in time for a second meeting. He didn't want to meet anybody after 9 p.m. That just seemed stupid. Too risky, even in the well-lit public place that was recommended. But he didn't want to hang around Dallas any later than he had to either. And he couldn't stay overnight.

This fitted with his initial thoughts. Build in time to allow for a no-show, and then get out of Dallas as fast as you can. No dithering.

He looked on Greyhound. Forty-four bucks from Dallas to El Paso. A long journey, but the only option. He wondered if he'd missed a trick. He quickly checked the gun listings for El Paso itself, but the choice was far more limited than Dallas. It would be much quicker though. Ah. No, it wouldn't. No direct flights from LAX. Stick to Dallas. Or at least, get Dallas lined up and then pull the trigger.

He flicked over the page on his notebook where he was keeping count of the costs. Added a round fifty dollars underneath the hundred fifty he'd put in for the flight to Dallas. If he overestimated, that wasn't a bad thing. Gave him some wiggle room, just in case.

He opened up another tab on the browser and went to Amtrak. Two hundred bucks would get him a roomette on the Texas Eagle from El Paso. What the fuck was a roomette? Ah. Not much use. It was a room with a door you could presumably lock, two bunk beds but no toilet. It came with access to a toilet in the car. That was no use. Even if he could lock the door, he wasn't going to leave the weapon in the room when he went for a dump. He clicked on the next option. That was similar but it came with its own washroom, including a shower. Five hundred dollars. Jeez. No wonder nobody took the damn train when flying was so much cheaper. Or maybe the train was how lots of people did what he was going to do. Maybe he wasn't so unique after all. But surely most people moving weapons would drive. Whatever. He could afford it. it wasn't like he would need his savings account once this was over anyway.

He clicked on the room-with-a-washroom option. There was only one left. Fuck. Adrenalin exploded within him. It fizzed within his hands first as he held them over the keyboard. Then he noticed it in his heart, pumping faster, his biceps growing. His feet were drumming under his desk. Now or never?

He clicked on the 'reserve' button. As he'd hoped, that gave him some time to complete the transaction before releasing the room. He hit refresh on his fake email and checked the burner app on his phone. Nothing yet. Fuck. He needed at least one of the sellers to come back to him.

He took a deep breath and tried to calm himself. It didn't work, but that was OK. He was full of adrenalin, but he wasn't actually scared. More, excited. Felt like he was about to take a snap for the Chargers and explode up the field with the ball, or walk out to the plate at Dodger Stadium, bottom of the Ninth, tied ballgame. He actually felt *good*. He clenched his jaw and chewed an imaginary piece of gum.

Clarity revealed itself in front of him, an invisible apparition between his eyes and his screen.

You need to execute. Right now. There's a finite number of rooms on the train. If you don't make the booking, you definitely can't do this. If you do make the booking, you still could.

He made the booking. Five hundred dollars came off his debit card. He quickly scribbled the amount onto the tally in his notebook. Total was now seven hundred dollars.

The jigsaw now had the first fixed piece in it. That meant the rest of the pieces had less freedom about where they would go.

He was returning from El Paso on the Texas Eagle at 1.47 p.m. on the Thursday. That meant he had to get from Dallas to El Paso in time to catch it. He went back to Greyhound and booked that leg. Paid the extra ten bucks for a flexible booking in case. Amended the tally on the notepad.

He paused briefly but there had been no replies to his emails. He went back to American, and booked his flight. It was only an additional thirty bucks to make it a return, so he put in a return for the Thursday. He would only need it if all his sellers blew him out. Or if Mom told him on Wednesday that she was coming home Thursday. If she told him any later, he'd be halfway to home on bus and railroad, and arriving too late to beat her home.

He went back to his notebook. Sketched out his itinerary. It worked. He nodded his head, and his eyes took on a faraway gaze as he went through the steps in mid-air. Home to LAX to Dallas to El Paso to home. It worked.

Now all he needed was the gun.

Chapter Forty-Five

It wouldn't help if I moved anyway. You can't leave cyberspace. But maybe I have moved, because I kinda left cyberspace. But every so often, I can't help going back there.

I haven't left Whittlesford though. The name still feels warm to me. It reminds me of when Jonathan and I first moved out west. Whittlesford, California. It brought up images of sun and beach, baseball and surfing. Tanned kids with shiny white teeth. It just sounds healthy.

To everyone else, Whittlesford has become a name that means something different. Hiroshima. Pearl Harbor. It's become a shorthand. I guess whenever a town earns its place in history, it's remembered for something bad. Sandy Hook. Columbine. A whole city, full of people, reduced to an abbreviation for a specific unspeakable horror. Whittlesford will be remembered, across the country. But how many people remember Jack? Who he was, what happened to him and what happened on that day?

I made the mistake of googling Whittlesford, maybe a month after it happened. I make that mistake again sometimes. I can't stop myself. There's a Wikipedia article that shows up first. It varies in its accuracy. Every so often, someone edits it. One time, someone added totally fictitious details about Jack, saying he was a child rapist. Maybe that's the only thing they could think of that was worse than actually happened. Someone else edited it and said it was a hoax, that everyone was alive. Neither edits lasted. They were reported – not by me – and then the article changed back. It's now a sober, factual account of that day.

After it happened, social media was ablaze with descriptions and reports and opinions. Why. How. Constant opinions from everybody on earth with a computer and internet access. Europeans using Jack to support their view on gun control. Southerners using Jack to support their view on gun control. Jack became a pawn for whatever view people had already. I just scrolled down, fixated. I wanted to scream, this is my baby. He's dead. He's not a poster child, he's not a buttress for whatever ramshackle argument you're making. He's dead. My seventeen-year-old boy is dead.

I fell down the rabbit hole of the conspiracy theorists. Sandy Hook didn't happen. Columbine was a set-up. Nobody died at Whittlesford. Truly bizarre and twisted. Photoshopped fakes of my baby spotted in Hawaii, India, the South China Sea.

When it happened, the press tried to get me to speak. Demanded it. An opportunity to put the record straight, give my side of the story. I said no. I figured that if I didn't say anything, it couldn't be twisted. Turns out it doesn't work that way. If you don't say anything, then they will make it up and say it for you. And then cyberspace will twist the twist. I'm the real villain. I made him do it. He's still alive. I'm making money from all the visitors who come to Whittlesford. It's beyond insane.

I still get emails. No matter how I try to filter and screen and block and junk. I still get emails. Anonymous, for the most part. The signed ones tend to come from burly men with beards and guns. I've ruined their enjoyment of the right to shoot guns. I should be ashamed. What happened is the price of a free society. The anonymous ones are worse but better. I'm a bitch. A whore. I'm evil. They're glad Jack is dead. Jack is alive. I put him up to it. Jack deserved what he got. Jack escaped and is in Australia.

I changed my email address after it happened, but I still get emails. I need email, like everyone else does. How else can I communicate professionally? I have to earn a living. I have to pay for food. The court case was expensive. I need email. But emails by definition have to be sent, and that gives away your email address and then it gets forwarded and then someone posts it online and then you're back to square one. Nine days out of ten, I just delete and block, delete and block. But once in a while, I can't help myself and I read them. It doesn't usually bring tears. It's a quiet kind of horror, a fascination.

There's paper mail too, of course. Some of it is just crayon scrawled on notepaper. Whore. Bitch. You'll be next. That kind of thing. Sometimes, it's typed and printed. Postcards too. Biblical quotes about vengeance and damnation. I went to the post office to try and have them stopped. They weren't sympathetic. It's only a small town.

Our postbox is at the end of the drive. It's a bit cute and Americana, but it was like that when we bought the house, and we thought it was quirky, so we kept it. When the letters came after it happened, I was glad. I didn't want anything coming directly into the house. Immediately after, Jonathan was home on leave, but he had to go back at some point. And yes, I felt vulnerable. But the postbox is outside, and that's a good thing. One time, someone had put in an envelope of faeces. It had leaked. I couldn't smell it before I opened the postbox, but I sensed something was amiss. That envelope was obviously hand-delivered, not through the Postal Service.

I went through a stage of wondering who was sending the letters. You can't always read the postmark. Were they really sent in Dallas, or Iowa or Tulsa? Or were they sent by people I knew? The hand-delivered ones, who sent those? One time, during the day, I resolved that I would stay up all night, and look from the front bedroom onto the postbox and see who it was. By the time I went to bed, I'd decided I'd rather not know.

So why not move? What's the point? I don't think I should have to. Jack is dead. His ashes are in an urn on his desk in his bedroom. We can't bring ourselves to scatter him yet. What use would moving be anyway? By definition, the post follows you around. And once one person found out who I was, they would tell another person and then another and then it would be on the internet, and it would be back to square 1 again. And this is our home. Jonathan, me and Jack. One day, not long away, Jonathan will complete his commission and he'll retire. And then this will be our home again, just the two of us. Because Jack is dead.

Chapter Forty-Six

Jack had sent eight emails or texts to potential sellers and was impatient for a reply. Not 'waiting-for-Santa' impatient. Annoyed kind of impatient. He'd already booked his travel, and these were the last remaining pieces of the puzzle. He needed them to fall into place.

He left the cell in his room while he went to eat lunch and watch college ball on the couch. He didn't want to, but he knew it would be unusual if he didn't go and watch the game. The TV downstairs was much bigger, and it was rare that he watched live football in his room for that reason. His mom might suspect something if he didn't have a good reason. A good reason to trump watching live football…well, that was kind of hard to think of. If it was a poor game, there wouldn't be anything unusual about turning it off and going upstairs. But it would be unusual not to start watching it. And while Jack was just as addicted to his cellphone as everyone else, he usually focused more on the game than his phone. If he constantly checked his phone while the game was on, his mom might wonder what was going on. So it was safer to leave it upstairs, at least for the first quarter.

The game was absorbing, and Jack actually managed to concentrate on it. Razorbacks versus Crimson Tide on a hot day in Alabama. Two schools with excellent records, head-to-head, and knocking the crap out of each other. Sell-out stadium. Over a hundred thousand packed in. Must be impossible to get tickets. Jack had read one time about fans who would drive a hundred miles in the pre-internet days, just to be within range of college radio to hear the commentary. True commitment.

At half-time, he went upstairs to check for messages. He didn't want to use his cellphone browser to open his fake email, so he had to go through the rigmarole of TAILS and Tor. It was already losing whatever shine it had. At first, there had been comfort in secrecy and a degree of excitement, almost secret agent status. Now there was just grim realisation that this was the path he had chosen, and nothing could stop it. He had become the ball that rolled after Indiana Jones. Ain't nothing beats gravity.

He had four positive replies and one negative – *sorry dude, just sold it*. One email had bounced back, user unknown. He figured that might mean the seller had set up the email just for that transaction and was now done. Either way, not worth wasting time on. And three had either not replied yet, or weren't going to.

One positive reply was via email. The remaining three via text to the burner. His choice had narrowed to two Kel-Tecs, the white Steyr and a Chinese rifle he'd never heard of. He really wasn't keen on the latter. He didn't know why. He'd never fired one. He didn't hate Chinese people or things. He was texting the owner of the Chinese gun using a Chinese-made iPhone and yet the nationality of the gun put him off. Was he being irrational? Racist even? It didn't matter. It looked like he had enough choice. No biggie.

He considered his options quickly. Keep everybody onside. He sent broadly the same message to all four.

"Hi, thanks for getting back to me. Very keen to view and if it's as good as it looks, will buy. Does Wednesday after work work for you? I'm downtown that day. Oh, and can I check if you have extra mags and ammo too? Thanks, Jack."

Wednesday seemed an age away. Jack worried that someone else might beat him to the purchase before then but there wasn't much he could do about it. He had no idea how fast these things sold anyway. Presumably all a matter of supply and demand, price and need. But if he could keep all four warm until Wednesday, then he should be OK.

Two replies came quickly. Wednesday after work would be fine. Clips and ammo would not be a problem. The ease of

235

response to the request for extra bullets made him suspect he was actually dealing with a private individual who ran an unlicensed side-business buying and selling. Not technically legal, as he'd discovered when researching. Not technically legal for the seller, that was. Jack knew perfectly well his side of the transaction was illegal. Boy, did he know that.

He heard his mom calling. Second half about to start. He'd have to wait for any further replies. he shut down the computer, hid the flash drive and went back downstairs, pouring himself a large cold OJ and putting his feet on the coffee table. Football time.

When he returned, he had four replies. Three could do Wednesday, one wanted to meet earlier. He knew from his research that he couldn't say he was from out of town. He needed to be a legal Texas resident. He replied to that seller saying he was tied up until Wednesday, but hopefully nobody would jump ahead of him in the line. They agreed a soft Wednesday time, but Jack sensed the seller was likely to deal before he got there.

The other two were more promising.

A gentleman called Clay had both a Kel Tec and ammunition for sale. He would even throw in a semi-rigid carry case. Jack paused. The last thing he wanted was a case that made it obvious what was in it. But he figured he couldn't say no. He thought most buyers would want one, especially in Texas. He agreed enthusiastically. They agreed to meet downtown in Dallas just after 6 p.m. on Wednesday.

The second seller, Drew, had the Steyr and also wanted to meet just after 6 p.m. on Wednesday. Jack pushed back, asking if 7.30 p.m. was possible, claiming college pressures. He didn't want the Steyr if he could get the Kel Tec. He had no idea which was actually better. But if he could, he would stick with the one he'd already shot. Drew agreed but wanted to meet in the parking lot of his gun range, which was halfway back to the airport, on Mockingbird Lane. Jack quickly did the math. If Clay was a no show, or the sale was a bust, he could just make it. He confirmed 7.30 p.m. He had his insurance seller.

The matter of the case vexed Jack. He needed to be able to bring the weapon and the ammunition back, without it being obvious. He was breaking the law the second he undertook the transaction. But anybody would be breaking the law with that weapon in California. He pondered.

You can't carry a gun case because you can't legally carry a gun. So you need something else.

OK.

You still need to transport the weapon back though.

OK. What if it wasn't a gun? What do I actually need to transport?

Ah. Clever. You need to transport something that's twenty-seven inches long and weighs about seven pounds. And some ammunition that weighs another three or four pounds.

Hockey.

Hockey?

How do people carry hockey sticks? They have bags for those. Field hockey, not ice hockey. They have long bags that you see girls carry over their shoulders.

Yes, dumbfuck. Girls carry them. Boys don't. You've never even played field hockey. If anyone sees you with a hockey bag, they're going to wonder what the fuck is going on. When did you start playing hockey? And more to the point, who do you play with? You can't just wake up and decide to play hockey without there being a team or a club to play with. Is there even a field hockey team in Whittlesford? A boys' one? No. There isn't.

All true. Pity though. The bag would have been plenty long enough.

OK. If not hockey, then what?

How long is the weapon?

Twenty-seven inches.

Could you take it apart? Would it be easier to carry then?

Yes. But then how would I get it into school?

Take it to school broken down into pieces. Go into the washroom, put it together. Come out blazing.

Forget it. Dumb idea. The whole point of getting a bullpup was that they're compact. Small. Easy to transport. About the

237

size of a tennis racket.

A tennis racket?

Yes. A tennis racket.

Oh. This is good. Yes. Google says a tennis racket standard length is twenty-seven inches. That means a tennis racket bag must be longer than twenty-seven inches.

Tennis is a game anyone can play. You don't need someone to play with. You could just be getting lessons. There are public courts everywhere. It isn't impossible that you decide to learn tennis and bring your stuff so you can play after school. Nobody gives two shits what you do anyway.

He went onto Dick's Sporting Goods website. Seventy bucks would get him a bright red semi-rigid Wilson Federer tennis backpack. Twenty-seven and a half inches long, twelve inches wide, twelve inches deep. Apparently big enough for twelve rackets. Not that he cared. He used his ruler to measure out the twelve inches wide and twenty-seven and a half inches long. Then measured the diagonal. Thirty inches, and that didn't include the depth. Plenty big enough.

He moved the mouse toward click and collect and reserved the bag. Almost as an afterthought, he added a special offer racket for twenty-nine bucks. Problem solved.

Chapter Forty-Seven

Jack took a deep breath of smoggy air, his last before running the gauntlet of smokers outside the terminal building at LAX. Some were airport workers in uniform, with their ID cards on lanyards around their necks. Others had clearly just arrived and were sucking down nicotine at their first opportunity since touchdown. He thought they were more stupid than the ones who were taking their last drags before flying away somewhere. The arrivers had obviously gone for enough hours without a cigarette on their journey. They'd clearly managed without one. Those heading for departures, well, it kind of made sense. If the airplane crashed, even Jack wouldn't begrudge them a final cigarette. Heck, even the American Cancer Society would probably understand.

He pushed his way through the ditherers and looked up at the departures board. AA2855 from LAX to Dallas-Fort Worth running as scheduled. He had plenty of time before departure. He could feel the clock ticking down, nonetheless, although that clock was measured in days rather hours.

He felt his wallet tight against his thigh in his jeans pocket. He'd never carried this much cash in his life. Why would he have? Everything these days was done with chip and pin, PayPal or Venmo. Nobody carried cash around anymore. And certainly not over a thousand bucks. His mind wandered, coming up with disaster scenarios where he was interrogated. Why did he have that much cash? Why did he have a return flight to Dallas, but also a single Greyhound bus ticket from Dallas to El Paso? Why go all the way to Dallas, just to spend a few hours there? He didn't have any detail as to who was doing the interrogating, just dark shapes in ominous black uniforms in a police interview room, like in the movies. He found himself mouthing potential excuses and explanations, just talking to himself with no sound. He realised what he was doing and caught himself.

You're not breaking the law flying to Dallas, he told himself. *You're not breaking the law having two ways of getting back. Nobody will stop you, because you're not doing anything wrong.*

Yet. His inner fear counter-punched back. *You're not doing anything illegal yet. But you will be.*

He took another deep breath. *Cross that bridge when you come to it. So far, so good. You've done nothing wrong. You're doing nothing wrong.*

He reached back into the side pocket of the backpack across his shoulders and pulled out the sport water bottle. Drained the last half of it as he approached security and joined the line. The TSA agent at the head of the line barely checked his passport and boarding pass, scrawling a tick mark across the boarding pass with a red ballpoint. Bored. And not wearing ominous black but a gaudier royal blue. Hardly threatening.

In the line for the baggage X-ray, Jack could feel his heart beginning to beat a little harder. Beat, then thump. He focused his mind. Slid out his iPad from the backpack, and the empty water bottle, ready to put them into a tray.

"Shoes."

"I'm sorry?"

"Shoes, young man. You gotta take your shoes off too. Lemme see your belt." Another TSA agent motioned to Jack's waist from the other side of the conveyor. She was short, tubby, and black, efficient but not unfriendly. Almost maternal. She probably thought Jack was a novice or nervous flyer.

He hoisted up his baggy shirt.

"Yeah, we'll need the belt too. That'll set the machine off."

He set the iPad and water bottle in a grey plastic tray. Added his sneakers, wallet and cell. And then unbuckled his belt. It was an old belt, from when the Chargers were in San Diego, but the enamel hadn't chipped off the metal and it still shone. He slid the leather through the loops and took it off. Leaned forward and gently placed it on the tray.

As he straightened up, he felt his jeans start to slide. He had to hastily grab the waistband to stop them falling, although truth be told, it was unlikely they'd have come all the way down. Probably.

The TSA agent was amused and smiled warmly at him.

"You lost a little there, honey? Wish I could!"

He tried to think of a witty answer, but nothing came, so Jack just smiled at her, his face reddening. Stood there like a lemon, waiting his turn to walk through the scanner. A blushing red lemon, but less round than before.

He retrieved his items from the belt on the other side and carried them to the nearest bench. Tucked away the iPad and water bottle, replaced his wallet and carefully threaded the belt back around his waist. Definitely needed it for these jeans. He smiled to himself. It was a gentle little happy smile, that turned sad. A recognition of what he'd achieved, and a recognition that it could never be enough. Would never be enough. Hardly worth trying, but at least he had.

He leaned forward to sling the backpack behind him and stood up. On the way out of security, there was a polling machine where travellers were invited to grade their security experience from a choice of four buttons, each with an emoji ranging from very angry to very smiley. He pushed the very smiley one. He wondered what happened to the results. Would happier travellers make the kind TSA lady's life better? Probably not, but that wasn't a reason not to click it.

Jack still had an hour to kill before boarding. He wandered aimlessly around the terminal, looking at stores who earned most of their money through boredom. Lakers and Dodgers T-shirts that were short on fabric quality and long on price. Bright red hoodies declaring the wearer to be an Official Lifeguard. Fridge magnets as far as the eye could see, gaudy and garish, showing everything from the Hollywood sign to surfboards and bikini bodies. He wasted a few minutes at

Hudsons, skimming through the articles in Sports Illustrated but balking at the six-dollar cover price.

He continued his meandering through the terminal. Saw Starbucks and contemplated a coffee. Declined. Jack figured he looked nervous enough already and caffeine wasn't going to help that. He refilled his water bottle at a faucet instead and sat down near the gate to wait for the flight. It wasn't going to be an especially full flight judging by the other passengers seated there, but that didn't stop three guys in suits aggressively forming a line by the little sign marked for AAdvantage frequent fliers. Jack snorted. Status, status, status. If they had any sense, they'd be sitting down before their flight. It wasn't like they'd have to stand if they didn't board first. But then again, nobody would know they were frequent fliers if they didn't stand by the little sign. *Dicks.*

Activity increased at the gate, and soon Jack and his fellow passengers were filing past the human automata wishing each and all a pleasant flight. Jack had been right. The 11 a.m. flight was barely half full and after take-off, the cabin crew were relaxed about letting passengers spread out and take a little more room. Jack moved back from his aisle seat to let the neighbouring couple have the whole row to themselves, and found an unoccupied row for himself, near the back.

Without Wi-Fi or phone signal, Jack was somewhat lost. No Twitter or Insta to scroll through, no YouTube to kill time. Instead, he pulled out his iPad and plugged in his headphones. He'd downloaded a Netflix documentary series about Aaron Hernandez, the Patriots tight end who'd been convicted of murder and then killed himself in prison. Hernandez had been a ridiculously good player, an absolute beast who'd been feted from high school through the Gators and then in the NFL. And he'd thrown it all away with five bullets in a parking lot in North Attleborough. Jack watched in silence, fully engrossed. His Chargers had drafted Mathews, Butler and Stucky ahead of Hernandez. Maybe it would have ended differently for Hernandez if he'd moved to the west coast, away from his old roots. Maybe, maybe,

maybe. It was all down to chance. Everything was.

As one episode finished, the next started. Jack was rapt with attention. Even though he obviously knew what had happened, the tension was running high. The stewardess had to gently nudge his arm to gain his attention as she pushed the beverage cart back down the aisle. He relented on the caffeine this time, and took a coffee, stifling a yawn. He always yawned on airplanes whether he was tired or not.

He felt his ears start to pop, and squeezed his nose as he blew, to equalize the pressure. The plane was clearly starting to descend. He clicked off his belt and made his way to the restroom at the back. There was no line, but clearly other passengers were starting to have the same idea, stirring to take a last-minute leak before the seatbelt sign came on. He crammed himself into the tiny cubicle and relieved himself. Even with the weight he'd lost, it was still a tight squeeze and he sighed. He cast a glance at himself in the mirror. He'd lost a lot, but he was still a pretty big guy. An inch taller than Hernandez at six foot three, but clearly still a bit heavier than him. Well, maybe not heavier. Fatter for sure.

He returned to his seat and folded up the table. Without iPad or phone, he just stared out of the window as the plane flew down. It never occurred to him to read the in-flight magazine tucked into the pocket in front of him. He just stared and sighed out the window. His escape to the NFL was long forgotten and he felt the pressure build a little in his chest. Even though he could feel his wallet in his jeans pocket, he touched it again through the denim. Still bulging. Still safe.

The ground accelerated up under the wing in front of him. A short screech of tires and then the brakes went on. The belt bit into his waistline as the airplane slowed down. The few passengers in the cabin were reaching for their cell phones, almost synchronised. Jack followed suit.

"Ladies and gentlemen, welcome to Dallas-Fort Worth, where the local time is two minutes to four, Central Standard Time, and the temperature is sixty-eight degrees.

For your safety and comfort, please remain seated with

243

your seat belt fastened until the captain turns off the Fasten Seat Belt sign. At this time, you may use your cell phones if you wish.

Please check around your seat for any personal belongings you may have brought on board with you and please do take care when opening the overhead bins, as heavy articles may have shifted around during the flight.

Dallas-Fort Worth is a non-smoking airport, and we would remind you that you may not smoke at any location inside the terminal building. If you wish to smoke, please refrain from doing so until you have left the terminal.

On behalf of American Airlines and the entire crew, we'd like to say thank you for choosing American for your flight today. We appreciate you have a choice, and we appreciate your custom. We look forward to seeing you on board again in the future and have a nice day."

As Jack joined the line, his phone found signal and flashed up notifications. Group WhatsApp messages. One from his mom. And an SMS alert from the burner app. He opened that first.

Hey Jack, just wanted to make sure you're still good for this evening. I might be a little late but shouldn't be later than half-past, C.

He took a deep breath. So far, so good. He texted back.

Sure, no worries. See you then, J.

He opened WhatsApp. Opened one from his mom. His only message.

Hi honey, hope you're having a great day. All good here, love you xxx

He quickly typed.

All good here too, love you too xxx

He quickly went to the burner app. Sent *Just checking we're still on for this evening* via text to Drew.

He made his way through the terminal. The same tired stores as in LAX, except they'd swapped out the Lakers and Dodgers for the Mavericks and Rangers. Different fridge magnets on the rotating roller displays. One caught his eye and he stopped. It had on a flag of Texas – red, white and blue, with a Colt .45 revolver in the centre. Across the top, it said, "Welcome to Texas." And on the bottom, "We don't dial 911." He snorted and spun the display around. Kept walking to the exit.

He followed the orange signs to the DART Rail and spent three dollars on a ticket. According to his planning, it was about fifty minutes to downtown. He walked to the far end of the platform, figuring he'd be more likely to get a seat than in the middle, even though it was a pretty small train. Strange. On the plane, he'd felt hemmed in and confined and would have been happy to stand. But even after a twenty-minute amble through the airport, he wanted to sit down again.

He found a place and rested. The thin fabric cushion was barely worthy of that description, and he could feel the bones in his butt. Still, better than standing. A family of Far Eastern tourists boarded after him, bouncy kids pointing out of the windows and chattering excitedly to their parents. He craned his neck to see their luggage tags, to try and work out where they were from. The tag said DFW. Doh. Of course it would. Tags say where bags are going, not where they're from. So much for that idea. He scratched his stubble and continued looking around the car.

One of the kids made eye contact with him and he quickly looked away. Stupid, he thought to himself. If you make eye contact with someone, then they're making eye contact with you. So don't look around. It was only then that he realised almost everyone else in the car was on their cell. For some reason, he wasn't. He leaned back a little to make extracting his phone easier. Went to ESPN. As long as he just stared at that, all would be well.

The DART pulled into the West End stop and he lugged his backpack off the tram. Google Maps told him Southern Grit was about a half mile walk. He had time so he walked down Main. Even though it was a pretty simple route – walk one block south and straight along Main for five blocks, he found it hard to resist watching the blue glowing circle record his progress on his cell. *Stupid sheep*, he thought to himself

245

and put the phone back in his pocket.

He started suddenly. *WTF.* Standing in the middle of a neat grass square on his left was a thirty-foot-high plastic eyeball. Shimmering in the afternoon sunshine, a black pupil inside a cornflower blue iris. Thin red blood vessels decorated the white. It stared blankly out. Not at him or anyone else passing. No expression at all. Some kind of modern art. Jack's lip curled down. It didn't even look real. Well, obviously it wasn't real. But good art was all about eyes, making them look happy or sad or piercing or anguished or whatever. Maybe it was the lack of lids or lashes or brows. This just looked like a ridiculous giant toy that had rolled and come to a halt on the lawn outside an expensive hotel, tucked away behind a low metal railing. It reminded him of the Indiana Jones ball. He clenched his jaw and felt his hands go to his hips, his shoulders tight. *Fuck them.*

He kept walking down Main, conscious of time. He didn't want to hang around too long in the diner, even though he wasn't breaking the law. Well, not until the deal was done anyway. He saw a sporting apparel store a half block down and wandered in to kill some time. He idly went through the game jerseys. Something about football jerseys just lifted his mood, even if they were from the Cowboys.

At the back of the store, he saw a bargain bucket, full of remainder items. An idea jumped into his head. His plan did have a weakness, he knew that, but this might help address it more. Without being too obvious. He rifled his way through the T-shirts, looking for what he needed. Found it. A burnt orange Texas Longhorns football tee, in Large, and most importantly with the letters printed high on the front of the chest. He grimaced at the fabric quality. Or lack of it. One of those annoying tees where the block print itched and scratched. Ten bucks plus tax. Worth it.

He paid for the tee with his bank card, holding his wallet low behind the counter, not wanting the clerk to see how much cash he was carrying. Then jammed it into his backpack. He didn't want a plastic bag with the store's logo on it. On its own, it might have been OK. Together, it might be overkill. He left and returned to main. It was nearly six. Showtime. He could feel his heart start to quicken in and of itself, but he didn't feel especially nervous. What was going to happen, was going to happen, and nothing could stop it. Ain't nothing beats gravity.

The diner was busy at the bar, locals staring at sports on screens above the shelves of spirits, but quiet in the seating area. A diminutive server in a denim blouse and pink cowboy boots approached but he motioned that he needed the restroom first, and she smiled and nodded, pointing in back, down the stairs. He pushed on the door marked for men with a foot high cowboy riding a bucking steer with what looked like plastic horns at the front. The women's door had a line-dancer in pink boots and check shirt contrasting her blue denims.

The restroom was an odd shape, jammed into the cellar and way too small for the size of the bar. Its saving grace was that its solitary cubicle was an actual separate room, with a proper wooden door. A tiny room, yes, but better than one of those metal cubicles, with a big gap under the door and a crack that always made Jack feel he was being watched while he took a dump. Inside, he put on his new tee and replaced the shirt over the top. He was going to be too warm, and the tee itched already, especially the label at the back. He took it off again. Jammed his finger in the loop and ripped the label off. It came away, tearing a hole in the back of the collar. Didn't matter. That would be hidden by his shirt collar anyway. And Clay would be sitting opposite. He replaced the shirt. Paranoia made him flush the cistern. He didn't want anyone to know that he had gone to the bathroom not to use the bathroom. Overthinking it.

He came out of the cubicle and noticed a guy at the urinal. Golden rule of anywhere, never talk to a stranger in the restroom. And definitely not in Texas. He turned on the faucet and washed his hands. As he soaped, he noticed his Chargers belt buckle, blue and gold. He quickly pulled his shirt out of his waistband so the tail would cover it. The movement was not without irony. He'd worn baggy tops

247

forever and being able to tuck them in without tapping a huge gut bulge had been an achievement. Now he needed to go baggy again. Overthinking it again? Probably.

He went back into the diner and found himself a booth in the corner. It was a dark, rustic kind of place. Wooden booths and dark red plastic tabletops. Almost every spare space on the wall was covered in football memorabilia, Cowboys and college ball. What wasn't covered with football pictures was pretty much covered with Rangers baseball prints or Texas flags. And what was left was covered by pictures of real cowboys, not the ones with helmets and image rights contracts.

He pulled out his phone and saw a text from Clay to the burner app.

On my way. Should be on time, C.

He typed back:

Cool. Just arrived. Seated in back corner. Want anything? J

Fuck. He shouldn't have done that. What if Clay wanted a beer? And the server carded him? Even his fake ID said eighteen, not twenty-one. Then everything would be fucked. Fuck, fuck, fuck. Stupid, stupid, stupid.

His cell pinged again.

I'll have a Deep Ellum, thx, C.

Fuck. Here goes nothing. And everything. A thought crossed his mind.

He made eye contact with the server, and she made her way over. As she did so, he pretended that his eye had been caught by one of the pictures by the booth and he stood up to get a better look at it, craning his neck in the dim light. When she arrived, he towered over her by a good foot. Six foot three versus five foot three. The top of her head barely reached the bottom of his chin.

"What'll it be?" she smiled up at him. Smiles mean tips. Or maybe she was just a smiley person.

"Uh, can I get a coke please. And…" He looked at his phone even though he knew what the order was. "And a Deep Ellum?"

"Sure, you want me to start a tab? Will you be dining?"

"Uh, yes to tab, maybe to dining." He handed her his bank card and received a laminate card in return. Number nine. Obviously not busy yet. Or maybe the locals at the bar didn't need laminate cards to run their tabs.

She headed back to the bar and Jack consciously carried on staring at the wall as he took a deep breath. That could have been disastrous.

He settled in his seat and prepared to wait. Undid the top two buttons of his shirt. The horns of the steer and the Texas letters were now much more visible. His San Diego belt buckle was hidden below his untucked shirt and in any case, below the line of the table. He had a good view of the diner, had a good view of the sports on TV, and had a good view of the entrance.

A different server came over with the drinks on a tray. A younger guy, maybe a student himself, with an aggressively sculpted beard. But also, maybe better at determining the ages of those close to him in age. Jack imagined that he hesitated as the server looked at the beer and then at Jack.

Jack took the initiative.

"Coke for me, and the beer goes there." He motioned to the empty seat opposite and then checked his watch.

"Ah cool."

Jack took a sip of the coke and checked his cell. Nothing from the burner app. Suddenly a WhatsApp from his mom.

Clay had arrived. Jack couldn't be sure it was Clay, but the man who had just walked in the diner had looked straight to the back corner and mouthed "Are you Jack?" at him. Jack gave him a friendly wave and nodded. Thank fuck. Clay was short, maybe five foot eight at most, but obviously in his thirties or forties. His beard was grey, and his eyes lined. On his hip, he nonchalantly wore a brown leather holster with the black grip of a pistol protruding. He had a Cowboys backpack on his shoulders and a long-padded Remington bag in his left hand. His right hand was free to reach for the pistol if he needed.

The server followed Jack's wave with his eyes, saw Clay

approaching. He waved. Clay was obviously a regular. Then placed the beer down opposite the empty bench.

"Well, good evening, Clay. How are you today?"

"Hey Tommy, I'm good, thank you for asking." He motioned to the gun case. "Are you OK if we do this in here, or you want that we go out back to the parking lot?"

"Clay, you're part of the furniture. Y'all can stay in here. It'd be nice if you actually ate something once in a while though." The server smiled and glided off in the direction of his station.

Jack stood to greet Clay, dwarfing him by a good six inches. They shook hands.

"Thanks for the beer, you not having one?" Clay drawled, the words as smooth and southern as stoneground grits.

"Nah, I'm thinking I might shoot this evening."

"Hell, that shouldn't stop you," cackled Clay. "God bless Texas." He chuckled, and Jack joined in.

"How come you're selling it?" asked Jack. "Beautiful gun like that. You trading up?"

Clay's face fell a fraction.

"I wish. Long story short, my wife got sick plus they cut her hours where she works. And we don't got good medical insurance, so I need to thin down the collection some. I sold the foreign guns first, obviously. Wanted to hold on to my American ones. At least, as long as I could. But now, she got to go."

Jack etched sympathy on his face. Brought a hand up to his thick stubble and scratched.

"Man, that's tough. I'm real sorry to hear that. I hope she's well now, well, better anyways?" Jack wasn't stupid enough to try and match Clay's southern accent, but he figured that matching the vocabulary wouldn't hurt. Although of course, this could be a bargaining ploy by Clay to avoid discounting.

"Yeah, she's mending. Just a little tough, and that's why this needs to go."

Clay placed the case on the table between them, the zip facing Jack. He reached over and deftly opened it up. Inside was the gently gleaming black rifle. The saw-toothed rail on the top for fitting the scope gave it additional menace.

"Here she is. One Kel Tec RDB, as discussed." He slid the case across the table.

Jack looked around the diner. Nobody had batted so much as an eyelid. He realised now that Clay was far from the only person wearing a pistol on his hip.

Clay chuckled again.

"It's OK, Jack. I've sold a couple in here, and they don't mind as long as you don't wave it around any. Heck, they got quite a collection in back themselves, but I didn't tell you that."

Jack slid toward the outer edge of the bench seat, freeing up some room between him and the wall to examine the weapon more closely. It looked and felt exactly like the one he'd used on the range in Vegas. The grip which had a little wear on it but nothing too major. The manufacturer's name and origin were marked out on the side, above the grip. He held the gun in his right hand and ran the index finger of his left along the barrel. The markings felt solid.

He thumbed the safety on and off. It snapped into place with a reassuring noise. No travel, no play in the switch. Good.

The weapon already had a magazine in it. He thumbed the release catch and it clicked cleanly, the magazine falling out into his hand below. He inserted the other two magazines from the case into the gun and repeated the process. They both fit, and they both released smoothly. He pushed down on the magazine springs, and they felt firm and strong. Good so far.

Clay watched over the top of his beer.

"Were you in the service, Jack? You look like you know what you're doing. Most folks check the gun and forget about the magazines."

"Nah, Dad is, though. Maybe I'll follow." Jack could have kicked himself. He'd meant to just be polite, even though he knew he wouldn't get the choice to do anything once it was done. And now he'd opened up a potential conversation.

Clay barely noticed.

251

"I, uh, found another magazine for her," he said. "Hence why you've got four there, rather than the three we discussed on the phone."

"Cool. That'd be great."

Jack held the weapon below the line of the table, pointing toward the wall. Racked the slide back to cock the action and then dry-fired it. It was smooth. He repeated the test a couple of times and then put each of the magazines back into the pistol in turn to make sure they caught the action when he racked it back on empty. All good.

"That looks good to me," he said. "Did you remember the ammunition too?"

Clay nodded but didn't move.

Jack took the hint, and replaced the weapon and magazines in the case, and zipped it shut. Slid it along the table against the wall. Demonstrably a bit further out of reach. Public place or not, pistol on the hip or not, no seller in their right mind would ever hand over a loaded gun to a potential buyer.

Clay reached into his backpack and pulled out an olive green metal ammunition can. The sticker on the side stated the contents, along with a barcode. 420 rounds of Federal 5.56 millimetre, fifty-five grains in weight, full metal jacket.

Jack quickly opened the can, breaking the seal and checked the contents. He counted the cardboard boxes contained within. Fourteen boxes containing thirty rounds each. 420 shots in total. If he got one in four right, that covered a hundred. With twenty left over. He would need more magazines though. Ten more, in fact.

He nodded appreciatively as he placed the boxes back in the can.

"I've heard good things about these ones," he said. "Never shot them myself, though."

Clay cackled again.

"They're darn good," he said. "She's the last of my guns that fires those, so I figured you might as well take them off my hands in one go. Y'all getting a bargain there."

"So…"

"So…" and Clay laughed again. "Well, Jack, I'm thinking you want to pay less than I want you to pay, and I want you to pay more than you want me to accept. But how about we stick with the original amount, and you get the extra magazine for free?"

Jack scratched his stubble and pretended to think about it. He just wanted to get it over and done with. He smiled broadly and stretched his hand across the table.

"Eleven hundred?"

"Eleven hundred."

They shook for the second time that evening.

Clay made an apologetic face and pulled a piece of paper from his bag.

"I am sorry about this," he said, "but it's just easier to do the damn paperwork."

Jack was surprised but laughed, pulling the exact same form out of his bag. They'd both clearly downloaded and printed it from the same website. Clay had filled in his side already, so Jack took that. Scrunched up his copy and tossed it back in his bag. It wouldn't do to forget it. Just in case.

He checked quickly through the list of legal exclusions. Was neither a felon, a fugitive, nor a fruitloop. Under Texas law, he passed ten of the eleven exclusions to complete the sale. On the eleventh, he'd just have to lie.

He noted Clay's address on his side of the form. Pleasingly nowhere near Jack's fictitious address in Arlington, which he entered. He had a back-up address in case, one he'd found and memorised after a property search on Zillow. He reached in his pocket for his wallet and took out eleven one-hundred-dollar bills and counted them out on the table to Clay. Clay nodded and inspected them, counting them out himself. Satisfied.

Jack waited.

As Clay reached for his own wallet to put the bills away, Jack pretended to check his drivers' license in its wallet, to enter the number on the form. After all, who actually remembered their driver's license number?

He didn't slide the Texas license fully out of its little slip in his wallet, because it was a fake. It looked plausible to him, in fact it looked darn good, but he'd never seen a real one before. Why take the risk? The DL number was at the top, as was the Texas logo. So he just half slid the plastic card out and made a point of concentrating as he scribbled.

The fact that Clay had filled in his side of the bill of sale was helpful. It showed Clay's driver license number. A California license number was one letter followed by seven digits. A Texas license number was eight digits. If Jack had filled in a fictitious number first, there was an infinitely small possibility that he might have come up with the same eight digits as Clay. Unlikely. But not impossible. As long as the eight digits he wrote in weren't the same as Clay's, he was good.

He signed the form at the bottom. Didn't ask Clay to see his license to check his license. If Jack had asked for Clay's, then Clay might have asked for Jack's. So, he didn't. Just signed the form. Deal done. He took out his phone and took a picture of it.

"You can keep the paper," he said, sliding it back across the table to Clay. "I got my copy here now." He took the ammunition can and put it in his backpack. Zipped it shut.

"Sounds good."

Clay drained his beer.

"Well, Jack, it's been a pleasure doing business with you. I hope you enjoy her as much as I did."

Jack smiled.

"I'm sure I will, Clay. And I do hope your wife gets better."

"Thank you. So long."

Jack took a deep breath as he watched Clay's receding back. Saw him pause for a brief chat with the server. Jack took a sip of his coke. Looked at his watch. He'd made better time than he could have hoped for. But now he had longer to wait. With a gun he wasn't legally allowed to have. Even in Texas, that was bad.

First things first. Out of nothing more than decency, he texted Drew. Apologies but something had come up and he wouldn't be able to make it to the range this evening. Then he deleted the burner app and the number. He didn't need them anymore.

He then waved to the server and scrawled a signature in mid-air. The check came to twelve bucks. He tipped three but paid in cash. Not too much to be memorable, not too little to attract attention. And no electronic trail that he was ever in that bar. He finished his coke and went back to the restroom and into the tiny cubicle. He removed the itchy, scratchy Longhorns tee. He consciously buttoned his shirt higher, to hide the lack of the logo.

He then flushed the toilet to generate some noise to cover what he was about to do.

He took the fourteen carboard boxes of bullets out of the aluminium ammunition can, and placed the boxes back in the backpack, wrapping them in the Longhorns tee. The ammunition can stay on the floor, behind the cubicle door. The gun itself came out of the Remington bag and into the tennis backpack. It fit perfectly, the backpack's rigidity making it look full of tennis rackets. Innocent. There was plenty of room left in the bag.

He pondered. Which to dump? The can or the bag. The can, preferably. He rolled up the soft gun case into a fat burrito and jammed it into the backpack.

Then he paused, waiting for the cistern to finish refilling. He tried to listen through the door. What he'd gained in privacy, he'd lost in vigilance. It didn't sound like there was anybody in the restroom. He cast his mind back to the layout. Where was the trashcan? Under the towel dispenser. It was one of those stainless-steel ones, embedded into the wall.

He took a deep breath and opened the door. If another patron had been in the restroom, he would have just quickly rinsed his hands and gone, leaving the ammunition can behind the door of the cubicle. As it was empty, he quickly reached down and picked it up, walked smartly to the trashcan and jammed it to the bottom. He grabbed several fistfuls of paper towels and dumped them on top, concealing it. With any luck, nobody would notice until the end of the night. He wasn't breaking the law by throwing the ammunition can, but it felt like it. He was nervous and skittish and just wanted to leave the scene of the crime as quickly as possible. The door to the restroom opened and a patron came in. Another boot-wearing elderly cowboy, with a pancake holster on his hip. Jack rinsed his hands under the faucet and then dried, adding extra paper towels to the layers of concealment.

He doublechecked that the backpack was fully zipped shut, then hoisted it up onto his shoulders. The weight wasn't actually too bad. Not compared to all the crap he usually carried around, schoolbooks and iPad and so on. He walked up the stairs and then smartly left the bar. Nobody noticed him leave, but to Jack, it felt like all eyes were on him. He was openly carrying a gun he wasn't legally allowed to have, along with over four hundred rounds of ammunition. So what if carrying a gun in a case wasn't illegal in Texas? It was illegal for him. If they caught him, they'd throw away the key. He put his sunglasses on, imagining that they would stop him blushing.

He walked back along Main, past the staring, glaring eye. It knew his bag didn't contain tennis rackets. He needed to get back to California. Get away from the scene of the crime. Well, away from the scene of this crime. But he couldn't fly. He knew that. A flight would have been quicker and cheaper and more convenient. Three hours and fifteen minutes in the air. But for obvious reasons, he couldn't fly.

For a moment, he considered abandoning all his carefully laid-out plans and wondered if he could post the gun. Did USPS usually scan regular parcels? No. That would be madness. Stick with the plan. Plans are made in slow-time to stop you doing something stupid in quick-time. Stick to the plan.

He passed a hip coffee shop, advertising free Wi-Fi and the best buzz downtown. Five apple laptops sat at the counter looking out the window, like targets at a funfair, with their hipster humans tapping away behind them. Two bushy-bearded men in check shirts and boots, two relatively hot girls with white headphones, 1 harassed-looking mom-type. He ordered a decaf from the barista and found a seat in back. The tiny little tables with tiny little seats were taken, so he took a larger table and hoped nobody would join him. At least this was not the kind of place he would expect to bump into Clay. He needed to charge his phone and check his transport options in real time versus what he had booked. A better option might have presented itself.

He checked carpool and hitchhiker websites. No dice. Nobody leaving imminently from downtown Dallas to California. Unsurprising. And also, to be honest, a good thing. He really wasn't sure he could cope with any conversation.

He typed Greyhound Dallas into his iPad. Amid the first page of Google results, he saw a homeless man had stabbed a passenger the night before at the bus terminal. Another vote against waiting around the terminal at night. He'd have to find somewhere else to hang out. But the buses were running to time, according to the website. Good. Stick with the original plan then.

Bus to El Paso. Get out of Dallas. Maybe not as quick as he would have liked, but at least he'd be heading in the right direction. Then get the train from El Paso as planned.

He'd be sacrificing privacy on the first leg in return for it on the second leg. The first leg would be overnight. Even if his fellow passengers weren't asleep, Jack could pretend he was. Minimise contact. Minimise conversation. Avoid being memorable.

That left him a few hours to kill in Dallas before the Greyhound left. He needed to find something to do, somewhere to go, where nobody would look in his bag, nobody would talk to him, nobody would hear his heart pounding through his chest. He had planned to just wait at the Bus Terminal, minding his own business in a waiting room, but the news item had put him off. Even if nothing happened to him, he didn't want to be anywhere where cops might show up. Don't take the risk.

He tapped on Google Maps. All the attractions nearby

were closed or about to. Museums, zoo, gallery. All closed in the evening. And he didn't want to go to a bar or a diner. Too many people. He flicked his thumb on the map. Perfect. A movie theatre. He could sit in a movie. Kill time. Save battery. And be unnoticed.

It was about six blocks away from the coffee house, and two away from the bus terminal. If he killed a little more time while it was still light, he could watch a late show in the movie theatre and then go direct to the bus terminal.

He checked the listings. It was a multiplex with eleven screens. He scrolled down on his iPad, not looking at the movies, but looking at the start times. Amongst the blockbusters and the rom-coms and the CGI sci-fi, they had some classics. *Joker*. And a double feature. *Godfather* and *Godfather II*, back-to-back. Together they added up to over six hours of run time.

He bought a ticket on his cell. Belatedly realised it was even better than he had thought. A single man sulking into a rom-com might have been memorable. Unusual. A rom-com was more date night, he figured. For couples. Not for a single. Whereas two old classic movies would be for film buffs. Nerds. And nerds can go to a movie theatre on their own without attracting attention. He would have to leave before the end of the sequel, but no big deal. He'd seen it before. He knew how it ended. For Fredo, at least.

He had an hour to kill in the coffee place. Figured it would look more normally to be wasting time there rather than showing up at the movie theatre over an hour early. All around him, the other patrons seemed to be doing the same. The place was surprisingly busy. He plugged his cell in to recharge it and lost himself in ESPN.

"Excuse me, sir."

Jack was lost in his own world.

"EXCUSE me, sir!"

He jumped in his seat. Looked up, startled. His heart rate instantly doubled, trebled. Two cops towered over him. A man and a woman. Menacing midnight blue uniforms with shiny silver buttons. Shiny five-point stars over their hearts,

Dallas PD patches on the shoulder, name badges on the right chest. And dark, deadly guns in leather holsters on belts around their waists.

His mind raced as fast as his heart. How could they have found him so fast? How had he given himself away. He glanced involuntarily at the backpack by his feet. Why had Clay snitched? How had he given himself away? How was he-

The female officer spoke again, unsmiling. Officer Rosario according to her name badge.

"Excuse me, sir, do you mind if we sit here?" she motioned around the room. While Jack had been lost on the internet, the room had filled up some more. Jack's table was the only one with spare seats.

"Um-sure-sorry-I-didn't-hear-you," he babbled, a bag of nerves. Was that all it was? Somewhere to sit? Or did they just want to make sure he couldn't reach for the gun. The illegal, felonious gun and over four hundred rounds of ammunition resting on his feet.

"Thank you, sir." Polite words but angsty. Maybe she'd been trying to catch his attention for a while. Maybe she'd had a shitty shift. Either way, the fabled southern hospitality was totally absent. He picked up his coffee cup and moved it closer to him, even though it wasn't in the way. Just to show that he was making space for them. A third officer joined them, carrying three cups.

Jack's heart was slowing its pace but still thumping intensely. What now? What if they wanted to talk to him? Should he leave now, or would that be more suspicious? Cops had a sixth sense, didn't they? Would they smell the liquid fear that was oozing out of his pores, that he was exhaling with every breath? He must be radioactive with nerves, positively glowing with fear.

Self-consciously, he smiled at the three of them and forced himself to stare again at his cell. Shifted to Sports Illustrated. Tried to pretend he was totally engrossed in a story he'd read already, while also trying to appear completely uninterested in their conversation, organising an inter-precinct softball tournament and barbecue. The officer who'd bought the coffees was making notes on a pad.

He'd figured out they hadn't come to arrest him, but that didn't mean they still couldn't. Or wouldn't. He had to appear normal. Yeah right. He couldn't even remember what normal was right now, whether in a coffee place or anyplace else. His mind couldn't help bouncing from one tangent to another. Could they search his bag? He knew he was nervous. He knew they knew. Would they assume he was carrying drugs? Surely that would be the standard suspicion? Student, college age-ish. Standard crimes of under-age drinking or smoking weed. He wasn't doing either but that didn't mean they couldn't search him. Did it? A nervous tic leapt in his gullet and made him yawn. He tilted his head back and covered his mouth.

To be normal, he had to do what he was going to do anyway. Kill time in the coffee place until it was movie time. Whether surrounded by Dallas' finest or not. He forced himself to scroll through sports he normally didn't follow. Forced himself to keep his thumb moving, to make it obvious that he was actually doing something. Every so often, even though he could see the time on his phone, he couldn't help looking up at the clock on the wall. The hands were crawling around. He'd never realised a minute could be so long. How would he survive sixty of them?

He didn't have to.

After twenty or so minutes, Officer Rosario looked at her watch. The three of them drained the dregs from their mugs, then stretched in synchronisation. Nodded briefly at Jack and then departed, placing the cups back on the counter as they left.

Jack exhaled for a long, slow minute. He couldn't believe his luck. Both the bad and the good. It could so easily have been over. He'd have been locked up. He'd have been famous at Whittlesford as the kid who couldn't even buy a gun in Dallas. He could imagine the conversations.

"Hey bro, did you hear about Shamu?"
"No, what?"

260

"He thought he'd go get a gun and shoot up the school. But the fat fuck couldn't even get that right!"

"No way! What happened?"

"He got arrested with a rifle. In fucking Texas!"

"Oh man. In Texas?" How the fuck do you get arrested in Texas? Did he try and hold up a Krispy Kreme full of cops?"

"Lol. Probably"

Fuck them. He had what he needed, and he was coming.

He killed time in the coffee place until the patrons started thinning out. He didn't want to be memorable and be asked to leave at the end. Walked the half a dozen blocks to the theatre, arriving in perfect time. He loaded up on candy and a coke. For the next few hours, he needed to stay awake and anonymous. And within reach of the restroom.

There was a small line waiting to go into that auditorium. He was right. It was mainly men on their own, mainly pallid, and more than half wore eyeglasses. Film nerd night. The bored teller barely glanced at their cells. They all had e-tickets. Nobody had bought a paper one at the desk. Nerds are good with tech.

He took an aisle seat near the back of the theatre. Back right, close to the exit for the restroom. The cushion was firm, not well-used. But not on the back row in case any couples came in and started fooling around. Stay solitary. The theatre was barely a quarter full, with the audience concentrated in the prime viewing spots. Middle, middle. The clock ticked over to 8 p.m., the lights went down and Bonasera believed in America while Brando glowered at his desk. When Sonny got shot at the causeway, he used the loud gunshots as cover to quickly remove the gun bag burrito from his rucksack and jam it under the seat in front.

His bladder held out until about two hours in. He quickly went to the restroom, and took the opportunity to check his phone, using the cubicle even though he only needed a piss. Replied to his mom and sent a quick good night WhatsApp. *Love you too xxx*. Send. He didn't ignore his other messages because he didn't have any other messages. Just his mom.

He stayed in his seat during the intermission between the

movies. Head down, pretending to geek out and read his phone. Avoiding the conversations that were striking up between fellow movie buffs as they ambled out to stretch their legs, reload on snacks, or take a leak before the sequel.

Around ten to midnight, he got up and quietly left. There was only one clerk left in the foyer, disinterested and surfing the net on his phone. He only looked up as Jack pushed through the exit door and slipped away. All he would have seen was the backpack. Chubby tennis kid who liked movies. Whatever.

The streets were almost empty as he walked to the bus terminal. A couple of bums, snoring in their doorways. A smartly dressed couple holding hands as they walked to their car from an Italian restaurant. Late night date night. But no groups of young men. Or single young men. Jack was wary. He needed to get on the bus and get out of Dallas. That was all.

He'd catastrophised about every possible let-down at the bus terminal. He was wrong. It was brightly lit, antiseptic. No shadows or hidey-holes for bad guys to lurk. There were only five people waiting to board his bus. Two young black women, chubby in jeggings, standing next to each other but ignoring each other on their phones. Two men who looked military. Shaven heads and standing tall, even at midnight. Talking quietly to one another and watchful of everything around them. And a yawning blonde, maybe twenty, wearing a blue hoodie with Sverige picked out in bright yellow applique. She wanted to take her huge backpack onto the bus, but the driver insisted she stow it. She fished out her iPad and headphones for the journey and agreed, smiling at him.

Jack found an empty double seat, near the stench of the onboard restroom at the back. He figured nobody would want to join him. He placed his backpack on the floor in front of him and set his feet to the sides. It was a squeeze, but worth it. He leaned forward and untied his sneaker. Retied the laces around the shoulder strap of the backpack. Nobody would be able to move it without him noticing. He yawned and set his head against the headrest, smooth and cool. He was exhausted.

He woke up eleven hours later, on the outskirts of El Paso.

Initially disoriented, he couldn't believe he'd slept straight through. His first thought was the backpack. He pushed at it with his feet. He could feel the gun case in there, solid and reassuring. He undid his lace and hoisted the backpack onto his lap. Turned to the window to unzip it. All good.

He had just under two hours until his train left, but he wasn't in the mood to sightsee. He was stiff from the confined space, and he thought he stank. He'd been wearing the same clothes for more than twenty-four hours. He hadn't taken his sneakers off once. His jeans felt like they were sticking to his crotch and his ass. Disgusting.

He made the half mile to the train station on foot, shrugging his shoulders and clicking his back out as he walked the smooth asphalt. Started to feel a little more human again, yawning in the bright daylight. He hadn't realised he was hungry until he caught the waft of a food court by Union Plaza. Then suddenly he realised how empty his stomach was. Starving. He had time. He picked up a chicken burrito and ate it quickly at a metal table. He checked his watch. More or less the correct time to respond to the usual morning WhatsApp from his mom.

The train depot looked a little like a church, with a redbrick bell tower at one end. Maybe a lot like a church. It was nearly empty, save for a group of elderly women staring in unison at the announcements board, fixed to the checkered black and white floor like chess pieces. A dozen queens, with matching dark overnight suitcases on wheels. A tour group. Jack hung back, slinking into the corner.

The track was announced, and the white queens advanced in formation, heels clacking on the marble, overnight bags rolling in each wake. Jack followed suit, sneakers squeaking. The ladies boarded the front, their bags stowed by a tip-hopeful porter.

Jack checked his ticket and found his bedroom on the upper deck. It was smaller than it had appeared on the Amtrak website, but the same size as on TripAdvisor. Figured. The attendant greeted him with a plastic smile and reeled off a standard welcome, detailing sights along the way and mealtimes. He picked up on Jack's polite yawn and slid away. Jack locked the door behind him. For the first time since Clay had walked into Southern Grit, he felt he could relax a little. Breathe.

He opened his backpack and pulled out his cables. Started recharging phone and iPad. It was still a long way till California. He paused. He wanted to check the gun. He'd locked the door from the inside but still. The attendant could probably force it open. He knew he was being paranoid, but it was worth it. He double, triple-checked the door was locked and went into the tiny windowless bathroom cubicle. Sat on the rim and closed the door behind him. The gun was still there, the magazines were still there, the ammunition was still there. The train whistled and pulled off. Heading west.

Jack exhaled deeply. Then inhaled. He was sure he stank. He took a longer shower than he thought he would, the water hot and plentiful. The soap provided lathered into rich suds, and he enjoyed the sensation of being clean again. He scrubbed hard at his face and scraped dead skin away from the side of his nose and the dimple of his chin with his fingernail. Wrapped a towel around his waist and sat lengthways on the couch, staring out the picture window at the passing dry scenery as he dried. He felt human again. Normal. Even with an illegally purchased rifle and 420 bullets tucked away at the bottom of his backpack.

The Wi-Fi on the journey was crappy, so he had to resort to stuff he'd already downloaded on Netflix. No big deal. He had a ton of sports documentaries, and he left the iPad plugged in so he didn't drain the battery. He kept a close eye on the time and made sure he didn't go onto WhatsApp at a time when he wouldn't usually be able to access his phone. The time passed in comfort. The couch was a decent size, even for a big guy. A fresh set of underwear and a clean tee had made all the difference to his mood.

He took what felt like a chance at dinner time. He was hungry again. He could have ordered a tray dinner to his compartment, but the menu was uninspiring. The pictures on the card looked good in quality but lacking in quantity.

He decided to risk the dining car, where there was a greater choice. He took his backpack with him and pretended to be engrossed in the news from his iPad while he ate. The dining car was quiet. Who travelled on overnight trains anymore anyways? The attendant left him alone while he ate his flat iron steak and a baked potato. New York cheesecake after. He needed it.

After dinner, he went back to his compartment. The couch had been turned into a bed. It was actually a decent size. And comfortable. He locked the door, pulled the curtain closed and turned the lights down. Whatsapped good night to his mom.

He stretched out, a full stomach of contentment. Closed his eyes and enjoyed the rhythm of the train, a repetitive and soothing lullaby from the rails below him. His mind wandered. He checked the signal on his phone. Five bars. He figured the train Wi-Fi would block what he needed. He double checked the door. Still locked. He kicked off his jeans and his T-shirt. Went onto PornHub. Scrolled through thumbnails. Gonzo, gonzo, gonzo. He selected a cute young brunette college girl with a nice smile. Demure. He started playing with his cock while he watched her seduce the nerdy stud. He kept the noise down low, even with the locked door and the sound of the train. Imagined her lips on him, on his mouth, everywhere. He brought himself close and then backed off. Did it again. And then accelerated until he came all over his stomach, thick and heavy. He paused and sighed. It was good, but. But, but, but. He sighed again and walked gingerly to the little bathroom to clean himself up.

The train pulled into Los Angeles just before 6 a.m. the next morning. Must have picked up some delay overnight. Jack had woken early, after a short but thoroughly refreshing sleep. Beating off had relaxed him, and it had also driven his dreams. His mind had wandered to a world where the girl in the porn flick was his sweet girlfriend and they hung out and did boyfriend/girlfriend stuff as well as fuck. She held his hand and made out with him and slept with her head on his lap while he watched football. Sometimes she made him a sandwich. Despite the early hour and the reality which greeted him, he felt warm and content as he showered and dressed. And even though he still had an illegally held rifle and 420 rounds of ammunition in a state which really didn't like them, he was much more relaxed now he was back on home turf. Time to get back to Whittlesford.

Chapter Forty-Eight

Jack had less than twenty-four hours left.

He hadn't put it in the diary on his phone, hadn't set a countdown. But he knew he had less than twenty-four hours left. He wasn't sure what he felt about that. Surely he should feel something. But he just didn't. It was going to happen, and nothing was going to change that. In less than twenty-four hours. He couldn't stop it if he tried. And he wasn't actually sure if he wanted to. Stop it, that was. It really wasn't up to him anymore. It never really had been.

He looked around his room, neatish and tidyish, like normal. No cat on the bed today. He didn't read anything into it. Cats did what they liked, when they liked, after all. Besides, he'd be back at some point. For food or attention or just a comfortable spot to stretch out. It was probably better that he wasn't there. Jack had a couple of things to do before his last day.

He quickly walked downstairs and checked that his mom was still out. He could have called, but then what if she had answered? Better to pretend he was going downstairs for a drink or a snack. She wasn't home yet. He looked at the clock on the stove. He definitely had another hour at least. And if she was early, either she might call to ask if he wanted take-out on the way, or he'd hear the car arrive.

He went back to his room and thought for a moment. He stood by the door, looking in, and pulled out his phone. He took a picture of his room, of what anyone would see if they were looking in. Then he folded the duvet back. If he was interrupted, he could just dump the evidence on the sheet, pull the duvet over it and hope the bumps weren't noticed.

He put his cellphone on the mattress, face up. He needed to see if it rang. For the next fifteen minutes, he carefully loaded bullets into magazines. Counting them in, as he pressed his thumb against the shiny brass casing. They came packed in groups of ten so he didn't need to count. The first cartridge of each magazine slipped in easily, becoming progressively harder until the thirtieth. The spring was pushing back much harder by then, and it left a mark on his thumb. No matter, it would fade quickly.

When he had finished loading, he checked the time again. Still plenty of time. He placed them back in the tennis backpack, added in his racket, then threw in a towel. He considered adding smelly, worn kit for a moment. Would that discourage Mom if, for some unknown reason, she looked? Probably not. She would more likely shout at him and tip the bag out. But she wasn't likely to look. She never had before. Not as far as he knew. He added in clean kit. If she opened it, which she wouldn't, there would be no reason to go digging deeper into the bag.

The weapon itself, hmm. He could put it in the bag. But it wouldn't be hidden. He slid it under the mattress, tucked up against the wall. He slept in the middle of his bed. He wouldn't notice it. And the weapon was thin enough and the mattress soft enough, even at the edges, that you couldn't tell there was anything hidden.

He replaced the bag at the bottom of his wardrobe then stood at his bedroom door, looking in. He compared what he saw to the picture he'd taken before starting the task. Like a spot the difference competition in the funny pages when he was a kid. He couldn't see any difference. His room just looked normal.

He went to his bed and sat on it, as he had done thousands of times before. Leaned against all his pillows and cushions and the headboard. He exhaled, a long breezy sigh. It was a resigned sigh. Not long to go.

Chapter Forty-Nine

Jack had awoken early that morning. Or maybe he hadn't slept. A bit of both. He stayed under his duvet, in the middle of the mattress. If he pushed his weight into the side near the wall, he could feel the weapon underneath him. But who sleeps right up in the corner of a double bed, when they sleep alone? Nobody. And Jack slept alone that night, as he always had. He levered himself up and stared into space. He knew he would never share a bed with a girl. He hadn't managed it yet. And today was his last day. It was a shame. He would have liked to wake up with a girl one day. Maybe make her breakfast and bring it to her as she dozed, bedswept hair and cute tousles. It was not to be. Today was his last day.

Mr. Orange was at the foot of the bed, in the corner. During the night, if he joined Jack, he would usually seek out comfortable bends in Jack's body, like behind his knees. If Jack was having a restless night, he would retreat to the foot. Close enough for protection, but not so close he would be woken. He had snuggled up to Jack when he couldn't sleep but was still, then moved when Jack had sat up. Now he was curled up like a shrimp, his front paws holding his back paws, and his tail half resting over his eyes. His own private curtain. He was half awake, his eyes were open, but the grey of the inner eyelids visible through the orange tufts of tail.

Jack tried to call him over. He sucked on his lip and then flicked his tongue against the roof of his mouth. His cat stirred. His friend. Mr. Orange slowly raised his head and yawned. Stretched out front paws while lying on his side. Then stood and stretched again before prowling towards Jack. He walked around in a little circle next to the warmth of Jack's thighs under the duvet before settling down. He leaned against Jack and tilted his head back. Either so he could see Jack or because he wanted rubs under his chin. He got both. Mr. Orange always did.

Jack had a huge lump in the back of his throat. He remembered when Mr. Orange had been hurt, clipped by a car they thought, and he'd gotten home hobbling. He'd needed an operation to set his leg. Jack had been about ten, terrified the cat might die. His mom had told him then the kid's version of when pets die. They go to heaven, and it doesn't hurt any more. And they wait for you so when you get old and go to heaven, you walk onto a cloud, and you meet God and then all your pets wake up and come and sit on your lap. It had been a nice image his mom had painted, but he still didn't want Mr. Orange to die. He'd prayed so hard, so often. He'd convinced himself that if he prayed every hour on the hour, then Mr. Orange would be ok. Every hour, he knelt on his knees by his bed, hands pressed together, eyes screwed firmly shut. He even did it as long as he could manage to stay awake during the night. And Mr. Orange had survived the operation and come back to him. A little hobbly at first, but he had come back to him.

Since then, he'd known Mr. Orange wouldn't live forever. Nobody does. But he was getting on for twelve years old now, and he was still pretty spry. He didn't chase pieces of string or tinfoil balls anymore. He wasn't a kitten. But Jack knew one day he would get old, like real old. He had dreaded it. And it had turned out that Jack would die before Mr. Orange. It was a shame. He knew his mom loved him too, but Jack indulged him more. It would have been better if they could have gone together, but he knew he could never have done that.

He carried on scratching under the cat's chin and listened to the gentle purring. He wondered if he would get to wait for Mr. Orange on a cloud. He hoped he would, even after he'd done what he was about to do. He remembered the scene from Titanic when Rose finally met Jack again after she died. Maybe it was like that. He would wait for Mr. Orange, in a way that he didn't notice the years passing. He wanted his cat to carry on having a good time even without him. He wasn't going to take him with him. That thought made him shudder. But maybe he could do what he needed to do, and then time travel forward to when Mr. Orange would join him. One day. When it was time. When it was his time. Because today was Jack's time. His last day.

He looked over at his alarm clock. It was a minute away from getting up time. He reached over and switched the alarm off before it rang. He wouldn't usually do that, even if he woke early, because then he would forget to turn it on again for the next morning. He'd usually wait until it rang out, and then shut it off, ready for tomorrow. But he didn't want it going off tomorrow. He wouldn't be here.

He got out of bed and showered like usual. He washed his hair properly and stole some of his mom's conditioner. It made his hair feel silky. He didn't jerk off. Just slowly cleaned his body. His big wobbly disgusting body. He towelled himself dry back in the bedroom, watched by the cat who had moved onto the warm patch he'd left. He dressed in his usual clothes. No trench coat or anything stupid like that. Cargo shorts. Chargers shirt. Comfy sneakers.

He retrieved the tennis bag from the bottom of his wardrobe and briskly unzipped it open. The noise annoyed the cat and he glared. Jack slid his arm under his mattress incredibly carefully, so as not to disturb Mr. Orange any more, and retrieved the weapon. The ammunition was already fed into magazines in the bag. He had done it the night before. Not too long before he needed them that the springs might suffer. That could cause a jam. But he didn't want to rush on his last day. He picked out one of the magazines at random and pushed the shiny brass bullet at the top. It pushed back hard against his thumb. It was fine. He clicked it into the weapon and cocked it. Made sure the safety was on. He almost wanted to repeat the process, but he knew he shouldn't. Cock it. Check it. Leave it. He put the weapon in the bag and zipped it shut.

Mr. Orange was awake now. He had been watching Jack,

his bright green eyes wide open. Did he know what was happening? How could he? He was just a cat. Tears welled up in Jack's eyes. Was it too late? Could he just forget about it? His hand opened by itself and the bag fell to the floor with a soft thud. He went to his cat and stroked him. Mr. Orange knew something was wrong. He submitted to the overly firm strokes with good grace, leaning into Jack's hand. Jack gave up on trying to blink the tears away. He bowed his head and kissed Mr. Orange on the top of his head, where three dark orange stripes ran front to back between his ears.

"I'll see you soon. Promise."

Mr. Orange rolled onto his back, looking at Jack through blinking eyes. He held Jack's hand between his front paws, white socks and pink paw pads. He wanted more strokes and more rubs.

The tears flooded out of Jack's eyes. He grabbed a T-shirt from the laundry pile and tried to wipe them away.

"It's OK," he said to his cat. "It's ok. I don't mind. Honestly. It won't hurt. It'll be really quick. It'll be OK. And then it won't hurt any more. It'll be over. And I'll be waiting for you, when you want to come. I'll make sure there's chicken for you. Lots of chicken. And fish. You can sit on my lap, and I'll feed you."

He sniffed. Why did tears end up coming through his nose? Was there some tube he hadn't learned about in biology? He sniffed again, a great big snivel to retrieve the snot that was about to drip out and onto his top lip. He gave up and blew his nose on the T-shirt and then let it drop to the floor.

He kissed Mr. Orange again.

"Love you," he said, and then straightened. Picked up the tennis bag and his school bag and quickly went downstairs. He covered his wet eyes with his Oakleys and locked the door behind him before walking like a zombie to the bus stop.

It was time.

272

Chapter Fifty

The average human heart beats seventy times a minute. Until it doesn't.

Jack is sitting in his usual seat at the back of the class. It's been his usual seat for each of the three years and five months he's been at Whittlesford. At the back, on the right. He can slump against the pale blue wall if he wants to. He can stare at his classmates if he wants to. He can pay attention if he wants to. He can write studious notes if he wants to, or he can quietly read if he wants to do that. Sometimes it seems that as long as he's quiet and not disruptive, Mr. Merle is happy to forget about him. Same as everyone else.

He has planned this moment for months. He's considered it in his head. He's researched, and checked, and planned. He's imagined every possible scenario. He's had out-of-body visions where he's seen himself from the outside. He's heard himself shout. He knows to be aggressive and threatening. He's considered hundreds of reactions to hundreds of potential shouts. He's scribbled down possible complications and how he would react. He's listened to podcasts, true crime, and fiction. He's watched movies. Documentaries. He's read magazine articles. He's spent time in chat rooms, occupied by faceless keyboard warriors. Some sound plausible, ex-military or law enforcement. Others sound naïve, kids messing around.

He is an expert in the theory. But he's never put it into practice. By definition. Nobody has ever carried out two school shootings. That's why you need to get it right first time. You don't get two goes at it. You have to get it right first time. If you get it wrong, it'll just be another one. Immortality requires careful planning. If you want to be remembered, you need to sweat the small stuff. Where are the minnows? How do you get it done. And then you have to actually do it. Execute. Immortality. Execute.

Jack has read some basic strategy. Battle plans rarely survive first contact with the enemy, if you want to be historical. Everybody got a plan till they get punched in the face, if you prefer Mike to Moltke. If he is to be remembered, he knows he has to adapt to how the battlefield develops. He's read thousands of words, thousands of pages about previous shootings. And nobody has seen him do it. He has reworked, reconsidered, refined his strategy. There is one thing he has thought about that he is completely sure, one hundred percent convinced, nobody else has ever thought about before. He would bet his life on it. He will execute the plan. He will be remembered. He will not be forgotten.

He looks down at his watch. A cheap Casio, the digital numbers counting down. He can feel his heart beating faster. He has time though. His plan is detailed and exact, but he has built in flexibility as to the exact start time. He has anticipated heightened nerves. He slides his chair back behind him and then leans his forehead into his right hand, propped up on the elbow. He looks down at his watch. From a distance, he looks like he's reading. He's not making any noise or disturbance. Neither teachers nor classmates have any reason to notice him never mind call him out.

The minute passes. His heart is still beating fast, but it's a little less than it was. It seems to be beating harder though. Louder. Thumping. He's OK with it. In his mind, he sees the checklist he wrote out by hand, and neatly ticks it off. The checklist was blue ink. He ticked it off one at a time with a red pen. He looks around the room. Mr. Merle is drawing on the whiteboard, his back to the class, supporting himself with his free hand. Even though he's writing, he's turned his head sideways so the class can hear. His voice is loud and clear, but Jack isn't taking in what he's saying.

Jack's gaze maps around the room. It's deliberate.

Targeted. He sees Trent, Skyla, Brie, Luke. They are in front of him, to the left. The rest of the class are likewise in their usual seats. They are spilled around the classroom, occupying seventeen of the twenty-five seats. Five-by-five rows and Jack is in back. His classmates are paying the usual amount of attention, which is to say varied. But nobody is looking behind them.

Jack reaches down to his rucksack. From the netting side pocket, he pulls out his water-bottle. It's a squeezy plastic one, with a rubber mouthpiece he can pull open with his teeth and close by pushing against it with his tongue. He takes a brief swig of lukewarm water. He doesn't put it back in the bag, but on his desk. This is not a coincidence.

He reaches back down to his rucksack. It's the same tennis backpack he bought from Dick's. Spacious. It's very heavy today, much heavier than it usually is. Without looking, he unzips the main compartment. It's silent. He's practised that movement many times in his bedroom, sitting at his desk, looking straight ahead while reaching down. The zipper is silent. He's rubbed it with a pencil to reduce the friction and it slides soundlessly open.

He slides his hand into the rucksack. His hand touches the grip of the Kel-Tec. It's warm, rubber wrapped around metal. Now or never.

Now.

Jack stands up, pulling the gun out of his backpack. It's a big aggressive movement. Designed to intimidate. His chair squeaks on the floor. At the same time, he shouts, as loud as he can. Intimidation. Control the room. Execute.

"Nobody *fucking* move!"

Every pair of eyes in the classroom is on him. Total disbelief. Classmates are frozen to their chairs. What the fuck? Mr. Merle is half-turned toward Jack. He is the first to think. He is about to speak when Jack aims just to the left of him and fires a single shot into the wall. A single shot. A flat, loud crack. The ejected brass cartridge tinkles as it hits the floor by Jack's feet.

"I said nobody fucking move. Nobody say a fucking word.

One word, and I *WILL* kill you."

Jack is loud. Confident. Terrifying. He is standing at the back of the class, holding a black, shiny weapon, with a large magazine. He has full vision of everybody in the class. He is forcing eye contact on each of them. His heart is racing, big strong beats pumping oxygen around his body. The velocity of blood is rising.

"Everybody, both hands on the desk, palms DOWN! Look straight ahead. NOW. You too, Mr. Merle." To Jack, calling him Mr. Merle sounds natural. What else would he call him?

Every student places their hands palms down on their desk. They stare blankly ahead. Mr. Merle does the same, half bending over his desk at the front of class. Outside the classroom, there is a pick-up in background noise. Nobody is screaming. Nobody outside knows for sure that a gun has been fired. But something is happening. Jack can hear urgent footsteps slapping down on the corridor outside.

Jack stays at the back of the class. He is in perfect position. He has full view of the class. The only person who can see him is Mr. Merle.

Jack calls to the students seated nearest the window, down the left-hand side of the classroom. He's not yelling any more. He's more confident. Calm.

"Mike. Andrea. Joe. Slowly reach over and pull the shades all the way down." They do as they're told. The blinds are down. Nobody can see out. Or in.

Jack breathes. So far so good. His plan has survived first contact. Now for the trickier part.

He calls out to the class. A raised voice. Powerful but calm.

"If you do exactly what I say, you'll be OK. If you don't, you'll die. Nod if you understand."

Eighteen remaining heads nod, including Mr. Merle.

There are now police sirens in the distance. Jack ignores them. He steps towards his backpack.

The loudspeaker in the top corner of the classroom bursts into life and he starts a little. The alarm tone. A two-tone horn. A recorded voice follows, artificial and somehow plastic. "Lockdown - Intruder. This is not a drill. Lockdown. Intruder. This is not a drill."

Jack takes careful aim at the loudspeaker and shoots. It fractures shards of sharp grey plastic and falls silent. Another student bursts into tears, sobbing. This is part of the plan. The loudspeakers can continue elsewhere. It can be heard, muffled, from other loudspeakers in safer classrooms. In this classroom, Jack needs everyone to listen to him. Jack has fired two shots so far. Nobody is hurt. They are terrified. But they are not hurt. And they hope.

Jack now approaches the maximum risk part of his plan. This is where all could be lost. He stands over his bag and quickly glances down. He can see the package. He takes another glance around the room. They are all staring ahead.

Jack quickly bends his knees and retrieves the package. An orange plastic bag. He throws it to the front of the class. It lands on the floor, not far from Mr. Merle. The students jump. They don't know what it is.

Jack positions himself behind Adam and Sarah, who have sat close to each other since they first made out after a party that Jack wasn't invited to three months ago.

"Adam. You're going to do something for me. Nod if you understand."

Adam nods. He is an amiable enough young man. His interests are music, surfing, and Sarah. He cannot believe he is in this situation. But he nods, continuing to stare straight ahead. He is smart. He does not know what the plan is. But he knows he is still there and so there is hope. He nods.

"You're going to lace your hands behind your head so I can see them. The you're going to get up and SLOWLY walk to that bag, with your hands still on your head. In it are cable ties. You're going to pick out four with one hand. Then you're going to SLOWLY walk back, toward Trent. You're going to slowly kneel down on both knees. You're going to tie his left leg to the left chair leg, and his right leg to the right chair leg. And then you're going to tie his right wrist to the right arMr.est and the left wrist to the left arMr.est. If you do *anything* but that, I'm going to shoot Sarah in the back of the head first, and then everyone else. Do you understand what I just said? Nod if you do."

Adam nods. He steals a glance at his girlfriend, seated at the desk next to him. She is deadly quiet. No tears.

"Trent, if you do anything but sit still, I'm going to shoot Skyla in the back of the head first and then you. Do you understand? Nod if you do."

Trent nods. He does not know what is going on. He cannot comprehend the events unfolding around him. But he is still alive. There is still hope.

Adam has not yet moved.

"OK, Adam. Now would be good."

Adam takes a breath. He laces his hands behind his head. He slides his chair back and stands. He walks slowly toward the package on the floor at the front of the class.

He walks toward Trent. He avoids eye contact. He sees Jack commanding the classroom from the back. The weapon is pointed in Sarah's direction while Jack watches Adam slowly kneel down. Adam ties the first cable tie around Trent's left leg and the chair leg.

"Tighter."

He fastens it tighter. He moves to the right leg.

"Tighter."

He fastens it tighter. He moves to the wrists. He does not need to be told to do it tighter this time.

When he has finished, he looks in Jack's general direction. No eye contact. But can he go? Can he go on his own, or can he take Sarah? But can he go?

"Nice job. Now go back to the package and do the same but with Luke."

Luke takes half a breath. His chest swells. He still faces forward but he's becoming angry, his shoulders are rolling. He's about to say something, but he can't quite bring himself to speak.

Jack has noticed.

"Not a fucking word, Luke. Not a fucking word. Nod if you understand."

Luke nods. Adam stands up and repeats the process. He

walks to the package and pulls out four more cable ties. He seems to relax. He is smart. He thinks he knows what will happen. There are eight ties left in the bag. He walks slowly to Luke and ties his legs, then his hands, to the chair. He does not need to be told to tie them tightly. Jack remains in place. The gun is pointing toward Sarah.

"Now, Skyla."

Skyla can't help herself. Without looking around, she speaks.

"You are so fucked up. What the fuck is wrong with you? You are just so fucked up. No wonder everyone ha-"

The gunshot surprises everyone. Jack has fired his third shot just to the left of Skyla's ear. She flinches, and her left hand flies to her ear. Her ears are ringing. The bullet has torn straight through Mr. Merle's desk, ripping through the wooden pedestal. The stench of gun smoke wafts around the classroom, acrid and sour.

"Open your mouth again and I'll shoot you in the back. Put your hand back down on the desk."

Skyla's bravado is gone. She meekly places her hand back down on her desk, palm facing downward.

"Now, Skyla. Please, Adam."

Adam moves slowly, again. He ties Skyla. Brie is next. In the middle of the room, in the Cool section, Trent, Luke, Skyla and Brie are cable-tied to their chairs.

Adam looks up from binding Brie's wrist. Awaiting further instructions. None are immediately forthcoming.

The room is eerie. Four students are bound to their chairs with shiny black cable ties. One is crouched where he just finished tying one of his classmates. Twelve remain seated in their chairs, hands on their desks. Heads either face forward or down. There is some snivelling but for the most part there is quiet. Mr. Merle is the only one actually facing Jack. His hands remain planted on his desk, supporting his elderly bones. His eyes are weeping silently as he looks down.

There is confusion mixed with hope in the room. There is a gun, and it is pointed at them. Four of them are shackled to their chairs. But it is now more than fifteen minutes since

Jack Tolleson first fired a gun at the wall just to the left of Mr. Merle at Whittlesford High School, California and nobody is hurt. There are sirens wailing and yelping and nobody is hurt.

Jack pauses. Step one accomplished. He takes a deep breath. It does not go unnoticed. He motions Adam to his nearest empty chair, ensuring compliance by pointing the gun directly at Sarah's head.

Jack looks toward the front of the class.

"Mr. Merle, I'm going to need you to stand up. You can use your stick. Do you understand? Nod if you do."

Mr. Merle nods, slowly. His arms are shaking. He strains himself upright from his bent-over lean and he stands. He reaches for his stick and holds himself up. He is old and kindly and no threat at all. He is terrified.

"Now, turn and face the door. And leave the room."

Mr. Merle hesitates.

"Jack," he begins weakly, his voice quivering. "Whatever this is about, we can talk it out, we can-"

Jack fires the gun, again, just to the left of Mr. Merle. As the fourth shot reverberates, Mr. Merle's grey pants are colouring with a dark stain. His arms continue to shake as he pisses himself. He stares straight at Jack through thick horn-rimmed spectacles.

"You need to leave now or never." Jack looks down the sight of the gun and aims at Mr. Merle. "Now or never," he repeats.

Mr. Merle bows his head. He turns and walks to the door. Tears are now streaming down his cheeks. What choice does he have? He is slow and unsteady, leaning on his stick. He leaves without looking back. He does not run because he cannot run.

Jack speaks to the student seated nearest him.

"Tom. Put your hands on your head. Then slowly stand up. Then walk slowly straight to the front of the class and then to the door. You can go."

Tom slowly stands up, his fingers laced on his head. He walks to the door and pauses. His hands are on his head. He can't see but he knows Jack is pointing a gun at him. Should he take his hands off his head?

Jack recognises his dilemma. "You can take your left hand off your head. Open the door, slowly. Then go."

Tom, in slow motion, follows orders. The door swings closed behind him. Jack can hear him run down the hall, his sneakers squeaking on the linoleum. Jack isn't fazed.

"Jenny. It's your turn. Put your hands on your head. Then slowly stand up and walk straight to the front of the class and to the door." Jenny is second nearest Jack. She follows the same procedure.

There is hope in the room. Some students are sobbing, some breathe heavily, but there is hope. Two students have been released.

One by one, he releases more students, in order of proximity to himself. When they are released, they walk slowly to the front of the class, then turn right and toward the door. Some are shaking. Some are crying. Some are blank. Some have soiled themselves. But they get to the door. And all of them, as soon as the door swings shut behind them, run as fast as they possibly can, away from Jack, away from the gun.

The penultimate release is Adam.

"OK. You can go now. Stand up slowly. Walk to the front of class. Then walk out."

Adam's eyes flicker toward Sarah. It is not unobserved by Jack.

"It's OK. She will be right after you. But only one of you can leave at a time. It's OK. Just go."

For the first time, Adam risks eye contact with Jack. He notices the water-bottle on Jack's desk and nods, grateful. He stands slowly. Walks to the front of class. Turns and walks to the door. He alone does not run down the hall. He alone understands what is coming next. He alone knows the significance of the bottle.

"Sarah. Your turn."

She nods. Slowly stands. She does not look at the four who are bound to their chairs. She walks slowly to the door.

The door swings shut behind her and she runs, runs, runs.

Jack double-checks that the four are securely tied. Satisfied, he walks to the door. He turns the lock from the inside and then quickly shoves a desk against the door, barricading them in. He walks to Mr. Merle's desk and sweeps all the papers off it, onto the floor. He is standing in Mr. Merle's piss, but he doesn't notice.

He faces the four.

The room is quiet.

Chapter Fifty-One

Could I have seen this coming?

I've asked myself this a hundred thousand times. Was something off? Could I have known? Did I miss anything?

The police came and searched our house. They took away Jack's computer. They already had his cellphone. And they found nothing on there. Not on either. No Google searches about guns, no Google searches about shootings, or revenge or anything like that. His internet history was pretty normal, they said. Sports, and music, and a bit of porn.

The officer blushed when he told me about the porn, but I waved it off. He clearly wasn't a parent, or at least if he was, he didn't have a teenage boy. You practically have to walk around wearing a bell when they get to that age. Hormones all over the place. And porn is free. Jack was a perfectly normal teenager in that regard, or at least in-line with what other moms and the internet said. We'd had Net Nanny when he was pre-teen, but when we switched broadband providers when he was about fourteen, we didn't bother renewing it. It avoided having to have that conversation. And fourteen, well, it's that kind of age. It's normal. So you just avoid ever walking in on your teenage son and you try not to think about when he was tiny and new-born and you thought, how on earth did I ever grow a human? It's just part of life.

I know why he did it, obviously. I was told what he said, and I have to believe that when he said what he said, he meant it. But believe me, I've gone over pretty much every single interaction in my head a thousand times.

I've lain awake at night, trying to attach a meaning, or a clue, a tell to every time I spoke to my son in the last year

283

before it happened.

I've gotten organised and sat down at my computer with a legal pad and my calendar. I've tried to recreate every conversation, using the planner as a prompt. Nothing. There is not one thing I can point my finger at and say, *that was it*. That was when, if you'd been paying attention or listening harder, you could have known. And if you had, then your baby would still be alive.

I think one of the hardest things about not knowing was that he'd clearly planned it for a while. Obviously that means he was lying to me. That hurts. A lot. For a lot of reasons. Jack was always an honest child. He wouldn't tell lies, not even white lies. Jonathan was always very hot on owning up to stuff. When Jack was about eight, he dropped a glass he'd been told not to touch, and it smashed. Shards all over the kitchen. But he owned up to it, and Jonathan actually gave him an ice cream for being honest. But obviously he didn't tell me about a lot of stuff. The trip to Vegas. Well, yes, I knew he was going. But it was a Sunday football day trip. I'd never have let him go to Vegas overnight and he would never have asked. And Dallas.

I've started wondering now, how much of the last year was actually Jack. He'd always liked football and we'd always watched it as a family when we could, when Jonathan was home. Especially the Army-Navy game, I suppose. But then we found out that Jack had been to that shooting range in Las Vegas and he hadn't even been to the game. It sounds stupid in the grand scheme of things but that was a real blow. Finding out how much he'd lied. I remember when he got home that evening. I made sure I had food for when he got back – ball game food never fills you up – and we talked about the match-up and the trip. He wasn't as enthusiastic as I thought he might have been – he'd never seen the Raiders live, and it was one to cross off his list. Plus, the Chargers had beaten up on the Raiders by quite a bit. So he wasn't maybe as energised as he could have been, but I put it down to being tired and hungry. He demolished the dinner I'd made for him. And of course, I keep telling myself it's a long way from your teenage son being tired and hungry to thinking that he's actually spent the day at a shooting range. Practicing for, well, practicing for what happened.

So obviously one thought leads to another, and now I have doubts about almost everything. Did Jack even like football that much? He certainly seemed to get more into it in the last year. He was always on SI.com or ESPN. And we always watched the games on Sundays on TV. Sometimes college games on Saturday too. I wouldn't really watch, of course. I don't dislike it, but I'm not as keen. Well, not as keen as I thought Jack was. But now I don't know if he was really keen at all. Or whether he was just pretending, so he had reasons to go out of state and do what he did. So I guess I look back at those memories, of afternoons on the couch watching the games and I wonder if he really wanted to be there. It was usually just the two of us. Jack could get quite vocal watching games and if he got too loud, the cat would usually go upstairs for some peace and quiet. But maybe even Jack's cheering wasn't real? I just don't know.

When the police searched the house, they sent dogs in first. To try and sniff out if there were any explosives. Apparently sometimes they leave booby-traps. I can't believe I just said *they*. Excuse me. They were worried that Jack might have left a booby-trap. Explosives. So they sent in sniffer dogs. Scared the crap out of Mr. Orange. He sprinted out of the house as fast as he could and then leapt over the neighbour's fence. Watched everyone from their lawn. They didn't find any explosives or guns or ammunition in the house, but they had been stored there before. The dogs could smell the residue under the bed. They barked like crazy.

After it happened, the police obviously put it together. Where Jack had actually been. They didn't find it from his internet history, but more from his transactions. There was a lot of bullshit printed in the press about that. They claimed we'd given him a credit card and that was how he did it. All bullshit. He didn't have a credit card. He had a perfectly normal checking account, like most kids. He had a perfectly normal savings account, like most kids. He was really good at saving, and didn't waste money, which I guess is not like most kids, but you don't get suspicious because your kid isn't spending his money on crap. I was pleased, not suspicious. He was into sports, and you can be into watching sports without spending a lot of money on it. it's not like playing sports like golf or cycling, where I see guys Jonathan's age spending thousands of dollars on equipment and looking stupid.

Anyway, the police worked out that Jack must have gotten the gun and the ammunition in Texas. He'd bought it and brought it home and hidden it under the bed, but only for a couple of days. They asked me if I'd seen it, which I get, but that pissed me off. If I'd seen it, we wouldn't be here. Jack would be alive. And so would everyone else.

As for why I hadn't seen it, that's just as ridiculous. I didn't search his room. He was a typical seventeen-year-old boy. A teenager. They want privacy too. He never smelled of cigarette smoke, or beer or marijuana, and his grades were good. He didn't have any sketchy friends. Nothing had 'gone missing' from the house or school. Nothing expensive had ever shown up without any explanation. So no, I never had any reason to search his room. If his door was shut, I would call from halfway up the stairs in case he was being a teenage boy and jerking off, and I would knock loudly anyway. He would bring his laundry basket downstairs on a Saturday morning, and I'd put the washed clothes on the corner of his desk every Sunday for him to put away. I'd occasionally tell him to tidy his room, but to be honest, that was more in the pre-teen years. The Lego years. Once he got older, he was pretty tidy. As teenagers go, I suppose. Certainly not like some of the horror stories I heard, of kids throwing their discarded clothes over half empty cereal bowls and not realising what lay beneath until it smelled really bad. So I never had any reason to search his room. Why would I? I trusted him.

When I think about this, my head goes one of two ways. It either turns into a computer, where I see a list of options in front of me, and then I tick them off. I call that my blue head, it's something from a psychology book I read one time. It's supposed to help you think clearly. And my blue head is rational, and it explains why I didn't see any warning signs. Because there really weren't any warning signs. No moodiness, no withdrawal, no fights, no obsession with guns, no drug use, no drunkenness. Nada.

I try to keep my blue head working, most of the time, because when I don't, my guilty brain kicks in. I hear this voice, smack bang between my ears, dead centre. You should have known. He was your baby, and you were supposed to protect him. And you didn't. And because of that, he's dead.

When I hear that voice, I try and switch on the blue brain. And then I feel shit about doing that. Because what I'm trying to do is deaden the pain. And I should feel pain. All of it. Because my baby boy, my sweet baby boy, grew from eight pounds the day I first held him to two hundred sixty pounds when he kissed me goodbye that morning, and now he's six pounds of ash in a fucking urn because nowhere would let us bury him in their church.

Chapter Fifty-Two

The classroom is still. There is a pool of urine on the floor where Mr. Merle was standing. There are shards of plastic from the loudspeaker on the floor and desks, shattered when Jack shot it. There are holes in the walls from where Jack has shot. But nobody has been hurt.

There are discarded papers and textbooks on the desks where students left them behind. Likewise, rucksacks and sports bags underneath desks. There is a caddy full of cellphones near the door. It is the scene of a classroom after a fire alarm, save for one detail.

There are four students cable-tied to their chairs. And there is one with a gun.

Trent is staring resolutely ahead, his eyes burning a hole into the whiteboard opposite. Skyla is shivering with fear. She cannot hear out of her left ear. Her jaw is quivering up and down, her breath shallow. Luke is defiant. He has strained his biceps against the cable ties, but they have not yielded. His jaw is firm. Brie is hunched over, her eyes clenched shut.

None of them knows what is about to happen. But they know what they have done to Jack.

Jack has planned this moment in infinite detail. He has sketched it, scribbled it, imagined it, researched it, and strategised it. He has looked for weaknesses in his plan and incorporated adaptations. He has prepared tactical amendments if the situation were to develop differently. He has lain awake, night after night, waiting for this moment to come. And now it has.

He reaches for his water bottle and walks to the front of

the class. His sneakers squeak on the linoleum and four pairs of eyes turn to follow him.

He pauses. He does not drink from his bottle. Instead, he places it on its side on Mr. Merle's desk. He looks at each of them in turn. And then he spins the bottle. He is looking in their eyes.

There is no longer hope. There is recognition. And there is dread. They remember. And they know.

The bottle spins on its axis, a little water spilling out as it rotates. It decelerates and slowly comes to a halt. The nozzle is pointing at Brie, seated at the end of the row. Brie shudders and hyperventilates. She hunches over once more and looks down at her knees. Her breath is short, great big noisy gulps of air.

Jack's face is expressionless. He walks slowly toward her. Stands behind her. Bent forward, she can see his sneakers behind her. He speaks only four words.

"You made this happen."

He raises the gun and touches the muzzle to the back of her head. She flinches at its touch, and he pulls the trigger. Her head explodes. There is blood and brain everywhere.

Skyla screams. She is screaming as loud as she can. "Daddy. Daddy. Daddy. Please, Daddy!"

Trent is yelling at the top of his lungs. "Help! Help! We're in here. Help. Somebody. Please. Come help us. He's gone crazy. Please help us!"

Luke is determined not to go down without a fight. "You motherfucker. You stupid fat motherfucker. When I get out of here, I'm going to beat you to fucking death, you lame ass fat motherfucker!" He is glaring right at Jack. "You useless fat motherfucker."

Jack will not tolerate this. He holds the gun in his left hand and sucker punches Luke with his right fist. Anger and fury ignite inside him. He slugs Luke above his right eye, his entire weight behind it. Luke cannot defend himself. His head snaps back and the skin splits against his eye socket. Blood oozes out and drips into his eye and down his cheek. Luke falls silent.

Jack repeats himself. "You made this happen."

He walks back to the desk and stares at Skyla, Trent, and Luke. He picks up the bottle. Takes a swig this time. And then he places it on its side again, on Mr. Merle's desk and spins it again. Water again dribbles out of the end as it rotates around.

It comes to a halt with the nozzle pointing toward the door. Away from his hostages. He snorts.

"No winner. I guess I have to spin again." He spins it.

Luke finds his voice.

"Seriously, man? This is about a game of spin the fucking bottle? This is about *us*? You are so fucked up."

Skyla is smarter.

"Jack, we're sorry. We really are. We were just being assholes. We didn't mean it. We didn't mean it. We didn't mean it. We're sorry. Honest to god, we are."

Jack stops the bottle, catching it mid-spin. He stares at Skyla. Then Luke. Then Trent. Then Skyla again. They have fallen silent.

"You made this happen," he says. "Everything that happens today is on you. You made it happen."

He spins the bottle again. Three pairs of eyes stare at the bottle as it spins and scuffs on Mr. Merle's desk. It slows and comes to a halt. It is pointing at Luke.

Luke stares up at Jack through one good eye and one bloodied one. He knows what is coming next. He glares, full of hate.

"Fucking cocksucker. Did you ever stop to think why we did that? Because you're a disgusting fat cocksucker. A disgusting fat cocksucker. A revolting, hideous, disgusting-"

"YOU MADE THIS HAPPEN!" Jack has to shout over Luke. He touches the gun to the back of Luke's head and pulls the trigger again. A fragment of skull, scorched black at the edge, lands on the desk.

Jack walks back to Mr. Merle's desk. His foot kicks the ejected brass cartridge case, and it shines as it rolls across the floor.

"And then there were two," he says.

Skyla looks at Trent. Trent looks at Skyla. They are covered in the blood and brains of their friends.

Trent finally speaks.

"Jack...dude...I'm sorry. I really am. I was an asshole. An absolute asshole. I am an asshole. Whatever it takes, I'll do it. Whatever it takes. We can make this work out, Jack. Whatever it. takes, we can make it work. Just put the gun down and untie us and we can talk it out. We can talk anything out if we try. We just need to talk."

Jack pauses. He is amused.

"Now?" he asks. "*Now*, you want to talk to me?"

He walks to a desk and pulls out a chair. Spins it round and sits opposite Trent and Skyla. The gun is loose in his hand.

"I'm listening," he says. "Talk."

Trent is struck dumb. He doesn't actually know what to say. He babbles. An incoherent stream of bullshit sounds.

Skyla butts in.

"Jack, the most important thing to say is that we're sorry. We really are. We were such total assholes, we-"

Jack raises a hand to silence her. His voice is even. He's been planning this for a long time.

"The thing I don't understand is why," he says. "I never did a thing to any of you. I never did one thing to any of you. I was just doing my thing. I never hurt any of you, never talked shit about any of you, never did *anything* to any of you. And somehow you decided that you got to decide what happened to me. You got to decide not just how you treated me, but how everyone else treated me. You made it impossible for anyone to hang out with me, because then you'd be assholes to them too."

Skyla just stares. Trent too. They don't know what to say. But if Jack is talking, then he's not shooting. And if he's not shooting, then they have hope. Hope. Not much hope. But some.

Skyla bows her head. She knows she needs to appear contrite. She might even be.

"I'm sorry," she says. "Truly I am."

"We both are," adds Trent.

"So why? What made you decide to pick on me? Why ruin my life? Why me?"

Trent and Skyla look at each other. They are blank. They cannot remember.

"Seriously?! You can't even fucking remember?!" Jack's voice is raised now, angry.

"Um. Um." Skyla simply cannot remember. She is casting her mind back. But she cannot remember.

"Um. The Diet Coke." Trent has found his voice.

"What?"

"You took a Diet Coke one day. At lunch. In the cafeteria. And Skyla saw it and told us, and we all laughed at you. Because you were heavier back then. I'm sorry, Jack. We were being assholes." Trent decides honesty is the best policy.

"*Seriously*? I took a Diet Coke because I wanted to lose weight and that was why you started being assholes? Because I took a *Diet Coke*?" Jack is angry now. His voice is raised. The gun is in his hand. He points it at Skyla then Trent then Skyla again.

"Is that why, Skyla? Is that why you decided to be such a bitch to me? Because I took a *Diet Coke*?"

"I don't remember. I'm sorry, Jack. Whatever it was, I don't remember. But I'm sorry. Truly I am."

Jack stares at her. Total contempt. She doesn't remember. She knows at that moment that he does not believe she is worthy of a single breath more. She has foregone that right.

He stands. Looks at the bottle. Spins it. It judders its way around. Comes to a halt with the nozzle pointing somewhere near Trent, but not directly at him. Trent breathes a sigh of relief. Skyla too.

Jack looks at Skyla. "Close enough, don't you think?"

He walks behind Trent. Whispers into his ear "You made this happen."

"No," shouts Skyla. "It's not pointing at him. That's not fair. It's not pointing at him, it's not pointing at him, it's not-"

Jack fires. A single shot. Trent dies. Messily. The

classroom is an abattoir.

Jack walks back to the front of the class. It is just him and Skyla. He sits in front of her. Her head is now bowed. She is snivelling. She knows she is next.

"You can't even remember why. You can't even remember why you did this. But you did. You did do it. You did it. You made this happen. Brie. Luke. Trent. This is all on you. You need to remember this. This is all on you. *All* of it."

He stares at her. She is covered in the blood and brains of her friends. Her hands and are legs are tied. But she is still alive. She slowly raises her eyes to meet his gaze.

"You need to know this is all because of you. Remember that."

He reverses the gun. Puts the muzzle in his mouth and pulls the trigger. His last thought is that he will be remembered. She will remember this.

Every. Single. Day.

Fantastic Books
Great Authors

darkstroke is
an imprint of
Crooked Cat Books

- Gripping Thrillers
- Cosy Mysteries
- Romantic Chick-Lit
- Fascinating Historicals
- Exciting Fantasy
- Young Adult and Children's
  Adventures
- Non-Fiction

Discover us online
www.darkstroke.com

Find us on instagram:
www.instagram.com/darkstrokebooks

Printed in Great Britain
by Amazon

18916598R00174